SICILIANA

A NOVEL

CARLO TREVISO

Trevixo
ORIGINALE

Published by Trevixo Originale Books
www.carlotreviso.com

Edited and designed by Girl Friday Productions
www.girlfridayproductions.com

Cover design: Rachel Marek
Project management: Katherine Richards
Editorial: Tiffany Taing
Illustrations: Josh Lynch
Image credits: Unsplash/Rishabh Pammi, Shutterstock/photopalace, Shutterstock/Peyker, Shutterstock/Inara Prusakova, Shutterstock/tugol, Shutterstock/Johan Larson
Image retouching: Scott Giannini

ISBN (hardcover): 978-1-7374577-1-8
ISBN (paperback): 978-1-7374577-0-1
ISBN (ebook): 978-1-7374577-2-5
ISBN (audiobook): 978-1-7374577-3-2

Library of Congress Control Number: 2021925173

For Andrea

*There are three things that are perilous to man:
fire, the sea, and Sicilian women.*
　　　　　　　　　　　　　　—A Sicilian Proverb

Inspired by actual events

WHY I WROTE *SICILIANA*

I'M THE first-generation son of a Sicilian immigrant family.

Growing up, if I mentioned Sicily or my Sicilian heritage to anyone unfamiliar with its past or culture, the typical response included some use of the notorious *M* word. "Oh, like the *Mafia*?" Mention Sicily in literature or film, and one might imagine an aging don stroking a white cat or a low-level mobster running a casino outfit.

In all fairness, the general public can't be faulted for making these connections. More often than not, Sicilians are portrayed and perceived in popular culture in a negative context—hustlers, gangsters, grifters.

My Sicilian heritage deserves better.

As a lifelong *aficionado* of fiction and cinema, I believe in the transformative power of storytelling and determined that the only way to confront and change these negative perceptions was to change the narrative.

This would become my knight's quest.

My hero's journey.

Enter *Siciliana*.

In writing this novel, I set out to paint a portrait of a tempestuous time when the island of Sicily was still considered its own kingdom. Originally known as the *Kingdom of Trinacria*, Sicily was once a grandiose and evocative realm of forbidden knights, forgotten fortresses, and fallen kings.

Readers of *Siciliana* will discover a moment in history that is not particularly well known. The period is focused on a brief era in thirteenth-century Sicily when a people's revolt against the island's French occupation single-handedly sparked a world war and forever altered the face of the Mediterranean as we know it. The uprising was called the *Sicilian Vespers*. It was a violent, harrowing, world-shaping event that delivered an oppressed people from the scourge of tyranny and fundamentally forged the identity of a Sicilian nation.

By opening a window into this dramatic era, I hope to shine a new light on Sicily's engrossing past and resilient culture, and celebrate my heritage in a way that I wanted to see in popular culture growing up.

Perhaps one day, when a Sicilian daughter or Sicilian son tells someone about their family's heritage, the response they receive will not be "Oh, like the *Mafia*?" but rather "Oh, like *Siciliana*!"

Carlo Treviso
March 30, 2022
Chicago, IL

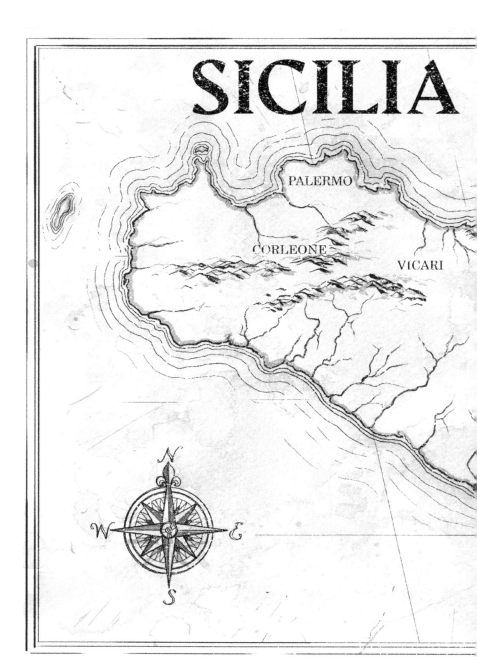

SICILIA

PALERMO

CORLEONE

VICARI

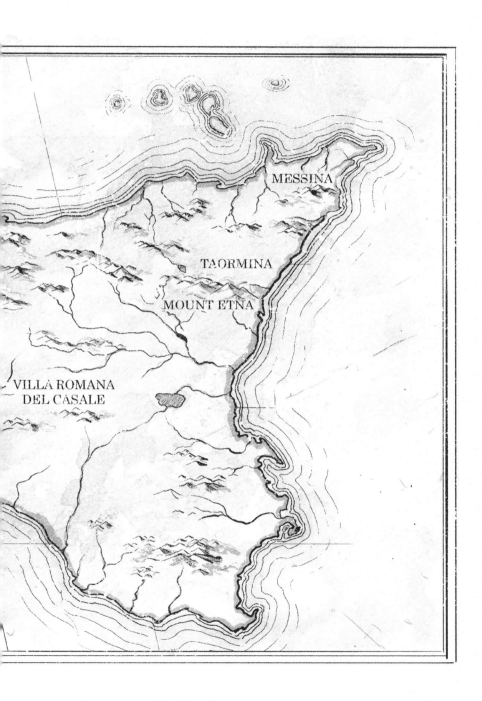

FACT:

On March 30, 1282, as the bells of Palermo tolled for Vespers, a Sicilian woman crying "Death to the Angevins!" led a people's uprising against the French garrison occupying the city. Within six weeks, Sicilian rebels slayed more than three thousand Angevin soldiers across the island. The turbulent events of 1282 became known as the Sicilian Vespers.

· ❧ ·

A stiletto is a long, razor-sharp blade with an ornamental hilt and cross-guard. The Sicilians were deadly with the stiletto blade—and their menacing flair gained notoriety throughout Europe—coining the phrase, "Only saints and Sicilians dare clash with the devil." A master of the stiletto was called a *cavaleri*, a Sicilian knight.

· ❧ ·

The Knights of the Teutonic Order, or *Ordu Teutoni*, was founded in 1190 during the Third Crusade. The Teutonic Order was charged with protecting the pilgrim path to the Holy Land and providing care for crusaders who had fallen ill. A decade later, the *Teutoni* Knights became a powerful military force throughout the Mediterranean. The order's fealty was toward the great dynasty of Sicilian kings. The Teutonic Order exists today as a chivalric sect of the Catholic Church.

· ❧ ·

All named locations, architecture, and historical symbols depicted in this novel are real, and their remnants can still be seen today.

IN THE early 1960s, volcanologists digging on a crater of Sicily's active volcano, Mount Etna, found an ancient papyrus scroll wrapped in preserved sheepskin. The fragile missive read:

> *Aprili 1282*
> *I've forgotten much about my childhood*
>   *years, but I remember the lava.*
> *The roaring fountain of red molten rock*
>   *erupting from the black earth.*
> *The glowing orange serpents slithering*
>   *down the flanks of the volcano.*
> *Deliberately.*
> *Violently.*
> *Yet in the path of its devastation came new*
>   *growth from the ugly soil.*
> *New life.*
> *A new era.*
> *I am lava.*
> *I am* Siciliana.

PROLOGUE

Castello di Vicari
Vicari, Sicily
March 30, 1282

DEATH CAME at sundown.

"Rapidement!" shouted Angevin lieutenant Guiscard, staggering through a vaulted archway and into the castle's dining hall. Only seconds behind him, a squad of twelve Angevin soldiers dragged the justiciar of Palermo, Jean de Saint-Remy, into the dark dining hall, the toes of his boots scraping across the stone floor.

Far off, an alarm rang out. The cliffside fortress awakened with a clamoring of urgent activity. The grizzled lieutenant pointed to a wooden chair near the center of the cavernous chamber. "Set him down."

Two soldiers thrust the forty-three-year-old justiciar onto the chair. The other men hurried to the corners of the room to ignite the torches, which blazed to life and cast long, flickering, contorted shadows across the high walls.

Justiciar Saint-Remy clutched his left eye, which hung from its gaping socket by a nerve fiber beneath his grisly palm. His cheeks were bruised and swollen. He glanced down in panic as blood ran down his face and caked in his gnarly gray beard.

A physician pushed through the group and started dressing the justiciar's facial wound in a linen cloth. Some of the men shot anxious glances at one another. Others were transfixed with astonishment. The justiciar of Palermo was barely recognizable.

"I rode directly from Palermo," Saint-Remy said. He grabbed a soldier's collar in his fist. "War is upon us."

The soldier studied Saint-Remy's misshapen face for a long moment. Then he burst into laughter. The other men shot nervous glances toward one another and joined in the laughter.

Saint-Remy bared his teeth. He lunged from the chair, clenching his hands around the soldier's throat and pushing him to the ground. The two men grappled on the stone floor.

"You think this is a game?" Saint-Remy growled. His cries echoed through the hollow chamber.

Two hulking Angevins wrestled Saint-Remy off the man and pushed him back into the chair.

Lieutenant Guiscard furrowed his brow. Justiciar Jean de Saint-Remy was the most powerful Angevin in Palermo, cousin to the royal vicar of Sicily himself. Seeing him reduced to such a wretched state sent a cold chill down his spine.

"Tell me," Guiscard asked carefully, "what foreign army has invaded Palermo?"

Saint-Remy shook his head. His eye darted around the room. He saw nothing but men blinking back at him.

"Not an army . . . ," Saint-Remy stammered. "*Siciliens* . . . hundreds of them . . . thousands . . ."

The Angevins' eyes widened in unison.

A soldier ran forward and handed a glass of wine to Saint-Remy, who quickly drained the tart red liquid down his throat.

"Sicilians, you say?" Guiscard said.

Saint-Remy nodded, exasperated, and wiped the wine from his beard.

Guiscard observed the honest terror gleaming from Saint-Remy's eye. He couldn't fathom what kind of primeval nightmare had fallen upon Palermo this night, but whatever it was, it would soon be beating a path to their doorstep. In that moment, the lieutenant made up his mind. The justiciar was telling the truth. The harrowing task before them would require every ounce of their resolve. He turned to his men and issued his final command. "Barricade the gates and ready the garrison . . . War is upon us."

Sobbing, Saint-Remy leaned back in his chair as the men stumbled from the room. He placed his quivering hand over his wounded face, feeling his own blood soaking through the cloth.

Guiscard stood over Saint-Remy in silence, cringing at the severity of the justiciar's facial wounds. "Who in God's name did this to you?"

Saint-Remy lifted his gaze to meet the lieutenant's. A long, uncomfortable silence hung between the two men.

Saint-Remy finally opened his mouth and muttered only two words: "A woman."

BOOK I

O SANTO CAVALERI
1269

THIRTEEN YEARS BEFORE VESPERS

MOUNT ETNA

MESSINA

MEGALITI
DELL'ARGIMUSCO

TAORMINA

MOUNT ETNA

VALLE DEL BOVE

VITICULTURA
VESPIRI

IONIAN SEA

PRINCE CONRADIN was dead.

After vanquishing the last prince of Sicily in battle, a monstrous French lord named Charles of Anjou, known in Sicilian as Re Carlu, ordered his army of Angevin soldiers to seize the kingdom of Sicily and invade its capital city of Palermo.

The Angevin army—a brutal outfit of drunkards and deviants—established a military occupation on the island and plundered Sicily of her treasures. The Angevins bullied, molested, and subjugated the Sicilian people, who submitted in fear under this dangerous new power.

But among the Sicilians themselves festered a muted, primeval rage. A seething resentment perhaps no different from that of a young woman who had been too often betrayed and was no longer fit for love.

—From *War of the Vespers*
by *Don Rapaci*, 1282

CHAPTER 1

Mount Etna, Sicily
August 20, 1269

THE CRIMSON glow of twilight washed over the volcanic countryside as seven-year-old Aetna Vespiri and her nine-year-old brother, Cicero, darted toward a festival gathering outside a nearby village. The August night was crisp, tingling their small lungs as they gulped in the cool, fresh air. Ragged tents were strewn across the field. Colorful banners snapped in the breeze. Women in silk garments beat sheepskin tambourines and pranced round one another, kicking their legs in a spirited *tarantella* dance. Orange torchlight cast long shadows across the black earth.

Aetna and Cicero entered a tent and took a front-row seat on an oaken bench. Inside, stage performers held life-size marionettes: two knights named Orlando and Rinaldo. As the story went, Orlando fought his cousin, Rinaldo, over the love of the beautiful princess Angelica. It was known as *The Song of Orlando*.

A tinkling lute that had played continuously as patrons first entered the tent suddenly fell silent. Aetna watched with anticipation as a skinny stagehand pulled on a gnarly rope, lifting an ornamental scarlet curtain and revealing an order of knights warring in front of a crude forest backdrop. All eyes in the audience glistened with wonder.

"Con un colpo della mia spada faccio saltare la testa a cento Paladini!" the virtuous Orlando boomed as the tumultuous rage of battle swirled around him. "With the stroke of my sword, I will slay one hundred knights!"

Vibrant blue and gold plumes stemmed from Orlando's helmet and visor; a crimson skirt wrapped around his thighs. His silver breastplate, gauntlets, and shield were all meticulously polished and worked, gleaming in the firelight for all the world to see.

A perfect Sicilian knight.

Lunging forward, Orlando struck blows with his cousin, Rinaldo, in an elaborately choreographed dance. An electric current seemed to surge through Orlando's armor as sparks burst from the clashing swords.

Taratata! Taratata!

Cicero leaned over to Aetna. "I can't believe Orlando would fight his own family."

"He has no choice," Aetna said, her eyes glued to the action on the stage. "Rinaldo wouldn't reason with him."

"But Rinaldo loves Princess Angelica, too," Cicero said.

Aetna nodded vigorously, her lips curling up into a knowing half smile. "Then they'll fight to the death."

Shushing sounds came from the crowd. Aetna and Cicero clasped their hands over their mouths, stooping their heads lower and snickering to themselves.

In that instant, Orlando twirled to face the audience, and it appeared to Aetna that the valiant knight's eyes flashed with fire as he swept his sword out over the children's heads. Silver volts seemed to crackle from Orlando's sword, bristling the hairs on their heads. The children yelped in surprise and delight.

Aetna watched as Orlando approached the front row, his boots stomping, one in front of the other. She jumped as the knight came to a stop right in front of her, their faces nearly touching. Orlando snapped to full attention as only a knight could. He then extended his sword outward, holding it over Aetna's head for a long moment. His piercing gaze stared down on her from a chiseled face. Aetna's green eyes glimmered in the firelight as she looked upward. Orlando gently lowered his blade, tapping Aetna on each shoulder.

"Cent'anni, Siciliana!" he bellowed. "May you live till kingdom come!"

Aetna's jaw dropped. The knight had spoken only to her, his words brimming her ears like a sacred command.

Glowing, Aetna turned to Cicero.

"Why did he say that?" she whispered.

Cicero shrugged, his eyes still marveling at the display on the stage.

Whatever the reason was, she knew something incredible happened to her that evening because of Orlando. He bestowed upon her a galvanizing feeling of significance, of greatness. In that very moment the young *Siciliana* made up her own mind.

She would live forever!

CHAPTER 2

Mount Etna, Sicily
August 22, 1269

THE FUGITIVE, wrapped in a black cowled robe, serpentined down the face of the volcanic crater. The thirty-one-year-old was a lean man. Dark and agile. His muscles felt starved of energy, sustained only by the primeval thrill of being hunted.

It's the panic that betrays you, he reminded himself.

Panic inhibited a fugitive's ability to think and act rationally and strategically. Panic kept his mind obsessed with an unrelenting paranoia. Never knowing when to expect a strong grip on the arm or a barn door crashing in.

Nearly a year earlier, the *Ordu Teutoni*—the Knights of the Teutonic Order, loyal to Prince Conradin—were outlawed by the French tyrant *Re Carlu* after the young prince's beheading. The arrest edict charged *Teutoni* Knights with treason and punished them with imprisonment, torture, and death. There was no safe haven for the *Ordu Teutoni* in the entire kingdom of Sicily. Many knights went into hiding. Most attempted to escape *Re Carlu's* reach and fled Sicily for the Holy Land.

To the knight on the run, the most effective antidote to panic was a clear plan, assistance from allies, and a sustained state of *calmo*—a calm mind. He knew that the most successful prisoners of war spent as much time planning their life after their escape as they did planning the escape itself. His safety came from constant secrecy, a new name, even a new means of livelihood. A knight with no plan and no support was in constant danger of betraying himself.

The *Teutoni* Knight winced in pain, his stomach growling with sharp pangs of hunger, as he made his way down the face of the crater, one foot in front of the other. It had been days since his last meal, but he couldn't stop now. Reaching Mount Etna's southeastern foothills meant he was close.

I must find the winemaker. The knight thought only of the mission with which he was now entrusted. He was the sole carrier of a powerful message that could alter the course of Sicily forever.

If I fail, all is lost . . .

The knight lifted his eyes to the sun, gauging the time of day. Beads of sweat trickled down his olive-skinned forehead. He'd been moving for over twenty-four hours straight. The human body could sustain long periods without eating, but sleeping could not be put off beyond the point at which the body absolutely demanded it, and then the fugitive was at his most vulnerable. Even the toughest battle-hardened knight was as helpless as a stray dog when in the black oblivion of slumber.

The knight's dark eyes flashed with desperation as he scrambled down the slope. Reaching the bottom of the crater, he suddenly found himself moving through a lush green field of shimmering grapevines, endlessly stretching out along the craters of the rolling foothills.

His ears perked up to a sharp snapping sound. He spotted a single flag, a *bannera*, fluttering violently in the wind.

The *bannera* was adorned with the likeness of the *Gorgoneion Trinacria*—an ancient Greek symbol depicting the shrieking face of Medusa, her hair slithering with serpents, surrounded by three human legs bent at the knee.

Embroidered beneath the horrific symbol in a strong Roman-style script were two words.

Viticultura Vespiri.

The cowled knight pondered the *bannera* as it blew stiffly in the wind.

The winemaker's vineyard, he told himself.

Suddenly, the knight was overwhelmed with a wave of exhaustion. He felt his knees give out and collapsed face-first into the dirt.

Then everything went black.

CHAPTER 3

Viticultura Vespiri
Mount Etna, Sicily
August 23, 1269

DON VITTORIO VESPIRI lurched up in bed, letting out a gasp of anguish as he awoke from his nightmare. Drenched in sweat, he felt his head still spinning as he tried to focus his blurry vision.

The room was dark except for the red light of dawn trickling in through the curtains. Panting, he felt the brisk air rush in and out of his lungs as he tried to control his breathing. He *had* to control it.

"*Patri?* Are you okay?"

Don Vespiri turned at the sound of the faint voice and saw her, illuminated by the red light pouring through the window.

His young daughter, Aetna. Her thick raven-black hair fell to her shoulders, framing a distinctive crescent-shaped scar on her right cheek. Nearly a year earlier, she and Cicero were climbing the surrounding slopes when a volcanic crater erupted beneath them. A molten rock fragment flung through the air and grazed Aetna's face, searing her olive skin. Forever branded by the lava.

Don Vespiri felt himself fixed in her strong gaze. The dark cloud hanging over him had begun to evaporate with the morning mist, leaving nothing but the damp smells of the room, his wooden tools, his musty clothing.

"*Santuzza,*" he muttered to Aetna. The Sicilian expression for *little, holy knight* was a term of endearment he had called her since birth.

Aetna just stood there, though, as stubbornly as the volcano she was named for.

"You had another dream again, didn't you?" she asked. Her piercing green eyes were filled with concern. And willfulness. "About the Angevins?"

"Go wake your brother," Don Vespiri said, trying to sound stern.

Aetna hesitated for a moment, then spun on her small heel and headed back through the doorway. She was as self-willed as her mother.

Rubbing his eyes with his knuckles, Don Vespiri stood up and walked barefoot across his bedroom, a familiar sigh escaping his lips.

Pull yourself together, Vittorio.

The twenty-seven-year-old winemaker wandered wearily over to his bedroom window. Outside, a morning mist drifted quietly over acres of *nerello mascalese* grapevines laid out in harmonic rows, their leaves dark green, their velvet fruit ripe and voluptuous.

Pale sunrays broke through the fog and slowly crowned over the slopes of the volcano, Mount Etna, painting the tops of the vines with a fiery red-orange glow. A gust of cold wind sent ripples across the top of the grapevines. Don Vespiri felt as if he were gazing upon the waves of the Mediterranean Sea itself, stretching far into the horizon.

Turning away from his bedroom window, the winemaker slid into his tunic and work boots. He grabbed a small torch hanging off the wall and slipped quietly outside.

Finally, he felt his blood begin to flow.

CHAPTER 4

SAUNTERING THROUGH the lush vineyard fields alone, Don Vespiri passed row upon row of grapevines glistening with dew. His torch spilled orange light across his face as he made his way toward a cavernous opening tucked into a steep slope of the volcano. He approached a set of narrow steps carved painstakingly into an ancient lava flow that led underground.

A wine cave.

Don Vespiri followed the steps downward and made his way through an arched passageway that opened into a vast barrel chamber. Rows of aged oak barrels were stacked atop one another in alternating patterns down the length of the cave walls. The air was thicker here. The aroma of fermenting grapes hung in the darkness, lingering in the winemaker's nostrils.

Don Vespiri half smiled as he approached his workbench, placing his torch gently into an iron sconce. The flickering flame cast dancing shadows across the cavern as he pulled a clean white tunic down from a hook on the wall, draping it over his torso like a magician's robe. He lifted a golden pendant off the table and hung it around his neck. Its shape was that of the *Gorgoneion Trinacria*—the face of Medusa surrounded by three human legs bent at the knees.

As he glanced up, his eyes caught on a mirrored silver plate that rested against the wall; in it, his own ghostly reflection stared back at him. Don Vespiri was a classically handsome man with curly dark hair, an aquiline nose, and olive Mediterranean skin hinting at an ancestral intermingling of the blood of various conquerors over the centuries. Greek, Roman, Arabic, Norman, all boiling together to form something strange and precarious: the true Sicilian. The *Don* at the beginning of his name was an honorific meaning *Sir*. Derived from the Latin *Dominus*, or *Lord*, it was a title bestowed only upon a master Sicilian knight. It was considered a term of *rispettu*—respect.

Don Vespiri was widely known among his peers to be a man who treated his fellow Sicilian with a keen sense of decency. One who would not stand idly by when others were greeted with insult or injury.

Last month, outside of Palermo Cathedral, he had broken up a stiletto duel simply by imposing his defenseless torso between the two quarreling men. He stepped between the razor-sharp blade tips the two angry Sicilians had aimed at one other. Both men stood in a firm guardian position—right foot forward, left foot back, a slightly crouched stance, dagger pointed outward. Even the faintest slash across the arm could cut a gash so deep, it meant certain death by blood loss or infection, as some blades were even dipped in diseased goat's blood before a duel.

"My friends," Don Vespiri had interjected, carefully raising his palms toward the blade tips.

The two men kept their eyes trained on one another, each ready to strike. A patrol of Angevin soldiers observed the gathering from the street, sharing a bottle of cheap wine among themselves as they laughed and jeered.

"This *Mamluk* insulted my sister," the first man said, eyes glaring with fire. "He dishonored my family's name and must pay with his life."

The second man growled, baring his teeth. "Your sister is a whore, and her bastard child is not my son," he said.

"Come on, then, you pig!" the first man shouted, beckoning him forward. "It's a good day to die!"

Don Vespiri took a deep breath, slowly placing his palms on top of each blade and pushing them downward. "We are not each other's enemy. We cannot be."

A man in the crowd stepped forward. "Don Vespiri, the deadliest *cavaleri* in all Sicily, telling others not to shed blood!"

There was a burst of uncomfortable laughter.

"My friends, I beg of you." Don Vespiri shook his head, thrusting a finger toward the horizon. "*Re Carlu* sits on a throne in Napoli, ruling our island from afar and subjecting us to his vile, drunken army."

Don Vespiri turned to face the gathering throng of spectators. "How many times have the Angevins stolen precious heirlooms from your homes, and livestock from your farms? How many times have they violated the innocence of your wives and daughters in the streets for all to see, while you were helpless to stop them?"

The two quarrelling men dropped their eyes.

"*Re Carlu* is our enemy," Don Vespiri said. "The Angevins are our enemy. Kings may be the judges of Sicily. But *we* are the judges of kings."

A man piped up. "The archbishop of Palermo will save us!" he said, pointing to the edifice of Palermo Cathedral looming over them. "He will lead us to salvation!"

In that instant, Don Vespiri felt the blood rush to his face. "The archbishop cares for no one but himself. Do not be fooled. He plays to the vices of our Angevin molesters for his own selfish gain. He serves only one master. Himself. And he seeks nothing more than to expand his own power. He is not *cosca*. He is not family. And I am ashamed to call him a Sicilian."

Don Vespiri hissed the *shh* sound in *ashamed* like a seething snake.

The two dueling men looked upon him with wide eyes. They had never heard another Sicilian speak with such ruthless courage and solidarity. By that time, the two men had lowered their blades, captivated by Don Vespiri's natural command and comfortable confidence. The dons of antiquity called it *occhinero*—literally meaning the black of the eyes. The name evolved into a term embodying the fierce quality of looking danger and adversity in the face . . . eyeballs to eyeballs.

Shaking the memory from his head, Don Vespiri grabbed his stiletto hanging from the wall, admiring it carefully in his palms. The blade was long and slender, with two snakes coiling around its crossbar. His eyes traced the length of the blade. If only the world knew how much blood had been drawn by its razor-sharp tip. Now, it drew only the red fluids of his own grapevines.

In that moment, he heard a faint rustling stir from under his workbench. Don Vespiri held his breath, feeling a chill as he placed his hand around the hilt of his blade.

A feral dog, he thought. A common menace he'd been dealing with since the beginning of time, it seemed.

Don Vespiri slowly tightened his grip. He had to be quick, for a bite from a sick dog was a certain death sentence. The infection could kill a man by slowly driving him mad, ultimately closing up his throat and drowning him in his own spit, if the violent muscle spasms didn't suffocate him first.

Steadying his blade in an attack guard, he quickly lifted the tablecloth, when a grinning face framed in raven-black hair suddenly emerged.

CHAPTER 5

"AETNA!" DON VESPIRI exclaimed, stumbling backward. Laughing, Aetna crawled out from underneath the table.

"*Santuzza*," he said, trying to slow his breathing. "You shouldn't scare *Patri* while he's working."

Aetna was still cackling as she climbed up onto his oaken stool, flashing her big eyes.

But then he smiled. It felt good, he realized, sharing this moment with her.

Aetna jumped to her feet, waving a small wooden sword. "I am Orlando, Sicily's perfect knight!"

Don Vespiri picked Aetna up and placed her firmly on the chair. "You know what made Orlando a great *cavaleri*, don't you?"

"His blade!" she exclaimed, hoisting her sword into the air.

Don Vespiri shook his head. He then pressed his finger into Aetna's forehead. "It was this," he said. "His mind was as sharp as any blade."

"Sharp, how?" Aetna said, rubbing the spot where her *patri's* finger jabbed her head.

"Sharp with ideas," he said. "Ideas that might inspire any woman, man, or an entire people to rule a country of their own." Don Vespiri paused for a moment, choosing his next words carefully. "Ideas of *rebellamentu.*"

"Rebellion?" she said. "Against who?"

"Not against *who.* Against *what.*"

"Against what, *Patri?*"

"Greed, oppression, the abuse of power," Don Vespiri explained. "Bad ideas that weak, lazy, selfish men use to expand their stations in life."

"How do we stop them?"

Don Vespiri smiled, leaning in to address his daughter. "By protecting the helpless," he said. "Defending those less fortunate than you so that they may become the best version of themselves. Sicily can only stand tall when all of her families and orphans stand together. These are the ideas of a great Sicilian *cavaleri* like Orlando."

With that, Don Vespiri gripped the golden pendant in his palm and extended it toward Aetna.

Aetna's eyes fell to the pendant, enthralled.

"It's called the *Gorgoneion Trinacria,*" Don Vespiri said.

"What is it?" Aetna asked, pondering Medusa's shrieking face and slithering hair frozen perpetually in time.

"A symbol of protection," Don Vespiri said. "Guarding all who display it from harm and evil influences."

Aetna reached out for the pendant and held it in her hands. The *Gorgoneion Trinacria* gleamed in the firelight, reflecting shards of golden rays into her green eyes.

Don Vespiri pressed his finger into the pendant. "Medusa was once a bright, happy Sicilian woman. Her beauty was so magnificent, in fact, that it caught the eye of Poseidon, the dastardly god of the sea. Though Medusa wanted nothing to do with him and resisted all of his advances. Until one day, she was praying alone in the temple of Athena, the goddess of wisdom, when Poseidon cornered Medusa and forced himself upon her."

Aetna felt a sudden chill. She glanced up. "Did she fight back?"

"She fought like the strong woman she was. But it was too late. The goddess Athena became furious with Poseidon and the terrible acts that took place in her temple. In an attempt to protect poor Medusa, Athena transformed her hair into slithering snakes and gave her the deadly power to turn to stone any man who gazed upon her."

Aetna's eyes flashed with surprise.

"And from that day forth, Medusa lived the life of a misunderstood monster," Don Vespiri continued. "Upon Medusa's death, the goddess Athena honored her by displaying her head on the aegis of her own shield—a warning to evil men that they act with respect and goodwill, or else be turned to stone." Don Vespiri paused, seeing the intrigue build in his daughter's eyes. "Medusa was a tragic victim . . . a misunderstood monster . . . and now"—he tapped his fingertip gently against Medusa's face on the pendant—"she is *our* Great Protector."

Aetna stared at the pendant. The image was unsettling and profoundly strange. Her initial awe gave way to a sudden upwelling of sorrow. "I feel sad for Medusa."

Don Vespiri's eyes fell upon Aetna, watching her face as he beheld her mind working behind her eyes. Processing. Forming an idea. "How so?"

"She was punished for being who she was," Aetna said. "For being a girl . . . like me."

Don Vespiri frowned. "And now she protects us so that you may one day grow up to be a strong woman."

Aetna's attention suddenly shifted. She noticed the three human legs spiraling outward from behind Medusa's head. "What are these strange-looking legs for?"

Don Vespiri smiled, leaning in closer. "That's the best part. These legs represent the three corners of Sicily, our home." He traced each bent leg with the tip of his finger. "More important, they serve to teach us a powerful lesson. No matter where we are thrown, a Sicilian will always land standing."

Aetna gazed down assuredly at the pendant. "I will be a great protector one day."

Don Vespiri smiled. "That's my *santuzza*," he said, leaning in and planting his lips on her forehead. With that, Aetna hopped off the bench and dashed up the stairs to the surface above.

As Don Vespiri watched his daughter leave, he felt a sudden surge of uneasiness. The same feeling that tortured him in his dreams, hanging over him, blocking his light like a solar eclipse.

Who will protect the families of Sicily against the Angevin threat?

Don Vespiri glanced down to his stiletto holstered on his hip. The blade was the embodiment of Sicilian courage. Where corrupt men in power failed to uphold justice, a *cavaleri* with a sharpened stiletto had to administer his own. *Swiftly. Viciously. Effectively.*

In that instant, Don Vespiri snapped out his blade with deadly speed and lifted it to his face, seeing his own reflection staring back at him. A master of *occhinero*. A man who looked danger in the black of the eyes. Like all *cavaleri* who came before him, he had learned to find courage in the assured voices of his own mind. Today, however, those voices were as dead quiet as the empty wine cave around him.

CHAPTER 6

VITICULTURA VESPIRI was an expansive vineyard estate nestled against the southeastern Ilice Crater on the active volcano Mount Etna. Along Etna's lower slopes, row upon row of grapevines and almond trees blossomed from the black soot. This ugly soil was among the richest earth in the *Regno*, holding the roots of Sicily's ancient vines in a lover's embrace. Mount Etna was at the same time a menace to those nestling into her slopes. Glowing orange fissures and hot-steam vents regularly burst from the flanks of the mountain. During these frequent eruptions, lava flowed relentlessly from her core, weaving webs of fire that could be seen through the hot summer nights, destroying everything in its path.

Vineyard overseer Paola Sinibaldo knelt down and brushed the cindery volcanic dust from a handful of violet-blue grapes as she inspected the satin fruit closely between her fingertips. The grapes were plump and strong, blooming year after year without a care for the troubles the world brought down around them. Every harvest then became an act of defiance against the waves of conquerors that slammed against Sicily's shores.

At twenty-four years old, Paola had supervised the vine-yard grounds for her entire young-adult life. She assumed the hectic role shortly after her older sister died giving birth to her niece, Aetna. It was the least Paola could do to help in the face of her family's loss.

Paola stood up, shielding her round, olive face from the glaring sun as she gazed out over the expansive property. The Vespiri farmhouse, a humble structure made of gray volcanic stone, sat atop a small hill overlooking the entire estate. Flying above the main entrance to the property was the vineyard's *bannera*, or flag. The words *Viticultura Vespiri* were sewn across the top in strong Roman-style script. Embroidered just below in the center of the *bannera* was the shrieking face of the *Gorgoneion Trinacria*.

Moments later, Paola saw the vineyard's very own daunt-less winemaker emerge from a nearby supply barn. A crooked smile broke out across her dry lips.

Don Vittorio Vespiri maneuvered an empty wheelbarrow through an endless row of bustling workers clipping ripe purple grapes from their vines. The tireless winemaker brought the wheelbarrow to a heavy stop in the middle of the field, leaving a large plume of dust in his path.

Paola picked up her feet and walked over to meet Don Vespiri.

"Bon jornu," she smirked. "If the sun beat us any harder, I'd think it was *Re Carlu* himself."

"How are the south fields coming along?" Don Vespiri asked sternly.

"Picked clean this morning," Paola said. She moved quickly out of the way as workers lumbered over with bulging woven baskets, dropping the freshly picked grapes into the wheelbarrow's hull. "Would you like to ride out and inspect the grounds?"

"I don't think that will be necessary," Don Vespiri said, dropping to his knees. He buried his hands in the plump grape bunches, examining the satiny fruit between his fingers. He plucked a single grape from the bunch and bit into it carefully. The cool, sweet juice exploded in his mouth.

Don Vespiri closed his eyes, concentrating on the sublime flavor coating his tongue, freshening his mouth. In that brief moment, he felt his troubles melt away.

Swirling around him, *Viticultura Vespiri* was alive with a cacophony of activity. The smell of horses and fresh soil hung in the air as rows of men and women roved through the fields, pruning grapes from their vines and dropping them into baskets below. In the kitchen, workers were already preparing lunch, stirring ruby tomato sauce, grilling various meats with onions and eggplant, pulling steaming bread from the oven, and rolling yellow pasta dough into broad *pappardelle* ribbons. At harvest time, they worked all day and, on some occasions, into the night. The fruit had to be picked on time: too early and the resulting wine would be tart and overly herbaceous; too late and the wine would be ruined in a more tragic way, flowing from the bottle like a flavorless brown syrup.

Don Vespiri rose to his feet, standing up straight and wiping his dirty hands against the front of his pants. "Not even *Re Carlu* could oppress this year's harvest," he said defiantly, smirking up to Paola.

There was a high-pitched whinny of a horse in the distance. He glanced up to see his son, Cicero, emerge from the barn, chasing a black *San Fratello* pony, a smile beaming wide across his determined face. His black curly hair flopped in front of his gentle hazel eyes. Aetna followed close behind, a crimson shawl flying out from her neck. Her long hair blazed in the sunlight as she ran.

The children dashed through the row of grapevines, right past Don Vespiri. He jumped out of the way, shaking his head.

"Don't run off too far now," he said.

It was enough that his heart already prickled with that constant worry for his children so ingrained in Sicilian fathers—but knowing his wild-hearted daughter, he found that his patience was stretched that much more.

"*Sì, Patri,*" Cicero called back over his shoulder.

Don Vespiri watched vigilantly as the children chased the pony down the rows of vines. Suddenly, they stopped dead in their tracks, distracted by something among the fields.

The pony bucked and whinnied, tearing back toward the barn.

Don Vespiri squinted into the distance, moving toward the two children. As he approached them, his eyes widened.

Lying among the vines was an unconscious Sicilian man who looked to be in his early thirties. Don Vespiri pressed his fingers into the man's neck, feeling the slow beat of his pulse.

"He's alive," Don Vespiri said.

Don Vespiri then bent over and slowly opened the man's cloak. His heart leapt into his throat as he beheld a white shield emblazoned with a black cross. He immediately knew what he was looking at.

The coat of arms of the *Ordu Teutoni.*

A Teutoni *Knight,* Don Vespiri thought to himself. The outlawed protectors of Sicily's vanquished prince.

CHAPTER 7

DON VESPIRI studied the unconscious man lying in the soil as Aetna and Cicero inched closer with wide eyes. The knight's pants and boots were stained with dirt, his olive face beaten and bruised, his thick black hair gnarled and matted with sweat. Dried blood stained in long streaks on his white tunic.

His heart racing, Don Vespiri pulled up the tunic and found a deep laceration across the man's lower rib cage and abdomen. The gash looked dangerously deep but seemed to be well treated and wrapped.

Aetna peered out cautiously from behind her aunt Paola, who along with the other vineyard workers had gathered round Don Vespiri, forming an artichoke-like protective shield around him.

Aetna stared for a long moment, feeling the searing images of the wounded knight pierce through her.

Kneeling down next to the knight, Don Vespiri carefully pressed his fingers into the man's throat. He then craned his head back to Paola. "Take the children and ready the back bedroom. Prepare water, fresh fruit, and clean linens."

Paola gazed at him in shock for a long moment.

"*Ammunini!*" Don Vespiri shouted. "Go!"

The workers quickly approached and lifted the knight from the ground, wrapping his body gently in a blanket.

Don Vespiri pressed his palms into his knees and stood up slowly, stealing an anxious glance toward his children. Seeing their worried faces, he felt like a hammer was slamming through his chest. The Sicilian people had grown accustomed to cruel abuses at the hands of *Re Carlu*'s soldiers, but he knew one thing was certain—he never wanted his children to feel unsafe.

In that moment, Don Vespiri's fists tightened in frustration, and helplessness.

Cicero ran up behind the workers and pressed his hands underneath the man's body as they sauntered across the field. Don Vespiri watched as his son's small hands tried to support the weight of the large man swinging to and fro in the blanket. He had his mother's kind and determined heart.

Paola scooped Aetna into her arms and hurried back toward the farmhouse with the other field workers. In a wave of distress, two workers flashed grim looks at each other. Together they expressed one final cognition, a strange set of words that Aetna didn't recognize.

"*Simmo surfaru,*" the first worker whispered.

The second worker shook his head and frowned. "*Simmo surfaru.*"

CHAPTER 8

THE VESPIRI farmhouse looked tired that night. A great blanket of darkness fell over the mountain, the night pierced only by a dim fire flickering red and orange in the windows.

Paola Sinibaldo carried a fresh jug of water into the small back bedroom, where the wounded knight had been laid. She kept her gaze on the man, who had since relented to the comfort of the straw mattress and slipped in and out of sleep.

Resting the jug gently on a wooden nightstand, Paola took a seat at the bedside and finished re-dressing his old wounds. She wrapped clean linen bandages around his torso.

She grabbed a wet cloth and slowly dabbed the knight's glistening forehead, shaking her head.

What has he gotten himself into out there? she wondered.

Sitting in the master parlor, Cicero stared out into the darkness over a row of toy soldiers that lined the windowsill. There were no signs of life. All was quiet.

At the same time, Aetna sauntered in, carrying an armful of firewood. She tossed what she could into the hearth, then dropped to her knees and continued to stoke the small fire she'd started earlier that evening.

Don Vittorio Vespiri sat silently in his favorite chair, pinching a morsel of bread between his fingers and sopping up the last of the olive oil and ruby-orange tomato sauce from his dinner plate. He then moved up beside his son, helping him to take down the toy soldiers one at a time.

"The Angevins are coming, aren't they?" Cicero asked.

"*Patri* will fight them off," Aetna said over her shoulder.

"Aetna!" Cicero said.

"*Patri* knows all about knights," Aetna shot back. "He'll protect us."

"That's enough," Don Vespiri said, placing the toy soldiers carefully inside a wooden case.

"I can fight," Cicero said, nodding assuredly.

Don Vespiri looked over to his son, his face softening. "I know you can fight. But it's not our blades that makes us great *cavaleri*." Don Vespiri laid his palm on his son's chest and said, "Your measure of greatness lies here."

Cicero looked down at his father's large hands. They were rough and muscular, bulging with veins, dirty from a long day in the field, and yet his palms were soft to the touch.

"One day, you will have to care for this land and for the people less fortunate than you," Don Vespiri said. "You aren't measured by how many soldiers you slay or how many victories you tally in battle, but by your ability to understand and share the feelings of others. Strive to leave this world better than when you found it. *Sempri*. Always."

Cicero's face seemed to sharpen with an assured sense of resolve. "*Sì, Patri.*"

Don Vespiri leaned forward and kissed him on the head.

Aetna yelped with surprise as she poked over a piece of firewood that sent up a plume of glowing embers. She then craned her neck over her shoulder. "*Patri*, I have a question. What does *simmo surfaru* mean?"

Don Vespiri slowly turned his head, his expression suddenly turning grim. He set down the toy soldiers to give Aetna his full attention. "Where did you hear that, *santuzza*?"

"The workers said it today," she said, poking the firewood. "After we saved the man in the field."

Don Vespiri closed his eyes and shook his head. "Don't ever say that again, *capiche*?"

"Why?"

"Because it's a bad word."

Cicero glanced up, seeming to notice his father's scolding tone and sensing a possible confrontation.

After a moment of tense silence, Aetna gathered her resolve and pressed the issue further. "But what does it mean, *Patri*?"

Don Vespiri blew a long breath between his lips. "If I tell you, do you promise never to say it again?"

"I promise," she said.

"Do you promise, too, Cicero?" Don Vespiri said, spinning the boy away from the window.

"*Sì, Patri.*" Cicero nodded.

Don Vespiri shifted his focus between the two children. "*Simmo surfaru* means that we are nothing but sulfur."

"Sulfur?" Cicero said.

"You mean that smelly rock that comes from the volcano?" Aetna asked.

Don Vespiri nodded. "It's an expression used in defeat," Don Vespiri said. "It means we Sicilians are helplessly strewn about this earth like sulfur from Mount Etna, doomed to forever be at the mercy of those stronger than us."

"Is it true?" Aetna asked.

"Of course not," Don Vespiri said. "Nonsense that only fearful Sicilians believe." He then lifted his finger to the *Gorgoneion Trinacria* hanging from his neck. "But we are not fearful, because we know that as Sicilians, no matter where we are thrown, we will always land standing. You . . . me . . ."

"Aunt Paola?" Aetna chimed in.

Don Vespiri nodded. "*Sì*, Aunt Paola, too. As a strong Sicilian family, we have to help lead the people *in posterum*. Into *tomorrow*."

Aetna flashed Cicero an astonished look.

Don Vespiri gazed down at his two children, admiring their glowing faces. *Tomorrow.* It was a wonderous Latin concept that didn't quite exist in the Sicilian heart and mind. Life under Angevin rule came with the constant threat of physical assault. Sicilians were viewed by the Angevins as culturally backward and racially suspect. Their language and customs considered dirty, primitive, and uncivilized. Drunken Angevins soldiers vandalized churches, raided trattorias, and stole food and supplies. With no time to rest nerves or contemplate tomorrow, Sicilian life was lived fiercely in the present. To speak of the future was to speak of the language of the gods.

Don Vespiri smiled and clapped his hands together. "Well, that's enough excitement for one day. Off to bed, the both of you."

Aetna lowered her brow, pouting in defiance.

"*Ammunini*," Don Vespiri said, raising his voice.

Cicero stooped his head and leapt from his seat, shuffling off to his room.

Aetna just sat there, watching her brother leave. She then turned and locked eyes with her father.

Don Vespiri shook his head. *She gets it from her mother. Stubborn as the volcano she was named for.* He lifted a finger and pointed toward her room. "Off to bed now," he said again, attempting to sound stern.

Aetna hesitated for a moment, then finally picked up her feet and headed out of the room.

Don Vespiri watched carefully and waited to make sure the children were settled and in their beds. He then grabbed a candelabrum off the table and made his way to the back of the manor.

It was time he found out the truth about the mysterious stranger who had arrived at their doorstep.

CHAPTER 9

DON VESPIRI pressed his hand on the bedroom door and gently pushed it open. He saw Paola sitting with the wounded *Teutoni* Knight. Don Vespiri moved up behind her and rested an assuring hand on her shoulder. Paola placed her palm over Don Vespiri's hand, feeling a rush of relief wash over her.

"How's he doing?" he asked.

"He lacks sleep and nourishment. Nothing a glass of *Etna Rosso* can't remedy."

Don Vespiri did his best to feign a smile, his expression then turning solemn. "Leave me alone with him."

Paola nodded and stood up from her seat. She headed out the door, keeping it cracked open behind her as she slipped out.

Don Vespiri watched her depart; then he turned and slowly took a seat on the wooden stool next to the bedside. He gazed down at the wounded knight, who was muttering something unintelligible. It sounded like prayers.

The knight had olive skin, thick black hair, and a poorly shaven face. Where there was once a thick beard now revealed a pale chin and cheeks, much lighter in color than his skin above. Thrown over a chair was the notorious white tunic, emblazoned with a single black cross and adorned with a familiar high-ranking officer's seal.

Don Vespiri opened his mouth to speak, but no words came out. He felt his heart pound in his chest as a revelation struck him. *Cristu.* He suddenly realized the man in his presence was no ordinary man. It was the *capu*, the high commander of the *Ordu Teutoni*, Andrea Bonelli.

Capu Bonelli was last seen on the Palentine Plains nearly one year ago when Prince Conradin was decisively defeated by *Re Carlu*'s superior army. Soon after the young prince's capture and execution, the *Teutoni* Knights were driven underground. Bonelli had vanished. Some believed he was dead. Others that he slipped away into a life of obscurity within the safety of the brotherhood's clandestine network.

Now, standing in the dim light of his candelabrum, Don Vespiri felt he was forced to accept a very troubling truth. With the conquest of *Re Carlu*, and the *Teutoni* commander lying in his home, the kingdom of Sicily as he knew it was nothing but sulfur. *Simmo surfaru.*

Bonelli groaned, attempting to sit up. "Is there no help for a widow's son?"

Don Vespiri laid his palm on the *capu*'s chest, pressing him back into the mattress. "Save your energy, my friend. You're safe now."

Bonelli grimaced. "Don Vespiri . . . forgive me. I know my presence here is a grave risk to you and your family."

Don Vespiri looked troubled. "Were you followed?"

Bonelli shook his head.

Don Vespiri took a deep breath and gazed out the bedroom window into the expansive darkness. *Re Carlu*'s arrest edict included anyone who had information on *Teutoni* Knight whereabouts. Merchants, carpenters, fishermen, shepherds. In spite of this looming threat, Sicilians were sympathetic to the *Ordu Teutoni* and considered them protectors of the *Regno*, the old kingdom. The people banded together and created a secret network of concealment and lodging, helping *Teutoni* Knights move through towns and villages as they escaped to more friendly lands. They offered pasta, wine, and protection. A stable, a hunter's hut, anything to provide safekeeping for the night. It was here that *Teutoni* Knights received news, directions to the next hiding place, and depending on the generosity of the Sicilian, a few spare coins and pieces of bread for the next leg of their journey.

Bonelli took a labored breath. "I've traveled a long and treacherous road . . ."

"You could've smuggled yourself onto a ship with safe passage to the Holy Land," Don Vespiri said. "Why come back to Sicily?"

"To bring you Conradin's last command—the fulfillment of a promise."

"What kind of promise?"

Bonelli locked eyes with him. "One that gives power back to the Sicilian people, so that they may rule themselves as a free nation . . . *in posterum.*"

Don Vespiri's breathing quickened as he felt a shiver of anticipation. "What has the prince asked of me?"

Bonelli looked as if he were choosing his next words carefully. "Become the Protector of Sicily. Return this land to her families and orphans so that they may know a country of their own."

Don Vespiri's entire body went rigid. He couldn't believe his ears. *Become the Protector of Sicily?* Don Vespiri exhaled, motioning toward the window. "And what of the Angevin yoke that strangles our island?"

Bonelli's expression hardened. *"Rebellamentu."*

Don Vespiri's raised his eyebrows. "Incite rebellion against *Re Carlu*?"

Bonelli nodded grimly. "Will you accept this sacred duty being asked of you?"

Don Vespiri shook his head, feeling a knot tighten in his gut. "Surely a *Teutoni* marshal or general would be better suited. Somebody with command over an army—"

"*You* command the hearts and minds of the Sicilian people," Bonelli said, lowering his voice as if to make sure no one else was listening. "Kings may be the judges of Sicily . . . but *we* are the judges of kings. And the king's judgment has come. Raise your blade and return Sicily to her rightful heir . . . the Sicilians. The *Ordu Teutoni* stands with you . . . *O Santo Cavaleri.*"

Don Vespiri's shook his head. "That name died with Conradin."

"But his promise of a free Sicily lives as long as we carry breath in our lungs," Bonelli pressed.

Don Vespiri thrust a finger toward the commander. "Not even the *Ordu Teutoni* stands a chance against the Angevins. *Re Carlu*'s army is undefeatable."

Bonelli stared at him for a long moment. "Poor is the nation that has no heroes. I knew you to be a man of *occhinero*. A man who looks his enemies in the black of the eyes."

Don Vespiri blew hot air from his nostrils, feeling a tinge of anger. He knew in his bones that he could slay one hundred Angevin soldiers roughly, swiftly, and efficiently with the stroke of his blade. But he would not willfully incite open war on their island. Among their homes.

"There are alternatives to war," Don Vespiri said.

"What alternatives?" Bonelli scoffed.

"We bring our terms before *Re Carlu*," Don Vespiri said. "We plead with him for independence."

"Impossible," Bonelli spat.

"Well, we must try. And keep trying for as long as it takes," Don Vespiri said, his face souring. "Anything to avoid war."

In that instant, Bonelli raised his hand, revealing an ornamental gauntlet glimmering from his forearm—displaying the heraldry of a black Imperial Eagle on a golden shield. Its wings spread outward, its red tongue extending from its beak.

Don Vespiri's jaw dropped. *"La Guanto di Sfida,"* he muttered. "Conradin's gauntlet of defiance." Legend told of the day when the vanquished prince fearlessly mounted the execution scaffold and threw his royal gauntlet out into the watching crowd—a final act of defiance against Angevin power. It was even said that at the moment of his death, an eagle swooped down from the sky and dipped its right wing in his blood.

Bonelli's expression was grim. "I was there that fateful day when everything changed. *Re Carlu*'s thirst for power and bloodlust are insatiable. Not since Alexander the Great have I seen a ruthless would-be emperor loom so large over the Mediterranean. That's the measure of the threat upon us. He is immune to treaty or diplomacy."

"I have two children," Don Vespiri said. "What becomes of them if I do what is being asked of me?"

"The children of Sicily need you," Bonelli said. "You must think larger now."

Don Vespiri took a deep breath. "My place is here."

Bonelli locked eyes with Don Vespiri, struggling to sit up. He grasped Don Vespiri's hand, squeezing it tightly. "There will be no peace for us as long as *Re Carlu* sits on the throne. What makes this your place will soon be no more."

Don Vespiri shook his head. "Sicily is *cosca*. It is family, or it is nothing. Their protection is all that matters now."

"Family can be a convenient disguise for fear," Bonelli said.

Don Vespiri furrowed his brow. He raised his finger, pointing it toward Bonelli. "How dare you speak to me in this way."

Bonelli fell silent. A long moment passed between the two men.

"I was merely a boy when my village was destroyed," Bonelli said. "At a time when Arab Sicilians were deemed a threat to the monarchy and expelled from the kingdom." He paused, seeming to retreat inward. "Family *is* everything . . . to those who have one."

Don Vespiri had no idea how to respond. The commander's words landed like a sudden punch to his gut.

Bonelli's expression turned solemn. "What about the orphans?" He pointed to himself. "What if Sicily were the *only* family we had left? Wouldn't you die for your family?"

For several seconds, Don Vespiri stared into Bonelli's eyes, feeling the air hanging heavy between them.

"I think you need to rest, Commander," Don Vespiri said. He stood up to leave, never turning back. "You speak dangerous words."

"*Cent'anni,*" Bonelli muttered softly. "*O Santo Cavaleri.*"

As Don Vespiri left the room, a small figure crept out from behind the door where it had been hiding. Cicero could hear his own heart as he slowly peered inside the room. At that moment, Cicero's eyes connected with the wounded knight's, which were as dark as Mount Etna's soil. They held one another's gaze like two clashing blades. Cicero felt a knot tighten in his stomach as a strange mix of fear and curiosity overtook him.

The man leaned forward from his bed, his face illuminated by the candlelight. "Who's there?" he muttered.

Cicero's eyes went wide. In a sudden panic, he spun on his heel and disappeared silently into the darkness of the manor.

CHAPTER 10

ALL NIGHT, Don Vespiri couldn't sleep. The *Teutoni* commander's words still lingered in his mind. *Kings may be the judges of Sicily, but we are the judges of kings.* It was a stirring sentiment. But a foolish one. No brave Sicilian had dared stand up to *Re Carlu* and lived to tell the tale.

Groaning, Don Vespiri slid off the bed, donned a robe, and stepped out of the manor into the cool air. He took a deep breath as he stood in solitude, looking up into the night sky. The blanket of stars helped to suppress the rising uncertainty swirling in his mind. Scanning the heavens, he was looking for something. He knew it was up there this time of year.

The star Spica, his wife's namesake, glistened in the constellation Virgo every harvest season. The star represented the ear of wheat, the nurturing grain of Sicily herself. Finally, Don Vespiri saw it. It shined brightly from above, as if only for him.

Gazing upward, Don Vespiri retreated into his memory. He reached up toward the star and now found himself grasping his pregnant wife's hand as she screamed in agony. A midwife gently dabbed the sweat trickling from Spica Vespiri's clammy forehead. Don Vespiri noticed with worry that her breathing had become more labored.

"She's losing blood," the midwife said.

The old woman inspected the suffering mother. The white silk linens were stained red. Horseflies buzzed ferociously overhead, attracted by the salty scent of blood that lingered in the musty room. The midwife swatted them aside, shaking her head.

She looked up at the exhausted father, pursing her lips as she broke the horrific news.

"I'm afraid your child has turned the wrong way in the womb," she said.

Spica threw her head back and wailed into the air. Her screams frightened their toddler, Cicero, who lay crying in his crib in the corner of the room. Don Vespiri clutched for his wife's hand, squeezing it as hard as he could. His heart thundered in his chest.

"Will she live?" he asked, panicked, willing the news not to be true.

"We'll need to deliver the child as soon as possible," the midwife said quickly. She looked up at Don Vespiri, noting the despair on his face. She assumed a loud, authoritative tone and said, "Go fetch a set of clean linens from the shed."

Don Vespiri nodded and scrambled from the room. When he returned moments later, gripping the bedsheets in his hands, he felt a wave of relief wash over him to discover the midwife holding a baby girl in her arms. The child's cries pierced the delicate silence of the farmhouse as she inhaled air for the first time.

Aetna.

It was the name they had agreed on, a tribute to the temperamental volcano that towered over their vineyard estate, its rich black soil providing them with a livelihood.

Don Vespiri's smile suddenly faded as he gazed upon his wife in horror. Her eyes were glazed over, her face frozen in an expression of pain. Dropping the linens, Don Vespiri fell to his knees. He threw his arms over his wife and wept.

His greatest love. His guiding light. The nurturing wheat of their family.

Spica was gone.

Standing beneath the star, Don Vespiri suddenly felt the crushing weight of his sole responsibility—a father's immense obligation to protect his beautiful children from a menacing threat looming over the horizon.

If I take up my blade against the Angevins, he asked the glimmering star, *what becomes of our family?*

His eyes became liquid pools as he opened his conflicted heart to his lost love, waiting to receive her answer. As usual, his heart was never quiet enough to hear it, and the answer never came.

CHAPTER 11

SMOKE ROSE slowly from Etna's crater the next morning. She had awoken from her long slumber. The wind whipped across the foothills, carrying repugnant gaseous aromas down through the valley. Etna's smoke mixed with the cool morning air coming off the vines, draping the land in a veil of thick fog.

Don Vittorio Vespiri's pruning blade twitched and snapped as he clipped the grapevines with a sense of purpose. He glanced over at Aetna, who was working only a few feet away with her back turned to him. Her form was more spirited than usual.

"Rispettu," Don Vespiri said. "We must respect Etna's vines. Pruning too hard may bruise her fruit."

Stumbling among the field, Cicero struggled to hold a large basket bulging with grapes.

"Finuti," he grunted as he collapsed to his knees, letting out a long sigh of relief. He grabbed a few grapes from the pile and shoved them into his mouth.

"A bottomless pit," Don Vespiri said. "The harvest does us no good in your belly."

Cicero smiled, sneaking a few more grapes for good measure. Then he crinkled his nose, squeezing his nostrils with his fingertips. The fog carried a stifling aroma of rotten eggs.

"Is that what I think it is?" he grumbled.

"*Surfaru,*" Don Vespiri said. "Sulfur."

Aetna glanced sideways at her father through her long hair, recognizing the strange word the workers had used the day before.

Suddenly Cicero felt a rumbling coming from beneath the earth. He sat up quickly and pressed his palms into the damp soil. "Did you feel that?"

Don Vespiri felt a faint tremor beneath his feet. He turned to Cicero and smiled. "Even Etna's belly grumbles from time to time."

Shooting a glance down the field, Don Vespiri noticed that Paola and the other workers had stopped clipping the vines and were murmuring among themselves.

They must've felt it, too, he thought.

Silence hung.

Then the ground began to tremble violently beneath their feet as a thunderous sound rose louder and louder. Slowly, the menacing reverberation broke apart and separated into the sound of hooves beating in the distance.

"Vittorio!" Paola yelled, motioning toward the horizon.

Don Vespiri turned his head and peered down the road. In that instant, a primeval feeling of terror clenched his gut as he beheld a dreadful figure emerging from the fog.

In his tired bones, he knew that everything was about to change for the worse.

CHAPTER 12

AETNA LOOKED on in shock as a single Angevin horseman rose up over the foggy horizon, wielding a flaming torch. The horse was bigger than any horse she had ever seen, and covered in more metal than a Greek armada. It was truly a warhorse. Rising behind the soldier, the smeared glow of hundreds of red-orange flames penetrated the thick blue air as an entire horde of Angevin cavalry materialized through the fog. The horsemen were armed to the teeth. Carrying long, razor-sharp rapiers, holding lances pointing upward to the sky. They rode forward in two columns, hoisting royal blue Angevin flags patterned with golden *fleurs-de-lis* that snapped in the wind as they barreled forward.

Don Vittorio Vespiri carefully unsheathed his stiletto and twirled it in his fingers, turning it backward and upward, concealing the length of the blade from view behind the back of his forearm. *Indraga Mano.* The hidden-handguard.

Cicero rolled onto his knees to get a better look. His eyes narrowed. "Angevins."

Don Vespiri shot a concerned glance toward his son. "Take your sister and go hide in the field."

"But, *Patri*, I can help—" Cicero protested, eyeing the approaching soldiers.

"Go!" Don Vespiri growled.

Cicero clutched Aetna by the hand, and together they scampered off into the vineyard. The children dove hard onto the ground and crawled under a tangled grapevine, peering out carefully from the brush.

All of the vineyard workers turned their heads toward the road and watched as a large group of Angevin horsemen galloped toward them. The Angevin cavalry was the most dangerous fighting force in all of the Mediterranean. With polished armor and razor-sharp weaponry, they were a terrifying sight to behold and struck fear into the hearts of anyone who stood in their path.

The soldiers fanned out around the property with deadly precision, kicking up enormous plumes of blackened dust in their wake. The ground rumbled as their hooves beat the earth like war drums. A worker made the sign of the cross with a trembling hand.

God be with us, Don Vespiri told himself.

In that instant, a towering figure trotted forward from the tumult of the soldiers—a hulking man who, boasting a shining steel breastplate and a wolfskin draped around his shoulders, sat tall on his horse. He was the commanding officer, General Guy de Rochefort. The general had a pale complexion with icy gray eyes and the repugnant disposition of an aristocrat.

Gashed across his left eye and down his cheek was a sizable grotesque scar. He was a powerful horse-master on the largest steed in the cavalry. The general advanced with a chilling authority.

Rochefort pulled hard on the reins of his horse, bringing the beast to a heavy stop.

Don Vespiri felt the general's weight towering over him.

Rochefort snapped his sharp chin upward to survey the scene before him. "Search the house and stable."

A haggard Angevin with drunken eyes named Sergeant Drouet grinned deviously and strode to the front of the line, beckoning his men forward. The soldiers barreled toward the farmhouse, shoving Don Vespiri with their shoulders as they ran past him.

Don Vespiri looked up at Rochefort, studying the general's face to try to get a read on the situation. He stared deep into Rochefort's reptilian slits for eyes as the general scanned the workers standing in the vineyard. Don Vespiri knew what he was doing. The general was calculating a head count.

In that instant, Don Vespiri felt a surge of fear course through his veins. He didn't want to feel it. He was ashamed to feel it. But the fear came to him anyway. He stood silently as the Angevin soldiers sparked their torches and fanned out around him in all directions. Soldiers rammed their way into the manor while others headed around the perimeter toward the stables.

Paola looked on from across the field, shaking her head in disbelief. "You must do something!"

Don Vespiri's brow furrowed as he raised his hand to silence her. His children were hidden, and all of his workers were within sight and unharmed. They had to remain calm. Any brash moves would ensure the swift death of them all.

Moments later, there was a commotion coming from inside the farmhouse. All heads turned to the sounds of men shouting, furniture crashing. Soldiers emerged from the threshold dragging out the helpless *Teutoni* commander, *Capu* Andrea Bonelli, his bare toes scraping the black volcanic soil.

Watching from beneath the grapevine trunk, Aetna clasped her hands over her mouth to prevent a scream. Cicero squeezed her arm, his fingernails beginning to dig in.

Don Vespiri stood as still as stone. He watched as the soldiers dragged Bonelli past him and pushed him in front of Rochefort's horse. Another soldier came up from behind and threw a white tunic emblazoned with a black cross onto the dirt at Rochefort's feet.

The coat of arms of the *Ordu Teutoni*.

Rochefort glared down at Bonelli. In that instant, he seemed to determine the fate of *Viticultura Vespiri*. The general lifted his chin and called out to the soldiers surrounding the estate. "Burn the house and grounds."

CHAPTER 13

DON VESPIRI'S eyes widened in shock. His worst nightmare was materializing before him.

"Seize the horses, save the valuables," General Rochefort continued. "Let it be known that all who harbor enemies of King Charles will lose their home."

Sergeant Drouet nodded his head with satisfaction, flashing a devious grin. The Angevins hoisted their torches and ran off toward the farmhouse, touching the tips of their flames into the vines as they fanned out through the field. Fire spread quickly across the top of the vines and roiled upward toward the sky. Soldiers approached the stable, wrapping a rope around the black snout of Aetna's *San Fratello* pony. The terrified creature recoiled as two strong men tugged it away with the other horses.

Rochefort looked down at *Capu* Andrea Bonelli. "This *Teutoni* Knight is a traitor. Take him back to Messina. Mount his head on the castle embankments. Send his limbs to all three corners of the island."

A pair of soldiers nodded and moved in to bind Bonelli, shoving a dirty rag deep into his mouth. Weakened and overpowered, Bonelli submitted to his captors. He shot one final glance toward Don Vespiri, his eyes filled with apology, before he was dragged away.

In the distance, Paola and the other workers were being rounded up and forced into lines at the tips of Angevin rapiers. "Vittorio!" she cried out as the soldiers closed in around them.

Don Vespiri felt the earth spin beneath his feet as all of his options vanished like ill-fated ghosts. He felt a rush of blood course through his veins. Survival instinct took over as only one desperate thought gripped his heart and mind. *Cosca.*

I have to save my family, he told himself.

Don Vespiri inhaled a deep breath, feeling his heart beating against his chest. He tightened his grip around the hilt of his blade, still tucked behind his forearm. He carefully adjusted his footing, placing his left foot back and his right foot pointed forward, triangulating his weight into a guardian stance. *The foundation for everything.* He bent his knees, sinking slightly, lowering his center of gravity, making himself a small target. He then tightened his grip around the hilt, feeling its weight in his hands.

Don Vespiri snapped his gaze upward, his eyes two sharp blades. He remembered how to kill swiftly, and efficiently.

A master don.

A perfect Sicilian knight.

O Santo Cavaleri.

CHAPTER 14

DON VESPIRI bared his teeth and snapped his blade upward, thrusting for the nearest Angevin soldier with all of the selfless bravery of a father desperate to save his family.

A man of *occhinero*.

The sharp tip of the blade zipped through the air and punched straight into the soldier's exposed jugular. A fountain of blood spouted from the soldier's neck and onto Don Vespiri's face. The soldier's eyes shot open. He dropped his sword and struggled to clutch his throat through his heavy gauntlets. The soldier gurgled for air as his tongue thrashed in his mouth. Don Vespiri jabbed his foot into the man's abdomen and kicked him to the ground.

The Angevins looked on, stupefied. They beheld the Sicilian standing over their fallen comrade covered in blood, his chest heaving up and down. His blade glimmered in the sun as if it were a ray of fire, like that of Saint Michael the Archangel, who drove Satan from paradise.

An Angevin unsheathed his rapier and barreled forward. He flashed his sword upward and lunged for Don Vespiri's cheek.

Don Vespiri lifted his wrist to block the blow with his blade, deflecting it away. In the same motion, he grabbed the soldier's forearm and spun behind him. He slashed his blade across the soldier's throat, severing his windpipe, and then jammed the sharp sword tip into the back of the soldier's kidney. He gave the blade a few quick twists to grind up the man's internal organs.

Another soldier moved up from behind. Don Vespiri spun quickly, catching the soldier's incoming blow. He pushed the soldier's arm upward and sliced his blade across the man's jugular, then rammed it into his sternum.

Rochefort looked on, unimpressed. He turned a stiff neck toward Drouet and nodded grimly.

Drouet grinned and barked an order. A dozen hulking men moved in from all sides and tackled Don Vespiri to the ground. The soldiers drew their daggers, steadying their blades to gut Don Vespiri into pieces.

"Stay your weapons," Rochefort ordered, throwing up a hand. "Sicilians are a dirty people with dirty blood. Blood of gypsies. Savages. They must first learn their place." With that, the general unclipped an iron vise from around his belt. He threw the vise to Drouet.

A deadly grin formed across Drouet's lips as he extended his hand to catch it.

Rochefort nodded grimly. "Do us the honors, Sergeant."

The soldiers hoisted Don Vespiri to his feet, clutching him tightly from either side. Overwhelmed by their strength, he was no longer able to move. A soldier slugged him across the face for good measure. Don Vespiri's cheekbones throbbed painfully as he gazed upon the sergeant cantering toward him, carrying the iron vise. It was well worked and polished. Whatever it was, he decided it was efficient. Deadly.

"Your king does not tolerate traitors," Drouet said, sauntering forward. "You will submit to me. For God and for France."

Don Vespiri spat at his boots. "If that disgrace of a tyrant sitting on our throne is God's measure of a king, then I do not recognize your god."

Drouet growled. "Sicilians never learn to keep their big mouths shut!"

Don Vespiri felt fixed under the sergeant's gaze, powerless to act. For the first time in his life, the revered Sicilian knight faced the crushing inevitability of defeat.

Suddenly, a small voice cried out in the distance.

"*Scuzi . . .*"

Don Vespiri slowly turned his head. His eyes widened in horror as he watched his son, Cicero, saunter forward, his palms raised in the air.

CHAPTER 15

CICERO MOVED slowly, his eyes darting from man to man. He cautiously approached the Angevins as if they were rabid animals.

Don Vespiri bit hard into his tongue as the soldiers tightened their grip around his arms. Every instinct told him to yell for his son, but he knew the slightest reaction would bring them all instant death.

Sergeant Drouet turned his head to see the young boy. A devious grin crossed his lips.

Cicero approached the group of soldiers. He kept his chin high. A true *cavaleri* never showed fear. Cicero cleared his throat, attempting to sound assured. "I wish to speak with the commanding officer."

The Angevins stared blankly. Then they burst into laughter.

Cicero furrowed his brow. "A knight is entitled to parlay with the commanding officer."

Drouet snorted air out his nostrils and sauntered over, bending down to look the boy directly in the eyes. "You're a knight, are you?" Drouet said. "Then where is your sword? A knight is no good without his sword."

Cicero's bottom lip trembled.

Don Vespiri looked on with a pained expression.

"I'm afraid the general doesn't speak to Sicilians," Drouet said. "But I'm happy to take a message to him."

"I propose terms for *Re Carlu*," Cicero said, remembering the words he overheard his father use the night before.

Drouet snorted. "Terms? What kind of terms?"

"*Diplomazia*," Cicero said. "Peace."

The soldiers' eyes widened, their brows touching their foreheads. They howled with laughter.

Don Vespiri hung his head.

General Rochefort glared down at the boy, unmoved by his display of courage. "Take him. Put him with the prisoner."

A group of Angevins lumbered up behind Cicero and easily yanked him off the ground, throwing him over their shoulder. Cicero grimaced as the men's armor dug into his stomach.

"*Patri!*" Cicero cried.

"Cicero!" Don Vespiri growled. Baring his teeth, he yanked his arms forward, struggling to break free from the soldiers' grasp, until a heavy fist crashed into his cheekbone.

Rochefort nodded as the boy was carried past him. "He'll make fine soldier material."

"*Patri!*" Cicero screamed again as the soldiers fixed craggy ropes around his small wrists. "*Patri*, I'm sorry!"

Don Vespiri was at a loss for words. Never in a million lifetimes could a father know what to say to his own child being ripped away from him. His face soured as the only words he could muster finally croaked from his dry mouth. "Don't be afraid, Cicero! You will always be a *cavaleri*! You will always be my son!"

"*Patri!*" Cicero screamed again, his voice trailing off.

Don Vespiri's face contorted with grief as, powerless to save him, he watched the Angevin soldier drag the young boy off into the sulfuric fog.

Don Vespiri's eyes shot upward as a panicked realization hit him. *Where's Aetna?*

Drouet snapped his head back to face Don Vespiri and growled. "Time to shut that stupid Sicilian mouth."

With that, Drouet gripped Don Vespiri by his collar and yanked him forward so their noses almost touched. Drouet's gray beard was gnarly and unkempt, his teeth rotten and breath reeking of sour wine. He snapped the vise around the winemaker's neck, watching the fear flicker over Don Vespiri's face as he tightened the iron vise in place.

Feeling the crushing pressure around his windpipe, Don Vespiri tugged at it viciously, instinctively. He felt the muscles in his chest tighten. His red Sicilian blood boiled with an impossible rage. *"Curnutu fetusu,"* Don Vespiri growled. "Burn in hell." He gripped the vise as it seemed to tighten harder with each passing second. His breath grew shorter and more labored as he tried to focus his thoughts.

"It's the panic that betrays them," Rochefort said icily.

The soldiers around him nodded.

Rochefort surveyed the scene before him, pleased with what he saw. Soldiers emerged from the farmhouse, their arms laden with valuables and heirlooms that they tossed into piles. The soldiers spread out and organized the contents by gold, silver, precious jewels and stones, ceramics, fine linens, weaponry.

The general lowered his gaze to Don Vespiri and spat at his feet. "A dirty people with dirty blood." He then kicked his horse, tearing off to join his men pillaging the grounds.

Don Vespiri sank to his knees in the dirt. In the distance, he saw a group of Angevins muscling Paola and the workers into a straight line. Their faces trembled as archers loaded razor-sharp arrows into enormous longbows. The bows groaned as the men pulled the nocks taut against their cheeks. Silence hung in the air as the workers stared at the arrow tips bearing down on them.

Paola held her chin up in defiance as a tear trickled down her cheek. *"Simmo surfaru."*

"Loose!" the soldier ordered, dropping his forearm forward.

Thip! Thip! Thip!

The arrows screamed through the air and smashed into the torsos of the vineyard workers with a sickening thud. They dropped to the ground, some shrieking as they clutched their chests.

A young worker thrashed violently in the dirt, blood gurgling from his lungs with every strained breath, until an archer reloaded his longbow, stood over him, and shot another arrow directly into his heart.

Paola squeezed her eyes shut as she felt the barbed arrow tear into her sternum. She took one last breath and fell facedown in the dirt.

Then there was silence.

CHAPTER 16

DON VITTORIO VESPIRI groaned as his entire world caved in around him. Suffocating him. Killing him. He finally collapsed backward into the dirt, continuing to tug in vain at the tightening vise.

At that moment, a figure crawled out quickly from the flaming vines, perhaps a wild animal fleeing the field. Aetna emerged, moving fast on her belly, her elbows and knees scraping through the coarse soil. Fire whirled in tall pillars around them, licking hungrily at the gray sky. She pulled herself up onto his heaving chest and grasped the iron vise around his neck, trying to release it. *"Patri!"* she cried, keeping her head down, smoke billowing around them.

Don Vespiri tried to speak, but only strained noises came out. *"Santuzza."*

Aetna immediately refocused on the vise around his neck, struggling to remove it. "They took Cicero," she cried.

"Santuzza, listen," Don Vespiri groaned.

"I can help you," she said. "We have to save him."

Don Vespiri shook his head, pressing his palms firmly on Aetna's cheeks and forcing her gaze into his own eyes.

"Do you remember the Cistercian trail to Palermo?"

"*Sì, Patri,*" she said.

"The secret trail I taught you," he said. "The trail the Angevins don't patrol."

Aetna nodded, tears trickling down her face.

"Good girl," he said. "You have to run now, *santuzza.*"

"*Patri . . .*"

"Run to the church of the Cistercian nuns in Palermo, and don't stop," he said. "They will protect you."

"I can't leave you," she cried, blubbering through her tears.

Don Vespiri's face contorted into a tortured grimace as the vise crushed his windpipe. He gazed up into the liquid pools of his daughter's eyes as his vision became blurred, unfocused. Her stifled cries reverberated in his eardrums, traveled down his chest, and shattered his heart.

"Don't be afraid," Don Vespiri whispered. He grasped the *Gorgoneion Trinacria* pendant from around his neck, pulling it up over the tightening vise and hanging it around Aetna's small head.

She looked down at the golden pendant hanging heavy around her hair. Medusa's face and three spiraling legs gleamed in the firelight.

"No matter where you are thrown," he said, "you will always land standing."

A weak smile spread across his face. Aetna's bottom lip trembled. "*Patri,*" she sobbed.

"Go, *santuzza,*" he said. "*Ammunini.*" He rested his head in the dirt and closed his eyes, struggling for gulps of air.

Aetna lay on top of her father, fire swirling up around them in an inferno. She felt something inside her begin to boil up—a churning angst she had never felt before, coursing through her like lava, as if she would soon erupt.

In the distance, several Angevin soldiers perked up, hearing Aetna's cries echoing in the air. Rochefort heard them as well. He strode forward on his horse, emerging from the smoke.

"No survivors!" his voice bellowed through the thick air.

The sound of shimmering metal rang through the air as the soldiers unsheathed their rapiers and charged forward.

Aetna's fear broke in an instant, dissolving into resolve. She squeezed her eyes shut, shrieks racking her body uncontrollably. Instinct taking over, she grabbed her father's stiletto off the ground, sprung to her feet, and darted straight for the flaming fields.

The Angevins closed in quickly. One soldier lunged for her shawl, yanking her backward and spinning her around. Aetna lurched forward desperately and rammed her foot into the man's kneecap. There was strength in her kick. The soldier toppled backward and fell to the ground, writhing violently.

Aetna slipped out of the shawl and scurried away into the burning field.

The men gave chase, then slammed to a stop at the end of the clearing. They peered out into the raging inferno moving over the surface of the vines.

They exchanged anxious glances. "She's as good as dead," one soldier muttered. The other men nodded and turned away, lumbering back toward the farmhouse.

"Don't be afraid," Don Vespiri croaked, watching his daughter disappear into the fire forever. No longer able to breathe, he drifted in and out of consciousness. He would leave behind everything he had ever loved, everything he had ever protected. He would never see his children grow up; they would be left to fend for themselves in a cold and brutal world without a father, without a family.

A faint smile crossed his lips as he gazed up into the sky, his vision fading. Don Vespiri closed his eyes, resigning himself to oblivion.

Don Vittorio Vespiri, *O Santo Cavaleri*, was dead.

CHAPTER 17

A ROARING eruption of sulfur and lava spewed skyward from Mount Etna's cone, shooting out globs of flame from her throat like a Chimera monster. A horrific pillar of roiling smoke rose up from her crater, casting a hellish glow over the dark silhouette of the mountain.

Lightning crashed from the volcanic clouds above as Aetna scrambled for her life through the burning underbrush. She felt the fire sear against her cheeks and tear at her bare arms like the claws of a deranged devil from hell. Her instincts kept her moving as she serpentined through the labyrinth of blazing vines, finally coming to a clearing on the ashy slope of the volcano.

Aetna scraped her way up the shifting rocks until she reached a boulder jutting out from the flank. Crouching behind it, she peered carefully over the top. Her eyes were wide with liquid blurriness, reflecting the red-orange glow of the fire and embers swirling off the surface of the vineyard below her.

She watched the Angevins round up sacks of goods, tying them onto their horses. As they left the stone manor, they lobbed their torches through the windows. Horses whinnied as a few surviving attempted to flee, shot down in their tracks by Angevin arrows. The Angevins moved into formation, loading up their weapons and spoils as flames consumed the entire house and licked out the windows.

Aetna cried to herself as she fell to her knees, overwhelmed with the sudden realization that she was now completely alone, her entire life ripped away from her and shattered like the sulfuric stones being hurled from the volcano. As she knelt there on the black soil, a wave of fear and hopelessness washed over her.

Simmo surfaru, she told herself.

Heartbroken, Aetna tore her eyes away. She knew it was time to run. Taking a deep breath, she focused her thoughts inward. The Cistercian trail to Palermo was a perilous five-day hike through the island's interior. But she knew every cave, blood orange grove, and prickly pear patch along the way for continued sustenance. Her *patri* taught her well.

The young *Siciliana* picked up her small feet and ran, disappearing over the mountain.

BOOK II

PRIMA SANGUA
MARCH 1282

PALERMO

TYRRHENIAN SEA

CASTELLAMMARE
DISTRICT

PORTA FELICE

CASSARU

SERALCADIO
DISTRICT

QUATTRO
CANTI

KALSA DISTRICT

CATTEDRALE
DI PALERMO

LA MAGIONE

PORTA NUOVA

ALBERGHERIA
DISTRICT

PALAZZO DEI
NORMANI

ORETO RIVER

CHIESA DI
SANTO SPIRITO

SICILY SUFFERED under the Angevin yoke until March of 1282.

Messina was now the official seat of the Royal Vicar of Sicily, Herbert Orleans, who governed the island's affairs from the imposing fortress of Matagrifone.

The vicar's soldiers routinely patrolled villages and towns— seizing food and livestock to provide for Re Carlu's impending campaign against Constantinople—convinced that the Sicilians' bitter submission would endure forever.

As Easter approached in Palermo, the kingdom's fallen capital, daily acts of violence and molestation were being committed by Justiciar Jean de Saint-Remy and his hostile Angevin garrison occupying the city.

But as the Sicilians came together and prepared themselves for Vespers with their customary lambs and musical processions, a desperate anger was stirring beneath the surface. The mood in the streets was volatile.

Eruptive . . .

—From *War of the Vespers*
by *Don Rapaci,* 1282

CHAPTER 18

Palermo, Sicily
Kalsa District
March 29, 1282
3:23 p.m. // Twenty-seven hours to Vespers

DEATH CAME on the wind.

Gray clouds roiled in the skies overhead as an Angevin soldier stumbled alone through a crowded back street, splashing through muck and manure. The road itself was no wider than a one-donkey wheel cart, lined with endless rows of two-story houses squeezing the path like a vise. A teeming crowd of pedestrians swarmed around him, pushing their way past one another, up and down the length of the muddied passageway.

March was the rainiest time of the year in Sicily.

Clutching his lower backside, the soldier stared down in horror at a river of bright red blood coursing down his leg, leaving a trail in the mud as he walked. He removed his hand from the wound and looked at his stained palms.

I don't want to die, he thought.

Only minutes earlier, the soldier had felt the sharp pressure of a thin blade enter his lower-back cavity and retract just as quickly. In searing pain, he glanced around in a panic, seeking out the perpetrator, but all he saw were hundreds of faces milling around him. Nothing but the wind between them.

Splashing through the mud, the soldier stumbled into an open-air market.

Slipping into shock, the soldier unsheathed his rapier, swinging it violently at an unseen enemy as the pandemonium of the marketplace swirled around him. Losing strength, he dragged his heavy feet, finally coming to a stop against the stone wall. He clutched his lower backside as he slid down the length of the wall and into the mud. His steel helmet fell over his eyes as they fluttered shut.

The Sicilians milled about the marketplace, paying the soldier no special attention. There seemed to be as many drunk Angevin solders littering the streets as there were feral dogs in all of Palermo.

Drops of rain pelted the soldier's armor as he lay motionless, sinking into the mud. The *rat-a-tat-tat* of the rain clanking into the armor was like a thousand swords clashing in the tumult of battle.

A cold wind whistled through the narrow street as the shadow of a dark figure rose up over the soldier's corpse. Circling overhead, a golden eagle opened its hooked beak and shrieked down from the sky. The eagle's cry reverberated down through the narrow pathway.

The dark figure lingered for a moment, then as quickly as it appeared, suddenly vanished, obliterated by the passing crowd.

CHAPTER 19

Chiesa di Santo Spirito
Outskirts of Palermo
March 29, 1282
6:03 p.m. // Twenty-four hours to Vespers

No matter where I am thrown, I will always land standing.

Aetna Vespiri bobbed lightly on her toes, her calves taut like bowstrings. Her *patri's* words echoed in her ears. She bit her lip, gripping a stiletto tightly between her fingers.

A small crowd of Cistercian nuns and orderlies gathered around for the duel that would take place in the courtyard. Looming over them was the facade of the *Chiesa di Santo Spirito*, the Church of the Holy Spirit. Built of volcanic stone, the Gothic-Norman church was located within the boundaries of an old Arab cemetery sitting on the outskirts of Palermo's city walls, overlooking the ancient Oreto River. Tonight, the sky was black. Flickering torches blazed from the corners of the courtyard, casting the church in glowing orange firelight.

Directly in front of Aetna stood the Abbot of the church. The tall, lean Sicilian gripped a stiletto and paced in front of her.

Aetna had been looking forward to the duel for weeks. Her combat training was nearly complete. And today was the final test of *Prima Sangua*. First Blood. An honor that was not given. It had to be earned.

The flames flickered as a cold wind snapped between them.

Aetna glanced over to the crowd to see Tziporah Solazzo, a fourteen-year-old Cistercian orderly, standing among the nuns. Aetna flashed her a grin, attempting to project confidence. Tziporah nodded assuredly, her long black hair falling over her face.

Aetna then glared into the Abbot's eyes, baring her teeth. She remembered the chief tenet of *occhinero* during stiletto combat—a *cavaleri* locked in combat must hold eyeball-to-eyeball contact with her enemy. For this was her primary mental attack. Her eyes expressed the deadliness of her own blade. Her ability to spill her enemy's lifeblood in the street. It was the ultimate display of Sicilian bravery in the face of imminent danger and pain of death.

A Sicilian knight is always en occhinero . . . *even with a blade through the heart.*

She knew there was also a more tactical purpose to this ancient combat art. One that could ultimately save her life. Eyeball-to-eyeball contact allowed her to detect all of her enemy's movements through her periphery.

Aetna placed her right foot forward and extended her left foot back. She bent her knees slightly and held herself firmly in a crouched position, triangulating her center of gravity. She bobbed back and forth on her feet, feeling pure control over every motion in her body.

The guardian stance.

Aetna twirled her blade between her fingers. Leather chest armor covered her front torso, with sparring gauntlets strapped tightly around her forearms. Her raven hair was braided intricately in an updo fastened away from her face and neck, with

loose frayed strands falling over her shoulders. Tiny wall liz-
ards with pointed heads and slender bodies scampered over
her feet. She brushed them away with her toes. She gripped her
father's golden *Gorgoneion Trinacria* pendant in her palm and
raised it to her lips, kissing it. She then tucked it back under her
sparring armor.

The Abbot held out his blade and began to speak in Sicilian.
"Wielding a stiletto against your enemy takes extraordinary
nerve and a full intention to kill, cutting them open so their
lifeblood spills into the streets."

Aetna smirked. She gripped her own blade as the Abbot
circled her, her eyes locked with his.

Like lightning, the Abbot's blade snapped forward, aimed
for Aetna's chest. Aetna detected the sudden motion in her
periphery and knew instantly how to weave her upper body.
She quickly deflected the blow with ease. Sparks burst where
metal struck metal.

The Abbot twirled on his feet and grabbed Aetna by the
collar, pulling her close.

"Are you ready to prove your fearlessness in the face of
death?" he said.

The Abbot glided to his right, frosty breath snorting from
his nostrils.

"*Sì!*" Aetna said, sliding to face him.

The two Sicilians exchanged a series of blows.

"Are you ready to defend the helpless?" he said. "Protecting
them from men who abuse their power to advance their stations rather than lift up those around them?"

"*Sì!*" she cried a last time.

Aetna thrust again. The Abbot turned and caught the
edge of her blade with his own, pulling her close until their
faces were inches apart. She could feel the Abbot's hot breath
against her skin.

"Then let us have a duel of *Prima Sangua!*" he said. He shoved Aetna backward and crouched into a guardian stance, pointing his blade forward. The Abbot's expression turned grim. "Draw *first blood* . . . if you can."

The Abbot adjusted his footing and crouched lower, transforming his shape right before Aetna's eyes.

Aetna's heart pounded. *No matter where I am thrown, I will always land standing.* She adjusted her footing and narrowed her gaze.

Aetna twirled her blade between her fingertips and crouched into a guardian stance, staring the Abbot directly in the eyes. Aetna saw nothing but two black spots and a body becoming an ambiguous mass hovering in space. She was able to detect every motion he made. The Abbot would slightly waver forward, then back. His blade hovered out in front of him, swaying slowly to and fro.

Summoning her will, Aetna held a vivid image in her mind. She envisioned her blade flashing forward, streaking through the air, and drawing blood from her opponent's flesh. She knew that what she was thinking in this moment, her opponent was also thinking. *Tonight, one of us will bleed.* And she would make sure it was him.

Suddenly, the Abbot's blade flashed forward. Using the momentum of his strike against him, Aetna deflected the blow and glided out of harm's way.

Aetna swung forward. The Abbot caught her blade with his sparring gauntlet and twisted it from her hands. The blade tumbled across the ground.

Aetna reeled. The burning brightness of the torch fire filled her eyes.

The crowd reacted with a gasp.

The Abbot slashed downward at Aetna, who deflected the strike with her gauntlet. She then dropped to her knees and rolled past his legs. In one fell swoop, she dove to where her blade lay and landed at the foot of the crowd. As she snatched the blade and leapt to her feet, she quickly snatched a black shawl off a nun's shoulder.

Aetna slowly rose and adjusted her footing as the Abbot circled her. She twirled the shawl in the air and draped it over her free arm. She then raised the shawl in front of her to create a makeshift body shield and, more important, hide her blade from view. She flashed him a cunning smile.

The Abbot slowed his pace. "Cloak and dagger. *Bene.*"

Aetna held firm eye contact, piercing the Abbot with her burning green eyes. She didn't make a sound.

Aetna gritted her teeth and lunged forward, thrusting her blade out from behind the black cape. The Abbot parried downward, deflecting Aetna's strike. She thrust from behind the cloth again, and again, attacking with vigor and forcing him back across the courtyard.

The crowd murmured with muted excitement.

The Abbot struggled to maintain his footing as he defended against the vicious blows of Aetna's blade. The black cloth fluttered before his eyes again and again, filling his field of vision. Slammed back against the church stone facade, he ducked and spun away in time to avoid the deadly slash of Aetna's blade at his cheek. For a moment, their blades locked as they stood eye to eye with one another. Aetna pushed her blade forward, sending the Abbot back toward the center of the courtyard. Aetna sprung forward to meet him, her blade snapping out through the twirling cape.

The Abbot twisted, attempting to regain his balance. But the constant whipping and twirling of the black cloth in front of him distorted his field of vision. The direction of Aetna's incoming blade thrusts was impossible to detect. Suddenly, the black cloth snapped forward again and, like a snake, coiled itself around his right forearm, ensnaring his blade in its taut grip.

Aetna tightened her hold on the cloth and yanked the Abbot forward. As he fell toward her, she used his momentum to twirl around his back, bringing her blade's cutting edge into contact with his throat. Blood formed where even this feather-light touch cut his skin.

The Abbot didn't move. He watched a single drop of blood coagulate and run down the long edge of the blade, dripping off the tip and into the once-hallowed ground of *Santo Spirito*'s ancient courtyard.

The Abbot slowly lifted his eyes to meet his opponent's. He found himself scorched by two green balls of fire.

"You're doomed to the Valley of Hesitation," Aetna said, flashing a triumphant grin. *"Prima Sangua."*

The crowd applauded as Aetna and the Abbot turned to face one another, bowing their heads. Tziporah nodded and flashed an approving smile.

The old man turned to face the nuns and orderlies. Tziporah then stepped forward from the group and tossed him a small artichoke. He snatched the spiny bud from the air and held it up, admiring how its armorlike scales clustered around the flower bud.

Aetna sensed a lesson coming.

The Abbot smiled and pressed his finger into the artichoke. "As the prickly crown of the artichoke protects its heart, so our blades protect the tightness of our family. Our *cosca*," he said. "Always remember it's the charge of a *cavaleri* to protect herself and her *cosca* by way of her own personal influence, regardless of a king's authority."

"Re Carlu!" one orderly jeered.

"The Angevins!" a nun cried.

The Abbot nodded grimly. "*Cosca* is the only authority we recognize," he said, pressing a closed fist to his chest. "We are *cosca*."

The crowd cheered.

The Abbot closed his eyes and extended a hand over Aetna's forehead.

A sharp wind snapped through Aetna's hair. Her face was unmistakably Sicilian. The twenty-year-old woman was naturally beautiful; her once-glowing expression had hardened into a scowl as the years passed by. She was medium height with light olive skin and her father's dark eyebrows and aquiline nose, hooked like the beak of an eagle. As the wind whipped against her garment, it clung to her body, revealing the contours of her slim torso and small breasts.

"Bow your head now, child," the Abbot said. "Let us pray."

The crowd fell silent as they bowed their heads and clasped their hands.

God is within her. She will not fall . . .
God will help her when morning breaks . . .
Nations rage; kingdoms crumble . . .
The earth quakes when she lifts her own voice . . .

Aetna slowly raised her eyes. She never suspected that in less than twenty-four hours, in this very spot, her voice would quake the earth like the world had never seen.

CHAPTER 20

LATER THAT night, a shaft of pale moonlight poured into the *Santo Spirito* convent dormitory through an arched window. Aetna Vespiri lay on a straw mattress among the other Cistercian orderlies. The modest sleeping chamber had ten beds arranged in tight rows along the stone floor, roughly one arm's length between them.

Aetna lay awake, staring up into the silver moonlight. Her hands were clasped together, resting on her abdomen. Her breathing was slow. Measured.

In the next bed over, Tziporah rolled over to one side, and then back to the other. Sighing, she finally rolled onto her back.

"Are you still up?" Tziporah whispered.

"*Sì,*" Aetna said.

"What are you doing?"

"Thinking."

"About what?"

Aetna rolled her eyes. "Nothing."

Tziporah flashed a playful grin. "Nobody thinks about nothing." She then rolled over on her side to face Aetna. "Can I ask you something?"

Aetna blew air from her nostrils. *Will you go to sleep?*

"Sure," Aetna said.

"Tonight, when the Abbot spoke of *cosca*, it made me feel grateful. *Santo Spirito* is the only home I've ever known," Tziporah said, pausing for a moment as if collecting her thoughts. "I never knew my real mother. My *matri*. But sometimes when I dream, I can see her face. Do you ever dream about your family?"

Aetna could suddenly hear her own heartbeat. *My family?* The words sent an immediate surge of longing through her bones. In that fleeting moment, she saw images flash through her mind from a dream that had come to her countless times as a little girl: *My brother, Cicero, is still alive. He's coming home soon.* But, upon her awakening, those hopeful images evaporated with the rays of dawn.

I won't see Cicero again. My family is dead.

Aetna raised her eyes and gazed up into the moonlight. "Some nights, I dream of them. Mostly dreams I *don't* want."

Tziporah frowned, biting her lip. "The Abbot once told me we don't choose our dreams. They choose us."

Aetna flashed her eyes toward her young friend. "Do you know how hard it is mourning a loved one that you had to *decide* was dead? Because the thought of their death brings you more comfort than the agony of wondering if you'll ever see them again?"

Tziporah's face turned sour. She rested a hand on Aetna's arm. "I'm sorry."

Aetna tightened her grip around the hilt of her stiletto. She felt a sticky dryness in her throat. "When I lost my family, I thought the anger alone would kill me. Strangling my pain until the memory of them was just poison in my blood. For years, I've thought of nothing but bringing that pain to those who brought it to me."

Tziporah remained silent, looking at her friend with consternation.

Without another word, Aetna pulled up her blanket and rolled onto her side. "*Bona notti*, Tziporah."

Aetna closed her eyes and settled into the mattress. As she felt herself sinking into the pillow, she prayed for a fast and dreamless sleep. For dreaming was far too painful.

CHAPTER 21

Palermo, Sicily
Seralcadio District
March 30, 1282
8:04 a.m. // Ten hours to Vespers

PALERMO WAS at once a cosmopolitan metropolis and a provincial village. Both a bustling Greek seaport and a colorful Arabic bazaar set down between the sea and the mountains.

In Palermo, it was said, the streets were the key to everything. The importance of a street could be determined by whether it was paved or unkempt. Many streets were narrow, serpentine dirt paths squeezed between an endless row of two-story houses untouched by sunlight. Rivaling the labyrinths of Jerusalem, Palermo had streets for blacksmiths, for bankers, for glassblowers. Streets for merchants, for bakers, for citrus-fruit vendors. Streets for nuns and streets for whores. If there was a need or vice known to the Sicilian people, there was a street in Palermo for it.

The most ancient street in Palermo was called the *Cassaru*. A sparkling marble road laid down by the Phoenicians centuries before, the street was a perfectly straight main artery that ran the length of the entire city, with many smaller streets leading into it. The entrance to the *Cassaru* was found at the city's seaside gate of *Porta Felice*; from there, it carved its way through the city eastward and southward. The road came to an end at the Royal Palace of Palermo, known as *Palazzo dei Normanni*, on the far southwest end of the city's walls. The Arab-built royal palace was the seat of Angevin power in Palermo, and the residence of Justiciar Jean de Saint-Remy, administrator of the city.

Earlier this morning, Palermo's archbishop, Salvatore Malu, had decided to walk the stretch of the *Cassaru*. Headstrong pedestrians and donkey-drawn carts adorned with elaborate paintings and feathered plumes tore to and fro through the frenzied street.

Normally, the archbishop would've wrapped a gold-embroidered green vestment and cincture around his shoulders and waist, but today he would be traveling among the public and decided not to draw attention to himself. Only those with a trained gaze would recognize the bejeweled rings clinging to his thick fingers.

Archbishop Malu, known to the Sicilians as *Buccamazza* for his large, clodlike mouth, was an overweight Sicilian in his late forties. He had a bulbous face and burnt-red hair cropped short to his ears. His reddish locks served as a genetic reminder of the Norman conquerors who had ruled Sicily more than a century before. He often struggled with breathing, frequently breaking into cold sweats, especially in times of stress. And today was proving to be no different.

In the years since *Re Carlu* seized the crown, normal patterns of life in Palermo ground to a halt. The shining city of kings had decayed into a cruel, corrupt military state. Arab palaces and Norman cathedrals were fortified with elite Angevin garrisons and weapon stockpiles.

Angevin foot soldiers frequently patrolled the streets, harassing Sicilians without cause, robbing them of valuables, personal heirlooms, and their daily trappings.

Young sons were warned not to provoke Angevin *machismo* with the intimidating flair of their stiletto dueling skills. Young daughters were told not to venture into the streets alone, especially after sundown.

Sicilian culture transformed into a culture on edge. A wartime culture.

As he strode down the bustling *Cassaru*, Malu witnessed a contingent of hulking Angevin soldiers surround a young Sicilian boy as he pulled a stubborn donkey along the *Cassaru*. The lead Angevin stepped forward and yanked the bridle from the boy's hands. The soldier stood over the donkey, caressing the animal's snout. Then the soldier clenched his fist and smashed it directly between the donkey's eyes. The donkey let out a bloodcurdling groan before collapsing to the ground, its tongue hanging from its mouth. Dead.

The boy's eyes widened in shock. His face then seemed to sour with grief, then rage. Baring his teeth, the boy pounced on the Angevin, pummeling him in the face. Little did he know, the boy had just sealed his own fate.

The passing crowd screamed and scattered as the Angevins unsheathed their rapiers. They shoved the boy to the ground, taking turns plunging their sharp blades deep into the boy's torso again and again and again, leaving him to bleed out on the *Cassaru* next to the fallen donkey. Pools of dark blood spread slowly across the road's marble slabs.

Archbishop Malu kept his eyes trained forward, avoiding eye contact with the Angevin soldiers. He said a silent prayer as he turned off the *Cassaru* and entered the courtyard to the *Palazzo dei Normanni*.

Dangerous times are upon my station, Malu told himself as he ascended the steps of the Norman Palace. The archbishop had managed to survive regime changes in the past, ingratiating himself personally with past kings and foreign nobility with bribes of gold and otherworldly treasures kept safe in his cathedral's coffers. Though the Angevins had proved to be a new kind of threat. Appealing to greed alone seldom worked. Malu discovered that no amount of treasure could quench their insatiable thirst for power, lust, and total destruction.

As the archbishop reached the palace doors, he glanced back toward the streets of Palermo, never suspecting that tonight every street would become a pathway to hell.

· ❦ ·

Now, Archbishop Malu stood in the personal chambers of Justiciar Saint-Remy.

The wily-faced justiciar studied stacks of scrolls and parchments, signing them and passing them to a nearby attendant. He was flanked on either side by two half-naked concubines. One ran her fingers through his hair as the other poured a glass of wine. More women were sprawled around the room, talking softly with one another and eyeing the large bishop who had just entered their realm.

"I don't bother to read them anymore," Saint-Remy said, scribbling carelessly across the parchments.

Archbishop Malu smiled nervously. A bead of salty sweat dripped from his chin.

Saint-Remy glanced up, annoyed. "Has it already been seven days since my last confession?"

The Angevin guards in the room laughed.

"Or perhaps you come seeking some other vice?" Saint-Remy said, beckoning to the women around the room.

Malu dabbed the sweat from his chin. "My lord, permit me to speak on an issue that must be addressed immediately," Malu mumbled. His tongue was too large for his mouth. "Every day I walk the *Cassaru*, trying to build my congregation."

Saint-Remy yawned, continuing to scribble on documents. "And this concerns me how?"

"Every day brings some new offense or outrage against them," Malu countered. "Molestation. Petty larceny . . ."

Saint-Remy furrowed his brow. "Order must be maintained at all costs."

"But the more you keep taking from them—"

"The less goes into your own pocket?" Saint-Remy said.

Malu pouted. *That is precisely the reason.* Offerings were the lifeblood of Palermo Cathedral. Especially when he was used to skimming a hefty duty off the top for himself. "Attendance is down, and so are my profits."

Saint-Remy leaned forward, slamming his hands into the desk. "Which is why I am increasing your personal stipend," he said, pushing himself up. "Courtesy of King Charles."

Saint-Remy walked around the desk and put an arm around the archbishop, walking him to the Arab-style window overlooking the city. "Worry not, my friend." Saint-Remy paused, pressing a finger into Malu's breast. "Your patience and loyalty will soon be rewarded."

Malu wiped his sweaty palms on the side of his cassock. He knew the prize *Re Carlu* had pledged to him was astonishingly exceptional. It was also highly secretive. Known only to Saint-Remy and himself.

The justiciar beckoned out the window. "In the meantime, you will make the Sicilian people believe that their salvation from tyranny comes only through the grace of God."

Malu nodded, pleasantly surprised by how little remorse he felt at the thought of it. "Blessed are the meek, for they shall inherit the earth," he said. "They will submit faithfully, even as they are beaten."

Saint-Remy smacked Malu hard on the chest. "Now you got it."

The men in the room broke out into laughter.

Saint-Remy turned back to his desk, cracking a wolfish grin. "The appearance of hope must be upheld . . . especially because there is none."

CHAPTER 22

Chiesa di Santa Maria dell'Alemanna
Messina, Sicily
March 30, 1282
8:09 a.m.

TORCHES BLAZED from inside the crypt. Mummified corpses and skeleton heads were laid neatly among the five repository vaults built into either side of the stone walls. An ancient catacomb. The air down here was moldy and cold. Rats scurried along the length of the floor, their high-pitched shrieks echoing through the cramped chamber.

Sitting under a flickering torch, *Teutoni* Knight Bartolomeo Maniscalco buried his nose in a sheepskin book, gently flipping the pages as his eyes scanned the words inside. A small squad of *Teutoni* Knights sat beside him, reading, eating, and sharing stories. Etched on the book's cover in thick black ink was a single word: *Contrasto*. The book was widely considered a quintessential poem from the Sicilian School of Poetry established in the courts of the *Palazzo dei Normanni* only fifty years earlier. The school was established under the rule of the *Stupor Mundi*, the former Holy Roman Emperor and king

of Sicily, Frederick II—Prince Conradin's own grandfather—
and was held in the same palace where Palermo justiciar Jean
de Saint-Remy now kept his harem. A stark reminder of how
much of Sicily's culture they had lost since the conquest by *Re
Carlu's* Angevin military.

How our Sicily has fallen, Maniscalco thought.

Written in Middle Sicilian, the romantically charged work
about a damsel and her knight was hailed a milestone in what
became the eventual development of the formal Italian language centuries later.

A knight burst into the crypt. His face dripped with sweat.
"Angevins!" he gasped.

Maniscalco lowered the book from his nose and rose to
his feet, standing tall. His face filled with a mix of surprise and
conviction.

"Ready your weapons," Maniscalco ordered. He dropped
the book of poetry to the ground and unsheathed his sword.

The men sprung into action. They armed themselves with
long swords, blowing out the torches around the catacombs.

Then the crypt went black.

Angevin general Guy de Rochefort sat stone-faced atop an
enormous steed outside the *Chiesa di Santa Maria dell'Alemanna,* his chin held high. He wore a helmet, steel breastplate,
and gray wolfskin draped over his broad shoulders. Angevin
soldiers surrounded the edifice, fanning out around the
grounds. Prickly *opuntia* paddle cacti surrounded the church's
perimeter.

An Angevin lieutenant sauntered over and stepped up to
the general's side. "They're dug in good," the lieutenant said.

Rochefort lowered his frigid gaze to the lieutenant. The lieutenant winced at the sight of the large scar gashed over Rochefort's left eye.

"There may be twenty or more inside," the lieutenant added.

Rochefort studied the face of the church, noting the Gothic structure's famous grouping of three apse columns clustered together, topped by ornate pointed roofs.

"*Teutoni* Knights?" Rochefort asked.

The lieutenant nodded grimly. He then beckoned to the neck vise hanging from Rochefort's belt. "Should I do the honors?"

Rochefort lowered his eyes to the lieutenant. "Not today," he said, shaking his head. "Send in *Fra'Diavulu.*"

The lieutenant grinned, turned on his heel, and signaled to his men. Moments later, a dark and agile figure emerged from the contingent of Angevin soldiers.

The Messinese mercenary *Fra'Diavulu* stepped forward. Slender yet powerful, the knight was a truly imposing sight to behold. He wore a bloodred tunic chest plate and billowing cape with gold piping, and black leather boots. Two stiletto blades crisscrossed over his abdomen. A long rapier with an ornamental hilt hung at his side, the steel expertly worked and polished.

Fra'Diavulu lifted a ruby prickly pear fruit to his mouth and ripped into it with his front teeth. The fruit's red liquid dribbled down his chin like the blood that would soon be spilled on the stone floor of the crypt inside the church. The nefarious knight then tossed the fruit to another soldier and slowly lowered a silver Saracen war mask over his face. It portrayed the likeness of a scowling Satan with two horns protruding upward from the forehead. The mouth was downturned into a dramatic frown, a hooked mustache dangling over the upper lip and curving up the sides of the cheeks.

Fra'Diavulu unsheathed his rapier to the shrill sound of scraping metal and held it outward. An Angevin soldier ran up to his side, carrying a goatskin cask. The soldier removed the cap and tipped the cask forward, dousing the length of the blade with oil. Another soldier approached with a flaming torch. *Fra'Diavulu* extended his blade outward, touching its tip to the fire. The soldiers watched with wide eyes as the flame leapt from the torch and set the entire length of the sword ablaze.

Fra'Diavulu lifted the flaming sword high over his head, pointing it into the sky. "On my signal, break down the door."

Inside the crypt, the *Teutoni* Knights breathed heavily through the pitch black, gripping their blades until the blood left their hands.

Suddenly, they heard heavy footsteps approach from outside. With the footsteps came the glow of orange firelight shooting streaking columns of light through the cracks in the crypt's arched doorway. Then, rising from the silence, a blood-curdling cackle that sounded like Satan himself. The laughter became louder and louder, sending shivers down the spines of the knights.

"Fra'Diavulu!" a knight gasped.

"Steady, men," Bartolomeo Maniscalco ordered.

In that instant, the door came crashing down. The men's eyes widened with terror as the black crypt was filled with the blinding glow of a scowling devil's mask illuminated by a blazing sword.

The men screamed as a laughing devil swirled into the crypt.

Sparks of clashing metal flew in the darkness as the *Teutoni* Knights attempted to parry the incoming blows. But it was futile.

Maniscalco screamed as he was stabbed directly through the shoulder and singed by the scorching heat of the metal. The fire cauterized the gash wound as soon as the searing blade was painfully yanked from his body cavity.

Maniacal laughter came from behind the devilish war mask as he moved through the darkness. Stabbing and singeing.

One by one, the *Teutoni* Knights screamed in gut-wrenching agony as they were skewered and cauterized. The putrid smell of burning flesh filled the crypt.

Then as quickly as the laughing devil appeared, he was gone.

Lying on the ground, Maniscalco raised a shaking hand to his shoulder, feeling the closed wound. He gritted his teeth as powerful jolts of pain shot through his body and up into his brain. Losing his strength, he closed his eyes and rolled back onto the floor, his chest heaving.

Angevin soldiers rushed into the crypt, carrying torches, and surveyed the carnage.

The *Teutoni* Knights writhed and wailed, every single man wounded, but alive.

CHAPTER 23

Porto di Messina
Messina, Sicily
March 30, 1282
8:28 a.m.

DARK CLOUDS hung heavy over the *Porto di Messina* as cold rain pelted the Angevin warships plated with steel and armor. The ships seemed to arrive daily, amassing in Messina's large port. Sicily's most powerful maritime center, the Port of Messina was said to be famous for three things: relentless wind, swordfish, and bad news. The third usually came in the form of Angevin galleys that appeared to arrive daily carrying soldiers, mercenaries, and French nobility looking to lay conquest to their newest Sicilian fiefdom.

General Guy de Rochefort and *Fra'Diavulu* rode on horseback through the streets, their beasts kicking up mud and manure beneath their hooves. A contingent of Angevin horsemen followed close behind them, forming two columns. Donkey-drawn carts splashed through the mud mixed with manure, past merchants selling fish, squid, pistachios, and prickly pears. Row houses and private inns for sailors,

Crusaders, and pilgrims lined the port's perimeter, shaped like a farmer's sickle. At the end of the stretch of roads sat the taverns and brothels, famous for their *puttanesca*, or whore's sauce, a garlicky tomato concoction drenched with anchovies, capers, and black Gaeta olives. The flavors created such a pungent aroma that the prostitutes of Messina used it to lure sailors and soldiers into their brothels.

General Rochefort glanced down and noticed a sheepskin book tucked into *Fra'Diavulu*'s belt. He cocked his neck to get a better view of its cover: *Contrasto*.

"Why did you take it?" the general scoffed.

The Messinese knight looked down at the book, then snapped his gaze forward.

"Counterintelligence," *Fra'Diavulu* said. "*Teutoni* Knights have an affinity for the Middle Sicilian dialect of Frederick the Second's Sicilian School. The better I understand them, the faster I find them."

Rochefort snorted. "A barbaric language. I will choke it from existence." With that, he gripped the iron vise on his belt as if to make his point.

"An impassioned man does not fear death," *Fra'Diavulu* said, scanning the slew of Sicilians pushing their way through the piazza. He saw seething eyeballs shoot daggers at him as the Angevin contingent rode through the crowd. "A muted anger is boiling underneath the surface. I can feel it."

Rochefort rolled his eyes forward, shaking his head. He squinted out over the harbor, lifting a large finger in front of *Fra'Diavulu*'s face. He pointed toward the incoming Angevin warships lurching slowly in the sickle-shaped port. *Fra'Diavulu* glanced out over the harbor, observing the ships being stocked and armored.

"Angevin power reigns in the port of Messina," Rochefort said, staring at the massive warships groaning in the docks. "New ships come in every day from France, carrying soldiers and mercenaries. Soon King Charles will launch a thousand ships against the shores of Constantinople. Rome will pale in comparison to our Great Angevin Empire." Rochefort turned a stiff neck toward *Fra'Diavulu*. "Sicilians are a dirty people with dirty blood. Blood of gypsies. Savages. They are nothing."

Fra'Diavulu studied the resentful faces in the crowd glaring back at them. "But are they?"

Rochefort shot him a dubious glare.

Fra'Diavulu sensed the general staring a hole into his own head. The Messinese mercenary gazed forward for a long moment before shooting an assured glance back at Rochefort.

"They are nothing," he corrected himself.

CHAPTER 24

Palermo, Sicily
Kalsa District
March 30, 1282
8:36 a.m.

PALERMO'S OLD city center was known as the *Kalsa*. At the height of its glory, this Arab district served as the administrative center of the Islamic emirate, rivaling cities such as Cairo or Cordoba. The area once contained the sultan's government offices, lush gardens, fountains, baths, and mosques. Today, it was a twisting labyrinth of narrow streets, row houses, small piazzas, and open-air markets.

Aetna Vespiri felt the pangs of hunger as she moved through a twisting bazaar of vendor carts strung together along a warren of narrow streets. Her feet squished through the muddy street as rain pelted the balcony awnings hanging above, casting the streets in shadow. She wore a garment made of yellow and bloodred fabric, girdled at the thighs for better mobility. Gold hoop earrings hung from her earlobes, her hair tied up in a large braid that fell over her shoulder, pinned with an ornamental sapphire brooch. She pressed her hand against her thigh, feeling the reassuring shape of her blade holstered against her leg, hidden from view.

Carrying a straw basket, Aetna filled it with citrus fruits and various cured meats to be used for the *Santo Spirito*'s holiday feast later that night. Tziporah and a small group of Cistercian nuns walked beside her, doing the same as they moved together through the marketplace.

Tonight, the Norman church was observing Vespers, the sunset vigil marking the coming of Easter. To the Sicilians, Vespers rivaled Christmas Eve in importance. A solemn yet celebratory night when the people of Palermo came together to feast in solidarity, cast aside their troubles, and forget if for just one night the harsh realities of their oppressed existence. Reveling in the hope for a coming salvation.

Aetna observed the spectacle of human faces milling about the marketplace in a well-orchestrated pandemonium. Greek faces. Arabic faces. Christian women followed the fashion of the Muslim women and were fluent in Arabic, and vice versa, each wrapping their black, green, and scarlet cloaks and veils about their heads and face. Scrawny stray dogs scampered among the market stalls, noses hanging to the ground, searching for any scraps of meat they could find. Along the sides of the muddy street, men took naps in their doorways while with hypnotic shouts, vendors slung their goods and services to passersby in singsong voices.

"*Miele sono queste ciciri!*" a vendor shouted from behind his cart. "Chickpeas as sweet as nectar."

The man grinned at Aetna, gripping a palmful of small white peas as they slipped between his fingers.

"*Pira butiti, si mancia e si vivi!*" another vendor yelled. "Pears like butter! Drink while you eat!"

Aetna and Tziporah broke off from the group and roamed together among the melee of food stalls, scanning the wooden tables that groaned under the weight of freshly caught squid and octopus, lemons and blood oranges, turmeric and cinnamon spices, almonds and pistachios, *panelli* and *arancini*, chickpea fritters and sauce-filled rice balls that sizzled in olive oil. Eggplants gleamed in towering violet pyramids to the right, and to the left were pig heads strung on wooden poles, rimmed by rows of skinned rabbits dangling from clotheslines. Crates that once held lemons and prickly pears were now used as makeshift table legs and chairs.

Artisans and craftsmen launched their attack on unsuspecting passersby with a variety of ammunition: ceramic Moorish heads, candles, paintings of *Monte Pellegrino*, wooden rosaries, and statues of the Virgin Mary.

Aetna glanced upward, beholding an intricate canopy of balconies with red and yellow canvases stretched out over the sandy streets casting long, angular shadows below. Windowsills were festooned with wildflowers and cacti. Women stepped out from their balconies above, lowering straw baskets on a piece of handwoven rope. When a basket reached the street, workers would take the coins placed inside and fill it with whatever meats or fruits the woman had ordered. If she was unsatisfied with the quality, she would send the basket back down and haggle.

On the far end of the street, an Angevin patrol pushed their way carelessly through the crowd, drinking wine from a bottle and laughing obnoxiously. A soldier yanked a barb of *stigghiola* off its spit and shoved the sizzling sheep entrails into his mouth. The vendor clenched his fists, watching helplessly as the soldier made off with his product without paying.

As the Angevin soldiers sauntered past Aetna, one man shoved her with his shoulder. Aetna tripped forward into the mud, catching herself on the ground with her palms.

Tziporah caught her basket as it fell from her hands. "Are you okay?"

Aetna nodded, gnashing her teeth as she pushed herself up. "Angevin filth."

Tziporah glanced back and threw pointed blades from her small eyes straight into the soldier's back.

Aetna brushed the mud off her knees, grabbing the basket back from Tziporah. *"Ammunini,"* she growled. "Let's go."

Twenty minutes later, Aetna and Tziporah placed their baskets down and sat at a small bar table under a covered vendor stall.

Aetna bit into a fried *arancini* rice ball as she watched the foot traffic swarm through the narrow streets. A horde of dirty children scurried out from underneath the table and crowded around the table. The children argued and grappled with one another. A little boy picked up a stone and threw it at an affluent-looking man passing them in the street. As the guilty boy turned to run, Aetna reached out and caught him by the neck.

"Mamluk!" the boy protested, swinging his fists violently. "Let me go!"

"That's no way to treat a stranger," she scolded, shaking her finger in his face.

"Leave me alone!" he cried.

Aetna gazed down at the boy, kneeling to meet him at eye level. He looked dangerously thin. His face was covered in dirt, his hair smelling of mud and mold. Aetna reached into her basket and pulled out a lemon. The bright yellow fruit seemed to sparkle in her hand. The boy suddenly stopped moving, his eyes filling with wonder, as if he had just seen the crown jewels of Queen Constanza of Aragon, the former queen of Sicily.

"Take it," she said.

The boy eyed the lemon for a moment, then snatched it from Aetna's hand and broke free of her grip, scampering off into the alley.

Tziporah shook her head, then took a large bite of her *arancini*. She held it up to inspect it, admiring the deep-fried rice ball as if it were a coveted prize. She beheld the yellow saffron rice held together by melted cheese. A ruby meat sauce filled with peas oozed from its gooey center.

"*Beddu*," Tziporah declared, a smile crossing her lips. "The perfect *arancini*." She took another bite, closing her eyes as she slowly chewed. "Sicily's finest treasure, don't you think?"

Aetna, however, wasn't paying her any attention. Her eyes were drawn down the street to an Angevin soldier trudging aimlessly through the crowd, dragging his feet in the mud. He looked delirious, his face frozen in a state of shock. Furrowing her brow, she studied the soldier as he took a few more steps before unsheathing his rapier and swinging it wildly in all directions. He clutched his lower backside as he collapsed to his knees and fell face-first into the mud. Motionless. A pool of blood spread out beneath him.

Aetna's eyes narrowed. Suddenly, she flinched as a golden eagle shrieked down from the sky, sending a powerful echo through the streets. Aetna squinted up to see the large bird of prey circling overhead.

A Sicilian man dressed in black leaned into the table next to her, gazing up at the circling bird of prey. "He's been busy lately."

Aetna glanced toward the man. He had a slender olive face with a well-groomed black mustache tapered at both ends and a long beard shaped into a sharp point. He wore a gold-brimmed black cap low over his forehead. Beneath the cap, just at the nape, was a thick mass of dark curly hair. She noticed he was missing the thumbnail on his left hand.

"Who's been busy?" Aetna said.

The man's lips widened into a grin, his dark eyes revealing a roguish glint. He pointed his finger skyward. "When the golden eagle cries . . . an Angevin meets his demise." He then dragged his finger across his own throat. "The calling card of the outlaw *cavaleri . . . Don Rapaci.*"

Tziporah's eyes widened. "You mean the *Falcon of Palermo*? *Master of the Sky*. The stories are true, then?"

The man in black nodded. "As true as the generous bounty the Angevins placed on his head."

Aetna raised a skeptical brow. "He really kills Angevins in broad daylight?"

"Drunk soldiers are easy targets." The man in black smiled, peering out over the pedestrian heads passing in the street. "The *Falcon* moves among the crowd no different from you or I. And then . . ."

The man in black sat straight up, seeing something. He pointed over Aetna's shoulder. "Over there. Can you see it?"

Aetna craned her neck, observing the unconscious Angevin soldier across the street.

"Stuck by the stiletto of *Don Rapaci*," the man in black said, miming a swift stabbing motion with his fist. "Some even say he is the ghost of Prince Conradin himself. Doing the work of the people."

Aetna studied his face. She found something about him charming. And annoying. "How do you know he's a man? Has anyone actually seen this person?"

The man in black glanced over to Aetna, eyeing her with a teasing suspicion. "Ah . . . perhaps *you* are the great *Don Rapaci* . . . disguised in plain sight."

Aetna rolled her eyes and snorted. In that instant, she snapped out her *patri*'s stiletto, aiming for the man's neck. The razor edge of her blade hovered less than an inch from his throat. "Maybe I am . . . maybe I'm not. Now, get a move on. We didn't ask for company."

The man's eyes widened in surprise. They then narrowed, tracing the length of the blade from Aetna's hand to his neck.

Two engraved snakes coiled around its crossbar. He swallowed a lump in his throat. "Point taken."

Tziporah grinned impishly, glancing up toward Aetna with amusement.

Suddenly, the ground began to rumble beneath their feet.

Aetna glanced up and saw a contingent of Angevin soldiers barreling down the street. Their heavy armor clanked as they ran, long rapiers strapped to their belts. They moved like an unstoppable war machine. Screams of women and children pierced the air as they pushed their way through the throng of pedestrians.

Startled, Aetna leapt to her feet to get a better look.

The Angevins rounded a corner and entered a small piazza situated outside of the *Sant'Anna la Misericordia* church and convent. They approached the wooden doors of the church. A soldier lifted his leg, smashed his foot into the door, and led the men inside. There was the sound of a struggle.

Tziporah leapt to her feet, her face stricken with worry. "What is it?"

"Bastards," Aetna spat, feeling as if her face were drenched with oil and lit on fire. She sheathed her blade and erupted from her seat, knocking over her basket of fruit and meats from the bar top. She dashed swiftly toward the church.

"Aetna, wait!" Tziporah shouted.

But she had already disappeared into the crowded street.

CHAPTER 25

A THRONG of frightened spectators had formed around the *Sant'Anna la Misericordia* church when the wooden doors burst open. A patrol of Angevin officers rounded up twenty Sicilian women and pushed them into the center of a small square situated outside of the church where they had been attending service.

The frightened women kept their heads down as they shuffled single file, forming a line that stretched out throughout the square.

Aetna careened to a stop behind the perimeter of the crowd. Pushing up onto her toes, she peered over their heads to get a better look. Suddenly, a large Angevin soldier grabbed her forcefully from behind. Aetna winced as the soldier squeezed her arms tight in his large hands.

"Got another one!" the soldier growled.

"Get your hands off me!" Aetna cried. She thrashed wildly as the soldier dragged her toward the line of women and pushed her into the formation.

Tziporah rounded a corner and emerged from the street near the far end of the piazza. She looked on in horror as Aetna was shoved into the line of women. From across the square, Aetna and Tziporah made eye contact. Tziporah quietly reached under her tunic and half unsheathed a short sword she had concealed. Aetna shook her head.

Suddenly, a hush fell over the piazza as the crowd parted. Cantering forward on a black stallion was none other than the scourge of Palermo, the Angevin sergeant Drouet.

The sergeant wore a tunic adorned with the coat of arms of the Angevin Crown of Sicily—a series of golden *fleur-de-lis* stacked in rows against a royal blue shield. An ornamented rapier was strapped to his belt. His dirty gray beard was gnarly and unkempt.

A soldier picked up his feet and hurried toward the sergeant, carrying a sheepskin scroll.

"The justiciar's royal harem manifest, sir," the soldier said.

Annoyed, Drouet nodded, beckoning him forward. The soldier picked up his boots and shuffled over. Drouet extended his open palm as the soldier approached, grasping the scroll. The soldier then clasped his hands behind his back, standing at attention.

Drouet unwrapped the scroll, skimming the surface of the document. Twenty entries listed by only a number and approximate age. Number eight was scratched out in thick black ink. Scribbled beneath it was a single word: *Mort.*

Dead.

Drouet stared at the manifest for a long moment. He clenched the scroll, squeezing it tightly.

"The justiciar has been highly displeased of late," Drouet said.

The soldier nodded. "He disposed of another concubine just this morning."

"Her corpse was thrown to the vultures?" Drouet said.

The soldier nodded grimly.

"Bien," Drouet said, looking up. "Vultures pick the corpse clean. We can't afford the spread of disease, you understand."

"Yes, sir," the soldier said.

An officer walked the length of women standing in line in front of the church. "There you are, Sergeant."

Sergeant Drouet stood still as stone, scanning the line of women. After a long moment, he cantered his horse forward. "Today, good fortune smiles down upon one of you. Justiciar Jean de Saint-Remy has an opening in his royal harem," he said, beckoning his hand backward, "in the Norman Palace. Away from this pitiful existence." He reached the end of the line, then turned and trotted back to the other end.

"Who here has experience pleasuring a man?" he asked, reining his horse to a stop.

The leering Angevin soldiers smirked among themselves.

A few hands slowly went up. Drouet scanned the group of women. He shook his head as if unsatisfied with the selection.

Then, at the far end of the line, Drouet's attention was drawn to a young woman standing silently. Her hand wasn't raised. She held her chin high but kept her eyes trained to the ground, a hardened scowl on her face. Her olive face glowed like the golden wheat of Sicily itself. She had dark raven hair, piercing green eyes, and an aquiline nose. Golden hoop earrings hung from her ears.

Drouet grinned deviously.

"As I think about it, I don't want another man's whore," he sneered. He kicked his horse and rode over toward the young woman.

Aetna watched from her peripheral vision as the haggard sergeant approached on horseback, stopping directly in front of her. She felt the hot air on her face as the enormous beast let out a snort from its large nostrils.

Drouet reined his horse back.

"What's your name, *ciciri*?" the sergeant leered, hacking up the *r* sound from the back of his throat.

Aetna cringed. *Ciciri* was the Sicilian word for chickpea, used by the Angevins as a pejorative to describe youthful and attractive Sicilian women they believed were ripe for the taking. Chickpeas as sweet as nectar. Pronounced *chee-cheri* by the native Sicilians, *ciciri* was a tricky word the French tongue struggled to enunciate—incorrectly pronouncing it *see-sheri*. Adding further insult to injury, the sergeant's guttural *r* was unmistakable—a hoarse growl-like sound produced deep in the gullet. It sounded nothing like the harplike rolling of the Sicilian *r* pronounced with a trill of the tongue. This strange sound from the Angevin throat served as yet another reminder of the foreign oppression plaguing the Sicilian people.

Scowling, Aetna knew the last thing she was going to do was give the vile Frenchman her name. *"Siciliana,"* she spat.

"I can't hear you," Drouet said.

"Siciliana," Aetna said again louder, stronger.

Drouet nodded to a nearby soldier. The soldier reached over and grabbed Aetna's shawl, opening it. Drouet gazed down from his horse at her slim torso and small breasts. "Look at me."

Aetna raised her eyes slowly, feeling her blood run hot. She grimaced as she looked upon the sergeant's gnarly beard and rotten teeth.

Drouet stared at her for a long moment, then turned to another officer. "This one," he said, nodding toward Aetna.

The group of women flinched as they heard the sharp sound of singing metal as the officer unsheathed his blade, pointing its tip away, toward the street. "The rest of you, get a move on!"

The women nodded and shuffled away one by one, keeping their heads down.

Aetna stood alone with the Angevin unit, glaring at the sergeant in the black of the eyes. A *cavaleri* was always *en occhinero* . . . even in the face of death.

For a brief moment, she calculated the distance between her and the sergeant. The amount of time it would take for her to unsheathe her stiletto, spring from her feet, and smash it directly into his chest cavity.

Three seconds, maybe fewer.

Aetna glanced around as the men closed in on her. Her hand slipped slowly down her hip, where she had concealed her stiletto. In three seconds, she could be on top of the sergeant. But in four seconds she would be dead. She knew this was not the time for brash action. Aetna retracted her hand, relaxing her arms at her sides.

As the men moved in on her, she curled her lips back, baring her teeth like a wildcat. The soldiers grabbed her forcefully by the arm and dragged her away.

She didn't make a sound.

A dark figure emerged from the shadow of an alleyway, peering out toward the small piazza of *Sant'Anna la Misericordia.* He was a large man, ominous and menacing. His face obliterated in shadow. He watched vigilantly as Angevin soldiers dragged a young woman away and hurled her into the back of a garrison wagon.

The dark figure watched with a keen gaze as the soldiers piled into the wagon, lashed the reins on the horses, and barreled away. He waited for the men to turn a corner, then extended his forearm.

Suddenly, a large golden eagle swooped down from the sky, flapping its enormous wings. It came to perch its large talons onto the dark figure's ornamental gauntlet.

The dark figure fed the enormous raptor a small piece of bloodied meat from his hand before sending the beast back into the air. Gazing up into the sky, watching the bird of prey take flight, he imagined his ancestors smiling down at him. He was fighting their war. Coming to blows with the same oppressive forces they had been grappling with since the Norman invasion of Palermo nearly two centuries earlier. Back when the Norman kings had first pillaged their homes, and raped and murdered their people.

The dark figure lingered for a minute in the alleyway, a roguish glint flashing in his eyes. Then as quickly as the wind blew, he disappeared into the shadows.

CHAPTER 26

Macalda's Tower, Matagrifone
Messina, Sicily
March 30, 1282
10:16 a.m. // Eight hours to Vespers

***MATAGRIFONE* WAS** known as the *Terror of the Greeks*. The imposing fortress was built during the Third Crusade by Richard the Lionheart to intimidate the Greeks of Messina, who did not welcome his presence on their island. Crouching about two hundred feet above sea level, situated on a dominant hill, it was a privileged point for control over the city and its port.

The royal vicar Herbert Orleans, governor of Sicily, watched *Fra'Diavulu* enter his office chamber alone. The Messinese knight walked stiffly through the threshold with a stern look on his face, carrying his devilish war mask at his side. Two elite sentries then assumed their positions on either side of the entryway.

Vicar Orleans poured the entire contents of a wine cask into a large goblet. His third already that day. He lifted the cup to his lips and gulped down the entire thing. He was a large man in his early fifties, tall and slightly overweight. He was clean-shaven, and his gray hair was cropped short, much like that of the pope. He wore a purple velvet robe with a white collar; a large gold amulet hung around his neck and jewel rings adorned his fat fingers.

The vicar's office was a stark, cavernous stone chamber. Woven tapestries depicting the great Norman invasion of England hung down in massive sheets from the ceilings. A map of the old kingdom of Sicily was sprawled out across a large oaken table in the center of the room. Tokens in the shape of Angevin foot soldiers and horsemen were spread around the map, depicting the various fortresses and strongholds they had managed around the island. Messina. Palermo. Corleone. Vicari. This was truly the office of a militaristic administration.

Vicar Orleans felt a burp come out of his throat as he watched *Fra'Diavulu* draw closer. The knight approached the vicar and snapped to attention, lifting his chin upward.

Vicar Orleans reached across the table and grabbed a black olive from a ceramic bowl. He popped it into his mouth and chewed it loudly. Orleans pressed his palm into his belly and massaged out a light burp. He grinned sheepishly. "I understand you are especially feared among these people."

Fra'Diavulu stared forward sternly, his lips pursed. "I have a reputation."

"And why do you imagine that is?" Orleans asked.

"The Sicilians are a superstitious people. I exploit that superstition."

"Yes, what is that funny name they call you?" Orleans said. "I can never properly pronounce it."

"*Fra'Diavulu*, Your Grace," the mercenary told him. "The Brother Devil."

Orleans studied the knight's extravagant bloodred uniform. His eyes traced the gold piping lining his cape before falling down to the devilish war mask in his hands. An image of scowling Satan, a mustache hanging on his lips over a dramatic frown. Orleans snatched a loaf of bread and tore his teeth into it, washing it down with a gulp of wine. He then narrowed his gaze. "You don't kill like the others. Why?"

"To instill obedience, Your Grace," *Fra'Diavulu* said. "Obedience through fear."

"Seems like a lot of work when a simple swing of the ax across the neck will do, don't you think?"

Fra'Diavulu shook his head. He then pressed his fist slowly into his sternum, mimicking a blade stab.

Orleans raised an eyebrow.

"A deep, hard stab will cause the body cavity to close around the blade, impaling itself around its razor-sharp edges," *Fra'Diavulu* said, tightening his fist in a squeezing motion. "The pain is excruciating, if not worse than death, Your Grace."

Orleans's jaw dropped in disgust. He pressed his palm to his chest as he considered the thought.

"Normally the wound would kill a man from infection," *Fra'Diavulu* continued. "But my flaming sword instantly cauterizes the wound so that they live in fear of facing my blade again. This is how you control them."

"Is it?" Orleans said.

Fra'Diavulu pursed his lips. "Your Grace, more soldiers arrived from France just this morning," he said. "Every day your army grows larger. We need labor to till the land, build our ships and castles, provide services to our garrisons and nobles. We will destroy the *Teutoni* Knights, but the Sicilians are no good to us dead."

Orleans nodded, seeing his point. He took a swig from his chalice, staring down into the depths of the glass for a long moment. An impish grin formed on his lips. "You have eyes for my daughter?"

Fra'Diavulu kept his gaze trained forward like two pointed spears, but he couldn't help swallowing a lump in his throat. "No, Your Grace," he said. "She is betrothed to General Rochefort."

Orleans shifted in his chair. "You wrote letters to her from the Albanian trenches," Orleans said. "All correspondence to and from my daughter comes through me, you understand. You two have developed quite a close friendship."

Fra'Diavulu continued to stare ahead. "Your Grace, you summoned me from the front to hunt and maim *Teutoni* Knights, and that's what I came here to do."

"Good," Orleans said. He then grimaced and pressed his hand to his stomach before leaning over and letting a burst of gas rip from the seat of his loins.

"She is feral and insubordinate," Orleans said. Then he paused for a moment. A resentful glint seemed to linger in his eyes. "She shows no respect for me or my soldiers."

"You must feel incredibly affronted, Your Grace," *Fra'Diavulu* said. "I'm sorry."

Orleans nodded, clenching his jaw. He thrust a finger forward and wagged it in the air. "General Rochefort is exactly the type of man that will set her straight." He lurched for his wine bottle and sloppily poured himself another glass.

"A father can only hope, Your Grace," *Fra'Diavulu* said.

CHAPTER 27

Palazzo dei Normanni
Palermo, Sicily
Albergheria District
March 30, 1282
12:02 p.m. // Six hours to Vespers

SOMEWHERE BENEATH the *Palazzo dei Normanni*, Palermo justiciar Jean de Saint-Remy sauntered down a stone ramp and into a subterranean tunnel. Torches cast ghastly shadows against the walls as he marched down the long passageway. Turning a sharp corner, he descended a set of small steps into a dark basement chamber. Saint-Remy felt the air becoming thick and murky. There was the sound of water dripping down the walls.

Saint-Remy's eyes narrowed as they fell upon Aetna standing in the center of the basement.

Aetna stood alone. Her skin was clammy and damp, her face stricken with a harrowed gaze as she stared a hole into the wall.

Saint-Remy leered as he circled Aetna like a panther, tracing her figure downward with eyes from head to toe, admiring the lean curves of her arms and legs. He raised his large hand, pressing his palm into her face.

"To think I questioned your beauty even for a second," he said.

Aetna breathed heavier, her face turning to a scowl.

"You will make a wonderful concubine," he said. "As long as you are obedient." He circled her. "You must feel unwanted down here alone. Do you feel unwanted?"

Aetna said nothing.

Saint-Remy cracked a grin. "You can tell me the truth. Everyone feels unwanted at times."

He ran his fingers through her hair, admiring each ebony strand between his fingertips. "If only you had someone to touch you so you didn't have to feel unwanted."

Aetna's chest heaved up and down, her eyes trained to the wall.

Saint-Remy laughed to himself, extracting his hand. "They say Sicilians are beneath us. But perhaps the problem isn't you. Perhaps the problem is them." He gestured broadly. "After all, when they compare you to vermin . . ." He moved up behind her, pressing his torso against her back. He let his nose drift over her hair, smelling her salty skin. He circled around, coming face to face with her. He lifted his hand and brushed his fingers gently down her scarred cheek. "Is this the skin of vermin? The hair of vermin?"

Aetna glared forward. Saint-Remy closed his eyes, taking a deep breath as if overwhelmed by her youthful beauty. He clasped his hands together as if in prayer.

"I feel for your kind, *Siciliana*," he said, running his hand down her neck, over her firm breast.

Aetna remained silent. She would give him nothing.

"Why don't you be a good girl and slip out of that garment," he whispered, his voice almost fatherly. He ran his hand down the side of her torso, feeling her lean, concave waist.

Aetna's face hardened into a scowl. She remained motionless, keeping her eyes trained on the wall ahead.

Saint-Remy glared at her. His face flushed red, the white of his eyes widening with rage. "Why don't you obey?"

Aetna's heart pounded harder and harder against her chest.

Saint-Remy stared at her for a long moment. He swallowed a hard lump in his throat. "Filthy bitch."

In that instant, Saint-Remy raised his palm and struck Aetna across the face. *Smack!* There was the loud cracking of skin hitting skin, bone hitting bone.

The force of the blow sent her sprawling backward and tumbling across the floor. She crashed face-first into a rack of ceramic wine casks. She scrambled to her feet, grimacing and pressing her hand to her face. Blood came trickling down from her mouth.

Saint-Remy charged her like a bull. He grabbed her by the shoulders with his thick hands and threw her across the room toward a straw mattress. Aetna was no match against his brute strength and missed the mat completely. She hit the wall face-first, cracking her head against the stone and falling to the ground.

Saint-Remy stood over Aetna and hit her hard across the cheek. *Smack!* He then brought his arm back down and backhanded her across the other cheek. *Smack!*

Saint-Remy screamed as he pushed over the rack of wine casks, onto Aetna. The casks smashed to the ground around her, covering her silk garment in their bloodred liquid.

Aetna didn't make a sound as she lay in the cold pool of wine.

Saint-Remy clenched his fists as he stood over her, wheezing. "Look what you've made me do." He spat venom, gesturing to the destroyed wine shelf. He then turned on his heel, his cape billowing behind him as he sauntered toward the staircase.

"Sergeant!" he cried.

Minutes later, Sergeant Drouet led a group of soldiers down the staircase. The sergeant's eyes bulged with fury as he scanned the room and observed the utter destruction.

Aetna spat blood onto the floor and pushed herself to her feet. Her face was bruised and bloodied. She couldn't think of anything but the throbbing pain in her skull.

"Do you have anything to say for yourself?" Saint-Remy said.

Disoriented, Aetna attempted to focus her blurred vision. She refused to plead for her life. Glaring up at the justiciar, she spat at his feet. *"Vaffanculu."*

The room fell silent. In that moment, Saint-Remy decided her fate. "Cut off her head. Stick it on a pike on the highest tower of this palace."

Drouet stabbed a large finger toward Aetna. "I get a piece of her first."

Saint-Remy raised his hand. "Do not make a mess in my palace. Take her into the alley. Leave her corpse to the dogs. Bring back her head."

The men cheered as Drouet barreled forward.

Aetna braced for pain as Drouet extended his hand and yanked her by the hair, pulling her hard into his chest. He inhaled deeply, smelling her clammy skin. "When I'm done with you, *ciciri*, you'll be begging for the ax."

With that, Drouet tightened his grip around a clump of Aetna's hair and dragged her away by her roots.

CHAPTER 28

Cattedrale di Palermo
Palermo, Sicily
Seralcadio District
March 30, 1282
12:14 p.m.

CATTEDRALE DI PALERMO, the Palermo Cathedral, was erected in 1184 on the site of an old Muslim mosque, set back from the *Cassaru* and facing a large courtyard lined with towering palm trees. Clad in brown Norman stone, the massive structure looked more like an Arabic fortress than a place of holy worship. The cathedral was flanked by two soaring steepled towers at each corner, covered in intricate Byzantine-style mosaics and statues. Two arcades arched over a busy cross street and connected the cathedral's main facade with the looming bell tower, annexed by the archbishop's own palace and residence. The cathedral looked like no other edifice in all of Europe.

That afternoon, Archbishop Salvatore Malu entered the cathedral and flattened himself against the wall, feeling cool stone against his back. Burning beneath his cassock, he took out a silk cloth and dabbed the sweat from his forehead. He repeated the justiciar's words in his head:

The appearance of hope must be upheld.

Malu had been using all of his religious sway over the past decade to persuade the people of Palermo that salvation could be found only through the grace of the church. He reminded them that as Jesus went to the cross, they would pray together even as they were beaten by the oppressor. His manipulative sermons extolled the "good Sicilian virtues" of staunch faith and muted submission.

"*Simmo surfaru,*" Malu insisted to the full congregation. "Remember that we are nothing but sulfur. Only through unwavering faith in God's grace can we be freed from the Angevin yoke."

But regardless of these efforts, Mass attendance of late neared an all-time low. The few donations the people could make barely kept the baskets full. The Angevins had been taking too much from the people. Expensive duties owed to *Re Carlu* kept the Sicilians in a constant state of debt. Random home invasion and petty theft of personal property in the streets kept them afraid. Every day was getting worse.

This afternoon, Palermo Cathedral was quiet, a gaping marble cavern filled with the usual suspects—frail nuns grasping wooden crucifixes, clusters of bleary-eyed Sicilian men and women deep in prayer.

As Malu let his eyes drift upward, the true magnificence of the place radiated like an exultant choir of angels, comforting him even under the gray skies of March. The spicy smell of incense burned his nostrils. The Arab-Norman church was so lavish, he had to close his eyes and reopen them to take it all in. He gazed high overhead upon the enormous apse, a half-domed roof vault above the altar, adorned in gold. His eyes then traced the enormous pillars downward, where he beheld the sarcophagi of royal rulers, including the tomb of Frederick II tucked away in the aisle. Surrounded by a templelike canopy held up by reddish igneous columns, the sarcophagus urn was cradled by two pairs of lions on either side.

The resting place of the *Stupor Mundi*. The world's greatest emperor. Sicily's greatest king.

The crown of Queen Constanza of Aragon, wife of Frederick II, was displayed on a royal mantel nearby. The so-called crown was actually a Byzantine kamelaukion, a gold brimless skullcap bedecked with pearls, sapphires, and other precious red and green gems. Constanza, a woman possessing a radiant intellect, was twenty-four when she married Frederick, then a boy of only fourteen.

Malu's eyes finally fell upon a specific pew somewhere near the center of the cathedral. He suddenly felt his face growing hot. It was from that pew over a decade ago that a Sicilian challenged his authority and put his own future at risk.

The archbishop retreated into his memory. He now found himself standing at the altar. The seats were full. A few Angevin guards lingered in the corner of the room, sharing a bottle of cheap wine among themselves. Rarely did Angevin soldiers attend Mass. But Justiciar Saint-Remy had ordered them to keep an eye on Malu, and today they were in for a show.

Malu opened his palms outward. *"Simmo surfaru,"* he said to the full congregation. "We are nothing but sulfur. God does what he wants with us. Put your faith in him and this church, and you will find salvation. As Jesus went to the cross, we will pray as we are beaten."

The Sicilians nodded, grasped their hands tightly in prayer, and bowed their heads in submission. They offered up their hard-earned coins to the cathedral every Sunday in hopes of one day being freed from the yoke of their hard existence.

"No," a voice boomed from the back of the church.

The cathedral fell silent.

Malu recognized the man who was adorned with a pendant displaying the likeness of the *Gorgoneion Trinacria*—Medusa's shrieking face from which radiated three human legs bent at the knee. The winemaker from Mount Etna was a well-known figure in the community. He had adopted the ancient Greek symbol for the island as his heraldry. It was unmistakable.

Don Vittorio Vespiri, he told himself. *The one they called* O Santo Cavaleri.

"Brothers and sisters," Don Vespiri said, "we must resist Angevin aggression at all costs. This offense against Palermo is only the beginning."

Every day under French rule seemed to bring a new atrocity or outrage, but on that day, *Re Carlu* had issued a shocking new decree. He would displace the kingdom of Sicily's royal capital city from Palermo, where it had stood for a thousand years, to the shores of Napoli, on the mainland of Italy. The decision impaled the hearts, minds, and pride of the Sicilian people. For the French tyranny now ruled from afar, treating the Sicilians as nothing more than subjects, and Sicily itself an annexed island to be exploited and plundered for resources.

"Next, they come for our farms, our homes, our loved ones. Their vile natures know no bounds," Don Vespiri continued, his eyes moving from man to woman.

The crowd murmured with concern.

Malu glared at the young man.

"It is our charge to protect this land," Don Vespiri shouted above the crowd. "We didn't inherit Sicily from our ancestors; we are borrowing it from our children."

The men and women looked around and nodded to one another.

Don Vespiri beckoned with his hand back toward the archbishop. "Where are Sicily's clergymen in our time of need? They have become soft and comfortable. They neglect the plight of their brethren and instead indulge themselves in sport, pleasure, and useless pastimes." He then thrust a finger toward the altar, making direct eye contact with Malu. A *cavaleri* always *en occhinero*. "Let the chaplain of this church hear these words," he said. "Through the authority of the pope, he ought to protect the helpless among us in the face of our Angevin overlords. But instead, he seeks the admiration of the oppressor, accepting their gifts, pandering to their interests, and worse, enabling the rape and murder of our people."

The entire crowd gasped, all eyes turning toward the archbishop. Malu's bulbous face burned red with fire. He thrust a thick finger out into the crowd like a dagger, stabbing it directly at Don Vespiri's heart.

"How dare you," Malu growled.

Don Vespiri spat at his feet. "Kings may be the judges of
Sicily, but *we* are the judges of kings."

Malu's eyes widened. "Guards, arrest that man for
blasphemy!"

Don Vespiri stood unshaken. Angevin soldiers scrambled
forward and shackled his wrists together. He flashed a defiant
grin at Malu as he was marched away.

Stricken with fear, the Sicilians kept their heads down as
the soldiers left the cathedral with their prisoner, and over the
coming months submitted to the yoke of the Angevin military.

Don Vespiri was held for only twenty-four hours in the
Palazzo dei Normanni. He was released through the involve-
ment of Justiciar Jean de Saint-Remy, who had thought the
entire episode was daft and harmless.

Shortly after, Malu confronted Saint-Remy in protest.

"Vespiri is a dangerous man. He spoke out against *Re Carlu*
and my own station," Malu said. "He deserves to rot in a prison
cell."

"Now, what fun would that be, Archbishop?" the justiciar
said.

Malu fumed. "You think this is a game?"

"The appearance of hope must be upheld," Saint-Remy
said, grinning. "Especially because there is none."

Archbishop Malu retreated from his memory, finding himself
gazing out over his church. He eyed the very pew where Don
Vittorio Vespiri had once stood up and defied him. Feeling his
blood begin to boil, Malu took a deep breath to slow his racing heart. He reminded himself of the retribution he felt when
word of the winemaker's death at the hands of General Guy de
Rochefort reached Palermo.

A rightful punishment.

Malu snorted with delight and turned on his heel, his cape flowing behind him. A decade ago, he had feared for the future of his station. But today, the ultimate reward for his loyalty to the Angevins was within reach. If all continued as *Re Carlu* had promised, Malu would soon find himself the most powerful man in Christendom.

CHAPTER 29

Palazzo dei Normanni
Palermo, Sicily
Albergheria District
March 30, 1282
12:36 p.m.

AETNA VESPIRI braced herself as Sergeant Drouet smashed her head into the side of a stone wall. Bursts of light flashed before her eyes as splintering pain racked her skull.

She had been dragged into an alley just beyond the palace perimeter, near the Punic city wall. Thrashing with all her strength, she had struggled to resist as her toes carved chaotic lines into the dirt behind her. Confused and frightened pedestrians darted in every direction at the sight of Drouet. A mother clasped her hands around her young daughter's eyes, shielding her from the sight of yet another Sicilian woman molested at the hands of Angevin soldiers. An act that had become all too common of late.

Keeping Aetna's face pressed against the alley wall with his strong hand, Drouet scrambled to unbuckle his armor. Two of his men stood close behind him, laughing and cheering him on. The balcony awning and hanging clothes above created a canopy over the narrow alleyway, casting the street in dark shadow. A biting wind blew, chilling Aetna to the bone. She felt a sullen dread inside as she heard Drouet remove the heavy belt from his uniform.

"Help!" Aetna cried out. "Somebody help me!"

The alley filled with sickening laughter.

Drouet leaned in and licked the sweaty skin of Aetna's neck, catching the trickles of salty fluid running down the back of her ear.

"Open your legs," he snarled, shoving his knee between her thighs and spreading her legs apart.

Aetna felt a surge of panic rush through her veins. Her muscles became tense and engorged with blood. *I'd rather die.* In that instant, she gnashed her teeth and with all of her strength lunged her head backward. A sickening crack rang out as the back of her skull smashed into Drouet's forehead. Drouet yelled as he stumbled backward, holding his hands to his face.

Still reeling from the blow, Aetna spun around to face her attacker. Drouet seemed unfazed, scorching the earth she stood on with his fiery eyes. He lowered his hands from his face to reveal a river of blood streaming freely from his nose, down the front of his mouth, soaking his gray beard. His breathing became heavier.

Aetna's head turned over and over with pain as she tried to retain consciousness. She wanted to fight but felt dizzy with concussion.

"No *ciciri* is worth this," Drouet snarled as he gripped the hilt of his rapier, ripping it from the sheath. With a merciless glare, he lumbered toward her with the sword held steady at his side.

Aetna felt a foot shove into her calf, forcing her to the ground. Drouet lurched forward and grabbed a tuft of her hair, yanking her head backward.

As Aetna squinted up at her attacker, her vision blurred, she thought she saw a large golden eagle swoop down from the sky. The feathered beast seemed to perch its claws on a donkey cart far off in the distance.

Then, at the end of the murky alley, the silhouette of a large man seemed to rise up from the shadows. His face shined with the black ebony of a Saracen war mask mimicking the shape of a falcon's beak. His head was wrapped in a dark cloth like a turban. His eyes were lined with eye shadow. The man quickly approached, not making a sound.

"Who the hell are you?" a soldier growled.

With lightning speed, the masked man snapped out a stiletto that flashed silver in the moonlight.

"He's got a sword!" a soldier cried, unsheathing his rapier.

But before the Angevin could steady himself, the stiletto flashed forward and knocked his sword away. Sparks flew where the two steel blades connected. Seconds later, a fist smashed into the soldier's face. *Crack!* Blood spurted from his nose as he fell backward, unconscious.

Aetna could only watch the ensuing whirlwind that followed. It was hard to comprehend the tumult of violence. The masked man moved so fast, so silently. One moment he was there; the next, he was gone. He twirled out from the shadows and swung the hilt of his blade upward, smashing it into a soldier's chin. *Crack!* At the same time, he spun backward, stabbing the chest of another. The mortally wounded Angevin howled. The masked man then tried to retract the stiletto from the soldier's body, but it became stuck. With a swift motion of his leg, he kicked the man away, using the momentum to dislodge the weapon. His moves were fluid. Precise. No wasted energy. A true stiletto master.

Then he was gone. As if consumed by the dark.

Drouet glanced frantically around the alley. Silence hung in the air for a long moment. Growling, he shoved Aetna face-first to the ground and steadied his blade over her neck. "This is going to hurt." In that instant, a large figure rose behind him.

Drouet froze as if sensing the looming presence. He then spun on his heel and thrust his rapier forward with all of his strength. Seconds later, a sharp blade screamed through the air, blocking the force of the strike and locking the two blades together.

The masked man ripped the sword from Drouet's hand. He simultaneously wrapped his dominant arm around the sergeant's throat, squeezing him tightly like a python. He then pushed the sergeant's head forward into a sleeper-hold position. Drouet thrashed violently in his arms before finally falling limp. Unconscious.

Aetna looked on, stupefied. *The Saracen mercy lock.* A combat technique when the shame of being spared was deemed a crueler fate than death.

She watched the masked man drag the sergeant to the gutter of the alley, moving deliberately and silently. He threw Drouet next to the other Angevin soldiers already strewn on the ground. The man then turned his head slowly toward her.

Aetna's eyes widened in terror. She clawed her fingers into the mud, trying to pull herself away. But her field of vision suddenly narrowed, as if the world were closing in around her. Her skull rang with pain as she felt waves of dizziness overcome her. As the dark figure approached, she felt her strength give way beneath her.

Aetna collapsed to the mud. Then everything went black.

CHAPTER 30

Monte Pellegrino
Palermo, Sicily
March 30, 1282
3:30 p.m. // Three hours to Vespers

AETNA VESPIRI let out a tormented scream as she awoke, drenched in a cold sweat.

"Patri!" she cried, jolting upward, her head throbbing with a dull pain.

Letting out a deep groan, Aetna pressed her palm to the side of her head, feeling the pulsing blood pound angrily beneath her bruised skin. A linen cloth compress was wrapped around her forehead. She tried to remember the last thing that had happened. She was beaten senseless by Angevin soldiers. She recalled Sergeant Drouet's dirty beard against her skin, his rotten breath in her nostrils.

She fought to clear the haze in her mind. Squinting, she slowly focused her eyes on her surroundings—she lay on a straw mat against the corner of a rock wall. A dim streak of light flickered into the windowless chamber. An orange candlelight glow spilled across the walls and onto her mat. Her eyes slowly adjusted as she took in her surroundings.

Where the hell am I?

She peered upward to behold a vaulted cave, its jagged stalactites hanging down over her. Drops of water dripped from above, hitting the ground in evenly timed intervals and echoing through the chamber. Stacks of ancient books and scrolls were strewn about the uneven floor. She tilted her head and scanned one of the titles: *The Art of Falconry* by Frederick II.

Growing up, she had heard all about King Frederick II. The greatest Sicilian ruler the world had ever seen. A man of extraordinary culture and intellect. The *Stupor Mundi*. The Wonder of the World. *The Art of Falconry* was his most famous text and was long considered to be the first scientific treatise ever written. The *Stupor Mundi*'s legacy in Sicily was cut short when *Re Carlu* executed his descendant and rightful heir, Prince Conradin.

Aetna groaned as she pushed herself to her feet. In a sudden panic, she pressed her hands to her chest. She dug her fingers frantically under her tunic and pulled out the *Gorgoneion Trinacria* pendant. She let out a long sigh of relief. She hadn't lost it.

Along with the candlelight trickling in came the rhythmic sounds of a singing voice reverberating through the cave. For a moment, it startled her. It resonated like a man's voice. Deep and gruff, yet with the soft cadence of a Sicilian father singing his child to sleep.

Aetna gulped in a deep breath as she left the small nook and turned a corner into a narrow passageway, moving along the walls of the enormous vaulted cavern. She was reminded of her *patri*'s wine cave in which she played as a child. Keeping her palm pressed to the cool rock, she sauntered slowly down the passageway. The cave looked thousands of years old.

Aetna gazed up, admiring crude paintings left behind on the smooth walls. The paintings revealed the animals of the island—a mountain lion, an eagle, a lizard. Moving farther down the wall, she laid her eyes on a series of human handprints patterned up and down the wall. Gazing upward, she extended her own palm against the rock, laying it to rest gently on top of a small hand the size of a child's.

The sounds of singing were becoming clearer as Aetna pushed herself forward. She smelled the pungent aromas of onions and garlic sizzling in olive oil. Her mouth watered. She realized she hadn't eaten in what felt like days.

Aetna maneuvered through the narrow passageway leading to an even larger chamber. Like a great museum, the place was packed with a collection of trinkets and artifacts from every corner of Sicily. Ceramic heads sculpted in the shape of Moorish kings and queens wearing fruit baskets for crowns. She saw rows of marionette knights strung up together and hanging on a wooden rack. There was a dilapidated donkey cart, depicting great battle scenes from the Crusades. Ceramic wine casks were strewn about, painted all over in crude colors of red, green, yellow, and blue, colors meant to symbolize Sicily's citrus fruits, grass, sun, and sea. A neatly organized armory of weapons: Arabic scimitars, Norman broadswords, French rapiers. There were paintings of the Madonna and other religious mosaics stacked against the cave walls.

In the corner, Aetna spotted a small wooden table with two stools. And just beyond, from out of the shadows, a man in dark clothing emerged, crouching over an iron pot that hung over a small fire. An enormous golden eagle sat on a perch nearby. The man was humming an indistinguishable tune to himself as he appeared to stir the contents of the pot with a long wooden spoon. He then suddenly left the pot and disappeared into the dark, still singing to himself.

Aetna waited until the coast was clear, then slowly entered the chamber. The eagle watched her with its large black pupils. The beast ruffled its feathers, not making a sound.

Approaching the pot, Aetna heard the gurgling of a boiling liquid coming from inside. She peeked her head slowly over the rim of the pot. Her nostrils were suddenly hit with a blast of steam filled with the poignant aromas of hot, thick tomatoes. She picked up the spoon, gave it a quick stir, and tasted the tangy liquid. She closed her eyes as her mouth burst with comforting flavor.

Salsa rubbinu, she thought.

In that moment, the simple yet piquant tastes of the Sicilian ruby sauce brought her back home. She remembered the sauces her *patri* had made. Meat sauces, winter sauces, sauces bathing freshly cooked squid and peas. He would sit in his favorite chair, sopping it all up with a large piece of bread.

Suddenly, a deep voice bellowed out from the darkness behind her. "Say *ciao* to Rosalia," he said, gesturing toward the eagle. "The queen of Sicily."

Aetna's heart leapt into her chest. In a flash, she twirled on her heels, unsheathed her stiletto, and flicked it upward toward the man's throat.

"Mi dispiace," he said. "I didn't mean to startle you."

The man had tough olive skin and a black angular mustache and beard whose tips seemed as sharp as blades. He wore a gold-trimmed, brimless black cap that covered most of his head, with curly black locks twirling out from underneath. He looked to be in his midforties. She noticed the missing thumbnail on his left hand.

Aetna's eyes widened in recognition. *The annoying man from the market.*

"You!" she said, thrusting her finger toward him and taking a step backward.

The man in black carried a handful of tomatoes and coolly stepped forward. "Your reflexes are extraordinary," he said.

"Get away from me," Aetna said, her blade pointed forward. She backed away from the man, holding him at arm's length as he moved around her.

"Are you feeling all right?" he asked.

"Where have you taken me?"

"My home," he said. "I call it the *Grotto Santuario*. The Sanctuary Cave."

Aetna suddenly turned inward, pressing her hand to her forehead. "Good God, what did I do? I attacked that Angevin sergeant."

"You did what you felt was right," he said.

Aetna paused, considering his words. She realized it felt good inflicting pain on that soldier. *It was the least he deserved.* Even so, the mere thought of it created an ominous pit in her stomach. She was in deep enough as it was. She gulped in a short breath, then snapped her blade forward. "I have to leave."

She glanced around frantically, searching for an escape. She decided she had overstayed her welcome. A sharp gust of wind came from around a bend. *That must be the way out.* Aetna spun on her heel, sheathed her blade, and powered toward the exit.

"Where are you going?" the man in black asked softly, patiently.

"Home," she called over her shoulder, shaking her head. *The Abbot is going to kill me.*

The man in black stared a hole into her back for a long moment. Finally, he said, "You're the winemaker's daughter."

Aetna stopped dead in her tracks. *What did he say?*

"I lost my family, too," the man in black said.

Aetna hovered for a long moment, a pained look crossing her face. "I really must be going."

"Those soldiers in the alley were going to violate you. And kill you."

"Tell me something I don't know," Aetna said.

"They are no doubt looking for you now," he said. "Norman deerhounds have tracked down many a Sicilian fugitive. I had no choice but to take you with me. For your own protection."

Aetna searched her feelings, knowing deep down he was telling the truth. She turned to face the man. "Who are you?"

The man in black blew out a snort from his nostrils. "*Mi dispiace* . . . how rude of me," he said, bowing his head. "You may call me . . . *Don Rapaci.*"

Aetna's eyes widened. She thrust a finger toward him. "You're the *Falcon of Palermo,*" she said. "*Master of the Sky.*" Aetna was beside herself. The floor seemed to tilt beneath her feet. "You're the deadliest don in all of Sicily!"

A beguiled grin crossed *Don Rapaci's* bearded lips. He raised his hands quickly, like a sorcerer summoning a spell. Two gleaming stiletto blades flashed forward as if he conjured them from thin air. He twirled the blades effortlessly between his fingers, bringing them to a guardian stance. "Like I was trying to tell you," he said, pointing to Aetna's own weapon. "Your reflexes are extraordinary."

With that, he twirled his dueling blades downward into two leather scabbards hanging on either side of his rib cage. "You're also extraordinarily wrong. I'm not the deadliest don in all of Sicily."

A look of puzzlement crossed Aetna's face.

"That honor belonged to one of the greatest Sicilians ever to walk this land," he said. "Don Vittorio Vespiri."

Aetna's jaw dropped. "You knew my *patri*?"

A knowing grin crossed *Don Rapaci's* lips. "And the truth prevails."

"*Sì,*" Aetna finally admitted. "Don Vittorio Vespiri was my father. I'm Aetna."

"With a volcanic spirit to match."

"But how could you possibly know Vittorio was my *patri*? Is it some kind of magic trick?"

Don Rapaci lowered his eyes to the golden pendant dangling from Aetna's neck, glimmering in the dim candlelight.

"*Gorgoneion Trinacria*," he said. "The ancient Greek symbol for Sicily, and adopted coat of arms of Don Vespiri."

Instinctively, Aetna glanced down and clutched the pendant in her palm. "He said it means protection from man's corrupt forces."

"Protection, indeed," *Don Rapaci* said, a knowing smile crossing his lips. He turned around, sauntering back to the saucepot. "Of course I knew Don Vespiri," he called out over his shoulder. "He was my best student."

Aetna stood transfixed.

Don Rapaci came to a stop in front of the pot. He gave the sauce a stir, then lifted the spoon to his mouth.

"Student?" she asked.

Don Rapaci slowly craned his neck over his shoulder. The firelight created an ominous rimmed halo down the length of his face. His eyes flashed with intrigue. "You look hungry," he said. "I've started a ruby sauce. My *nanna*'s own recipe. What kind of *Siciliano* would I be if I didn't invite you to my table?"

Aetna felt her stomach grumble at the mere thought of a warm meal.

Don Rapaci turned back toward the saucepot. "Come," he said, beckoning with his hand. "Let us drink from the same cup."

CHAPTER 31

Matagrifone
Messina, Sicily
March 30, 1282
3:34 p.m.

BARTOLOMEO MANISCALCO awoke with a scream. The *Teutoni* Knight had been beaten senseless earlier that day. Trying to focus through his blurred vision, he found himself in a dark stone chamber that smelled of mold and rat feces. He dangled from a chain hanging from the ceiling with two rusted shackles clenched around his wrists. Another *Teutoni* Knight hung next to him; his chest heaved up and down, his head hung low.

As he trained his gaze forward, Maniscalco beheld General Guy de Rochefort. And behind the hulking general, he noticed the glint of firelight flickering from a reflective silver surface. His eyes widened in recognition. Standing silently in the corner was none other than the Brother Devil himself, *Fra'Diavulu*— the notorious Messinese mercenary who was summoned from the cold, diseased trenches of Albania to hunt *Teutoni* Knights in Sicily.

A traitor to his own blood kin.

General Guy de Rochefort scorched Maniscalco beneath his glare. He approached the young man strapped stiffly against a wooden beam, who dripped in a cold sweat. The moldy air hung heavy between them. *Fra'Diavulu* stood silently in the dark corner, observing the interrogation through his silver devil's mask.

"Who are you?" Rochefort said, his breath reeking.

"Bartolomeo Maniscalco," the man growled. The Sicilian was in his midthirties with olive skin, a clean-shaven face, and ebony hair tied back behind his head. He held his pointed chin high.

Rochefort stared icily at him for a long moment. He lifted the back of his hand and smacked the young man across the face with his gauntlet. "The correct answer is *Teutoni* Knight and traitor," he said.

Maniscalco spat blood from his mouth.

Rochefort then turned to the other knight, whose head stooped toward the floor. "And you?"

"*Vaffanculu,*" the man spat.

Rochefort lurched forward and gripped the man by the collar of his tunic, pulling him close until their faces almost touched. The general then reached down to his hip and yanked off the neck vise hanging from his belt as the guards moved in to unshackle the knight. "Do you know what this is?" With a sudden jerk, Rochefort snapped the vise around the man's neck and clamped it tight. "It's for Sicilians with big mouths."

The man fell to his knees, tugging desperately as the device around his neck tightened, his eyes bugging out from his head. Cries of pain echoed down the dungeon halls beneath *Matagrifone.*

"It's the panic that betrays them," Rochefort said.

The knight croaked. He pulled at the device, but the more he struggled, the tighter it squeezed. The knight stared directly into *Fra'Diavulu*'s silver mask, its face frozen in a perpetual frown as he watched the man's futile effort to save himself.

"Brother Devil," the knight muttered, grabbing at the vise. His face turned completely blue. Suddenly, his heart seized up in his chest. His eyes rolled back into his brain, severing all signals to his legs. He collapsed to the floor. Dead.

Bartolomeo Maniscalco grimaced as he gazed upon his fallen brother. Cold beads of sweat dripped down his face. He squeezed his eyes shut, shaking his head in despair. He knew he was next.

Rochefort's chapped lips curled up in a dubious half smile as he bent over and unclipped the vise from the dead knight's throat. He then slowly lifted his eyes to meet Maniscalco's pained gaze.

"This time last year I was hunting *Teutoni* Knights in the city of Augusta," Rochefort said. "The people there wouldn't talk. All to protect enemies of the king. They defied me much like your friend here." Rochefort pointed to the knight as the soldiers dragged him away by his boots.

Fra'Diavulu stepped up behind the general to provide proper cover.

"Do you know what I did to them?" Rochefort said.

Maniscalco refused to look.

"I put the city under siege," Rochefort continued. "Over the course of three long nights, my men rounded up every Sicilian down to the last man, woman, and child. We lined them up in the main piazza and beheaded them, one by one, for all to see. We piled their heads neatly on the coastline and burned the city to ashes."

Rochefort turned and flashed a grim look to *Fra'Diavulu*, who nodded silently through his devilish mask.

Maniscalco grimaced in pain.

Rochefort snapped back toward Maniscalco. "Where are the other *Teutoni* hideouts?"

"Kings may be the judge of Sicily, but we are the judges of kings." Maniscalco spat at the general's feet.

Rochefort snorted. He glared at the knight for a long moment. He tossed the neck vise backward to *Fra'Diavulu*. "Please do us the honors."

Fra'Diavulu snatched the device from the air.

Maniscalco's eyes filled with dread as the imposing masked figure sauntered forward. The multiple blades strapped to his body clinked together as he walked.

Fra'Diavulu stepped up to the prisoner. Maniscalco watched in horror as the scowling mask of Satan grew larger in his field of vision, the flickering torchlight reflecting off its polished surface. The Messinese knight came to a stop in front of Maniscalco. The grinning face of Satan lingered over him for a long moment.

Maniscalco detected an air of hesitation hanging between them. *What is he waiting for?*

"No," *Fra'Diavulu* said from behind the mask. Suddenly, he turned on his heel and extended the vise back toward Rochefort. "I think it's better if you do it."

Rochefort sneered, yanking the vise back. "The devil knight who doesn't kill." The general stepped forward and gripped Maniscalco by the collar. "Where are the *Teutoni* Knights hiding?"

"I don't know," Maniscalco said, staring forward with conviction.

Rochefort grabbed Maniscalco's chin, squeezing it between his fingers. The general studied him for a long moment. "Either he's telling the truth, or he's a cunning actor."

"I don't know where they are," Maniscalco said. "But if I did, I certainly wouldn't tell you."

Rochefort stared down his nose, then turned to *Fra'Diavulu*. "Brand him. Let it be known that a *Teutoni* Knight was spared in shame by his king, Charles the First of Sicily."

A prison attendant stepped forward and handed *Fra'Diavulu* a glowing iron rod. Its white-hot tip was forged into the shape of the royal arms of France, the *fleur-de-lis*.

Fra'Diavulu nodded his head and took the iron rod.

Maniscalco's chest heaved as he looked on in terror. The mercenary slowly turned his head toward Maniscalco. Maniscalco's eyes widened as he stared into the scowling face of Satan. The knight grimaced, bracing for pain.

Fra'Diavulu adjusted his footing into a striking position. In that instant, the mercenary lunged forward, the iron rod snapping out like a viper.

The white-hot tip of the *fleur-de-lis* flew forward and seared into Maniscalco's cheek. The knight's skin sizzled as the excruciating pain shot up from his face and through his skull.

There was the putrid smell of burning flesh.

CHAPTER 32

Monte Pellegrino
Palermo, Sicily
March 30, 1282
3:48 p.m.

AETNA SHOVED a forkful of plump penne noodles into her mouth. The pasta dripped with ruby sauce and was laced with olive oil, onion, garlic, and basil. The tang of the sauce hit the back of her tongue. She tore off a small piece of bread and sank her teeth into its crusty surface. Her mouth watered with satisfaction. "My *patri* was a *cavaleri*?" Aetna asked. "He hated violence."

"That's what he wanted you to believe," *Don Rapaci* said. "He was a master Sicilian knight . . . a don. Like me." He pressed his finger into his chest. "He also knew that sometimes violence is the strong color of life when nobly evoked against tyranny and oppression."

Aetna nodded, furrowing her brows. She missed him. His quiet strength. "That's my *patri*," she said.

"He was the deadliest *cavaleri* in all of Sicily," he said. "A real devil with the blade. Not unlike you."

Aetna lifted her eyes through her strands of hair, studying *Don Rapaci's* face. A knowing grin crossed his lips. He then shoved a forkful of pasta into his mouth.

"And he was my best pupil," he said. *Don Rapaci* wiped his lips, then fell silent for a moment, as if reflecting inward. Then he leaned forward, lowering his face. "For over a millennium, *cavaleri* like your father have protected Sicilian families from the corrupt authority of kings and conquerors. It's how we, as a people, survived through the stomping of history. *Cavaleri* were the spiny thorns of our island's *cosca*. And *cosca* is everything."

Aetna nodded. "Why did the Angevins kill my *patri*?"

Don Rapaci's face turned grim. "The brutal Angevin general Guy de Rochefort was charged by *Re Carlu* to hunt down and murder those loyal to the *Ordu Teutoni*."

"The outlawed order of Teutonic Knights," she said.

Don Rapaci nodded. "Conradin's elite bodyguard and protectors of the kingdom of Sicily. *Teutoni* Knights swore an oath to defend Sicilian lands, homes, and families. After Conradin's execution, *Re Carlu* deemed them enemies of the state and ordered them to be hunted down and eradicated from the *Regno*. Your father's vineyard was believed to be one of many safe havens for these men on the run. Which must have led the general right to your homestead."

Aetna listened, her eyes two pools of water.

"Now, the *Ordu Teutoni* is all but decimated in Sicily. Driven underground," *Don Rapaci* said. "They lie waiting with hopes to rise up once more with a fearless *cavaleri* of the people who walks the path of *rebellamentu*."

A flash of recognition crossed Aetna's face. *"Rebellamentu?"* she said, remembering her father's words. "Against bad ideas. Men who would rather abuse their power than lift up those around them."

"*Precisamenti,*" *Don Rapaci* said, studying Aetna for an uncomfortably long moment.

Aetna shifted in her seat. "What are you looking at?"

Don Rapaci grinned. He dabbed the sauce gently from his mouth, then rested his utensils on the table. "Tell me. Did your father use any nicknames with you as a child?"

"What does it matter to you?" Aetna said.

"Did he call you *santuzza*?"

Aetna's jaw dropped. "How could you possibly know that?"

"Little, holy knight." *Don Rapaci* nodded.

"He used that name only when we were alone together," Aetna said. "Nobody else knew of it. Not even my own brother."

Don Rapaci took a deep breath, seemingly unable to believe what he was about to tell her.

"He was preparing you," *Don Rapaci* said.

"Preparing me for what?"

Don Rapaci extended his finger and pressed it into the protective pendant hanging from Aetna's neck. "Instilling your heart with the values to continue blazing the path he started."

"Path?" she said.

Don Rapaci smiled. "Don Vespiri was the best of us. A man of virtue. He loved his people and protected the helpless, always putting himself in harm's way for those less fortunate than he. He became known throughout the *Regno* by a single name: *O Santo Cavaleri.*"

"The Perfect Sicilian Knight," Aetna said.

Don Rapaci nodded. He leaned in closer. "The story goes that Don Vespiri was so respected in the eyes of princes and kings that he was charged by Prince Conradin to fulfill his last promise."

Aetna was transfixed. "What kind of promise?"

"It was said that upon being led to his execution, Conradin granted his power back to the people of Sicily and threw his gauntlet out into the crowd in a final act of defiance." *Don*

Rapaci pressed his finger into the *Gorgoneion Trinacria* pendant. "The vanquished prince charged *O Santo Cavaleri* to become the Protector of Sicily and end the oppression that has crippled it."

Aetna shook her head. "This doesn't make any sense. How could Conradin expect my *patri* to protect Sicily alone?"

"He wouldn't be alone."

"Then who would help him?"

Don Rapaci leaned forward, his voice lowering. "The *Ordu Teutoni*."

Aetna stared in shock.

Don Rapaci smiled, making his final point. "That is the path, Aetna. The path your father started down. The path he wanted you to continue blazing. The path of *O Santo Cavaleri*."

The Perfect Sicilian Knight, Aetna thought. Her heart hung heavy like Norman stones. Aetna gazed up into *Don Rapaci's* eyes. She saw his face turn sour.

"When news of Don Vespiri's murder spread, all hope was lost," he said. "But fate, it seems, was *en Indraga Mano*. Had a hidden blade at its back. Today I witnessed a *Siciliana* rise up without fear."

Aetna glanced up, her eyes welling with tears.

"Become the knight your father was preparing you to be," *Don Rapaci* said. "Awaken the *Ordu Teutoni*. Command their loyalty. Walk the path of *rebellamentu*."

Aetna was silent for a long moment. Then she snorted through her nostrils, wiping her nose.

"Walk the path of *rebellamentu*? How am I supposed to do that?"

Don Rapaci's black eyes sharpened. "You've already started. Back in the square in front of *Sant'Anna*. When you stood up to those men. You displayed true *occhinero*. Fearlessness in the face of death. Now do it again." *Don Rapaci* pressed his hand over his stiletto lying on the table. He pushed it toward her. The metal scraped across the wooden surface.

Aetna's eyes fell to the blade on the table. She scoffed. "I hate the Angevins. My hate is so strong, it's become a poison in my veins. But I want nothing to do with this. Sicily never belonged to princes and kings to begin with. It's not theirs to give away."

Don Rapaci's face softened, his eyes pleading with her. "That is why it must be you, Aetna."

Aetna took a deep breath. She shook her head. "I'm only one woman. What possible difference can I make?"

Don Rapaci bit his lip. "Your father suffered from the same reluctance."

Aetna's eyes become two balls of green fire. Her eyebrows furrowed. "How dare you? Are you calling my *patri* a coward?"

"That's not how I meant it," *Don Rapaci* said.

Aetna threw down her utensils and pushed herself from the table. Startled, the golden eagle, Rosalia, ruffled her feathers in the corner. "Maybe this was a mistake. I can't stay any longer," she said, standing up.

"Where are you going?" *Don Rapaci* said.

"Back to *Santo Spirito*," she said, pressing her hand to her forehead. "The Abbot is probably worried sick."

Don Rapaci sat still, seeming deflated in the face. "Then you readily invite death into your home."

Aetna turned on her heels. *"Bona Pasqua,"* she said over her shoulder, *"Falcon of Palermo."*

Don Rapaci watched her leave. His curly locks fell over his dark eyes. "And a blessed Vespers to you, *Siciliana*."

BOOK III

VESPRI SICILIANI
MARCH 1282

PALERMO

TYRRHENIAN SEA

CASTELLAMMARE
DISTRICT

PORTA FELICE

CASSARU

SERALCADIO
DISTRICT

QUATTRO
CANTI

KALSA DISTRICT

CATTEDRALE
DI PALERMO

LA MAGIONE

PORTA NUOVA

ALBERGHERIA
DISTRICT

PALAZZO DEI
NORMANI

ORETO RIVER

CHIESA DI
SANTO SPIRITO

CHAPTER 33

Chiesa di Santo Spirito
Outskirts of Palermo, Sicily
March 30, 1282
5:32 p.m. // Twenty-eight minutes to Vespers

HALF A mile from Palermo's southern wall, clinging to the brink of the ancient Oreto River ravine, stood the *Chiesa di Santo Spirito*—the Church of the Holy Spirit. Shaded by dusky cypress trees, the lonely church's surrounding grounds were honeycombed with tombs adorned with dismal urns and dilapidated monuments. Legend told of the day a century earlier when the church's first cornerstone was laid. The sun was suddenly obscured by an eclipse, casting the land in total darkness. Stricken with dread, the original Norman builders considered it a foreboding omen that the edifice would be forever cursed.

Tonight, storm clouds hung in the night sky as a throng of people from Palermo and the surrounding villages came crowding together from across the countryside. Sicilians from all walks of life descended upon the grounds of the *Santo Spirito* in a festive parade led by bands of musicians and dancers. They

were celebrating the coming evening vigil of Vespers marking
the beginning of Easter.

There were men who proudly carried wooden crosses
alone, and others who were flanked by their wives and children
holding large candles. Teenage boys showed off their physical
prowess by racing one another, attempting to draw the attention of the other girls.

Spectacular donkey carts were festooned in dazzling feathers, tassels, and colorful blankets. Some carts were dedicated
to towing jugs of fresh wines. Others were loaded with cooking pots, crates of various pastas, tomatoes, eggplants, olives,
cheeses, and wooden bowls. Small lambs recently sacrificed for
the festivities were to be roasted with onion and parsley. The
tradition of the lamb recollected a time when God told Moses
to order the Israelites to smear lamb's blood on their doors so
that the angel of death would pass over them.

Upon reaching the grounds of the church, the crowds
were greeted by the Abbot and Cistercian nuns before they
fanned and formed into numerous clusters. The grounds were
carpeted with spring flowers. Torches cast flickering shadows

across the solemn face of the church's volcanic stone. Men spread out long serving tables. Women boiled water for pasta and chopped meats for sauces. Children played upon the courtyard and in the grass. A troupe of young girls beat sheep-skin tambourines as they pranced round one another, shouting and chanting in a spirited *tarantella*. The air was filled with gossiping and playful banter as everyone waited for the vigil service to begin.

Standing on the courtyard's perimeter away from the main crowd, Tziporah Solazzo, the Cistercian orderly, gripped a longbow and pulled back the bowstring taut against her cheek. She stared down the length of the arrow, directly toward a straw dummy placed across the other end of the cemetery.

Several children gathered around her.

"Aim small, miss small," Tziporah said, her arm absorbing the tension of the bow. "If you aim for the entire man, you risk missing the man completely. But if you aim for a specific point on the man's chest, a button or a seal, you still hit the chest."

The children's eyes were wide with anticipation.

Tziporah narrowed her focus to a single *fleur-de-lis* painted on the dummy's torso. Staring at the French seal, she felt her chest suddenly tighten as her mind reeled to the men who took Aetna earlier that morning. She shrank inward at the thought of what they would do to her. *Vile Angevin scum.* If only she could send an arrow directly into the flesh of a real Frenchman. They would wail and whimper on their way to hell.

Her face hardening with resolve, Tziporah gulped in a breath and fired the arrow. It zipped through the air and hit the *fleur-de-lis* dead in the center.

The children cheered and clapped their small hands.

Moments later, a voice called out from behind her. "Keep your elbow straighter."

Tziporah scoffed and rolled her eyes. "I hit the target, didn't I?" She nocked another arrow and drew back the bowstring.

She then held her breath and released the arrow, sending it zipping through the air.

In the same instant, Tziporah felt a short blade whip past her head. It whirled through the air and struck the dummy right in the center of the chest, deflecting the incoming arrow away and spinning to the ground.

Tziporah furrowed her brow. "You ruined my shot . . . ," she grumbled, spinning on her heel. But when her eyes fell upon the lean, feminine figure standing before her, she instantly felt as if her heart had burst open. All of the angst and consternation she had suppressed tonight came flowing forth. *Aetna!*

Aetna Vespiri's eyes filled with solace as she stepped forward directly into Tziporah's arms.

"I thought I lost you," Tziporah said. She felt tears come on suddenly but fought them back.

Aetna held her friend tightly. "It's okay," she whispered, her husky voice resonating in Tziporah's ears, comforting her. "No matter what happens, we'll always be *cosca*."

Aetna closed her eyes and lost herself in the consoling arms of her young friend.

Moments later from across the courtyard, the Abbot lifted his head from a plate of pasta and spotted Aetna through the crowd. His eyes widened as he immediately leapt to his feet. He shuffled forward, pushing his way through the festivities. His expression was bewildered. When he finally approached Aetna, he pulled her into a hard embrace, studying the bruises on her face.

"Look at you. Are you okay?" he said. "We were worried to death."

Aetna felt her muscles stiffen instantly. She lifted her chin. "I came to say goodbye. I'm going away for a while."

The Abbot's brow furrowed. "Going away? What are you talking about?"

Before she could explain herself, Aetna's attention was drawn to a set of dinnerware on a nearby tabletop. It had seemed to her as if the cutlery were wiggling. She reached out and pressed her palm gently over a fork, stopping its movement. She looked out over the table. Every loose piece of ceramic was vibrating.

An earthquake?

She glanced around the *Santo Spirito* courtyard, seeing nothing but laughing faces and eyes bulging with enthusiasm. Kissing and dancing and singing. Sicilians smashed their chalices together, sending red wine erupting into the air before downing the full glass. Aetna furrowed her brow. No one else seemed to notice it. *It's probably nothing.*

Suddenly, her ears perked up to the unexpected sound of dogs barking in the distance and approaching fast. She felt her heart rate spike, her instinct flaring, sensing danger.

Aetna felt a dull rumbling vibration in the dirt beneath her feet. She craned her head back and peered out into the black oblivion of the cemetery as the rumbling grew louder and drew closer, breaking the silence of the night.

Suddenly, the smeared glow of torches materialized through the dark. Then, the thundering of warhorses. In her gut she knew the terrible truth.

The Angevins are coming.

CHAPTER 34

A **HORDE** of Angevin horsemen emerged from the darkness. They wielded torches and flew banners emblazoned with the Angevin coat of arms, the blue-and-gold *fleur-de-lis* topped with a red embattled partition line.

At the head of the patrol rode Sergeant Drouet, his eyes glazed over in a drunken stupor.

Aetna carefully twirled her stiletto in her fingers, turning it backward and upward, concealing the length of the blade from view behind the back of her forearm. *Indraga Mano.* The hidden handguard of a *cavaleri.*

Gasps of panic erupted from the crowd as the rumbling of heaving hooves pummeled the dirt.

The Angevin horsemen entered the courtyard and thundered to a halt in front of the crowd, who flashed icy glares toward the approaching soldiers.

Sergeant Drouet stared out over the grounds of the church. His drunken eyes moved across the top of a hundred heads. Soldiers fanned out and dispersed among the crowd.

Drouet lurched forward and swung a heavy leg over his horse, planting his boots firmly on the ground. He turned toward the crowd and staggered forward, a deadly grin on his lips.

The crowd moved backward slowly.

Drouet snatched a glass of wine from a nearby woman and gulped it down quickly, the dark red liquid dripping down his beard. Gagging, he smashed the glass to the ground. "I can taste their women's stinky feet." With that, Drouet pulled out a razor-sharp dagger. The crowd gasped as he pointed it aimlessly toward the terrified faces staring back at him. "I'm looking for a criminal. A *Sicilienne* who assaulted the king's soldiers."

The Abbot pushed his way through the crowd and stepped forward. He thrust a finger toward Drouet. "The only criminals here are your kind."

The crowd started to murmur.

Drouet nodded his head and showed his rotten teeth. He suddenly yanked a young girl by the arm, pulling her hard against his chest. He held the edge of his blade dangerously close to her throat.

"Where is my *see-sheri*?" Drouet spat the word *ciciri* into the girl's ear, taking extra care to gargle out the guttural *r* from the back of his gullet, his breath foul with the stench of decay.

The young girl squeezed her eyes shut when a voice called out from the crowd.

"*Chee-cherrri*," the voice said, trilling the *r* with harplike grace.

The crowd gasped.

Drouet craned his neck, his eyes narrowing on a woman sauntering toward him.

Stone-lipped, Aetna stepped forward and carefully approached the drunk sergeant. "It's pronounced *chee-cheri*," she said, rolling her *r*'s once more.

Drouet's eyes widened in recognition.

"You," he said.

Aetna lifted her gaze to his, locking eye contact. "You want me; here I am," she said, spitting at his boots.

Drouet turned and lumbered toward Aetna, snorting and licking his cracked lips. Instantly, his powerful arm was around her midsection as his hand crept firmly up her right breast. "Be a good girl, now," Drouet slurred, grinning.

Aetna felt her stomach turn in disgust. In a desperate surge of strength, she gritted her teeth and thrust her knee into his groin, shoving him backward.

The crowd gasped in horror.

The drunken sergeant staggered backward, groaning in agony. Instantly regaining his footing, he drew a dagger and suddenly barreled forward. He grabbed her throat and spun her backward into his breastplate.

Aetna gasped for air as the sharp pain spread through her chest, down her entire body.

Clenching her by the throat, Drouet gripped a tuft of her long hair in his fist and yanked her skull backward, pressing the sharp side of his dagger against the veins in her neck. Blood formed where even this featherlight touch of the razor-sharp blade made contact with her skin. Aetna felt the sergeant's hot breath as he pressed his gnarly beard against her cheek. She smelled stale wine and onions.

In the distance, Aetna thought she spotted a large golden eagle swoop silently down from the sky and land on a tombstone cross in the cemetery. As she turned her gaze out over the courtyard, a hundred horrified faces staring back at her, she swore she saw the beguiling smile of *Don Rapaci* materialize among the crowd. The roguish glint in his eye. The confident grin beaming from beneath his black mustache and beard, three long, pointed blades. He seemed to move silently through them, among them. But just as quickly as he had appeared, he vanished.

Drouet leaned in, smelling Aetna's hair. He rested the tip of the blade under her bottom lip. He placed his mouth next to her ear and whispered, "I'm going to fuck you like a French whore."

Aetna was utterly repulsed as her brain suddenly flipped into survival instinct like a cornered wildcat. *It's me or him.*

Aetna's heart pounded. She tightened her grip around the hilt of her blade, still tucked behind her forearm. She carefully triangulated her footing into a guardian stance. *The foundation for everything.* She bent her knees, sinking slightly, lowering her center of gravity. She tightened her grip around the hilt, feeling its weight in her hands. A flaming sword of Saint Michael in the hands of a *cavaleri*. Aetna snapped her eyes upward as she summoned her will to kill swiftly and efficiently.

Clang!

The *Santo Spirito*'s iron bells suddenly rang out. The powerful sound swelled and reverberated out over the courtyard and down across the countryside. Across Palermo and the rest of the island, all other churches were doing the same. In a brief moment, the people rejoiced as one and turned Sicily into a glistening bell of the Mediterranean.

Vespers had begun.

Clang!

Summoning all of her *occhinero*, Aetna took a deep breath and snapped out her stiletto. The blade glimmered in the torchlight as if it were a ray of fire. In a flash, she ripped herself out of Drouet's grasp and spun away to face him, glaring straight into his eyes.

Baring her teeth, she hoisted the blade high into the air, its sharp tip pointing downward from the sky like an eagle's talon.

The crowd gasped in disbelief.

Clang!

Aetna thrust the blade downward and smashed it into Drouet's neck. Drouet's eyes bugged outward as a fountain of blood spouted across Aetna's face—the sticky liquid covering her like grotesque war paint.

Drouet clutched his throat, gagging, his tongue flailing from his mouth.

Clang!

Aetna gritted her teeth and clung to Drouet, pulling him closer into the blade. *Be a good boy, now.*

Drouet gagged violently, hawking up blood down his wiry beard. His eyes were wide with horror. Struggling, his right hand came up and grabbed Aetna's shoulder.

Clang!

Drouet began to stagger sideways, but Aetna held him firm, keeping him upright. She would be the last thing he would see in his vile existence. Finally, the sergeant's eyes rolled upward into his head. His jaw fell slack.

Aetna released her grasp. With a push, she sent the sergeant's corpse hard into the ground. She then looked up into the crowd, her chest heaving, her face dripping with revulsion.

The Angevin soldiers gaped upon Aetna, frozen in shock. They were so stupefied, they hadn't noticed the Sicilians—men, women, nuns, orderlies—with stiletto blades drawn, closing in slowly around them. The spines of the artichoke. The *cosca*.

Clang!

Aetna tightened her grip around her blade. She watched as the men and women around the courtyard closed in silently behind the Angevin soldiers from all sides, placing one silent foot in front of the other, their sharp blades pointing forward.

Aetna's eyes filled with resolve. Her heart with solidarity. *For the* cosca, she told herself.

In that instant, the golden eagle opened its wings and took off into the sky.

Aetna gritted her teeth and pumped her fist high into the air. She squeezed her eyes shut and, over the roaring of blood rushing through her eardrums, yelled at the top of her lungs.

"Moranu li Francisi!" she cried. "Death to the Angevins!"

CHAPTER 35

To the sound of the tolling bells, every Sicilian man and woman from age twelve to fifty fell upon the Angevin soldiers with their blades.

"*Moranu li Francisi!*" the crowd cried, becoming one voice in the night.

The cursed grounds of the *Santo Spirito* became a cursed killing zone.

Mothers wrapped their arms around their daughters, their eyes filled with terror as they scrambled down a nearby stone staircase into the fields below. Young runners immediately fled the cemetery to spread the word to Palermo.

Standing at the center of the chaos, Aetna spun to face four soldiers. The men barreled forward, rapiers drawn and pointed directly at her.

"*Siciliana!*" *Don Rapaci* shouted. He emerged from the crowd and whipped a stiletto toward her. The blade whistled through the air.

Aetna caught it by the hilt, now holding one sword in each hand. She pivoted on her right leg to parry an incoming blow from the first man. She adjusted her footing and kicked the second man with her left leg in one continuous, sweeping motion. The soldier whirled around and ran right into *Don Rapaci*'s blade. The soldier's rapier slipped from his trembling hand and fell to the ground. Aetna kicked it away. She then swung her blade forward, slashing the jugulars of the remaining two soldiers. The Angevins grabbed their throats, gurgling as blood spurted from their necks. Clutching her blades, she stared deep into the black of their eyes as they dropped to the ground.

Don Rapaci pressed his foot into a dead soldier's back and dislodged his blade from the man's torso. He immediately raised his fingers to his lips and whistled loudly.

The deafening shriek of the golden eagle Rosalia pierced the air. The large beast tore down from the black sky, plunging her razor-sharp talons into the eyes of a hulking Angevin. The large man thrashed at the animal, wailing in horror.

Tziporah burst from the crowd and leapt onto the soldier's back. She locked her legs around his torso, plunging a dagger deep through his collarbone. He cried out in horror and collapsed to the ground.

The Sicilians swarmed around the Angevin soldiers, sticking them with their blades.

Aetna's heart pounded as she moved swiftly between men, becoming a flurry of death as she struck with each measured step. Each time she thrust her blade, an arm flew from its socket, entrails spilled to the ground, and her yellow-and-vermillion dress became stained with blood.

The remaining soldiers took stock and began to overcome their fear. Summoning their training, they attempted to organize into a defensive formation. Suddenly, however, more Sicilians fell upon them, wielding short swords and throwing rocks. The Angevins were outnumbered.

"Every man for himself!" a frightened Angevin screamed.

The soldiers tripped over one another as they fled the grounds.

Raising their arms, the Sicilian mob charged after them. *"Moranu li Francisi!"* they cried. "Death to the Angevins!"

In the tumult, Aetna sheathed her blade and darted toward a warhorse, leaping into its saddle. She glanced down at *Don Rapaci*. He stared back at her with a harrowed gaze.

"You'll find the justiciar feasting in the Norman Palace," *Don Rapaci* shouted.

"Rebellamentu." Aetna nodded, a look of understanding passing between them. The dangerous task ahead, she knew, would require all of her *occhinero* training. She pursed her lips, raising her eyes toward the horizon. *Saint-Remy will pay for his crimes.*

She lashed the reins, digging her heels into the beast's torso. The large warhorse snorted into the chilled air and tore off toward Palermo's walls.

CHAPTER 36

Palermo, Sicily
Kalsa District
March 30, 1282
6:31 p.m.

DARK CLOUDS roiled above as an Angevin soldier scrambled down a narrow passageway, splashing through muck and mud and manure. The Angevin's fate was sealed by how well he could run. Behind him, an angry throng of Sicilians was gaining fast.

To the sound of the tolling bells, the Angevin barreled down the street and begged that a friendly door might swing open to offer aid. But aid never came.

"Get him!" the Sicilians cried.

Stricken with panic, the soldier rounded a tight corner and stepped into a mud slick. He slipped and landed hard on his back. The wind knocked from his lungs, he groaned for air as the Sicilians swarmed around him, thrusting their blades in and out of his chest and stomach.

The mud ran red with streams of blood.

As the bells tolled throughout the city like a call to arms, Sicilians poured into the streets from their homes, taverns, and churches. The rebels swelled to seven thousand strong, all united by a passionate fury and armed with swords, clubs, and carpenter's hatchets.

Tonight, all the streets of Palermo were a gateway to hell.

Castellammare District
6:42 p.m.

An Angevin regiment arrived at the foot of the *Cassaru* to meet a troop of drunken soldiers pouring out of an armory post. To their horror, the soldiers were being assaulted by Sicilian rebels hurling rocks and other makeshift projectiles.

The rebels stormed the drunken soldiers, felling them beneath their blades. They broke into the outpost and smashed tables and chairs, raiding the building for heavier arms and weaponry to use against their oppressors.

Outside raged a terror of the most primeval kind. The approaching Angevin regiment clustered as one, howling, arms waving madly.

A frenzied rebel circled the men and charged a dazed soldier. He swung his stiletto at the soldier's chest, the strike catching him just above the right clavicle, penetrating his rib cage and bringing him down, dying, to his knees. The Sicilians rushed the remaining soldiers, laying them low with unrelenting blade strokes.

Seralcadio District
6:56 p.m.

Inside his home, a French nobleman took a seat at the head of the dinner table where his family sat. "Amen," he said, making the sign of the cross as he finished blessing their meal.

Suddenly, there was a loud crash at the door. The roaring of a mob. The French family members leapt from their seats as sharp blades and clubs smashed through the wooden doors. The women and children scattered, shrieking in fear, as the nobleman grabbed his rapier and unsheathed the blade from its scabbard. "Get the children upstairs," he growled.

As soon as the words left his lips, the doors came crashing in as Sicilian rebels swarmed into the household, swords and clubs flailing.

From behind, a rebel struck the French lord's head with a carpenter's hatchet, the blow so ferocious, it cleaved his skull in two so that brain matter protruded from the gaping fissure. The lord fell forward onto the table, his head spouting blood, and then collapsed to the stone floor.

Castellammare District
7:01 p.m.

A Sicilian man dressed in his finest Vespers clothing emerged quietly from his home and snuck up behind an Angevin soldier lingering outside his doorway, separated from his unit.

The Sicilian screamed at the top of his lungs as he wrapped a frayed rope around the soldier's neck, squeezing it tight like a python. The soldier's eyes bugged out as the Sicilian grappled him to the ground.

Four other rebels suddenly moved in from all sides, bludgeoning the soldier's cheeks with their bare knuckles and breaking his bones so badly, his face no longer looked human.

Kalsa District
7:56 p.m.

A cluster of Sicilians held an Angevin soldier by his scalp as each took turns jamming their daggers upward into the man's sternum.

The Angevin's eyes rolled back into his skull as his legs gave out, his throat gurgling as blood rapidly filled his punctured lungs. The rebels dragged the soldier by the hair toward a nearby balcony, where they wrapped a gnarly rope around the soldier's neck and hoisted the corpse into the air for all to see.

A rebel ran forward with a burning torch and touched it to the soldier's leg. The corpse quickly caught fire as the rebels took turns ferociously beating it with the hilt of their blades.

An orange pyre of retribution burned into the night.

Albergheria District
8:04 p.m.

Rebels smashed down the oaken doors of a Dominican church filled with frightened bystanders. In the tumult of the chaos, they needed a quick way to unmask any French person who had sought sanctuary in this house of God. Petrified men and women were dragged out before the altar and forced to their knees. The rebels held blades to their chins and put them to a morbid test.

"Say *ciciri!*" one rebel cried out.

Anyone pronouncing the word with a guttural *r* was cut across the throat from ear to ear, their corpses strewn into the nave.

Another rebel discovered a pregnant woman hiding in a confessional booth. He grabbed her by the hair and pushed her to the stone floor.

"Say *ciciri!*" he yelled.

The woman clasped her palms together, tears streaming down her cheeks. "Please, show me mercy!"

Upon hearing a French accent, the rebel's eyes went black with murder. "Your kind didn't show mercy when they violated my wife and daughters," he said. "I will not see another Angevin child born on my soil, nor share it with a French whore."

The woman's mouth opened wide. A scream pierced the air. The rebel swung his hatchet down swiftly over her neck, cleaving effortlessly through the bone. The woman's head thudded to the ground and rolled into the aisle, an expression of fear still frozen on her face.

What happened next was even more terrifying, and would forever codify this violent night in the annals of crimes against humanity. Consumed by wrath, the rebel bent over the woman's headless corpse. He lowered his ax to her abdomen and cut out the unborn fetus.

No man, woman, or child was spared this night.

Seralcadio District
8:19 p.m.

Outside Saint Anna's Convent, a contingent of Angevin knights and squires merrymaking in the piazza had no time to don armor. Upon hearing the pained howls of their fallen comrades, they huddled together, rapiers pointed outward.

Without warning, the Angevins were charged by a wave of armed Sicilians flooding into the square from every direction. Outnumbered, they threw down their weapons and hoisted their palms skyward. They knew the codes of chivalry forbade the killing of a knight once word of surrender was given.

But tonight, chivalry was just another French word.

A hundred Sicilian blades flashed in the firelight and thrust straight into Angevin torsos, nailing their bodies into the ground. Their corpses were then piled into high pyramids in the center of the piazza.

The Sicilians would eventually mark the spot with an iron cross, to always remember the occasion. They would call it the *Croce dei Vespri*.

The Cross of the Vespers.

CHAPTER 37

Palermo, Sicily
Kalsa District
March 30, 1282
8:39 p.m.

A HALO of firelight seemed to glow over Palermo as Aetna Vespiri kicked her heels into her horse's ribs and tore down the *Cassaru*, dodging obstacles in her path: livestock, carts, men, and women. Angevin soldiers scattered through the streets in every direction, attempting to make order of the pandemonium. The first soldier, she trampled right over; the second, she struck down with a singular roundhouse swing of her blade.

In that instant, an Angevin dove in front of the galloping horse and slammed a spear firmly into the dirt. He thrust it upward into the beast's enormous chest. Aetna attempted to rein it in, but it was too late. The spear crushed the animal's rib cage and sent Aetna hurling into the air. She barreled into another armed soldier, knocking him to the ground with the force of her momentum. Reacting on instinct, she gripped the hilt of her blade and swung it quickly through the air, slashing the neck of the man kneeling before her.

"Rise up against the oppressor!" Aetna screamed into the night.

She moved through the chaotic streets, a symphony of death, striking down every Angevin soldier crossing her path. Overwhelmed with fear and shock, the Angevins didn't fight back. They turned on one another, pushing each other out into the tumult of battle, crying and screaming.

Moments later, a streetlamp was overturned onto a set of large oil barrels. A burst of flames exploded at her back. The heat from the blast hurled her forward, slamming her hard to the ground as hot embers flew and smoke plumed overhead.

Aetna lifted her head from the dirt, her ears ringing with concussion. Then the world suddenly went silent. She saw a hundred Angevin corpses littering the streets, staining the golden dirt red as fires raged in shops and homes. Countless other bodies thrashed on the ground, writhing like wounded animals, their mouths hanging open, some crying for their mothers as they were impaled by vengeful Sicilian blades.

But Aetna heard nothing. She watched in stupefied shock as the massacre played out before her like a grotesque, chaotic dance.

Angevin men and women fled from their blazing houses and into the street, where they were stuck by the sharp ends of a Sicilian blade . . .

Orphaned children wailed as they wandered aimlessly through the streets, carrying their straw-stuffed dolls . . .

Stray dogs yelped and scampered underfoot in large droves to escape the carnage . . .

Attempting to regain focus, Aetna pushed herself to her feet and grabbed her stiletto. She hurled herself into a horde of retreating soldiers, swinging her sword, moving fluidly among them. Slashing and thrusting. Every strike hit its mark.

Aetna spotted an Angevin warhorse a few feet away. Without hesitation, she sheathed her blade and dashed toward the beast, jumping onto its muscular back. Lashing the reins, she tore off toward the *Palazzo dei Normanni*.

Tonight, the justiciar's cruel reign over the city would come to an end. She would make certain of it.

CHAPTER 38

Palazzo dei Normanni
Palermo, Sicily
Albergheria District
March 30, 1282
8:59 p.m.

PALERMO JUSTICIAR Jean de Saint-Remy peered out from the second-story window of his personal chambers, hearing the approaching screams. A handful of guards had barricaded the palace entrance, watching the terrors unfold on the roads below. Men from their garrison who had been feasting in the city earlier that night were now mangled corpses sprawled in the streets.

The guards heard the cries and howls draw closer as the Sicilian insurgents stampeded toward them. One guard stared in shock as he witnessed three teenage boys swarm around an Angevin separated from his unit. The boys became a blur, falling upon the soldier and stabbing their blades repeatedly into his sternum. They killed swiftly and without remorse. They killed with a vengeance.

"Do not fear!" Saint-Remy shouted down, feigning an assured tone. "They are nothing but vermin to be stomped beneath our heels."

Though the justiciar knew that the few remaining guards would not be enough to protect the palace from the Sicilian insurgents. And his words brought no comfort as the men watched their comrades cut down in cold blood.

In that instant, Saint-Remy spotted a young woman on horseback on the street below, approaching slowly, as if she had nothing but time on her side. Even from a distance, he could see the fiery glare in the woman's green eyes scorching the road in front of her.

"A rider approaches!" he barked down to his men, stabbing a finger into the dark. "Prepare for attack."

The Angevins moved quickly into position, creating a protective semicircle around the palace entrance and each other. But before they could settle, the woman reined her horse back and disappeared into an alley. The men's eyes darted back and forth into the shadows, scanning for danger. "She's gone!" a soldier shouted.

Saint-Remy's mind raced manically about what he'd do next. He pressed his hand against the ornamental rapier strapped to his hip. He had never been in a combat situation in his entire life, let alone killed another man . . . or woman.

Suddenly, a thought stuck his brain as he remembered his training. The procedure for evacuation in the event of a military breach into the city walls. The fortress *Castello di Vicari*, situated in the island's interior, had one of the best fortified strongholds on the island. The castle was built high on a steep, jagged mountain cliff. He knew it was time to survive.

I need to find a horse, he thought.

· ❦ ·

Aetna Vespiri emerged from the darkness. She leapt off her horse and dashed in on foot toward the palace entrance. Screaming, she raised her blade over her head and smashed it into an Angevin guard. The sharp blade smashed into the man's chest, sending him backward to the ground.

Aetna's eyes shifted, lifting her gaze to Saint-Remy in the window above. For a moment, their eyes locked. She gnashed her teeth and clenched her fists. *You're mine.*

In that instant, the Sicilian rebels charged forward and rushed past her.

The Angevin guards broke formation and scattered in every direction. Panicked, Saint-Remy turned away from the window and tore off into the dark hallway and down the main staircase.

Growling, Aetna yanked her blade from the Angevin's chest and sprung herself over the top of his corpse. She plowed toward the palace entrance and crashed through the wooden doors. She found herself in the two-story open-air courtyard, where she had been dragged earlier that day on her way to Saint-Remy's concubine holding cell.

Aetna spotted Saint-Remy scrambling down a nearby staircase. Picking up her feet, she barreled toward him and leapt into the air, tackling him hard onto the marble floor.

He spun onto his back and grappled for her throat. "Bitch!"

Aetna lashed at his face with her fingernails, baring her teeth like a wildcat, her lungs heaving. She thrust her knee into Saint-Remy's groin. The shock from the blow immediately loosened his grip. She broke through his grasp with her slender arms. Curling her fingers into a claw, she dug her nails into his left eye, ripping the organ right from its socket.

Saint-Remy howled as a violent stream of blood spurted from the wound.

Directly behind her, an Angevin guard moved in, lunging his rapier at her back. The blade grazed her right shoulder as she rolled away. Springing to her feet, she snapped out her stiletto and swung it upward in an elliptical motion. The blade whistled through the air, ripping a deep gash across the soldier's throat. At the same moment, the soldier swung his heavy fist and clocked Aetna hard across the cheekbone. Aetna stumbled backward, seeing bursts of light dance in her field of vision, her skull racked with pain.

The soldier then gripped his neck tightly, cackling as he choked on his own blood. Aetna pressed her foot into his abdomen and kicked him to the floor. Grimacing, Aetna staggered a few steps, then fell to her knees. Out of breath, she looked down at the gash in her shoulder. It was bleeding, but the cut wasn't deep.

Saint-Remy was already on his feet and scrambling away. Aetna watched as he turned a corner and disappeared into the guts of the palace.

Then, the palace doors burst open as a throng of rebels poured in. Their cries echoed through the hall as they fanned out into the palace.

Aetna pushed herself to her feet, slowly regaining her focus. She gazed at the pools of red sanguine fluid on the floor. It stained her hands, her clothing, her *patri*'s blade.

Angevin blood.

Aetna felt a surge of retribution course through her veins. She would take back everything they had taken from her, from all of the families of Sicily. *Palermo is just the beginning.* She closed her eyes, tilted her head back, and screamed into the night.

Justiciar Jean de Saint-Remy's heart raced as he ran for his life. He climbed through a rear palace window and shinnied along the palace walls. Turning a corner, he crossed a short pathway and stumbled toward a large wooden structure.

The royal stables.

Saint-Remy plowed through the stable gates. Startled, the horses snorted and twitched at the unwelcome visitor. Plugging his bleeding eye with one hand, he harnessed the closest beast to him and jumped on its back. "Arrrghh!" he howled as he steadied himself in the saddle. Every slight movement sent searing jolts of pain from his eye socket into his brain.

Groaning, Saint-Remy gritted his teeth and lashed hard on the reins. The horse whinnied and pounded its hooves into the stable gate, tearing off into the black of night.

CHAPTER 39

Castello di Vicari
Vicari, Sicily
March 30, 1282
11:58 p.m.

THE SETTLEMENT of Vicari lay twenty-two miles southwest of
Palermo in the Sicilian interior. A massive limestone fortress
known as *Castello di Vicari* clung desperately to the sheer face
of a jagged cliff formation towering two thousand feet over the
small commune.

Erected by the Romans and fortified by the Arabs and
Normans, Vicari Fortress had endured more than ten centuries of invasion and war. From its strategic elevated position,
the imposing fortification dominated the surrounding countryside and guarded the main crossroads of the central island.
A stretch of walls ran around the castle's perimeter. The structure boasted three large towers visible for miles, including the
infamous *Porta Fausa* tower, or false door, which contained a
secret staircase excavated into the stone leading down the face
of the cliff.

As the commanding officer, Lieutenant Guiscard was responsible for overseeing all aspects of the fortress's operations—general upkeep, drilling troops, and, as it was the most fortified position in the central island, managing incoming and outgoing correspondence with the other barracks and outposts stationed around the interior. If *Matagrifone* in Messina was the nerve center of Angevin power in Sicily, the *Castello di Vicari* was its beating heart.

Tonight, asleep in his bed, Guiscard awoke to the sound of a sudden pounding on his chamber door.

"Lieutenant!" a man shouted from the hallway.

Guiscard sat up. *What the hell?* He recognized the night sentry's voice, though in the decade running the fortress, he had never been disturbed by him at this late an hour.

Groaning, Guiscard swung his legs off the bed, shuffled over to the door, and yanked it open.

The sentry stood alone in the dark hallway, illuminated by only a single torch.

"What is it?" Guiscard grumbled.

"I apologize for waking you . . . ," the sentry stammered.

A scowl hung on Guiscard's face. "Can't this wait until morning?"

The sentry shook his head, his face stricken with alarm. "We have a situation that needs your immediate attention."

Guiscard's brow furrowed. He glanced down and noticed the sentry's hands covered with blood. "What the hell is going on here?"

Moments later, a squad of twelve men emerged from the dark passageway, dragging none other than Palermo justiciar Jean de Saint-Remy.

Even in the dim torchlight, Guiscard could see the justiciar's face was terribly wounded. The lacerations were still fresh. He immediately felt his skin crawl. *This man needs a physician!* In a breathless silence, he threw on his officer's uniform and holstered a rapier around his waist, then bolted from the room.

"Rapidement!" Lieutenant Guiscard shouted, staggering through a vaulted archway and into the castle's dining hall. The implications of Saint-Remy's dramatic arrival were unsettling. *What in God's name happened in Palermo?* Only seconds behind him, the squad of men dragged Saint-Remy into the dark dining hall. The lieutenant pointed to a wooden chair near the center of the cavernous chamber. "Set him down."

Justiciar Saint-Remy clutched his left eye, which hung from its gaping socket by a nerve fiber beneath his grisly palm. A physician pushed through the group and started dressing the justiciar's facial wound in a linen cloth.

The men shot anxious glances at one another. The justiciar of Palermo was barely recognizable.

In that instant, Saint-Remy lurched forward, grabbing a soldier's collar in his fist. His bloodshot eye widened with desperation. "I rode directly from Palermo," he said. "War is upon us."

CHAPTER 40

Palermo, Sicily
Castellammare District
March 31, 1282
2:05 a.m. // First day of Vespers

THE CLOUDS above Palermo were bathed in a hellish glow. An ominous halo of firelight and death hung over the city.

Sicilian rebels seized the stalwarts of the castle fortress of *Kala* overlooking the sea. The fortress provided them with a vantage point overlooking the entire city, from the bay to the mountains strangling the city from all sides.

Fires were set to Angevin warships throughout Palermo harbor.

Offices and houses of known Angevin officials were torched, the flames jumping from building to building.

The night was punctured by the occasional yelp of Angevin soldiers as they were stabbed in the streets.

The church bells continued to toll throughout the city.

· ❦ ·

Albergheria District
2:27 a.m.

Soon, the horrors of the evening gave way to celebration and merriment.

In the piazzas around Palermo, bonfires blazed as Sicilian men banged tambourines and women and children hopped and twirled around one another with silk ribbons in traditional *tarantellas*.

Near the Norman Palace, rebels dragged out fat boars found in livestock pens. Others raided the royal wine cellars, pilfering valuable chalices and filling them up by the goblet.

On the edge of the city, rebels broke into a royal pavilion and freed a pack of royal Norman deerhounds.

The slender, shaggy dogs barked and scampered out into the streets, finally disappearing into the surrounding woods.

It would be the last time the ancient Norman deerhound, known as the *cerveru*, would ever be seen in Sicily. The purebred bloodline mixed and mingled with the feral dogs on the island and finally disappeared altogether.

Seralcadio District
3:03 a.m.

Around the city, Sicilian rebels carried wooden crates full of tax records and other Angevin documents charging them with crimes they never committed and smashed them to pieces in the middle of various piazzas.

They gathered and pressed their torches into the piles of crates and papers and set them ablaze. Enormous bonfires burst into raging infernos, sending pillars of billowing flames, smoke, and glowing embers flurrying into the sky. A hundred volcanos erupted in the night.

The citizens of Palermo gathered round their fires in exaltation, fanning the flames of retribution. The word *vinnitta*—vendetta . . . vengeance—had sealed its place in the Sicilian psyche for all time, its legacy written in the Angevin blood that now flowed from Palermo's streets and into the gutters.

CHAPTER 41

Palermo, Sicily
Kalsa District
March 31, 1282
3:15 a.m.

EMERGING FROM a pile of dead bodies, an Angevin soldier scrambled to his feet and snuck hastily along the interior of the city wall. Stricken with panic and grief, he scrambled for an Arabian horse hitched near the *Porta Felice* sea gate. He ran and jumped up onto its back. Undetected, he lashed the reins, kicked his heels into the horse's rib cage, and tore off from the city perimeter.

A bolt of lightning flashed in the sky behind him.

The Angevin tore down the muddied winter road, sloping and twisting, hugging the rugged coastline where the sea crashed into giant rocks. The sea mist sprayed his face, stabbing his cheeks like a thousand little blades. He knew this route well, having traveled it hundreds of times, but had never galloped so hard, under such panic and distress. He rode eastward toward Messina at full gallop.

He forded the Oreto River. He rode past the convents, past the old palaces of the emirs, past the Phoenician ruins, never glancing back to check for possible pursuers.

The Angevin was armed with little more than his sword and the memory of the bloodbath he had just witnessed of his countrymen mangled in the streets.

Gritting his teeth, the rain pelting his face, the Angevin had only one thought racing through his mind. He had to warn the governor of Sicily, the royal vicar Herbert Orleans.

La vitesse de Dieu, he told himself. *God be with us.*

CHAPTER 42

Palazzo dei Normanni
Palermo, Sicily
Albergheria District
March 31, 1282
6:42 a.m.

THE BLOODRED sun broke the following morning. The rain had stopped. Only a crowing rooster shattered the silence. Red shards of sunlight sliced their way across the blood-soaked streets of Palermo. Two thousand Angevin men and women lay dead in the gutters.

From a vantage point atop the Norman Palace, Aetna Vespiri peered out over the city, her green eyes narrowing with resolve. She observed a moment of silence, feeling a conflicted mix of triumph and remorse for the acts of violence and blood spilled on Sicily's soil.

Don Rapaci approached her from behind. He stood beside her silently, taking in the moment with her. "Aetna's eruption last night was unlike anything the world has ever known," he said. "*Rebellamentu* is now upon us."

Aetna took a few steps forward, then dropped to her knees. She lifted her eyes to the sky, seeing Don Vittorio Vespiri's face materialize in the sunrise. She needed to speak to him and suddenly felt the words pour out of her. *"Rebellamentu."* She nodded to herself. "For *cosca*. For family."

A single tear welled up in *Don Rapaci's* eye and trickled down his cheek. His face hardened with pride and vindication.

With a half-trembling hand, Aetna lifted her stiletto and pressed the razor-sharp tip into her palm. She slowly applied pressure on her skin until she drew blood. Black droplets splattered one by one into a grotesque pattern on the stone floor at her knees.

"By my own blood, I swear to you, my dear *patri*, that I won't rest until Sicily is ours again," she said. "Or until I am with you in death."

Rising to her feet, she remembered her *patri's* words: *No matter how we are thrown, we will always land standing.*

Aetna looked out over the city of Palermo with a harrowed gaze. In the streets below, she spotted a group of rebels tearing down the Angevin French flag. In its place, they raised a *bannera* emblazoned with a black Imperial Eagle on a golden shield, its wings spread outward, its red tongue extending from its beak. The heraldry was originally adopted by Frederick II as a badge to the city during his rule. Another group raised a vermillion flag emblazoned with the official papal insignia and coat of arms of the Vatican—two crossed Keys of Saint Peter making the shape of the letter *X*.

Aetna's stomach churned at the sight of it. She decided in that moment that the flags would not stand. It was a new day. The beginning of a new era. And she knew Sicily would need a new heraldry. A coat of arms.

A *bannera* of its own.

CHAPTER 43

Matagrifone
Messina, Sicily
March 31, 1282
7:33 a.m.

THE LONG wooden table was as cold and hardened as the twelve officers and noblemen sitting around it. Angevin foot soldiers stood guard at the entrance of the war chamber, which was sparsely lit by torch sconces flickering from the walls.

One of the twelve men among them, Messinese nobleman Don Riccardo Riso, possessed a twisted, deadly shrewdness that had allowed him to maintain his station as the head of the most powerful Sicilian noble families in Messina province. His fine garments were neatly pressed and tailored perfectly to the shape of his skinny frame. Loyal to *Re Carlu* and the Angevin military, Don Riso commanded the largest private navy this side of the Mediterranean. He possessed a weaselly air, but despite this, he commanded respect. Or fear. His best and most loyal vassal knight, the notorious mercenary *Fra'Diavulu*, stood at full attention behind him. The knight's razor-sharp steel stiletto blades seemed to groan and hum quietly in the dank war chamber.

A map of Sicily sprawled out across the table, its surface littered with warship figurines. Don Riso leaned forward and pointed to a cluster of ships placed over Messina.

"Until Angevin warships are fully amassed in our eastern ports, we are vulnerable," Don Riso said. "Constantinople is too well protected. The Byzantine emperor is more dangerous than we realized."

A French aristocrat sneered from across the long table. "Dangerous to your galleys, perhaps, but not to the Angevin navy."

Don Riso's brow furrowed. "My galleys will support *Re Carlu*'s conquest of Constantinople, but you are not ready."

The men were suddenly cut off by the sound of heavy boots clanking into the war chamber. Foot soldiers snapped to attention. Don Riso's head turned, along with the other officers and noblemen in the room.

Two large men entered and marched together toward the head of the table. They were as different in appearance as they were united in resolve. The one nearer to Don Riso was an overweight man draped in fine purple garments, Vicar Herbert Orleans, the governor of Sicily. The vicar was dwarfed by the broad, imposing, fully armored hulk of General Guy de Rochefort, a wolfskin draped around his shoulders and breastplate, a large claymore battle sword strapped to his back. Don Riso cringed at the sight of the general's grotesque gash of a scar that cut over his left eye and down the length of his face.

Vicar Orleans assumed his place at the head of the long table. Rochefort stood at his side, a dominating presence behind the governor's seat.

Orleans carefully scanned the room. "Constantinople will no longer be of any concern to us. There has been an incident in Palermo."

"Incident?" an Angevin officer asked.

"A riot," Orleans said. "Blood in the streets. I am told it was started by a peasant criminal . . . a Sicilian woman."

The men shot glances toward one another, then burst into laughter.

"Impossible," an officer said.

Orleans's eyes widened in anger. He clenched a fist and slammed it down on the table. The men in the room fell silent. "Constantinople will soon grovel at our superior strength, yet we can't control the meager population on our own island?"

General Rochefort shifted behind him. His metal armor groaned under his weight.

The vicar's attention was diverted to the back of the chamber as he saw his daughter, Lady Manon Orleans, stride into the room with a confident disdain. She wore a jade silk gown with a golden lattice cinched at the waist. Her ashen-blond hair, usually dry and frazzled from too many hours spent out in the Sicilian sun, was pulled back in an intricate braid. She had piercing hazel eyes and lips that seemed perpetually curled upward into a mischievous grin. She had broad shoulders and lanky arms and legs with knobby joints. Black and blue bruises frequented her fair skin, the result of a condition she'd had since birth.

Orleans beckoned toward Manon as she moved across the chamber. "If my daughter intends to govern Sicily one day, the least she can do is be on time for an emergency council."

Manon flashed her father a scornful glare as all of the men in the room watched her stride coolly across the chamber. She brushed past *Fra'Diavulu*, handing him a small piece of folded goatskin before taking her place at her father's side.

Fra'Diavulu glanced down at the goatskin in his palm and slowly unfolded it. Inscribed in thick black ink on the soft skin was one word: *Megaliti*. He shook his head and raised his eyes to Manon. She was already holding eye contact with him, a playful smile crossing her lips.

Orleans narrowed his gaze back toward the men. "An attack made against our Angevin soldiers is a futile act. No matter how courageous they think they are. This army will be the most powerful the world has ever known." He shot an assured glance to *Fra'Diavulu*. "Fear will keep them in line."

Riso cleared his throat. "The Families of Messina are behind you. You have my knights." Riso beckoned toward *Fra'Diavulu*. "And my loyalty. For king and for France."

Rochefort peered down his nose in disgust. "A dirty people with dirty blood. Never trust Sicilian courage from a distance," he sneered to Orleans, quietly enough to make it look like a personal comment, but loud enough for Riso to hear.

Riso squirmed in his seat.

With that, Orleans picked up his feet and shuffled toward the exit. "The general and I leave for Napoli to celebrate King Charles's birthday. I want this little affair under control by the time we return."

"And what of this woman they speak of?" *Fra'Diavulu* interjected.

Manon seemed to perk up at the question, shooting the knight a curious look from across the room.

Approaching the threshold, Orleans turned back to face the men. He smiled. "Sergeant Drouet will set her straight, no doubt."

· ❧ ·

In Palermo, the Cistercian nuns dragged Sergeant Drouet's corpse across the *Santo Spirito* courtyard and threw it onto a pile of Angevin corpses stacked in a shallow grave dug into the surrounding cemetery grounds. The nuns knew that to prevent the spread of disease, the corpses would need to be burned.

The Abbot emerged from the cluster of nuns, carrying a flaming torch. He made the sign of the cross, then dropped the torch onto the pile. A burst of flames erupted from the corpses and licked upward into the sky.

Drouet's corpse was the first to burn.

CHAPTER 44

Cattedrale di Palermo
Palermo, Sicily
Seralcadio District
March 31, 1282
7:51 a.m.

AETNA VESPIRI'S movement down the marble-tiled *Cassaru* took on new urgency. *Don Rapaci* kept pace close behind her as they blazed a path down Palermo's main artery road. Throughout the city, the faint pounding of kettledrums echoed from the piazzas; horns blared from the rooftops. The citizens were agitated, anxious, restless.

The two Sicilians reached Palermo Cathedral, the edifice's Norman bell towers rising high into the sky like imperial spikes. Aetna pressed her palms into the heavy wooden doors and heaved them open, leading them into the nave.

The shouting inside Palermo Cathedral was deafening. The cavernous nave, supported by marble pillars running up the length of the space, was packed with Palermitans and reverberated with the electric murmurings of the inflamed crowd.

Aetna pushed her way through the assemblage of human bodies, down the central aisle. *Don Rapaci* moved behind her, his hands gripped on the hilts of his crossed stiletto blades hanging on his waist. A mixed sensation of triumph and horror washed over the makeshift assembly as they grappled with the horrific events that had transpired the night before.

On the far end of the nave, Archbishop Salvatore Malu emerged and approached the raised altar. He stood high above the crowd. His pale forehead beaded with sweat. The crowd was growing louder and more agitated with each passing minute. He saw in their eyes a mix of anger, terror, and resolve. A deadly and dangerous combination.

As Aetna surveyed the electric madness of the gathering, she spotted her dear friend Tziporah and the Cistercian nuns clustered together on the other side of the chamber.

Malu extended his palms outward. "Children of Palermo, please calm yourselves. What happened in our streets this past night was unthinkable."

As the crowd slowly simmered down, Malu dabbed the sweat dripping from his chin. He refrained from speaking until he could be heard by everyone. "Now is the time for somber reflection."

Several men on the opposite side of the nave shot to their feet.

"Reflection?" one man yelled. "*Re Carlu* will send his worst once he hears of this news!"

Heads nodded throughout the crowd.

"I'm not dying like a butchered hog!" a different man shouted.

"Hear, hear!" shouted another.

The crowd erupted in more shouting. Moorish kettledrums pounded throughout the nave.

Malu shook his head, waving his palms in the air, beckoning them into silence. "May God absolve us of the blood we spilled in anger, of the atrocities committed in the name of vengeance," Malu said. "I have faith we can beg *Re Carlu*'s forgiveness together."

Aetna pursed her lips, narrowing her gaze toward the archbishop. In that instant, she felt something bubbling in her gut.

God is within her. She will not fall . . .

God will help her when morning breaks . . .

The words moved up her stomach, through her heart, and into her throat. She felt her pulse thump louder and louder in her eardrums.

Nations rage; kingdoms crumble . . .

The earth quakes when she lifts her own voice . . .

"No!" Aetna shouted out above the crowd, thrusting a fist into the air.

In that instant, the entire cathedral fell dead silent. A thousand eyeballs slowly turned and blinked back at her.

Malu craned his neck and turned to face the direction the sound came from. He beheld a Sicilian woman with raven-black hair and green eyes step forward from the crowd. She was flanked by a man in black.

Sauntering forward, Aetna inspected her surroundings with sharpened eyes. By the time she reached the altar, the entire chamber had fallen silent except the sound of her feet on the marble tile. "We no longer recognize a king," Aetna said, stepping up to the altar.

Malu's eyes widened in disbelief. "How dare a woman address this assembly!"

Aetna scowled in indignation. She planted her feet firmly and spun toward the crowd. "Families of Sicily, I am Aetna Vespiri."

"Vespiri?" the people murmured to one another.

Malu furrowed his brow, recognizing the name. "Vespiri," he growled under his breath. Malu sweltered with sweat under his cassock. Saint-Remy had promised him the Pontifex's seat

as long as he kept the people of Sicily poor in spirit and bank-
rupt of any sense of manifest destiny. That future was now
crumbling down around him, like the Greek ruins frowning
on Sicily's hills. The last Sicilian who had attempted to disrupt
the life he had created for himself once stood before him in
this very church. *Don Vittorio Vespiri.*

Aetna scanned the faces of the crowd. "What we did last
night was unthinkable. Monstrous. But not as monstrous as
what they've done to us. Now is our time to rise up against our
Angevin oppressors and tell the world that the Sicilian people
will not be ruled."

The crowd nodded.

"Have you gone mad?" Malu shouted. "We'll all be executed with our heads piled neatly on the beaches of Palermo.
Or have you forgotten what they did to our kin in Augusta?"

Aetna narrowed her gaze to the bishop as he took a step
forward. And another step. And another.

"We will reestablish relations with *Re Carlu,*" Malu
declared, his face contorting with anger.

Aetna stepped forward to meet him. "We will take back
this land for the people of Sicily."

"With what army?" Malu said. "You have no soldiers, no
knights."

Aetna glanced out over a throng of hopeful Sicilian faces
beaming back at her. "I see a cathedral full of Sicilian knights."
With that, she felt a welcome rush of excitement in the air,
surging over the heads of the crowd.

Malu shook his jowls. "*Re Carlu* is amassing the largest
military force the world has ever seen, in Messina, on our own
shores. What possible chance do you stand against his fury?"

Aetna glared defiantly at the bishop. "No matter where we
are thrown, we will always land standing."

Malu took another step forward. "I should have you
arrested."

Aetna scoffed. "Under whose authority?" She then spun out toward the crowd, extending her palms outward. "Under whose authority?"

Malu's lips curled into a snarl as he stabbed a finger hard into his own chest. "Mine!" At that moment, Malu reached into his sleeve and unsheathed a short dagger, thrusting it toward Aetna's neck.

Aetna watched the dagger's tip slash toward her as if in slow motion. Suddenly, two blades emerged from the corner of her vision, parrying the blow and knocking the blade from the archbishop's grasp, sending it clanging to the floor.

The crowd gasped.

Don Rapaci stood like a rock, baring his teeth, his two stiletto blades crisscrossed out in front of him, creating a natural barrier between Malu and Aetna.

"Your authority ends here," *Don Rapaci* growled.

Malu's eyes widened in terror as he beheld the razor-sharp blade edges hovering over his throat.

Don Rapaci said sharply, "The oppressor now lies in pools of their own blood thanks to this *Siciliana*. You will show her your respect."

Malu's face contorted in panic, his forehead dripping with sweat. He stumbled backward, spun on his heel, and scrambled for the side exit.

Aetna gritted her teeth and picked up her feet to make chase, when she felt her arm yanked back.

"No," *Don Rapaci* said, his strong hand gripped tightly around her bicep.

"Get your hands off me!"

"Let him go," *Don Rapaci* said.

"He's getting away!"

"Your place is here now," *Don Rapaci* said. "His time will come."

Aetna glowered as she watched Malu burst through the exit. The archbishop then jumped onto a horse and lashed the reins, disappearing into the street.

"Judas rat," Aetna spat under her breath. She then spun to face the swelling congregation. A thousand eyeballs blinked back at her in disbelief. Silence hung for a long moment.

Then, in that instant, a military horn blared from outside.

Don Rapaci turned on his heels, his eyes widening.

"What is it?" Aetna said.

"That's no Angevin horn," *Don Rapaci* said.

In that moment, the cathedral doors banged open.

The crowd turned and peered into the blinding shaft of white light pouring in from outside.

Aetna's heart pounded as she stared into the intense brightness. Not until the approaching figures fully crossed the cathedral's threshold did Aetna recognize who they were. She found herself suddenly smiling. Her eyes teared up unexpectedly. "Well, I'll be damned."

CHAPTER 45

OUT FROM the pillar of white light materialized a troop of knights marching up the center aisle in two columns, led by a single captain. Their long swords and armor were expertly worked and polished, their tunics and regalia gleaming with the black cross against a white shield.

Ordu Teutoni. The outlawed Knights of the Teutonic Order.

Aetna looked on in wonder and disbelief as the crowd cleared a path for the *Teutoni* Knights marching down the center aisle.

"How is this possible?" one man whispered to his wife.

The knights marched to a stop in front of the altar. The *Teutoni* captain sauntered forward with a strong and upright gait.

"The streets have claimed a *Siciliana* has risen up against the oppressor," the captain said.

Aetna stepped forward from the altar. "Who are you?"

"I am Captain Roger Mastrangelo," the knight said.

A lean six feet tall, the young captain was in his early thirties with bronzed skin, a bright red beard, and curly auburn hair tied back behind his head. The young man exuded the regal fortitude of *Richard Coeur de Lion*—Richard the Lionheart, the legendary English Crusader king. Mastrangelo held his pointed chin up. His expressive blue eyes were buried in a hardened face that had seen too much war. His presence was commanding and authoritative, almost hypnotic.

"I bring word from the grand master of the *Ordu Teutoni,*" Mastrangelo said. "A promise was once made to the people of Sicily. Long ago, our order fought and died for the prosperity of this great island. We have returned to honor that promise and give power back to the people of Sicily, and end the oppression that has crippled it."

The crowd looked on in shock.

"The *Ordu Teutoni* is with you . . . *O Santo Cavaleri,*" Mastrangelo said.

At once, the *Teutoni* Knights unsheathed their swords and thrust their sharpened tips downward into the marble floor, genuflecting to one knee. They closed their eyes and bowed their heads before Aetna.

Aetna's heart raced as she beheld the contingent of *Teutoni* Knights kneeling before her. Their white tunics emblazoned with a black cross gleamed in the shafts of sunlight pouring in from the stained-glass windows above. Their polished swords glistened like fiery rays of sunlight.

Embarrassed, Aetna felt her face flush. "Stand up, man; I'm not the queen."

Captain Mastrangelo stood up slowly, giving her a nod of assurance.

The crowd erupted in applause, beating the Moorish kettledrums once more.

Aetna took a deep breath and turned toward the crowd. She looked around the cathedral at all of the faces staring back at her. In that instant, she felt her *patri*'s spirit, his essence, coursing through her veins and sharpening her mind.

"I am finding it hard to explain how it feels to say I'm willing to give my life for something that isn't tangible," she said. "It's one thing to say that a soldier has an arrow pointed at your mother, or sister, or friend, and that you're going to jump in front of that loved one and take that arrow in the chest. Because that's your mother, your sister, your friend. You can hold them; you can feel them. But when you speak of an idea, of *rebellamentu* . . . freedom from tyranny. Freedom to define our own lives as we see fit. Can you hold that? Can you feel it?"

Aetna looked around the room. All eyes were on her. "Will you fight for an idea?"

"For *Sicilia*!" a man shouted.

Aetna slowly closed her grasp around the hilt of her stiletto strapped to her hip. In one fell motion, she snapped it out from its sheath and thrust it high into the air. The blade caught a shaft of light pouring down from the apse windows above, sending golden rays gleaming outward over the crowd.

"*Rebellamentu!*" Aetna shouted.

The people roared like a thousand lions, pounding on Moorish kettledrums, the sound reverberating through the cavernous cathedral.

The crowd pumped their fists into the air and returned the cry.

"*Rebellamentu! Rebellamentu! Rebellamentu!*"

"*Rebellamentu!*" Aetna yelled at the top of her lungs.

Suddenly, Aetna felt two small arms wrap themselves tightly around the back of her midsection. She spun around to see Tziporah's smiling face beaming up at her.

Tziporah flung her arms around Aetna and buried her head in her chest. "We can be a *cosca* again."

Aetna pressed her palm into the back of the young girl's head and pulled her in close.

"*Cosca*." Aetna nodded.

The two friends shared a long embrace.

In that instant, a page burst through the cathedral doors, drenched in sweat. He jumped up onto a pew bench overlooking the crowd and cupped his hands around his mouth. *"Attenzioni!"* he shouted. "Justiciar Saint-Remy has fled to the *Castello di Vicari."*

The entire room erupted in murmuring.

Don Rapaci nodded grimly and leaned toward Aetna. "That's an hour's ride from here. We can still catch him."

The Sicilians pumped their fists into the air in unison. *"Moranu li Francisi!"* they cried as one. "Death to the Angevins!" The sound of pounding Moorish kettledrums once again reverberated throughout the cathedral.

Aetna's eyes filled with resolve. She knew exactly what she had to do. She turned to face the assembly. "We must strike before the Angevins can retaliate. Arm yourselves with anything you can carry. We ride for Vicari!"

CHAPTER 46

Megaliti dell'Argimusco
Messina Province, Sicily
March 31, 1282
10:41 p.m.

MEGALITI DELL'ARGIMUSCO, known as the Sicilian Stone-henge, was situated on a high plateau southwest of Messina and offered a sweeping panoramic view of Mount Etna, the volcano. A marvelous site of megalithic sandstone structures, the gigantic complex's rock formations were considered to mimic the constellations moving overhead across the night sky. Ancient tradition traced the megaliths to prehistoric civilizations. The massive rock formations took the form of various shapes and creatures: a swan, a lion, a giant eagle one hundred times larger than a human.

But perhaps most impressive was the monolith that struck the beholder's imagination more than anything, especially when observed in the sunset light, known as *Orante,* or the Praying Lady. Outlined along the sheer face of an eighty-five-foot-high cliff, a mysterious figure took shape, creating the profile of a tall woman with her hands clasped in prayer. An ancient legend said that the figure was once a young Sicilian maiden who was pursued by an unwanted suitor and, in order to avoid his constant harassment, sought protection in the stone. She remained frozen forever in time.

At the foot of the Praying Woman, a small bonfire flickered beneath the towering rock formation. The light of the flames cast an ominous glow across the sheer stone. Only the sounds of rustling ferns filled the chilly March air.

Standing beneath the cliff face, Lady Manon Orleans donned a hooded jade ermine robe. She gripped a Moorish throwing knife in her hand. It was a short, sickle-shaped blade specifically worked to achieve maximum damage when thrown straight at its target.

Manon felt the balanced weight of the blade. Furrowing her brow, she narrowed her gaze toward the straw dummy sitting twenty feet across the field, picturing the hideous face of General Guy de Rochefort.

"Damn him," she spat under her breath. "And my father." *Offering me up like a prize to be won.* She remembered it as if it were yesterday. Years earlier, Vicar Orleans and General Rochefort were hunting on *Monte Pellegrino* in Palermo when Orleans was suddenly attacked by a mountain lion. Rochefort threw himself at the mauling cougar and strangled it to death. He was nearly killed. The whole ordeal left him horribly disfigured. As a reward for saving his life, Orleans promised Rochefort claim to Manon's hand in marriage when she came of age.

Manon winced at the thought. She'd sooner run away and live in a cave like a hermit for the rest of her days than marry that vile thug.

Taking a deep breath, Manon extended her arm back and whipped the knife at the dummy. *Whoosh!* The razor-sharp blade whistled through the air and smashed dead center into the target.

A satisfied smirk crossed Manon's lips as she pulled another blade from her waistline. Suddenly, she heard the snort of a horse pierce the air. She spun around to see the Messinese mercenary *Fra'Diavulu* emerge from the darkness, illuminated by the orange glow of the fire. The horse blew frosted clouds from its nostrils as the knight dismounted.

"*Spinarosa . . . ,*" he called out, his voice cracking with an emotion she could not place. The Sicilian expression for "a rose among the thorns" meant a high-minded woman who was surrounded by vile, unscrupulous men. It was a nickname he had called Manon since they first met as teenagers.

Manon grinned and set her blades down. She removed her hood, revealing long, ashen-blond hair underneath. She strode toward the approaching knight and yanked him by the cheeks, pressing her lips against his. Her tongue moved down his throat. Her palm moved down the surface of his firm abdomen and gently pressed into his member.

Manon's lips lingered on *Fra'Diavulu*'s for a long moment; then she kissed him again. And again. Each kiss harder and with more purpose than the one before.

Suddenly, *Fra'Diavulu* shook his head, tearing himself away from her embrace. "We can't keep meeting like this."

Manon let out a sigh of frustration. Her gaze lingered on the knight as he moved toward the fire. "Do you think it's true?" she said.

"What's true?"

"The woman in Palermo."

"Soldiers under duress are known to exaggerate," *Fra'Diavulu* said. "Nothing but a routine arrest gone awry. Once the dust settles, they'll catch her."

"And then what?"

"If she's lucky . . . they'll kill her."

Manon recoiled. "Lucky? What will they do to her?" As soon as the words left her mouth, she realized she didn't want to know.

Fra'Diavulu shook his head, changing the subject. "Your father suspects something between us. If General Rochefort ever found out, he'd put my head on a pike."

Manon scoffed. She spun away from *Fra'Diavulu*, her muscles tensing up. "It gets worse," she said. "Once I inherit this realm from my father, Rochefort will become regent of Sicily."

Fra'Diavulu's gaze turned grim. "That's a lot of power for one man."

Manon turned and looked up at *Fra'Diavulu* with liquid eyes, pleading with him. "And the poor people of this island have suffered enough under his command."

Fra'Diavulu seemed to shrink back at the remark. "What am I supposed to do about it?"

"Choose to protect them," Manon said.

Fra'Diavulu studied her face for a long moment, then shook his head hesitantly. "I really must be going." With that, he pressed an object wrapped in sheepskin into Manon's hands.

Manon glanced down at it. She slowly unwrapped the cloth. A book of Sicilian poetry. On its cover was a single title: *Contrasto.*

Fra'Diavulu had already turned around and swung his leg up over his horse.

Manon didn't stop him. As she watched the knight mount into his saddle, she couldn't help but notice the devil mask strapped to his belt. She scoffed. "Maybe you have finally become that dreadful embodiment of evil you proudly display."

Fra'Diavulu glanced down at the mask, then lifted his eyes to catch her gaze. "Satan wasn't always evil."

Manon arched her eyebrow. "Then what was he?"

"The greatest lover of God," *Fra'Diavulu* said.

Manon's forehead crinkled. "Lover? That's not how I remember it."

Fra'Diavulu spoke thoughtfully. "The standard Christian story tells that when God created humankind, he ordered the angels to serve man. But Satan would not do it. This was interpreted as being the pride and ego of Satan. But in the Persian tradition, Satan couldn't bow down to man because he loved God far too much. So, then God said, 'Get out of my sight,' and cast Satan from paradise. Punished for nothing more than refusing to deny the love in his heart."

Manon was curt. "He was sent to hell."

Fra'Diavulu shook his head. "Hell wasn't a place in this story."

Manon furrowed her brow. "What was it, then?"

A look of longing crossed *Fra'Diavulu's* face. "A feeling. The greatest hell one can know is being separated from the one you love . . . and the suffering that follows."

Manon's gaze softened. She felt a twinge of sadness. *"Oui."*

The two lovers stared at one another for a long moment before *Fra'Diavulu* lashed his reins and tore off. Manon watched him disappear into the black oblivion. A cold gust of wind whipped through the valley.

Then we both know hell, she thought.

CHAPTER 47

Castello di Vicari
Vicari, Sicily
April 1, 1282
10:27 a.m. // Second day of Vespers

LOOKING OUT from his parapet chamber, Palermo justiciar Jean de Saint-Remy watched the bloodred sun creep over the horizon and make its way high into the clouded sky. Anxious thoughts turned over in his mind. *Palermo is lost.* How would he explain this to Vicar Orleans? His own cousin. *How would I ever show my face in another French court?* He clenched his fists, feeling the shame quickly boil into anger.

Saint-Remy glanced over to a silver-plated mirror hanging on the wall. He saw a ghostly reflection of his own hapless image. The fresh linen cloth wrapped around his wounded head was already soaked with blood. He cringed, tearing his eye away. *They'll suffer for their crimes.*

Saint-Remy turned from the mirror and suddenly found himself face to face with a soldier standing in his doorway. The man struggled to catch his breath.

A scowl crossed Saint-Remy's face. "What do you want?"

"You're needed at the main gate immediately."

"What is it?"

"Sicilians from Palermo are here," the soldier huffed. "They're offering . . . terms."

Saint-Remy's brow furrowed. "Impossible." He sprung into action, throwing on his bloodied tunic. "Take me to them."

The soldier nodded nervously and darted from the chamber.

Saint-Remy gnashed his teeth, grabbed a rapier hanging off the wall, and holstered it to his belt. In that moment, he decided he could not flee to Messina a humiliated man. He would utterly crush this Sicilian insurrection beneath his heel like a diseased rodent.

This ends today, he told himself.

CHAPTER 48

SITTING ATOP a black steed, Aetna Vespiri peered up toward the looming exterior wall of the *Castello di Vicari*. Tziporah sat on a horse at Aetna's side with a quiver of arrows strapped to her back. Two hundred angry Sicilian rebels amassed behind her. Some were on horses; some were on foot; all were armed with swords, and spears, and stiletto blades. Scowls hung on their tired faces, unable as they were to conceal their contempt. The golden eagle Rosalia circled the sky above.

Aetna watched as a squad of Angevin soldiers spread out along the fortress's perimeter. Then she saw him. Justiciar Jean de Saint-Remy limped out slowly onto the parapet. Aetna's lips curled into a half smile as she spotted the white cloth covering his left eye, admiring her handiwork.

Tziporah nocked a single arrow into her longbow, pointing it directly at Saint-Remy and straining to hold it steady against the string's groaning tension.

Saint-Remy glared down at the *Siciliana* on horseback. "You!" he boomed. "That bitch from my harem."

The Sicilians' eyes widened, all heads turning toward Aetna.

Aetna remained still, staring a hole into the justiciar's eyes.

Tziporah squeezed one eye shut, peering down the length of her arrow. "I could put one right into his mouth," Tziporah said. "That would shut him up."

Aetna smirked to herself. She then raised a palm, signaling Tziporah to hold her fire.

Saint-Remy scanned the faces of the Sicilian rebels staring back up at him. "All traitors to King Charles will lose their heads!" Saint-Remy cried down, a crack in his voice.

"We didn't come here to fight," Aetna said.

There was a murmuring of Angevin soldiers along the wall perimeter. Aetna noticed the men looked uneasy. Exactly what she had hoped for. "We have a galley waiting for you in Palermo," she said. "It will grant you safe passage back to Napoli. There you will tell your king that our soil is no longer his to rule. That Sicily's families are free."

Saint-Remy's gaze narrowed. "A galley in Palermo, you say?"

Aetna nodded.

"You attacked my palace, maimed my soldiers, tore out my eye," Saint-Remy shouted. "Why should I trust a Sicilian?"

"You shouldn't," she said. "But it seems you have to."

A long silence hung in the air as Saint-Remy turned away to address the commanding officer. He gripped the officer by the collar and pulled him close. A vigorous conversation seemed to be happening between them. Saint-Remy then turned back to face Aetna and the band of rebels. "Very well," Saint-Remy said. "Under these terms, I will depart for Palermo under your protection."

A beguiling grin crossed Aetna's lips. *Something like that.*

Seconds later, the bolts of the enormous gate began to move as it slowly creaked open.

CHAPTER 49

JUSTICIAR JEAN DE SAINT-REMY glared down at the Sicilian rebels spread out before the fortress gates. Not only had he lost Palermo; he lost it to a vulgar woman. The filthy *Siciliana* from his harem now sat atop a large warhorse, donned in leather armor with a long blade strapped to her waist. He shook his head, trying to comprehend how she could be the same woman he had beaten senseless just two days earlier.

Lieutenant Guiscard leaned over and whispered into the justiciar's ear. "We can sneak you out through the *Porta Fausa* tower. There is a hidden staircase that leads you safely down the face of the cliff and into the valley below. But we must go now."

Saint-Remy turned to Guiscard, his bloodshot eye wide with rage. "I will not tell my cousin I fled the greatest fortress in northern Sicily. Open the gates."

The lieutenant's eyes widened. "We are outnumbered."

"I know, you idiot," Saint-Remy said. "I will surrender myself to them."

"Sire?"

Saint-Remy gripped the officer by the collar and pulled him close. "Once I leave, you will catch up with us down the road and organize an ambush," Saint-Remy said. "Now, open the gates."

Guiscard nodded grimly, beckoning down to his men. Moving into position, the soldiers straddled the ropes on either side of the wooden doors and cranked the pulleys.

The fortress gate groaned to life, slowly grinding open.

Saint-Remy turned to the officer, straightening his uniform. "And be quick about it, will you?"

Suddenly, there was a hissing sound in the air, like a cobra leaping from the dirt.

In that instant, an arrow whizzed up from below and smashed directly into Saint-Remy's throat, crushing his windpipe. The arrow protruded from his neck. Saint-Remy's eye widened in shock. His mouth gaped open, already foaming with a mix of blood and drool.

Guiscard stood in terror as Saint-Remy stumbled forward. The justiciar slapped his palms hard onto the lieutenant's shoulders as his tongue flailed from his mouth.

Saint-Remy's knees gave out as he dropped hard to the stone floor. Dead.

Moments later, a golden eagle screeched down from the sky.

Guiscard spun around to face his men, but suddenly his jaw dropped. A large, dark figure loomed over him. Lean and agile, donned in all black. His face was covered by a Saracen war mask in the shape of a falcon's beak, two stiletto blades strapped to his abdomen, crisscrossed over one another.

"A hidden staircase, you say?" The man in black grinned.

Guiscard's face turned white with terror. *"Sicilien!"* But it was too late. As soon as he had opened his mouth, a blade shrieking through the air gashed open his jugular.

· ❦ ·

Aetna watched with anticipation as the large wooden gate doors slowly opened. She had already plotted the entire scenario in her mind, knowing exactly what she would say and how the Angevins would react. Sure enough, the enemy was willingly lowering its defenses to the most impenetrable castle, without the threat of a single catapult or siege machine.

Aetna glanced over to Tziporah and nodded. The young girl returned the nod.

Tziporah inhaled a deep gasp, carefully peering down the sight of the nocked arrow. "He talks too much," she grunted under her breath. Tziporah snapped open her fingers from the bow's taut string.

Thip! The arrow screamed as it tore through the air. It was an impossible shot from that distance, but it seemed to Aetna that her own hand had traveled with the arrow and smashed it directly into Saint-Remy's throat, crushing his windpipe.

Tziporah glanced assuredly over to Aetna.

Aetna kept her harrowed gaze trained on the justiciar stumbling forward. Saint-Remy's tongue thrashed from his mouth as he gripped his throat. Suddenly, she beheld *Don Rapaci* materialize on the wall perimeter, emerging from the hidden *Porta Fausa* staircase just as they had planned. His silver blades glimmered in the hot morning sun.

The golden eagle Rosalia circled overhead and cried down from the sky.

From her position, Aetna watched the Angevin justiciar spout a fountain of blood. She pursed her lips as her chest heaved with retribution. She then lowered her eyes to the gates as they ground to a stop. The strongest fortress in Sicily had just opened its doors.

She lifted her stiletto in the air and pointed it toward the fortress gate. *"Moranu li Francisi!"*

The Sicilian rebels raised their swords and roared into the morning sky.

Aetna jammed her heels into her horse's rib cage. The horse snorted and broke into a gallop. *"Assalto!"* she cried, charging upon the gate with irresistible fury.

A shaft of sunlight broke through the clouds as the rebels charged only seconds behind her. Plunging forward on horseback, Aetna ignored the burning sensation in her muscles, the soreness in her limbs. She did not stop. Her heart pounded heavily against her rib cage, her body hot and sticky, her mind sharpened by *occhinero*. She kept charging. The rebels struggled to keep up. Behind her, she heard the other horses snorting and stomping, and the cries and cursing of her men as they barreled forward on foot.

Aetna plowed through the main gate, into the inner courtyard, and leapt from her horse, slicing open Angevin soldiers with every swing of her blade, dropping them into pools of blood. She was fueled by a power beyond that of human capability, by the same rage that spawned on Vespers night.

The rebels drove back the Angevin soldiers into the guts of the fortress stronghold, putting the entire garrison to their blades and flinging their corpses into piles for the dogs and vultures.

Ahead, Aetna marveled at the sight of the remaining soldiers scattering in panic, hurling themselves from the castle embankments to the jagged cliffs below. The *Castello di Vicari,* the strongest fortress in Sicily, had fallen to a woman.

That bitch from my harem. She recalled Saint-Remy's insult.

Aetna threw her shoulders back and tightened her legs, standing tall as she surveyed the spoils of victory. In that moment, she felt she could fight forever.

CHAPTER 50

Matagrifone
Messina, Sicily
April 2, 1282
7:06 a.m. // Third day of Vespers

LADY MANON ORLEANS lay in bed, staring at the ceiling. Feeling a strange churning in her stomach, she rubbed her abdomen gently, attempting to relax what must have been her apprehension from the tumultuous events transpiring around the castle over the past twenty-four hours. Her muscles suddenly clenched violently; she thrust out of bed and vomited all over the stone floor. She spat the acidic bile from her mouth, before lunging over the bed and vomiting once more.

"Nurse!" she cried.

Manon lay on the bed as the nurse pressed a cold compress onto her forehead.

Attendants scurried to and fro, helping to keep Manon comfortable. They brought in fresh flowers, provided a pitcher with clean drinking water, and laid out a plate filled with fresh citrus fruits, such as lemons and oranges, and ruby prickly pear fruits. Vicar Orleans had contracted local nurses from Messina to work full-time in *Matagrifone*. Not because he felt their quality was any superior to what he could bring in from France, but simply that they worked for half the price.

"How long has this been happening?" the nurse asked. She was an old Sicilian woman with a leathery face, her midnight-black hair streaked with strands of silver.

"A few days," Manon said.

The nurse extended her hand and placed it on Manon's breast, massaging it gently. Manon grimaced.

"How does that feel?" the nurse asked, massaging the breast tighter in her palm.

Manon flinched. "Easy."

"I want you to lie still," the nurse said. She moved down the length of the bed. "I need to inspect your menses cloth," she said. "Please raise your knees for me."

Gently, the nurse ran her hands along Manon's legs and slipped the blanket over Manon's knees lying akimbo. The nurse removed the menses rag wrapped around her groin. The rag was clean.

The nurse glanced up with a look of concern on her face and turned to the attendants. "Everyone, leave the room at once."

The attendants froze in their place, seemingly unsure what to make of the sudden request.

The nurse grew impatient and raised her voice. "Leave, now!" she barked.

Confused, Manon watched as the young attendants quickly gathered their supplies and scuttled from the room. "What is it?"

"When was your last cycle?" the nurse asked.

Manon raised her eyes to her, a slow look of realization forming across her porcelain face. "A few weeks." She shrugged.

The nurse furrowed her brow, nodding her head in affirmation. She wasn't quite sure what to make of this.

"What is it?" Manon asked again.

The nurse let out a long breath. She lifted her eyes to meet Manon's. "Milady, you are with child."

Manon's face went white. "What?"

"But you are not yet married," the nurse said.

"Tell me something I don't know."

"General Rochefort is the father?" the nurse asked.

Manon shook her head and scoffed. "He'll never lay a finger on me." She then narrowed her gaze, turning inward. "I've only ever lain with one man."

"Who?" the nurse said.

Manon lifted her eyes to the nurse. Suddenly, an impish grin crossed her lips. She told the nurse the man's name.

The old woman clasped her hands over her mouth, her eyes widening. "What on earth will your father think when he finds out? What will Rochefort think?"

Manon looked unshaken. "Well, isn't it obvious?"

"Isn't what obvious?" the nurse pressed.

Manon lifted her chin and nodded. "I'm going to be one magnificent mother."

CHAPTER 51

Messina, Sicily
Harbor District
April 2, 1282
9:32 a.m.

TWO HULKING Angevin soldiers smashed down the wooden doors to a small homestead and stormed into the residence. The soldiers then parted, revealing *Fra'Diavulu* standing in the threshold in full regalia, complete with two stiletto blades and a glowering devil's mask. He took a step forward and marched in with a threatening gait.

An angry Sicilian woman flattened her back against the hallway, glaring at the soldiers as they pushed their way inside. "You can't do this."

Fra'Diavulu pushed past the woman. He smelled the poignant aromas of *puttanesca* sauce cooking over the fire. "We serve *Re Carlu*; there's nothing we can't do," *Fra'Diavulu* said, his deep voice muffled by his devil war mask.

The woman growled and pulled a knife from her dress. "Traitor!" she cried, lunging forward.

Fra'Diavulu caught her arm and spun her up against a wall tapestry. The woman gasped in panic.

"You're hiding *Teutoni* Knights," he said. "Where are they?"

"*Vaffanculu,*" the woman spat.

"Where are they?" *Fra'Diavulu* growled.

The woman scowled into *Fra'Diavulu*'s mask. Her chest heaved up and down.

Suddenly, *Fra'Diavulu* looked upon the wall tapestry hanging before him. It was an exquisitely woven fabric depicting the execution of Prince Conradin. The young prince was throwing his gauntlet out onto the platform in defiance of *Re Carlu*. *Fra'Diavulu* studied it for a long moment. He then gripped the tapestry and yanked it down, revealing an arched wooden door behind it. "Here."

Two soldiers moved up and kicked the door down.

Fra'Diavulu stepped forward through the door and entered a small hidden chamber. Ancient artifacts and weapons lined the room. White shields emblazoned with black crosses hung from the walls, the heraldry of the *Ordu Teutoni* illuminated by dim torchlit. A group of men huddled in the center, trembling at the sight of the imposing Messinese knight.

Fra'Diavulu stepped forward. "Who is your grand master?" he boomed through his mask, his voice deep and muffled.

The men remained silent.

Fra'Diavulu growled. "Speak or you will suffer by my blade of fire. Who is your grand master?"

The woman reached for a soldier's rapier and thrust it toward *Fra'Diavulu*. Another soldier unsheathed his rapier and moved to strike the woman down where she stood. In that instant, a blade tore through the air and caught the soldier's rapier midswing, inches away from the woman's neck.

Fra'Diavulu locked his blade against the soldier's. He stared at the soldier through his mask. "No."

The soldier looked confused.

Fra'Diavulu turned to the other soldiers blinking back at him. "Put her with the others."

The woman screamed as two soldiers moved in and shoved her into the hidden chamber with the other knights.

Fra'Diavulu reached into his chest pocket and pulled out a prickly pear. He sank his teeth into its red flesh and tossed it to another soldier. He then unsheathed his blade.

A soldier walked over with a sheepskin sack. He uncorked it and poured oil over *Fra'Diavulu*'s blade. Another soldier pressed his torch against the blade, igniting it.

Fra'Diavulu lifted the fiery blade in front of his face.

Seconds later, from behind his mask came maniacal laughter. The laughter grew louder and more sustained. *Fra'Diavulu* snapped forward into the chamber.

Then came the shrill screams of pain.

CHAPTER 52

Cattedrale di Palermo
Palermo, Sicily
Seralcadio District
April 2, 1282
8:42 p.m.

AETNA VESPIRI and *Teutoni* captain Roger Mastrangelo pored over a map rolled out over a wooden table, their backs facing Frederick II's tomb. Red-orange torchlight illuminated the darkness of the cavernous Palermo Cathedral, the roaring flames casting long, flickering shadows up the lengths of the vaulted marble walls. The air was thick and hazy, filled with the strong aromas of peppery incense.

Aetna glanced up to see a flurry of activity. Men and women moved to and fro, carrying food, supplies, and weapons. *Teutoni* Knights assisted in providing medical aid to the wounded sprawled about the floor of the cathedral. Mastrangelo was furiously signing orders and directing runners who were in charge of establishing a coordinated messenger network throughout the city and immediate province.

Palermo Cathedral had just become the makeshift barracks of the rebellion.

"We must seek the Vatican's endorsement," Aetna said. "The pope must view our actions here as a justified retaliation against a criminal tyrant, and not as a threat against his own seat of power over this realm."

Mastrangelo nodded. While Sicily would kneel before no king, he knew the necessity of the pope's recognition of Sicily as a sovereign nation under Christendom. "So be it. If this is God's plan for our poor Sicily, let him guide us in his perpetual grace."

Mastrangelo shot a glance over to his page, beckoning him forward. He directed the young boy on the contents of the letter written on the cathedral's official parchment.

Aetna picked up the letter and reviewed its contents. The letter spoke of the horrific treatment of the Sicilian people by the Angevin military and of the bloody insurrection as an act of defense against their abusive monarch, and provided assurance to the pope that they intended no infraction of loyalty against his station, looking to him only for recognition as a free people.

The parchment was then rolled into a tight scroll. The scribe dribbled hot red wax over the parchment and firmly pressed the archbishop's official insignia into the glob. Their fates had been sealed. Mastrangelo inspected the scroll and handed it to one of his personal attendants. "Send this letter with an envoy to Rome at once."

The page nodded and bowed, then turned on his heel and scurried away.

"The grand master will be pleased to hear of this development," Mastrangelo said.

Aetna nodded and leaned back against a cool marble column near the center of the nave, twirling her stiletto between her fingers. She studied a tapestry map of Sicily rolled out in front of her. The prospect of creating a country of their own excited her. But they still had much to do.

She directed her gaze toward Mastrangelo. "Perhaps one day I can meet him."

"Who?"

"Your grand master."

"I'm afraid that's impossible," Mastrangelo said.

Aetna scoffed. "*Teutoni* secret?"

Mastrangelo snorted. "The grand master's identity is unknown, even to us."

Mastrangelo scribbled his signature on a scroll and rolled it up before handing it to a page.

"Perhaps it is I, daughter of the great *O Santo Cavaleri*," Aetna said, a twinkle in her eye.

Mastrangelo raised a brow. He then pointed to a passing man. "Or maybe it's him. Or me," he continued. "That's the point, isn't it? Our grand master could be any of us, and all of us."

Aetna nodded, studying his face. He was telling the truth.

Don Rapaci set up a straw dummy in the shape of a soldier in the center aisle. The dummy was outfitted with old armor stolen off Angevin corpses. A small crowd of rebels gathered round as Tziporah moved up directly behind him. *Don Rapaci* spun around and pressed a stiletto blade into her palm. Gripping the hilt of the weapon, Tziporah inspected its long, slender blade and felt its weight in her hand.

Don Rapaci picked up a small bucket of red dye. He dipped a gnarly horsetail brush into the dye and swirled it around. The red dye dripped like blood from the tip of the brush as he pressed it against the dummy's jugular.

"Red dye reveals your enemy's kill zones," he said, addressing the group before him. He dragged the brush across the dummy's throat, leaving a long streak of red in its path. "The jugular, which carries blood to the head." He then painted a small circle on the dummy's sternum. "The chest holds his heart, which pumps his life's blood." He lowered the brush and applied globs of red dye across the lower stomach and groin, then raised the brush to paint spots under each of the dummy's arms. "Here you can puncture the organs that carry his breath." And finally, he traced the brush along the inside of the dummy's forearm, down to its wrists. "This area is laced with vulnerable arteries and veins."

Tziporah nodded, pondering the straw dummy marked up with red dye. She bit her lip, twirling the blade between her fingers.

Don Rapaci quickly unsheathed his blade, flicking it to the dummy's throat. "You want every stab to your enemy's body to cut deep and make blood spit forth," he said, miming slicing motions across each kill zone. "This makes his body go into a state of shock."

The rebels gazed on, transfixed.

"Within thirty seconds, the loss of blood will weaken your enemy, and you can easily finish him," he continued. "Though do not be fooled. Rage inspires strength. So if he charges you in a blind frenzy . . ." With that, *Don Rapaci* thrust his blade firmly into the dummy's sternum. He then turned to face the rebels, extending his palms outward and bowing as if to complete his demonstration. He saw their eyes glow with resolve.

"Stiletto combat is a life-or-death encounter," he said. "When your enemy draws a weapon against you, the only choice you have is to kill or be killed. The ability to harness your killer instinct is an essential step."

"A step?" Tziporah asked.

"Not until the fear of death runs cold through the heart of your enemy can you begin to contemplate something much more elusive . . ."

"What?" she said, hanging on his every word.

"Happiness."

On the opposite side of the nave, wounded rebels were being treated on mattresses laid down near the altar. A *Teutoni* Knight carrying a hot poker approached the group of rebels desperately trying to hold down a hulking man. The man's right arm had been pierced by an arrow, the sharp tip protruding out the back of his shoulder, with the shaft plugged into the meat of his upper body.

"Angevin bastards," the man growled.

"You must hold still," the *Teutoni* Knight said. "If we don't treat this now, you'll develop an infection and you will die, as certainly as the sun rises tomorrow."

The knight gripped the end of the arrow in his palm and snapped it clean off, leaving nothing but the shaft protruding from the man's arm. The man howled at the pain of the pressure. In the same instant, the knight pulled the arrow's shaft from the man's shoulder before stabbing the glowing poker directly into the wound. There was a horrifying sizzle and the smell of burning flesh. The men grimaced and gagged as the rotten fumes attacked their nostrils.

Eyes watering, the man jumped to his feet in anger and leapt for the closest man to him. The other men quickly grappled him to the floor. Then they burst into laughter.

Observing the scene from a distance, Aetna couldn't help but crack a small smile. Even in the face of adversity, they were able to find an inkling of joy together.

Moments later, *Don Rapaci* moved up behind her and pressed a fork and plate of creamy pasta into her hands.

Aetna recognized the pungent aroma steaming up from the plate. *Spaghetti alla Salsa Murisca Taratata.* Spaghetti with Moorish Sauce.

The Arabic-inspired dish consisted of a combination of strange ingredients such as *bottarga* fish roe, red pepper, cinnamon, garlic, pine nuts, and the citrus juices of lemon and orange. The *impasto* sauce was not cooked, but pounded in a mortar into a paste and served over the long pasta. In the local Sicilian dialect, *taratata* meant "clash," as in between two armies. The word itself sounded like the clanging of weapons that crossed: swords, scimitars, daggers, spears, *stiletti*. Traditionally, the exotic dish was served before a large battle and savored in honor of the Norman conquest of Sicily from the Arabs in the eleventh century.

Suddenly overcome with hunger, Aetna hastily twirled the creamy spaghetti and shoved a forkful into her mouth. Her lips smacked as the piquant flavors of fish roe, red pepper, and cinnamon clashed in her mouth.

"The men have fought well," *Don Rapaci* said, taking a seat beside her. "You've fought well. Don Vespiri would be proud of the woman you've become."

Aetna nodded and swallowed a large lump of pasta. She then glanced over to her friend. "Can I ask you a personal question?"

"Of course," *Don Rapaci* said.

"What happened to your family?"

"They were taken from me when I was merely a boy."

Aetna frowned. "I'm sorry."

Don Rapaci shook his head. "We cannot dwell on what has come to pass. We are now only what we do."

Aetna nodded. *Rispettu.* Respect.

She then lifted her gaze upward, pointing to the various red-and-gold flags mounted around the cathedral. The Vatican's Keys of Saint Peter. The Imperial Eagle of King Frederick II. "We say we are free Sicilians, yet we display the *bannera* of popes and kings," she said, a hint of contempt in her voice. "If Sicily is to be a new nation, she'll need her own heraldry, her own symbol."

"What symbol?" *Don Rapaci* said.

Aetna furrowed her brow, scanning the various flags hanging from the walls around the nave, searching for the right words. "Something provocative," she said, her eyes like steel. "Primeval."

Don Rapaci leaned back in his seat. "This symbol should serve to remind the Sicilian people that we don't have to be afraid of evil men who would rather abuse their power than lift others up around them."

Aetna nodded, keeping her eyes trained on the flags hanging around the cathedral.

Don Rapaci noticed a faint smile crossing her lips. "Nothing is more triumphant than a smile that has struggled through tears."

Aetna glanced up at him, catching his gaze. A moment of silence hung between the two Sicilians.

At that moment, two rebels emerged from the hazy darkness and approached Aetna's position. She looked up as they stepped forward. With some suspicion, *Don Rapaci* watched them approach.

As the two men laid their eyes on Aetna for the first time, their faces glowed with excitement.

The first Sicilian, a short, slender man with an Ericean accent from northwestern Sicily, bent down on one knee. "Aetna Vespiri," the man said, almost weeping. "I am Adrianu Amici." He then beckoned to the man behind him. "This is my brother, Gaetano. We have come to fight for you."

Gaetano stepped forward with a meek grin.

"You fight for Sicily," Aetna corrected him.

Adrianu nodded; then he reached into his cloak. But before he could remove whatever it was he had there, *Don Rapaci* swiftly produced a stiletto and held it to his neck.

"Slowly," he warned.

"We bring you a gift," Adrianu said. Carefully, he presented a bloodred pashmina. Gaetano dropped to his knees next to his brother and helped unravel it, revealing the other half made of golden thread that glimmered in the dim torchlight of the cathedral. The two fabrics were stitched together diagonally and embroidered with Norman floral patterns.

"Red and gold," Gaetano piped in. He placed his finger over the red half. "Emblematic of the Angevin blood spilled on Vespers night."

Adrianu then pressed his finger to the golden half. "And Palermo's extraordinary spirit."

Aetna glanced down at the shawl. She took it and laid it out carefully. She was moved by the fine artisanship and meaningful thoughts behind it. She noticed the ways the colors boldly complemented one another. She then lifted her eyes to the two men kneeling before her. "*Grazie mille* for this beautiful gesture of unity," she said, wrapping the pashmina around her shoulders like a cape.

The Amici brothers placed their hands over their heads, seemingly moved by her gratitude.

Suddenly, the cathedral bells rang out. There were noises coming from outside. A young Sicilian girl, one whom Captain Mastrangelo had stationed around the perimeter, ran bursting into the church.

"Men are coming," she screamed. "They look like soldiers."

In an instant, Aetna was on her feet. The sound of singing metal reverberated through the cavernous church as rebels and *Teutoni* Knights alike scrambled for their weapons.

"Angevins!" Captain Mastrangelo yelled. "It's an ambush!"

CHAPTER 53

"**PROTECT THE** entrances!" Aetna Vespiri yelled as she snatched up her blade, hoisted a small shield, and beat a path directly to the doors.

The Sicilians spread out through the church, taking positions in front of every vulnerable entry point. Some peered through the windows, trying to gauge the numbers they were faced with. Others looked for the best path for escape.

Aetna said emphatically, "We'll strike before they have a chance to react."

The Sicilians moved toward the heavy cathedral doors. Aetna nodded to her men. Together, they gripped the large rings and heaved the doors open.

To her surprise, Aetna beheld at least one hundred Sicilian rebels wielding stiletto blades, swords, spears, and clubs and carrying torches. Every man had been dressed in his finest handcrafted battle armor.

Mastrangelo pushed his way through the crowd and approached the leader of the men standing in the doors of the church. "Who are you?"

The group's captain, armed to the teeth, stepped forward and flashed a devious smile. "We come from the town of Corleone," the man replied. He was a dark Sicilian of about Mastrangelo's age, youthful and powerful. At least four men directly behind him looked ready for the fury of war. "Word of what's happened here has spread," the man continued. "And we're not going to let you take your swords to the Angevins without us."

Corleone was second to Palermo in terms of population and importance, for the city contained many noble families from the Lombardy region of mainland Italy, who especially abhorred the rule of *Re Carlu* and the cruel tax burdens he imposed on their farms and lands.

A smile spread across Mastrangelo's face. "Just like a *Corleoni* to butt his way into a fight."

The two men clasped palms and pulled each other into an embrace.

Aetna stepped forward from the center of the men and moved up among them. In that instant, the temperature of her eyes suddenly changed. Where they had once been colored by grief, they now turned to wintry steel, like a blade left out overnight on the mountaintop, covered with frost.

Aetna studied the angry young faces from Corleone glowing in torchlight. Then she turned around and observed her own men staring out from inside the cathedral. *The* rebella- mentu *is growing.*

"Many sleepless nights of cold and hunger are ahead of us," Aetna said, her voice strong. Determined. "We are all in this together now. Come, let us drink from the same cup."

At those words, the Sicilians cheered, and the two crowds merged. Men hugging men, kissing cheeks, helping one another carry weapons into the cathedral.

CHAPTER 54

Matagrifone
Messina, Sicily
April 2, 1282
9:36 p.m.

LADY MANON ORLEANS strolled into a small open-air court-yard, carrying a book tucked into her forearm. Genevieve, her handmaiden, walked by her side. Manon glanced up to see a scowling statue of King Charles standing in the center of the courtyard, glaring down with an icy stare to all who entered. The crisp evening air did nothing to calm her. *Fra'Diavulu*'s child was growing inside her. She couldn't fathom the conse-quences once her father discovered the truth. *Once Rochefort discovers the truth.* She winced at the thought of it.

In the main dining hall, a lively meal was already well underway. Don Riccardo Riso was seen at the head of the table sitting among a cohort of Angevin officers and Messinese noblemen. Swordfish, mussels, and boiled octopus were spread across the table. Pasta plates steaming. The pungent aroma of *puttanesca* sauce filled the air. The servants could barely keep the wine casks full before the men beckoned for refills, downing the fresh wine just as quickly as it came.

Genevieve looked upon the men in disgust. "When your father returns, he'll drown them in that wine."

Manon looked over to her friend. "What do you mean?"

"Palermo is in chaos," Genevieve said. "The woman they call *Siciliana* has led a rebel army to Vicari Fortress."

Manon's eyes widened. "A rebel army? How do you know this?"

Genevieve smirked. "Last night, I slept with an Angevin messenger."

"A messenger?" Manon asked. "He shouldn't be letting his tongue slip in bed."

A coy grin crossed Genevieve's lips. "It was quite satisfying, as it happens."

Manon's face flushed red. She smacked her with the back of her hand. "Is a retaliation being planned against the rebels?"

Genevieve shook her head. "The war council didn't believe him. It was determined to be nothing more than a story to incite panic. And an Angevin never panics."

Manon rolled her eyes. She watched the men at the dining table burst into laughter, clanking their glasses and downing their drinks. "Imbeciles," she said. "This Sicilian rebel . . . this woman. She led the uprising on Vespers night?"

Genevieve nodded. "Sergeant Drouet tried to capture her . . . and molest her. So she slit his throat and cried, 'Death to the Angevins!'"

Manon recoiled in shock.

Genevieve continued. "Fueled by vengeance, she mustered the people of Palermo and slaughtered every Angevin in the city."

Manon's mouth hung open.

"Now, that is a truly free woman, *oui*?" Genevieve said.

Manon composed herself and took a deep breath, blowing the air out her nostrils. *"Liberté."* She nodded. "I hope they find it."

"I hope so, too," Genevieve said, flashing a pointed glare toward the dining officers. She then glanced back over to Manon, noticing the book she had been carrying. *"Contrasto?"*

Manon followed her gaze downward, presenting the book forward. "A Sicilian poem."

"What's it about?"

"A bold maiden tries to resist the advances of a dastardly knight."

Genevieve watched as Manon thumbed to a page she had previously earmarked.

Manon cleared her throat. "'If I be your desire, sir knight, foolish indeed you are. For easier it is by far to strip of bark and bough all the forests of the world than to subdue my own heart. For if it were done, I would have shorn my hair off like a nun.'" With that, she snapped the book shut.

Genevieve bit her lip. "Romantic," she said glibly. "How does it end?"

"She gives in to the knight's seduction."

Genevieve scoffed. "Only a man would write such an ending. If it were written by a woman . . ."

Manon smirked. "She'd cut off his little prick."

The two friends exchanged half-suppressed laughs as they moved quietly through the courtyard.

CHAPTER 55

Cattedrale di Palermo
Palermo, Sicily
Seralcadio District
April 3, 1282
8:23 a.m. // Fourth day of Vespers

SHAFTS OF sunlight poured into Palermo Cathedral's windows as morning broke the following day.

Aetna Vespiri tied her red-and-gold wrap in a crisscross pattern across her chest. Over this she slipped on a leather chest plate, tightening the straps snug across her chest. She slipped leather gauntlets onto her arms and legs and slid her stiletto gently into the sheath strapped to her hip.

Don Rapaci moved up behind her, dressed in black leather armor, a black mask shaped like a raptor's beak covering his face. His long blades crisscrossed on his belt. He and Aetna exchanged smiles.

Aetna turned toward the enormous congregation of rebels and *Teutoni* Knights. Her heart pounded with anticipation for what was to come. "Families of Sicily," she said. "The blood that has been shed to date is not the seal of victory, but rather the provocation of a long and deadly struggle ahead. Soon, *Re Carlu*'s governor in Messina, Vicar Orleans, will no doubt receive word of what transpired here. The Angevins will be panting for vengeance and burst upon us. They will sow division among us, show no mercy, and drag us back into the shameful yoke of bondage."

The crowd booed.

"Remember the promise of Conradin!" Aetna cried. "To stop now will be the end of us. *Rebellamentu* is the only path to deliverance."

Aetna turned her head to the large map of the island of Sicily hanging over Mastrangelo's makeshift station by the cathedral's wall. The enormous fabric banner portrayed the three-pointed island with stunning accuracy. The names of cities like Palermo, Messina, Corleone, Trapani, and Siracusa were stitched into the fabric, along with rudimentary visuals of well-known monuments representing each area. Agrigento was portrayed by the ancient Greek ruins of the Valley of the Temples; Erice was represented by the ancient Phoenician citadel built atop the region's highest mountain, and Taormina for its gem of an ancient Greek amphitheater, the *Teatro Greco*.

"Our forces are now sufficient to raise the whole island as far as Messina," Aetna said. "All of Sicily is stained with the innocent blood of our families, yet she is strong. She is strong in the courage of her sons and daughters who stand today, in the ruggedness of her mountains, in the blades of *rebellamentu*!"

"*Rebellamentu!*" thundered the voices of a thousand men in answer to her words.

Aetna turned to Mastrangelo. "Captain Mastrangelo, I ask that you remain in Palermo with a contingent of *Teutoni* Knights to protect the city. Dispatch messengers to all towns and communes, fanning the flames of dissent and rousing them to unite with us for the freedom of Sicily. See to it that

Palermo does not aspire after dominion, but seeks freedom for all."

Captain Mastrangelo bowed his head. "Palermo will be safe as long as my knights protect it."

Aetna looked around the room. All eyes were on her. She tapped a finger against her temple. "*Rebellamentu* is a good idea. And the question you all must ask yourselves is, Will you give your life for a good idea?"

"We will fight!" one man declared.

"For *Sicilia*!" a woman shouted.

All of the rebels and *Teutoni* Knights raised their swords as one. With a marvelous display, the pages were dispatched, moving out in all directions. They would move discreetly and secretly, bringing a fervent message of revolt to the hearts of every church, every piazza, every trattoria.

The rebels raised the red-and-gold banners emblazoned with the Imperial Eagle of Frederick II and the papal Keys of Saint Peter. With the adopted flags of Palermo hoisted high into the air, the rebels marched from the cathedral, their stomping feet reverberating through the marble edifice like clapping thunder.

Aetna beheld the scene before her as she watched the men spread out in all directions. Her heart swelled with pride. *Sicily is ours.*

Shouldering a supply sack, Aetna nodded at *Don Rapaci*, and together they walked out the cathedral doors among the army of rebels.

They never looked back.

BOOK IV

SICILIANA
APRIL 1282

MOUNT ETNA

MESSINA

MEGALITI
DELL'ARGIMUSCO

TAORMINA

MOUNT ETNA

VALLE DEL BOVE

IONIAN SEA

VITICULTURA
VESPIRI

N

W   E

S

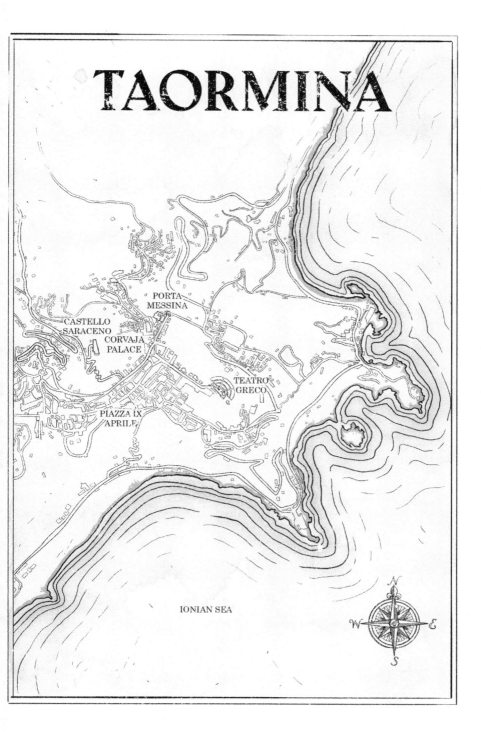

TAORMINA

PORTA
MESSINA

CASTELLO
SARACENO

CORVAJA
PALACE

TEATRO
GRECO

PIAZZA IX
APRILE

IONIAN SEA

AETNA VESPIRI led an army of three hundred Sicilian rebels over the backcountry hills of interior Sicily.

Over the next ten days, the Angevin soldiers were hunted down like wild animals in the dark forests and rugged mountains, attacked and vanquished in the Moorish castles, and chased with such fury that even those who had escaped from under the vengeful Sicilian blade could not find rest.

From the most remote outposts and most impregnable fortresses, the Angevin soldiers observed a single Sicilian woman rising up over the hillcrest, marching in solidarity, her gaze scorching the earth in front of her, her gait strong, her calves tightened like bowstrings. Materializing in the haze behind her, a clustered army of three hundred Sicilians stomped forward over the hill. The Angevin soldiers fled for their lives at the sight of the impending force, some hurling themselves from the highest towers, many surrendering themselves to the very people who had willed them to perish at their own hand.

The Sicilians fought with rancor and fury, engaging the enemy in swift and fluid close-quarter combat so near they could see the blacks of the Angevins' eyes—always en occhinero. There wasn't an outpost or fortress they couldn't overcome.

During one such incident, Aetna's army met a small fortified town built by the Arabs with enormous walls made of strong stone. French noble families had all but occupied the city, evicting the Sicilian inhabitants years prior. With no way through the main gate or over the fortified walls, she formed a brilliant plan. Sitting on a rugged overlook above the town's walls, she noticed many of the estate rooftops were made of straw thatch. And flocks of sparrows had created nests in the houses' thatched eaves.

Aetna observed that during the course of the day, these sparrows would fly from the thatched nests in the town out to the fields below, and then back again as the sun fell in the sky. She directed her men to capture as many sparrows as they could. They then strapped patches of dry grass and wooden splinters to the sparrows' backs, dousing the shrubbery with oil. They lit the makeshift splinter fuses with fire, sending the birds flocking back into the city to their nests in the thatched eaves. Just as she had predicted, the sparrows set the thatched homes ablaze. Aetna and her men stood ready as the gates of the town opened. Panic-stricken, the Angevin nobility fled for their lives from the burning town and directly into the sharp teeth of the Sicilians' blades. Not a single soul was spared.

By the light of the bloodred sunset, the Sicilians attacked Angevin outposts, torched barracks, ambushed sleeping garrisons, and raided prisons, freeing poor citizens jailed for nothing more than their inability to pay an impossible duty to the king.

Rumors about the merciless rebel army spread quickly through the interior as its notoriety only grew with each passing day, whispered from every farm to marketplace. "How many Angevin soldiers would meet the blade today?" became a common morning greeting among carpenters, fruit and seafood vendors, and clergy.

For the first time since hearing of Vespers and the fall of Palermo, the Sicilian people had dared to feel a tingling of hope in their wary hearts.

Tales of murder and intrigue poured out of village churches and trattorias throughout the interior . . . tales of a fearless woman rising from the fires of Palermo, blazing a path through Sicily, and bringing hell to those bastard Angevin soldiers . . . tales of the Siciliana.

—From *War of the Vespers*
by *Don Rapaci*, 1282

CHAPTER 56

Matagrifone
Messina, Sicily
April 15, 1282
9:04 a.m. // Sixteenth day of Vespers

VICAR HERBERT ORLEANS stepped into the war chamber, his face illuminated by the torchlights lining the room. General Guy de Rochefort marched close behind him.

Don Riccardo Riso and the group of Angevin officers were milling about the room, talking among themselves as the two men entered. *Fra'Diavulu* stood at attention against the wall behind Don Riso, ever watchful of his master's safety. The men snapped to attention as Vicar Orleans took his place at the head of the table. Orleans scanned the room with a cold glare, his eyes darting from officer to officer. He noticed his daughter, Manon, was nowhere to be found. He immediately felt agitated by her insolence, then just as quickly redirected his attention back to his men. "What's the news from the western provinces?"

Don Riso stepped forward, clearing his throat. "Nothing more to report, Your Grace."

Orleans raised a suspicious brow. "While leaving Napoli, where I am keeping our interests in the king's favor, they say Sicilian rebels have vanquished Palermo's garrison and taken control of the city."

"Nothing but rumors to incite panic," Don Riso said. "We should be receiving an update from Justiciar Saint-Remy any day now."

A Messinese page burst into the room, carrying a scroll. "Message, sire."

"You see?" Don Riso smiled, beckoning the page in. "The justiciar's timing is impeccable."

The page bit his lip and scrambled forward, handing him the document.

Don Riso unraveled the scroll and scanned its contents. His jaw dropped open, the blood draining from his pale face. "Vicari Fortress has been sacked!" Don Riso squealed.

Orleans furrowed his brow, leaned over, and snatched up the scroll. "Impossible."

Moments later, a group of pages burst into the war chamber, dragging a large, bulbous mass wrapped in bloodied linens. The pages approached the center of the room and dropped the mass onto the table.

The naked corpse of Palermo justiciar Jean de Saint-Remy.

The justiciar's hands and legs were tied. On his bare chest was carved a distinct pattern: three curved lines emerging from a center point. The wound oozed with pus. Horseflies buzzed around him. A parchment note was strapped to his lifeless body.

Hands trembling, Orleans leaned over and picked up the parchment. He slowly opened the letter and read its contents. Orleans's face turned sickly. "These people insult me!" he growled, crushing the parchment in his hands.

"Your own cousin," Don Riso said. "What savage is capable of such a thing?"

Orleans's thoughts raced as he reflected inward. "If they can sack Vicari, they can raid the whole of Messina province."

"You can stop them," Don Riso said.

Orleans glared at the Messinese noble, his face turning bloodred. The vicar snarled and lifted his arm, smashing the back of his hand into Don Riso's cheekbone. "Nothing but rumors, you say?" Orleans growled, drool spitting from his jowls. "Does this look like a rumor to you?"

Riso recoiled, whimpering to himself.

Orleans stared helplessly at Saint-Remy's corpse. "Damn, my impotent cousin."

"What are your orders?" Rochefort grunted from behind.

Orleans shook his head. "This is not an Angevin problem. Sicilians started this; Sicilians will finish it." Orleans turned to face Don Riso. "I want you to quell this insurrection. Or else your passage from this world will be through the portal of oblivion." With that, Orleans thrust a finger toward the neck vise dangling from Rochefort's belt.

Don Riso gulped, staring directly at the torture device. In *Matagrifone*, even the most powerful Sicilian in Messina felt powerless in the face of Rochefort's brute dominance. Don Riso turned toward his loyal knight. *"Fra'Diavulu."*

Fra'Diavulu snapped to attention.

"You are to lead a Messinese contingent of five hundred knights to defend Taormina," Don Riso said. "The king's favored resort city must be protected at all costs."

"Sì," *Fra'Diavulu* said. "What will you do, my lord?"

Don Riso looked at his page. "Summon my naval council."

With that, Don Riso twirled his cape and stormed from the room.

CHAPTER 57

Megaliti dell'Argimusco
Messina Province, Sicily
April 15, 1282
7:42 p.m.

LADY MANON ORLEANS lifted her arm in the air and whipped a Moorish throwing knife into the straw dummy. The blade stuck squarely in the dummy's chest. A small fire crackled at her feet, casting an orange glow across the sheer face of the Praying Woman cliff formation. Obsessive thoughts raced uncontrollably through her mind. *A child is growing inside of me.* She knew she had to tell him, but she didn't know how. *Would* Fra'Diavulu *make a good father?* His apparent disinterest and apathy for the plight of his own people seemed to tell her otherwise.

Manon snatched up another knife from her belt. Holding it steady for a moment, she noticed in the blade's reflection a blurry apparition of a figure emerging from the darkness, his face distorted by the polished metal surface.

Fra'Diavulu stepped forward. "An insurrection has begun."

"I know," Manon said, glancing up toward the target. She bit her lip and threw the knife straight at the dummy, this time puncturing its forehead.

Fra'Diavulu lifted his eyebrows in surprise at her deadly accuracy, then shook his head. "You shouldn't come here anymore. It's not safe."

"I think I'll decide what's safe for me," Manon said.

Fra'Diavulu sensed her pointed tone. "What's wrong? You don't seem yourself."

Manon scoffed, ignoring the question. She adjusted her footing, then threw another knife across the grassy field. The blade whipped through the air and stuck in the dummy's sternum. "Who is she?" she said. "The *Siciliana* they speak of?"

Fra'Diavulu blew a breath from his lips. "We don't know yet. But she fights with the heart of a *virago* . . . a savage."

"Savage?" Manon said. "Then she is no different from my father's men."

Fra'Diavulu pursed his lips and shook his head. "They say she razed an entire city to the ground . . . with fire on the backs of birds."

Manon whipped another knife into the straw dummy. "Good for her."

Fra'Diavulu approached her, taking her palm into his own. *"Spinarosa . . ."*

Manon looked down at his hand, then up to his eyes, yanking her hand from his grasp. "So, what are you going to do?"

Fra'Diavulu pursed his lips and took a deep breath. "I've been ordered to Taormina to protect it from the fury of the insurgency."

Manon's eyes flashed with concern. The ancient cliffside resort city, favored by King Charles himself, had not been occupied by an army since the time of the Norman conquest over two centuries ago. "The Families of Messina are behind this act?"

Fra'Diavulu nodded. "The Messinese nobles have renounced the insurrection, swearing allegiance to King Charles. They agree that the measures to protect Taormina are necessary. I am to leave tomorrow with a contingent of five hundred troops." He paused, seeming to scan his thoughts.

"What is it?" Manon said.

Fra'Diavulu lidded his eyes, his expression turning grim. "Don Riso spoke of a secret operation. The details of which were not disclosed to me. Whatever he is planning, I imagine it won't be merciful."

"Sicilians killing Sicilians," Manon said contemptuously. It was a shrewd act of cruelty to pit a people against one another. She shook her head and moved across the grass to snatch up the blades from the dummy.

Fra'Diavulu seemed to sense her consternation. "This is war, *Spinarosa*. There's nothing I can do about it."

Hearing his words, Manon felt her blood boil. Her hands suddenly became paralyzed, unable to yank the knives out from the dummy's chest cavity. She stood there for a long moment. *You mean there's nothing you* will *do about it.* She gripped a knife and ripped it from the dummy. Standing in silence for a long moment, she gazed with large pale eyes at *Fra'Diavulu* through the knife's reflection.

Fra'Diavulu turned his head. "What is it?"

Manon stared at him for a moment, a dismissive look falling across her face. "I see your meaning," she lied.

She yanked the remaining blades from the dummy's chest and moved over to *Fra'Diavulu*, planting a kiss on his cheek. "Be careful in Taormina. Don't catch a knife in the back."

Fra'Diavulu furrowed his brow. "Everything is under control. The insurrection will be quelled in a matter of days."

A gust of chilly air whipped between them, rustling the surrounding ferns.

Manon sheathed the throwing knives back into her belt. She picked up her hooded cape and wrapped it around her shoulders. "And what will become of this . . . savage woman?"

Fra'Diavulu spoke quietly, gravely. "If your father has his way," he said, "the *Siciliana* will burn at the stake."

CHAPTER 58

Mount Etna, Sicily
April 16, 1282
10:09 a.m. // Seventeenth day of Vespers

A **LIGHT** pillar of smoke drifted slowly from the coned summit of Mount Etna. In the black of night, streams of glowing red-orange lava were visible on the volcano's slopes, the hot molten rock carving forked lines down her mountainside like the crooked lightning bolts from Zeus himself. The temperamental volcano was considered by the locals to reveal glimpses of both hell and heaven. A force of destruction, consuming everything in her path, but also a force of creation, and abundance, providing nutrient-rich black soil for the surrounding farms and villages.

A patrol of Angevin horsemen serpentined along the volcano's black foothills, fully helmeted and armed to the teeth. Cresting the hill, the patrol's captain spotted a dilapidated stone farmhouse manor over the distant ridgeline, surrounded by endless acres of unkempt grapevines.

A decrepit, old vineyard, the captain observed.

A makeshift camp consisting of tents and fires had been built into and around the vineyard grounds, its grapevines wild and overrun. A modest squad of twelve Angevin foot soldiers inhabited the grounds. Far from the major cities and villages, they had been near-oblivious to the horrifying trials their fellow soldiers had gone through in Palermo, Vicari, Corleone, and other interior villages. The soldiers sat around a small fire, roasting pork and chicken and pouring wine for one another, laughing.

The incoming Angevin patrol approached the manor on horseback. The men dismounted and tied their horses to a long wooden post on the fort's perimeter.

"Come, the meat is ready." An overweight sergeant beckoned from the fire.

The patrol captain smiled and motioned to his men. At that moment, one of the patrols ripped off their helmet, revealing long, braided raven hair, blazing green eyes, and feminine features.

A woman.

Aetna Vespiri stepped forward, unsheathing her stiletto and twirling it in her fingers. Her gaze narrowed into a glare.

The full unit of patrolmen suddenly unsheathed their blades and surrounded the Angevin foot soldiers.

The sergeant's eyes widened. *"Siciliens!"*

Don Rapaci ripped off his helmet and grappled the sergeant around the neck, crisscrossing his dual blades against the man's throat, holding them firm against his jugular.

"Sicilian filth," the sergeant growled. "I have a squadron patrolling this region and due to return at any moment."

The Angevin soldiers shot assured glances to one another, nodding and laughing nervously.

"I wonder, Sergeant," Aetna said, pointing to her own chain mail, "if their armor looked anything like this?"

The sergeant's face turned pale. "It can't be . . ."

In that moment, *Don Rapaci* snapped his wrists, slashing his blades across the sergeant's throat. The rebels sprung into action and pounced on the remaining soldiers, running them through with their blades and bashing their heads into the black dirt with wooden clubs.

Suddenly, a single Angevin soldier tore out from behind the manor, hightailing it away on horseback toward the volcanic ridgeline.

"Over there!" a rebel shouted, thrusting a finger toward the rider.

The rider frantically lashed his horse as he galloped across the field, gasping for air, sweat pouring down his forehead.

Biting her lip, young Tziporah snatched up her bow. She pushed through the men, pulling an arrow from her quiver. "He's mine," she said, nocking the arrow into the bow. Tziporah dug her heels into the ground, yanking the bowstring tightly toward her cheek and peering carefully down the length of the arrow shaft. With one eye squeezed shut, she tracked the fleeing soldier with the razor-sharp tip of the arrow, taking aim. She felt the tension of the bow straining her forearm.

"He's getting away!" another man shouted.

"No, he's not," Tziporah said quietly, focusing her concentration. She inhaled a deep gulp of air, held her breath, steadied her aim. She released her fingers from the taut bowstring.

The arrow zipped through the air and smashed into the soldier's back, tearing through his heart. Black-red blood splattered across the gnarly grapevines as the man flew from his horse and hit the ground hard. The arrow protruding from his sternum snapped in half, knocking the wind from his lungs. He painfully gasped for air, writhing in agony for only a short moment before rolling over onto his back, motionless, gazing lifelessly into the sky.

Tziporah lowered her bow and nodded with satisfaction.

The men hoisted their blades into the air and roared as one.

Aetna looked on, her lips curling up into a half smile.

Don Rapaci turned to the men and beckoned to the surrounding grounds. "Spread out and gather all available food and supplies. We make camp here tonight."

The rebels picked up their feet and spread out around the manor.

"You heard the man!" a rebel shouted, clapping his hands. "*Andiamo*, you hapless bastards!"

Don Rapaci smiled. He then spotted Aetna sauntering away by herself among the dilapidated grapevines. He furrowed his brow, gripping his stiletto blades and wondering what danger she had detected.

Aetna let her weapon fall from her hand as she stepped slowly through the brush, allowing her fingers to glide along the tops of the wild leaf shoots. She scanned the terrain intently, looking for something.

Bending down on one knee, Aetna crouched low to the ground and peered through the vine shrubbery. Suddenly, a series of images flashed unbidden through her mind.

A hulking Angevin general sitting atop his warhorse, a grotesque scar running down his face . . .

Patri *tackled by soldiers, his face red with anger . . .*

Cicero kicking and screaming, dragged away into the sulfuric mist . . .

Like a wildcat picking up a scent, Aetna picked up her feet and scurried quickly through the vines toward a clearing ahead. Emerging from the brush, she stopped in an open patch of terrain.

She glanced down at her feet and knelt down at the very spot where she stood. *Patri,* she thought.

She extended her palm downward, touching her fingertips to the black cindery dirt. She squeezed her eyes shut. Hot tears welled up under her eyelids and trickled down her cheeks. *This is where I lost him.* This was the ground where her life came crashing down around her.

Suddenly, Aetna felt a strong hand press into her shoulder.

"Aetna?" *Don Rapaci* said, a concerned tone in his voice. "What is it?"

Aetna turned her head and lifted her liquid eyes up to him, then jumped to her feet and wrapped her arms around him.

Don Rapaci's eyes widened with tense surprise as he felt Aetna squeeze him tightly. He then relaxed his muscles, surrendering himself to the embrace. He pressed his palm to the back of Aetna's head, holding her against his shoulder. *Don Rapaci* wondered what on earth could have triggered such a vulnerable response from such a guarded soul. Then, out of the corner of his eye, he found his answer. Near the dilapidated entrance to the vineyard grounds, a tattered cloth *bannera* flapped from a decayed wooden pole, snapping defiantly in the wind.

Stitched into the *bannera* was the image of the *Gorgoneion Trinacria*, the shrieking face of Medusa with three curved legs emerging from the center. Above the terrifying symbol were two words embroidered in a strong Roman script: *VITICULTURA VESPIRI*.

In that moment, a sudden realization hit *Don Rapaci* like a ton of Moorish stones. They were standing on the fallen vineyard estate of *O Santo Cavaleri*, Sicily's great protector, Don Vittorio Vespiri.

Aetna had come home.

CHAPTER 59

Taormina, Sicily
April 16, 1282
3:22 p.m.

THE MESSINESE knight *Fra'Diavulu* trotted on horseback up the ancient stone path winding up the face of the steep cliff overlooking the sea, a long line of five hundred Angevin soldiers, archers, and heavy cavalry trailing behind him. He craned his neck skyward as he beheld the ancient city of Taormina towering over them.

Settled by the ancient Greeks in 395 BC, Taormina was a majestic eastern city hanging from a steep cliff high above the expansive blue gem of the Ionian Sea. The city once impressed the ancient Greeks, who admired it as much for its beautiful views as for its strategic position over the surrounding terrain. Now it had become Sicily's premier resort city reserved only for the Sicilian nobility and Angevin elite.

Taormina was perhaps best known for its Greek-Roman theater, the *Teatro Greco*, dramatically carved into the cliffs overlooking the city. The open-air theater hosted plays, operas, and concerts for the local citizens. Looming far in the distance on the horizon was the volcano, Mount Etna. Anything but extinct, her violent glowing eruptions provided a jaw-dropping spectacle to those lucky enough to bear witness to them.

The citizens of Taormina sneered in silence as *Fra'Diavulu* and his soldiers entered the city gates on horseback in single file. The Messinese knight was in full battle regalia, his boots shined black, his cape hanging over his broad shoulders, two sharp stiletto blades crossed over his abdomen, his scowling devil mask covering his face, freshly polished.

Fra'Diavulu glanced down at the icy glares and angry faces staring up at him. News of the uprising in Palermo, and the path of destruction being forged by a fearless woman across Sicily's interior, had already reached Taormina's streets. The crowd of people seethed with resentment as they helplessly witnessed armed soldiers entering their shining gem of a city.

The contingent of soldiers shot nervous glances among themselves as they rode up the city's narrow stone streets.

Fra'Diavulu pressed a palm assuredly into one of his blades, scanning the crowd for any signs of threat. The glimmer of a dagger. The flash of a blade.

Don't make me do something we'll both regret, he thought.

Moving through the main piazza, to his left, *Fra'Diavulu* beheld the road leading up toward the famous *Teatro Greco.* He pushed his men forward, passing vendor carts, shops, and trattorias that lined the narrow street. Women and children pointed down from balconies. Long, narrow staircases extended up and down on either side of the road, leading a strolling pedestrian into the labyrinth of side streets and alleys carved along the cliffside.

Suddenly, the main street opened up to an enormous piazza, clinging to the edge of the steep, jagged cliff. The city's prized square, *Piazza IX Aprile.*

Fra'Diavulu's eyes widened in amazement as he beheld the vast Ionian Sea spread out for miles like a smooth sheet of *azzurru* glass. In the distance beyond, Mount Etna was framed perfectly, looming on the horizon. A single smoke trail drifted up from her summit.

Fra'Diavulu continued up the winding streets until the contingent reached the foot of the road leading up to *Castello Saraceno*, the Saracen Fortress.

Built by Arab conquerors, *Castello Saraceno* was a trapezoid-shaped structure perched on the summit of *Monte Tauro*, the highest cliff, looming thirteen hundred feet over the entire city. It was distinguished by its imposing main tower, cistern, and underground corridors carved into the steep cliffs. Living quarters were crude and unrefined. Straw mats. Limited privacy.

Fra'Diavulu reared his horse to stop at the foot of the fortress's staircase, his men forming a semicircle behind him. He looked out over the crowd of Sicilians who had gathered around. He knew he had to say something. "Citizens of Taormina, I promise that no harm will come to you as long as order is kept within these walls."

The Sicilians sneered at their occupiers.

Fra'Diavulu jumped off his horse and snapped open a leather bag. He removed a large sheepskin parchment. He walked to the entrance of a nearby chapel and stretched out the skin along its oaken door. Another soldier moved in with a hammer and nail and pounded the letter into place.

"I want these edicts hung all over town and sent to the surrounding villages, for them to do the same," *Fra'Diavulu* ordered.

As he stepped away from the door, the Sicilian people pushed past one another for a better look. Written in black, inky script, the message read:

In the Name of His Majesty King Charles,
GENEROUS REWARD

For Information Leading to the Arrest and
Execution of the Insurgent Called
"Siciliana"
Signed, Your Royal Vicar Herbert Orleans

Upon reading the edict, one Taorminian man clenched his fist. He felt his heart harden with bitter indignation. The Sicilian people had their first true hero. One who fought for them, for their culture, for their history.

Siciliana *might be a nobody,* he told himself. *But she fights for us nobodies. The Angevins must consider us fools to think we'd betray her so easily.* He would rather burn in hell than turn in an oppressed brother or sister, a fellow *Siciliano* or *Siciliana.*

In that instant, the Taorminian made a decision to invoke an ancient Sicilian code. A code of defiance forged by centuries of foreign invasion, imperial oppression, and abusive authority. A code of deafness and blindness to the affairs of others. A code of silence.

The Taorminian spun to face the crowd standing behind him. *"Omertà!"* he spat, picking up his feet and storming away.

The remaining Sicilians shot pointed glances at one another, nodding their heads in agreement. *"Omertà,"* one woman muttered to another as they dispersed from the plaza.

An Angevin soldier waved mockingly into the air. *"Au revoir, Siciliens!"* he jeered as the Taorminians scuttled away in all directions.

Fra'Diavulu sat silently on his horse, studying the icy faces in the crowd. He was all too familiar with the ancient code of *omertà*. The same code adopted by the outlawed knights of the *Ordu Teutoni* that frustrated his manhunt at every turn.

The Messinese knight shifted in his seat as an uneasy feeling surged through him. It already seemed that the *Siciliana* had achieved victory in the hearts and minds of the people. That not even the prospect of a king's small fortune would turn them against her.

Instead, *omertà* was invoked. The final line of Sicilian defense against the oppressor. And as far as *Fra'Diavulu* knew, it had proved to be unbeatable.

CHAPTER 60

Mount Etna, Sicily
April 16, 1282
9:58 p.m.

THE PALE moonlight bathed Mount Etna's Ilice Crater in a silver glow, the volcano's cone jutting out ominously from the black starless sky.

Aetna Vespiri stood before a large fire, feeling the heat of the flames against her cheek. She watched, transfixed, as *Don Rapaci* seemed to dance ceremoniously in the open field with his golden eagle, Rosalia, illuminated by the bluish glow of moonlight. The eagle passed in large circles above before soaring down among the shards of starlight, beating her mighty wings as she wrapped her large talons around *Don Rapaci's* gauntlet. Smiling, he raised a piece of meat to Rosalia's sharp beak. The feathered beast snatched it from his fingers, taking it down in one gulp.

A dangerous beauty, she thought.

Aetna gazed into the sky for a long moment. She then glanced down to the stone-cutting tablet standing at her feet, a frying pan hanging over the fire nearby.

The piquant aroma of crackling olive oil filled the air.

Tziporah leaned over with a wide grin plastered on her face. "Let's eat."

"*Pacenza,*" Aetna groaned. "Patience."

Aetna smeared a glob of thick, creamy chickpea-flour batter over the surface of the tablet with a wooden spoon. She let the batter set for a few minutes as it cooled in the crisp night air. She then grabbed a knife and carved the firmed batter into squares.

Aetna poured the last of her olive oil into the frying pan. She then detached one of the chickpea squares from the stone tablet and tossed it into the pan. There was a loud hissing sound as the flour dough struck the hot oil. The *panelle* fritter popped and crackled, turning a crisp golden brown. She removed the finished fritter from the pan and placed it between two slabs of bread. She handed it to Tziporah, who immediately sank her teeth into the bread roll.

Tziporah closed her eyes, appreciating the comforting flavors of the hot chickpea fritter coating her tongue. She nodded and smiled.

"*Diliziusu,*" Tziporah said, chewing loudly.

Aetna smiled, enjoying the quiet moment with her friend. She picked up another square and tossed it into the frying pan. There was the sound of crackling oil.

"You used to live here?" Tziporah asked.

"*Sì,*" Aetna said. "A long time ago."

"*Bedda,*" Tziporah said, pondering the expansive grounds laid out on the slope of Mount Etna's Ilice Crater, etched in black against the night sky.

"It was my home," Aetna said.

Tziporah looked up at Aetna. "I'm sorry. No one should ever have to lose their family."

Aetna glanced down at her young friend and nodded, gesturing around the camp. "We're all family now."

Tziporah nodded, smiling to herself. *"Cosca."*

"Cosca," Aetna said.

The other men had spread out around the stone manor, setting up camp. They sat together in large circles, laughing and passing among themselves loaves of bread and bottles of wine left by the French patrol. Darkness had enveloped the surrounding terrain with a blanket of stars. A rebel rider, one of many commissioned as part of *Teutoni* captain Roger Mastrangelo's runner network, approached on horseback, toting a large messenger sack.

"Letters from Palermo!" he shouted as the men jumped to their feet. Adrianu and Gaetano Amici and a swath of dirty rebels crowded around the horse, extending their hands outward like hungry children begging for their evening supper.

Tziporah leapt from her seat and scrambled over to join in on the excitement. She watched as the rider took out carefully wrapped scrolls one at a time, calling each man by name. They reached out and grabbed their letters, eager to hear from their families, wives, mistresses, or any other business they had left behind.

Don Rapaci sauntered over to Aetna at the firepit, carrying Rosalia on his forearm. He presented her with a letter.

Aetna's brow furrowed. "What is it?"

"From one Bartolomeo Maniscalco of Messina," *Don Rapaci* said. "A man of the people with no particular prestige or family status."

"A mere supporter of our cause," Aetna said, pointing to a pile of letters near her tent. "Put it with the others."

Don Rapaci gazed at her for a long moment. Gripping the letter, he pushed his hand forward. "You might want to read this one."

"Why?"

"This mere supporter is also a *Teutoni* Knight."

Aetna's eyes shot open. "The *Ordu Teutoni* are in Messina?" Aetna said. She dropped her plate and eagerly snatched the scroll parchment. Quickly unraveling it, she scanned its contents.

"*Teutoni* Knights are hidden all across the island," *Don Rapaci* said. "Ever since the Teutonic Order was outlawed by *Re Carlu*, they went underground, clandestine, acclimating among the people and regular peasant life."

Aetna cut right to the point. "The *Teutoni* Knights in Messina will help us, then?" she said, her eyes lighting up.

"Not exactly," *Don Rapaci* said.

"Why not?"

"Every day, Angevin ships arrive from France, amassing in Messina's harbor," *Don Rapaci* said. "The companies of infantry arriving daily are brutal and bloodthirsty, the worst of men ready to do *Re Carlu*'s bidding. He is building the most advanced army in the Mediterranean, rivaled only by the great kingdoms of Spain and Constantinople. The people of Messina can barely take a shit without those Angevin bastards ramming their heels up their asses. They'd be slaughtered before they lifted a single blade." *Don Rapaci* paused, his eyes falling to the ground. "Messina will not rise up."

Aetna scoffed. She felt her face become hot, agitated. "The Angevins are cowards. You saw how they hurled themselves from great heights just at the sight of our stiletto blades. They are weak in mind and will."

"Killing scared Angevin soldiers is one thing," *Don Rapaci* said. "But Vicar Orleans is no doubt already aware of what happened in Palermo. He is angry and terrified. And a fearful man with that much military power at his fingertips is a volatile force. We must tread lightly."

Aetna sensed the impossibility in his tone but wouldn't let it seep into her heart. "I guess it could be worse."

Don Rapaci leaned closer. "It is." He pointed down at the scroll parchment. "The letter speaks of a deadly knight they call *Fra'Diavulu.*"

Aetna looked skeptical. "Brother Devil? Is that supposed to frighten me?"

Don Rapaci shook his head. "You don't understand. *Fra'Diavulu* is a cunning, ruthless mercenary. He hunts down and mutilates those unfortunate men suspected of being *Teutoni* Knights."

"Mutilates?"

"He doesn't kill," *Don Rapaci* said. "They say he carries a flaming sword that he uses to severely maim men near fatally."

"But they don't die?" Aetna asked.

Don Rapaci nodded. "The scorching steel immediately cauterizes their wounds. They live out the rest of their days riddled with pain and infection. A fate worse than death."

"*Cristu,*" Aetna said, her gaze turning to stone. "Who is he?"

"A Messinese knight," *Don Rapaci* said. "A dangerous mercenary who sold his soul to the Angevin tyrants. Loyal only to the head of the Messinese Families, Don Riccardo Riso. *Fra'Diavulu* has recently been deployed to Taormina with five hundred Messinese and Angevin troops to protect the city from insurrection."

Aetna nodded. "Then that is where we must go."

"Taormina? Why?"

"We cannot take Messina. As you said, they are much too powerful. Taormina is vulnerable." Aetna glanced up at *Don Rapaci*, a smirk crossing her lips. "A Messinese mercenary, we can handle."

Don Rapaci's face glowed with agreement.

"Besides, attacking Taormina will do two things to our advantage," Aetna said.

"Which are?"

"*Unu.* It's *Re Carlu*'s prized resort city and will make him fester with rage," Aetna said. "And there is nothing weaker than an angry, petulant man."

Don Rapaci snorted. "And two?"

"*Dui,*" Aetna said, throwing up two fingers. "We take Taormina and use the city's strategic position to establish our final defenses."

"Final defenses?" *Don Rapaci* asked.

"Where we make our last stand," Aetna said. "We'll draw waves of Angevin forces out of Messina, one squadron at a time, spitting them from our mouths like venom from a vein. We weaken their numbers until the people of Messina can rise up on their own, as we did in Palermo, and as the people of Sicily will do around the entire island until we can call it our own. As Taormina goes, Sicily goes."

Don Rapaci's breathing became heavier. "*Rebellamentu,*" he said. "You *are* Don Vespiri's daughter." With that, he turned and sauntered away.

Aetna watched as *Don Rapaci* headed back toward a clearing and released Rosalia back into the sky.

Don Vespiri's daughter, she thought. For over a decade, she had tried to bury the loss of her family deep within her. Though that loss hardened like a pit, numbing her to feeling and causing her to avoid real attachment to anything. In that moment, she suddenly felt that was no longer true. *Rebellamentu* made her feel alive. It gave her purpose. Purpose so real, she could feel it humming in her bones. The pit in her stomach hardened so much, it burst into flames.

It was that fire that fueled her now. It was that fire that she knew burned inside her *patri.* In that moment, Aetna felt connected to him, joined by an invisible energy thread stretching through time, bonding their hearts together.

Aetna knew what she had to do.

CHAPTER 61

Mount Etna, Sicily
April 17, 1282
6:01 a.m. // Eighteenth day of Vespers

AETNA VESPIRI gripped a flaming torch in her hand. Her heart pounded as she approached the side of the volcanic hill. She beheld the gaping entrance of the cave and stepped toward it slowly. Extending her hand outward, she brushed aside the wild vines growing freely along its opening.

Patri's *wine cave.*

Following the narrow steps down, she made her way through an arched passageway that opened into a vast chamber. Aetna peered into nothing but darkness. The black of oblivion. She extended her torch forward, throwing red-orange light against the arched walls of the cave. In the distance she saw the ghostly figures of enormous oak barrels stacked on top of one another, lining the length of the cave's walls. The air was thicker down here. The aroma of stale grapes hung in the darkness, stinging her nostrils.

She stepped forward slowly, breathing in the damp air, her feet pressing into the wet stone dirt. As the torch revealed more of the cavern, she finally saw it, sitting quietly against the wall, untouched for years.

Patri's *workbench.*

Slowly, she approached the table. It looked sturdy and untouched. As the day he last left it. She noticed the tablecloth still draped over its legs. She lifted the cloth up and peered underneath. The spot she used to hide in to scare him.

Aetna then noticed a large silver mirror sitting on the workbench, propped up against the wall. She brushed her hand across the metal, brushing way the dust and dirt that had collected over time.

Don Vittorio Vespiri stepped forward out of the darkness, looking at her longingly. Aetna's eyes widened in bewilderment, two large pools glistening in the dark.

"To see you standing there, a grown woman," the ghostly apparition said.

"*Patri?*" Aetna asked carefully.

"*Sì, santuzza,*" he said. "It is I—*O Santo Cavaleri.*"

"I have so many questions. Who am I?"

"You are my daughter—and a *true* Sicilian," *O Santo Cavaleri* said. "The ideals of *rebellamentu* flow through your veins as they did through mine."

"Why is all of this happening?"

"Long ago, in a more enlightened time, Sicily was safe under the guard of the last line of good kings. Prince Conradin and his loyal knights, the *Ordu Teutoni,* governed with honor and respect. They protected our land and the homes of our families. Sicily flourished, accomplished wonders. Great feats of architecture. The Sicilian Poetry School. But then . . ."

"*Re Carlu,*" Aetna said, her face turning sour.

O Santo Cavaleri's gaze narrowed. "The Angevins. Our land was overrun by corrupt men, lustful for power. Seeking new worlds to settle upon, to plunder and molest without shame. Military occupation was established. The *Ordu Teutoni* outlawed. Our natural resources exhausted. As a result, Sicilian families slipped into poverty. Our society became unstable. Eventually, Prince Conradin, the last of his bloodline, staged a counterattack against *Re Carlu*, facing him in battle. But by then it was too late. *Re Carlu*'s forces were far too strong. Prince Conradin was crushed and executed. I foresaw the coming calamity. Then, when you were just a child, a great *Teutoni* general showed up at our homestead, seeking my allegiance in taking up the blade once again. I decided instead to protect what I had left."

"*Cosca*," Aetna said.

O Santo Cavaleri nodded. "My only purpose became to ensure your survival."

A heavy air hung between them.

"This is my wine cave," *O Santo Cavaleri* said. "A sacred place where you decide what kind of Sicilian you want to be. A worker, a warrior. A leader. As time passed, I believed that Sicily lost something precious. Our people forgot the fierceness of *rebellamentu*. The fierceness to define our own destiny against greed, corruption, and evil."

"Against bad ideas," Aetna said.

O Santo Cavaleri frowned and nodded, then snapped his eyes up at Aetna with a piercing gaze.

"But what if a child could dream of becoming something greater than what this island intended for her?" *O Santo Cavaleri* said. "What if a child could aspire to something greater than herself? You were that hope, *santuzza*. That's why I risked so much to protect you."

Aetna's face hardened into a scowl. "You left us to fend for ourselves."

"I did what any father would when faced with an impossible choice."

"What was that choice?"

"My death . . . or yours."

Tears welled up in Aetna's eyes.

O Santo Cavaleri gazed upon her assuredly. "Aetna, you are now as much of a child of Sicily as you were of mine. You embody the best of both."

Suddenly, a rodent scurried, knocking over a broom. A large cloth rolled down from the ceiling where it had been tied up. Aetna turned to see where the commotion was coming from. Then, she saw it. Gleaming in the firelight hung the *bannera* depicting the *Gorgoneion Trinacria*. The shrieking face of Medusa crowned by three bent human legs spiraling out from the center. The ancient symbol of the island of Sicily itself. The symbol her *patri* had adopted as his own. *A true Sicilian heraldry.*

Aetna turned and slowly approached the tattered *bannera*.

"The people of Sicily are lost," *O Santo Cavaleri* said. "But ultimately, they are starving for a leader. You can guide them, *santuzza*. You can show them fierceness. Dare them to live a life without fear. Dare them to live a life *en occhinero*. That's what this symbol means."

Aetna tilted her neck, pondering the pained face of Medusa staring back at her. The once-beautiful *Siciliana*, turned monster, turned myth. *"The Great Protector."*

"Fierceness in the face of our enemy," *O Santo Cavaleri* said. "And embodied within that fierceness, within *occhinero*, is the fundamental belief that every Sicilian can be a force for change."

Aetna took the tattered flag into her hands.

"Your *occhinero* has grown more powerful than I could have ever dreamed," *O Santo Cavaleri* said. "The only way to know how powerful is to keep pushing forward."

Aetna stepped out of the wine cave into a shaft of sunlight breaking through the clouds. She carried the *Gorgoneion Trinacria* flag tied to a long spear. She gazed out over the vineyard, standing tall and holding a long wooden staff, the *Gorgoneion Trinacria bannera* waving stiffly in the air. She tilted her chin upward, exposing her face to the sun, feeling its warmth. She felt a power stirring within her. All of Sicily was inside her now.

Aetna peered out over the vineyard with a harrowed gaze, her hair whipping in the wind.

She heard *O Santo Cavaleri* speaking in her ear. Her *patri's* gentle voice resonating in her mind.

Show the poor families and orphans of Sicily a future to strive toward, he had said. *They may stumble and lose faith. But they* will *rise behind you. They* will *join you in* rebellamentu.

Aetna hoisted the *bannera* into the air. She felt the energy building in her calves, unable to contain it. Aetna burst into a run. She became a blur as she ran like the wind through the vineyard, the flag rising over the top of the vines, flapping defiantly in the wind.

Aetna reached the encampment as men were slowly waking and emerging from their tents. The smell of burning wood filled the air as the men boiled water over hot fires. Reaching her horse, she hitched the *bannera* into the saddle's stirrup. Then she quickly snatched up the flags flying on the perimeter of the camp. She snatched up the flags bearing the Imperial Eagle of Palermo, the heraldry of Prince Conradin. Next, she grabbed the Keys of Saint Peter, the heraldry of the Holy See. She bundled the flags up in a tight roll and shoved them into her horse's saddle.

Aetna jumped up on the horse and gripped the *Gorgoneion Trinacria* flag spear in her hands. She gritted her teeth and lashed the horse's reins. The large steed whinnied into the cold morning air and tore off toward the crater slopes.

CHAPTER 62

AETNA VESPIRI steered her horse up the same slope trail she and her brother, Cicero, used to sneak away against *Patri's* orders. Where she and Cicero used to battle hordes of iron-toy armies, clashing in glorious battles like the perfect knight Orlando and his notorious cousin, Rinaldo. Approaching the crater's summit, she stared down into its steaming cone.

Gripping the flag spear, Aetna leapt off her horse and thrust it into the black soil. Standing tall and holding her chin high, Aetna beheld the *Gorgoneion Trinacria* as the flag snapped defiantly in the wind.

Suddenly, Aetna was thrown violently backward as a burst of soil exploded from the crater and a gigantic geyser of lava gushed from the earth like blood from a punctured artery.

Aetna caught herself quickly and steadied her footing. She slowly approached the edge of the crater. The red-orange geyser sprung into the heavens, heating the air around her face. The heat was powerful. Invigorating. She lifted her fingers to the crescent-shaped scar on her right cheek—a scar from the lava. In that moment, Aetna felt her heart crack open. A stream of thoughts rushed through her mind.

I've forgotten much about my childhood years, but I remember the lava . . .

The roaring fountain of red molten rock erupting from the black earth . . .

The glowing orange serpents slithering down the flanks of the volcano . . .

Deliberately . . .

Violently . . .

Yet in the path of its devastation came new growth from the ugly soil. New life. A new era . . .

Aetna yanked the bundled flags of old from her horse's saddle and in one fell swoop whipped the bundle into the erupting lava. The bundle instantly burst into flames. Aetna's eyes flashed with fire as she watched the flags of old burn. The Imperial Eagle of Palermo, the Keys of Saint Peter, totally and utterly consumed by the lava.

Aetna inhaled a deep breath and let the roaring sounds of the eruption wash over her. She knew deep in her bones that the time of kings and conquerors was coming to an end. And as the flags of old went, so would her name. Aetna Vespiri would be no more.

I am lava, she told herself. *I am* Siciliana. And while she, an orphan, had lost her own family, she would fight to protect all Sicilian families and orphans so they could live together in a nation of their own . . . *forever.*

A sulfuric gust of wind blew up the side of the mountain, billowing the *Gorgoneion Trinacria* flag.

Suddenly, *Siciliana* sensed another presence on the volcano with her. She slowly opened her eyes, noticing a figure moving just behind her from her periphery. In that instant, three large men emerged from the sulfuric haze, moving toward her, three razor-sharp blades extended forward.

Siciliana's gaze narrowed. The three men weren't bandits. They weren't Angevin soldiers who might have somehow been patrolling the terrain. They were Sicilian rebels. Men from her own army.

The three men approached slowly, their pointed blades closing in on *Siciliana* from all sides.

"We have a message from Archbishop Malu," one man growled as the three turncoat rebels crept forward.

Siciliana glared at the approaching men, furrowing her brow tightly over the bridge of her nose. She took a deep breath, then slowly closed her eyes, remaining still. The sounds of the approaching men faded as she heard only her breathing. She gently ran her hands across both of her own blades.

One man adjusted his footing into a striking position.

"Burn in hell, bitch."

CHAPTER 63

THE THREE rebels snapped their blades forward at once.

Siciliana's eyelids drifted open. She felt time slow to a crawl, the sound of her escaping breath echoing through the air, sending puffs of silver clouds from her mouth, then . . . a blur of motion.

Everything had happened so fast, but all the men really knew was that *Siciliana* had leapt to the attack. Within seconds, *Siciliana's* blade whistled through the thick air, catching the three blades and locking them together. Then just as quickly, she snapped her arms outward and slashed her way through the men's jugulars in one fell swoop. Dropping their weapons, all three gripped their punctured throats, gargling viciously as they choked on their own blood.

Siciliana crouched over the three men, poised elegantly with her bloodied blades, her chest heaving.

As her vision readjusted, the men's faces materialized through the haze.

Siciliana loosened the grip on her blades as they slipped from her fingers, clanging to the ground. Her sadness was suddenly replaced by betrayal and rage. Gnashing her teeth, she gripped one rebel's collar. He was barely grasping on to consciousness.

"Where is the archbishop hiding?"

The man didn't speak, gripping his neck tightly to prevent the outpouring of his precious sanguine fluid. He glanced over to one of the other rebels, who had already stopped struggling. He had choked on his blood instantly.

"I don't know," the man said.

"Liar!" *Siciliana* said, pushing his head into the dirt. "You've already betrayed yourself. Will you also betray our families, our orphans?"

The man glared into *Siciliana*'s eyes, laughing through his bloody mouth.

"Speak!" she said.

"Don't you understand? The pope is loyal to *Re Carlu*. Whether from fear or promise of power, no one knows. But there will be no help from the Holy See. Nor will he endorse our cause. We're all alone now. It's us against the world. *Rebellamentu* is doomed."

"You lie!" *Siciliana* screamed.

The man spat blood, then shook his head, struggling to speak. "The Holy See denied an audience with Mastrangelo's diplomatic envoy. Instead, he issued a papal bull affirming *Re Carlu*'s right to retaliate and reclaim his dominion over Sicily."

"Where is this papal bull?" *Siciliana* pressed. "Have you seen it?"

"Malu has it . . ."

Siciliana gripped him by the collar, pulling him close. "Where is he hiding? Tell me!"

The man seemed to struggle to focus his vision. "He fled to the *Villa Romana del Casale*," he sputtered. "The villa ruins are heavily guarded. Attacking it is suicide. It's a fortress unto itself."

"Just like Vicari?" *Siciliana* sneered.

The man looked her in the eyes for a long moment, then released his own grip from his neck. Blood streamed down his chest, forming a black pool in the dirt beneath his head. He smiled as the life drifted slowly from his eyes. "*Vaffanculu . . . Siciliana,*" the man said before slumping, lifeless, in her arms.

Siciliana craned her neck backward and roared in anger. She took deep breaths, attempting to slow her racing heart that thundered against her rib cage. She glanced up to see the shrieking face of Medusa etched into the *bannera*. The black hole of the Gorgon's mouth gaping open, her eyes wide and filled with rage.

Siciliana's eyes filled with resolve as she beheld Medusa— the once-beautiful *Siciliana* turned victim turned monster— glaring back at her. She dropped the man to the black soil with a thud and rose to her feet. She took a step forward, slowly approaching the *bannera*. Suddenly, she remembered her *patri*'s words as if he had whispered them right into her ear: *No matter where a Sicilian is thrown, they always land standing.*

Siciliana slowly raised her gaze, her eyes two steely blades cutting through the sulfuric haze. She clenched her fists. Her breathing became more measured. She stared into the *bannera* waving defiantly in the wind, backlit by the roaring fountain of lava spewing from the crater's black soil.

Tonight, Archbishop Malu had a date with destiny.

CHAPTER 64

Matagrifone
Messina, Sicily
April 17, 1282
8:16 a.m.

THE CHAMBER was heavy with mist and steam. Behind a maze of silk screens, Lady Manon Orleans reclined in a warm milky bath. Her handmaiden, Genevieve, sat at her side, replenishing the bath with hot water from a nearby boiling crucible, while simultaneously pouring in aromatic lemon and floral oils. Manon stared forward, lost in her thoughts. "Can you I ask you a question?"

"Of course, milady," Genevieve said.

"Do you miss our home in Anjou?"

"Sicily is our home now," Genevieve said, running hot water over Manon's shoulders. "And one day, you will be countess of Angevin Sicily."

"Angevin Sicily," Manon said. "Tell me, would you want to bring a child into an Angevin Sicily?"

"I suppose I wouldn't," Genevieve said. "Not without a few changes first."

Manon nodded her head. She ran her hands slowly over her abdomen. Her thoughts reeled toward *Fra'Diavulu*. "I must go to him. He must know."

"The road to Taormina is dangerous," Genevieve said.

Manon glanced toward the open window, a shaft of sunlight pouring in from above. She observed her rack of Moorish throwing knives leaning against the wall, next to her riding boots. She smirked to herself. "So am I."

An hour later, Manon stepped from the bath and into her dressing chamber. She emerged wearing a long robe, arranging her wet ashen-blond hair into braids. "Genevieve, have you seen my . . ."

Manon came to a hard stop and let out a loud gasp. General Rochefort stood silently in her room.

He bowed his head, feigning an air of reverence.

Manon cinched her robe tightly around her body, feeling a chill run up her spine. "General, what are you doing here?"

Rochefort noticed Manon's throwing knives lying next to a pile of neatly folded riding gear and boots. "Planning a trip?"

"I don't know what you mean."

Rochefort eyed her suspiciously, seeming to sense her insolent tone. "The Sicilian insurgency is growing. I have ordered the closing of *Matagrifone*'s gates and am instituting a permanent curfew. No one will leave or enter these walls until this insurrection is ended. Punishable by imprisonment."

"I trust you have the situation under control."

"I have seen to it personally that four of my elite guards keep watch outside your chamber. For your safety."

If he thinks his guards can stop me . . . , she thought. "Whatever you say, General."

Rochefort moved around her. He watched the beads of water trickle down Manon's long neck and into her robe. His nose seemed to linger on the natural, sweet scents of her hair and skin. "You will either make the best of wives, or the very worst." Rochefort lifted his hand and placed the tips of his fingers gently on her shoulder.

Manon winced at the touch of his hand.

"I often consider all that you and I might accomplish together," he said quietly. "For Angevin Sicily."

Manon felt her insides twist at the mere thought of it. "If you'll excuse me, I must be on my way." With that, she picked up her feet and left the room.

Rochefort watched her leave. He then noticed something sitting next to her bedside table. An artifact that looked vaguely familiar. He approached the bedside table and hovered over it for a long moment. A book of poetry. With a stupid Sicilian title.

Contrasto.

Rochefort glared at the book, remembering exactly where he had last seen it. Clenching his teeth, he quickly snatched it up. Then turned on his boot heel and exited the room, his cape swirling behind him.

CHAPTER 65

Villa Romana del Casale
Piazza Armenia, Sicily
April 17, 1282
11:59 p.m.

THE ICY night wind whipped off the hills and into the valley below. A damp mist blurred the flaming torches and softened the various angles surrounding the massive ruins of the *Villa Romana del Casale*. Much of the villa had been destroyed nearly a century earlier, though at the present moment, the ruins of this once-extravagant estate made for a well-positioned and fortified outpost for the Angevin garrison overseeing the commune of Piazza Armenia.

Completed by the Romans in the early fourth century, the ancient villa was once an expansive single-story complex built around an enormous open-air courtyard. The estate contained various staterooms, gardens, a gymnasium, baths, and a basilica accessed through a majestic entrance divided by two Egyptian columns. The enormous ruin was perhaps best known for its intricate mosaic floors that covered over thirty-two thousand square feet.

The mosaics depicted a variety of scenes, from big-game hunting to sexual debauchery. But perhaps the most famous of them all was a series known as the *Coronation of the Winner*, consisting of young Roman women running, throwing discuses, and competing in athletic games. They wore scantily clad two-piece garments, with a top to cover the breasts, and underwear cut below the navel. The Romans effectively created the earliest known depiction of the *bandeaukini*, or *bikini*.

Two Angevin guards, Liam and Alexandre, patrolled the mosaic-floored hallways near the former open-air entrance of the villa ruins. Alexandre stood watch, staring out into the dark night, a layer of cool mist drifting ominously across the surface of the ground. The orange glow of torchlight did little to illuminate the expansive villa ruins, creating black voids among the estate's various hallways, staterooms, and *triclinia*. Even for a trained soldier like Alexandre, the unknown haunts of the dark wilderness terrified him.

Liam crossed the hallway from the other direction and came to a stop near a dark stateroom chamber. He turned his head, peering vigilantly out into the night. The only sound he heard was the howling of the wind through the surrounding hills. He then turned his back to the darkness of the chamber mere feet behind him. Suddenly, he felt a strong grip at his back and was yanked into the void with an echoing yelp.

Startled, Alexandre spun around. "Liam?"

There was no reply. Furrowing his brow, Alexandre unsheathed his rapier and stared down the long hallway into the black mouth of the chamber. He moved slowly down the corridor, his boots falling lightly over the colorful mosaics laid out at his feet.

"Enough of your games," Alexandre called out again.

Nearby, a third guard came around the corner, his sword drawn. The two men exchanged careful glances.

Suddenly, something heavy whooshed through the air from the shadows.

The approaching guard gasped, as if the wind had been knocked from his lungs. He looked down, horrified to see the tip of a large blade extending out from his sternum, creating a gaping wound at the base of his rib cage. Then the tip of the blade retracted and was gone. A pool of blood quickly expanded from the center of his torso.

Alexandre gazed on, terrified, as the soldier collapsed forward onto the hard stone floor. "Alarm!" Alexandre shouted as he felt a tight grip squeeze around his face. Suddenly, his chin was yanked sideways, a sickening snap echoing through the corridor.

In the villa's basilica at the far end of the complex, Archbishop Salvatore Malu had set up a makeshift workstation, where he pored over various dispatches from *Matagrifone*. Vicar Orleans had already set up a basic runner network to communicate with the archbishop, his former top agent from Palermo. A secret convoy had been deployed from *Matagrifone* to rendezvous with Malu and escort him back to Messina, where he would ultimately receive safe passage to Napoli, where a station serving the king's church would be waiting for him.

Suddenly, a soldier ran in, sounding an alarm.

"What is it?" Malu grumbled.

"Something's wrong out there. Possibly an intruder."

"You have swords, don't you?"

"*Oui*, Your Grace, but—"

Malu raised a swift hand, agitated. He was surrounded by one of the best Angevin units Vicar Orleans could provide, and they couldn't even take care of whatever trifling business was transpiring outside. Malu reached into his cloak, pulling out a stiletto. "If you want something done right . . . ," Malu muttered as he stormed from the basilica.

He and the other soldier went separate ways as they moved down the mosaic corridors toward the center of the complex.

Malu lifted his blade to hip level, hearing a commotion down the hall. He moved swiftly toward the central peristyle courtyard. He rounded a corner and observed about ten soldiers clustered together in a defensive circle, peering out anxiously into the dark.

Suddenly, a shadow dropped from the rafters above, landing in the center of the group. The soldiers scrambled backward, screaming in fear. Malu barely glimpsed a dark figure moving in the middle, severing the jugulars of his men one by one, each falling to the ground, tongues flailing as they choked on their own blood.

Malu's eyes widened in horror. He turned on his heel and bolted down the corridor. He ran outside and hobbled toward the equestrian stable. As he approached the stalls, his heart jumped into his throat at the grisly sight before him. All of the unit's horses lay lifeless on the ground, slaughtered mercilessly where they had stood.

There would be no escape.

Thinking fast, Malu unsheathed a rapier hanging from the saddle of one of the dead horses and ran back into the villa ruins. He stumbled down the corridor and turned into the basilica.

Suddenly, a shadow moved through the air and tackled Malu to the ground. Two muscular arms gripped him by the collar and yanked him upward, bringing him nose to nose with wild green eyes revealed in a shaft of moonlight.

A savage woman crouched over him like a mountain lion. Her raven-black hair was braided intricately above her head, so as not to interfere with her movement. Her face dripped with red-and-yellow war paint, bisected diagonally down the length of her face—red on the top half, gold on the bottom. Her teeth were bared like fangs. The shrieking face of Medusa with three bent human legs was embroidered over a red-and-gold pashmina wrapped around her chest.

Malu stared at the ferocious figure. "Who the hell are you?"

"I am *Siciliana*," the woman growled through her teeth.

Malu scrambled for his rapier with his free hand. He sure as hell wasn't going down without a fight. But in that moment, his fear was suddenly replaced by a keen look of recognition. He squinted in the darkness, peering closer.

Don Vespiri's daughter.

"You . . . ," he said. "Do you think you can alter the world? You're as mad as Vespiri."

"Don't you ever say his name!" With that, *Siciliana* lunged forward, smashing the top of her forehead into Malu's nose. The archbishop screamed as he heard the hideous crunch of bone reverberate through his skull.

Siciliana yanked him closer. "It is true?" she demanded, shaking him by the collar. "Did the pope refuse our plea for protection?"

Malu's face contorted in anger. He knew his men had talked. Malu lifted a heavy finger, pointing to the letters on his desk. "Read it for yourself."

Siciliana glared into his eyes. She thrust him to the ground and sauntered over to the wooden desk, snatching up the parchment and unrolling it in her hands. The letter was stamped with the Keys of Saint Peter, the heraldry of the Vatican.

Siciliana quickly scanned the contents of the letter, feeling her heart sink into her stomach. She read that the Holy See refused to acknowledge the Sicilian people as a sovereign state. He then declared *Re Carlu* within his right to retaliate against the Sicilian insurgency and reclaim his property by blood, if necessary.

In that moment, *Siciliana* felt the entire weight of the world on her shoulders. The worst was upon them now. They were truly alone. Sicilians against the world. The most powerful army in the Mediterranean. Like the three hundred Spartan warriors with their backs against the seawall, they were now on *terra morte*. Death ground. But like the three hundred Spartans, she knew that was when the truest of warriors had to dig in and fight.

Siciliana let the papal bull slip from her hands onto the table. She glanced down at Malu's desk. She noticed another letter sitting among a pile of parchments. This one was stamped with the *fleur-de-lis*. She pushed the other papers aside and picked up the letter. Her eyes widened in horror as she scanned its contents, which landed like shards of glass in her gut. As if matters couldn't get any worse, they just had.

Vicar Orleans had approved a Messinese naval strike against Palermo.

Siciliana stared at the letter in disbelief. *Our own brothers.*

Malu struggled to sit up. He cackled as he turned to face *Siciliana*. "Your little rebellion is finished," he spat through a bloody mouth.

Siciliana gnashed her teeth, clenching the letter in her fist. With her other hand, she slowly unsheathed the stiletto holstered to her thigh. There was the sound of scraping metal as the blade emerged from its scabbard. She slowly turned her head toward the wounded bishop, her eyes turning black.

Malu felt a corkscrew of fear run up his spine as he watched the humanity drain from the woman's eyes, leaving nothing but the empty shell of a cold-blooded murderer. Suddenly, he saw the shrieking face of Medusa lash toward him.

Malu's mouth gaped open. He wanted to scream, but *Siciliana* moved in, swinging her blade to stop the scream.

To kill the scream.

A convoy of elite Angevin infantry arrived on horseback at the entrance to the *Villa Romana del Casale*. The villa was disturbingly quiet. Archbishop Salvatore Malu was supposed to rendezvous at this location for protected extraction to Messina, where a ship for Rome had awaited him.

The convoy's commanding officer lifted his fist, signaling his men to halt.

"Where is everyone?" one soldier called out.

"Quiet," the officer ordered. By the pale light of the moon, the officer carefully scanned the terrain, attempting to detect any signs of danger.

"What is that?" another soldier yelled, thrusting his finger toward the villa's entrance.

The officer spotted a dark figure hanging from the rafters, swaying and creaking in the icy breeze by a gnarly rope. As the officer trotted closer to take a better look, the figure began to take shape in the darkness. He observed a large, rotund man with red hair, stripped completely nude. His throat was slashed open, leaving nothing but a gaping wound of bloodied, hanging flesh. His eyes were frozen in a state of shock, gazing lifelessly as his corpse swung to and fro. Finally, the officer realized whom he was looking at.

Archbishop Salvatore Malu.

The officer squinted even further, detecting what looked like a strange mark carved into the man's chest: three curved lines emerging from a center point. But it was what the officer saw next that drained the blood from his face. Just behind the dead bishop lay a pile of corpses stacked in a neat pyramid.

"My God," he said to himself.

Malu and the entire Angevin squadron of the *Villa Romana del Casale* had been slaughtered.

CHAPTER 66

Viticultura Vespiri
Mount Etna, Sicily
April 18, 1282
8:13 a.m. // Nineteenth day of Vespers

DON RAPACI tore down from the mountainside on horseback, approaching the vineyard encampment. *Siciliana* stepped forward to greet her approaching friend, her face dripping with red-and-yellow war paint. Tziporah and the rest of her men were scattered around the encampment, gathering up their tents and supplies.

"It's true!" *Don Rapaci* shouted, an urgent tone lacing his voice. "Our spies in Cefalù confirm that Messina has ordered a fleet of galleys to strike Palermo harbor, led by the head of the Messinese Families, Don Riccardo Riso himself." *Don Rapaci* looked down at her with a harrowed gaze. "Their arrival is imminent."

Siciliana felt her face set on fire. Unbelievable that times were so desperate, they would find themselves fighting their own brothers. She clenched her fists and lifted her eyes to *Don Rapaci*.

"Take the men and continue on toward Taormina," she ordered. "I'll meet you at the *Valle del Bove* in two days' time."

Don Rapaci nodded grimly, turning his horse around.

"Wait," *Siciliana* said, before running back into her tent.

Don Rapaci lowered his brow in confusion.

Siciliana emerged carrying a bundle in her arms, neatly wrapped in red-and-gold cloth. She carefully lifted the bundle up to her friend. "Take this with you."

Don Rapaci leaned over on his horse and grabbed the cloth bundle, gently hoisting it onto his lap. As he looked down at it, he saw hints of Medusa's face peeking through between the folds. He knew exactly what treasure she had just entrusted to him.

"Your *bannera*?" he said, a twinge of excitement in his voice.

"Sicily's *bannera*," *Siciliana* corrected him. "I've added a few finishing touches this morning that I think you'll appreciate."

Don Rapaci grinned from ear to ear. He pressed his fist to his chest. *"Rebellamentu."*

"Rebellamentu," she responded in kind.

With that, *Don Rapaci* lashed his reins and tore off into the field.

Siciliana watched him ride for a long moment, then jumped into action. She holstered her blade and strapped her personal effects to her horse's backside, tightening the leather ties in place. She then hoisted herself onto the back of the large beast.

Siciliana looked down at Tziporah. The two Sicilian women gazed at one another for a long moment. "Mount up and follow me," *Siciliana* commanded.

"Where are we going?" Tziporah asked carefully.

"We ride for Palermo."

"Only the two of us?" Tziporah squeaked. "Shouldn't we take more men?"

Siciliana flashed her a cold look through the red-and-yellow war paint smeared across her face.

Tziporah knew in that moment her friend was dead serious. She quickly gathered her weapons and supplies and jumped up on a horse.

Without saying another word, *Siciliana* looked at her and nodded grimly. *"Ammunini!"* she shouted, lashing her horse and tearing off.

CHAPTER 67

Cattedrale di Palermo
Palermo, Sicily
Seralcadio District
April 18, 1282
12:32 p.m.

TWO YOUNG spotters, siblings Concetta and Donato, peered down from the soaring bell tower of Palermo Cathedral. The tall spire jutted high into the sky like a sharp pike, overlooking the entire city. This vantage point provided a 360-degree view that extended far out into the green countryside beyond Palermo's city stone walls. Lying directly north was the flat horizon of the Mediterranean Sea, a sheet of pristine blue glass stretching to infinity.

Sitting alone in the belfry, the two young Sicilians, about ten years old, had sprawled out comfortably, each digging into a bowl of hot *pappardelle alla bolognese* delivered by a runner minutes earlier. The siblings groaned with delight as the warm, savory flavors of fresh tomato, olive oil, and cooked meats churned in their satisfied guts.

"I still don't believe you," Donato mumbled with a mouthful of starchy noodles.

Concetta lifted her eyes and glared at him. "Why would I lie?"

Donato smirked as he twirled the yellow noodle ribbons on his fork, shoving an entire bite into his mouth and chewing obnoxiously. "You mean to tell me that the *Siciliana* attacked a town by magically creating birds made of fire?"

"That's not what I said, *babbu*," Concetta shot back. She clenched her teeth, her eyes filled with annoyance for her brother's thickheadedness. "She seems to possess a special power."

"A power?" Donato said, raising an eyebrow. "You mean like a goddess?"

Concetta nodded, gazing down at her pasta bowl, picking at the noodles with the tip of her fork. "The way she uses her mind. She uses it like . . . a weapon."

Concetta retreated into her thoughts. The stories she had heard of the *Siciliana* overcoming impossible human odds excited her more than any Greek myth or Arabic fairy tale she had heard as a little girl. A long moment passed before she noticed the silence lingering in the air. Donato hadn't responded. Glancing up, she noticed his gaze was fixed on something far in the distance just over her left shoulder. "Are you listening to anything that I said?" she snapped.

Suddenly, Donato's jaw dropped open.

"What are you looking at—?"

Before Concetta had finished her thought, she was already craning her neck back over her own shoulder, peering out toward the horizon. Her hands trembling, she lost her grip on the ceramic pasta bowl. It fell into her lap and crashed to the floor, smashing to pieces. In that moment, she knew her worst nightmares had been realized.

"Concetta?" Donato muttered.

Without hesitation, Concetta sprung to her feet. She wrapped her small hands around the gnarly rope tied to the gigantic iron bells hanging above them. *"Andiamo,* Donato!" she yelled. "You must alert Captain Mastrangelo!"

Donato dropped his pasta bowl and leapt into action, diving for the belfry ladder and disappearing down the hatch below.

A bead of sweat forming on her forehead, Concetta bit her lip and yanked down on the bells' rope with all of her strength.

Clang! Clang! Clang! The earsplitting clamoring of the cathedral's iron bells resonated out over the entire city.

War was upon them.

CHAPTER 68

STANDING IN the nave of Palermo Cathedral, *Teutoni* captain Roger Mastrangelo quickly donned chain mail and forearm gauntlets. He then slid his shining white tunic emblazoned with a black cross neatly over his armor. A page handed him a long, polished sword. Mastrangelo raised it up in front of his face, admiring the steel sheen of the blade. He nodded and thrust the blade into a scabbard hanging from his belt.

The unforgiving Sicilian sun beat down from overhead as Mastrangelo exited Palermo Cathedral. He tightened his sword's holster around his waist and pushed his way onto the *Cassaru*. The ancient road carved a direct path from the cathedral to Palermo's monumental city gate called *Porta Felice*, which had served as the main seaside entrance to the city. Mastrangelo's vice-captain, *Teutoni* Knight Enzo Baverio, struggled to keep pace behind him as a throng of panicked Sicilian men and women scrambled to and fro across the muddy road and among the narrow passageways and alleys.

"Our runners can confirm that eleven warships have launched from Messina," Baverio said, briefing the captain with the little information he possessed.

"Messina, you say?" Mastrangelo shouted over his shoulder, pushing relentlessly through the crowd. "Who leads them?"

"Don Riccardo Riso," Baverio responded. "Head of the Messinese Families."

Mastrangelo dug his heel into the dusty sand, stopping dead in his tracks. He flashed his vice-captain an astonished look. "Our own brothers?"

Baverio nodded gravely.

Mastrangelo shook his head in disbelief. *After all we've been through these past two weeks, how did it come to this?* "God has abandoned this forsaken island," Mastrangelo said before tearing down the main road toward the harbor.

Baverio made the sign of the cross and scurried to keep pace with the captain.

Approaching the main gate, the two men passed through the enormous structure built of brown Arab stone. Upon exiting the city, they saw Palermo's expansive golden beaches suddenly come into view, disappearing into the blue sea that stretched endlessly into the horizon. The sun shimmered off the water like the exotic sapphire jewels of Queen Constanza of Aragon's royal tiara. To their left, the crown-shaped peak of *Monte Pellegrino* rose in the distance, materializing on the horizon through the salty haze.

Mastrangelo slammed to a stop, shielding his eyes from sun as he peered out toward the sea. There it was. A sight that made his blood run cold—the massive Messinese naval fleet slowly lurching up over the horizon.

"Do we know how many men?" Mastrangelo asked. As soon as the question left his lips, he knew he didn't want to know the answer.

Baverio swallowed a lump in this throat. "Two hundred, sir . . ."

"That's manageable," Mastrangelo said.

"Per ship. That's two thousand men strong."

We are not prepared for this, Mastrangelo thought. The *Teutoni* captain turned to Baverio with a grim look in his eyes bordering on desperation. "Muster every able-bodied man, woman, and child strong enough to carry a weapon. Our resolve must be as fierce as it was on Vespers night. We've faced these odds before, and we will again today."

Baverio stared blankly at his captain for a long moment.

"Ammunini!" Mastrangelo yelled.

With that, Baverio spun on his heels and tore off.

Mastrangelo stood quietly as he observed the approaching ships, getting larger on the horizon with every passing second. He estimated they'd slam upon Palermo's beaches in less than an hour.

An army of *Teutoni* Knights and Sicilian rebels swarmed around Mastrangelo, clustering into groups and preparing for the imminent naval strike. Mastrangelo watched the large doors of the city gate slowly crank closed, the groaning of ancient wood echoing through the thick, salty air. With their backs literally against a wall, there would be no retreating from this fight. Men and women scrambled to and fro, arming themselves with *stiletti*, clubs, swords, spears—the same weapons used two weeks earlier on that fateful Vespers night.

Mastrangelo saw men helping their sons put on homemade armor and gauntlets. Women scraped large rocks against the edge of their swords, sending sparks flying as they sharpened them to a razor point.

There was the sound of screaming children, their fear-stricken shrieks echoing from within the city's stone walls. Stray dogs darted through the streets, yelping through the pandemonium.

Directly above, Mastrangelo watched a group of women with their daughters spread out along the top of the exterior walls carrying bows and arrows, digging into strategic positions to help provide elevated cover. He knew in his bones that all of the citizens of Palermo had everything to lose on this day.

Mastrangelo sauntered solemnly down the line of his army, *Teutoni* Knights and Sicilian *cavaleri* standing side by side. He noticed a small boy of about twelve years standing alone, a long Angevin rapier trembling in his hands, his gaze trained at his own small feet.

The *Teutoni* captain walked up to the boy and touched the tips of his fingers under his small chin, lifting it gently upward. The boy looked up with fearful eyes.

"What is your name, son?" Mastrangelo asked quietly.

"Ignaziu, son of Luciu," the boy whimpered.

"And where are your parents?" Mastrangelo replied.

"Dead, sir."

Mastrangelo gazed at him for a long moment. He felt his heart tearing in two. *What on earth is this young boy doing out here alone, in the face of certain death?* "Do you have any other family left in Palermo?"

Ignaziu nodded. He lifted a trembling finger and pointed to the Palermo Cathedral bell tower, a tall spire jutting up from the distant skyline. "My little brother and sister. Watching over us from the bell tower."

Mastrangelo squinted up at the tall spire, and then lowered his eyes back down to the boy. "You're the man of the house now," he said in a fatherly tone.

"*Sì, Capitano*, I am all they have left," the boy said, lifting his chin. "I must protect them."

Mastrangelo gazed down at the boy for a long moment. *The heart of a true knight.* He extended an armored hand. "Let me see your blade."

Ignaziu gazed up at him before lifting the blade to the captain. "I stole it from an Angevin corpse on Vespers night," the boy said.

Mastrangelo smirked at him, gripping the hilt tightly in his palm. He swung the sword quickly up toward his own face, then swirled it in a figure-eight pattern. The blade whistled through the air with every strong swing. He then rested it lengthwise on the tip of his forefingers, testing its weight. Perfectly balanced. "This is a good blade," he said. "It will not fail you." He then spun the blade around and extended the hilt back to the young boy, who reached out with his small hand.

Ignaziu looked up with concern in his eyes. "The men are saying all is lost. That we will not survive to see the sunset."

Mastrangelo placed an assuring hand on the boy's shoulder. "We are Sicilians," he said. "If there's one thing our long history has taught us"—Mastrangelo flashed him a quick wink—"it's that we always survive."

Ignaziu nodded and grasped the rapier's hilt, squeezing it tightly in his palm. He then pressed the hilt proudly to his chest and looked up at Mastrangelo, wiping the tears from his face with his other hand.

Suddenly, a spotter sitting along the wall perimeter poked his head over the battlement, thrusting a finger to the street below. "Riders approach!" he shouted at the top of his lungs.

Mastrangelo peered down the length of the *Cassaru* through the slit of the closing city gates. His eyes widened as he raised a fist high into the air. "Stop! Open the gates!"

The order was passed up the length of the wall until the gears started grinding the doors back open. A rebel carrying a handful of swords stumbled up behind Mastrangelo. "Could it really be?" the rebel muttered.

The aggressive milling of knights and men ground to a halt as they gazed in fascination upon the imposing figure approaching on horseback.

A sudden burst of elation erupted behind Mastrangelo's eyes as he beheld two riders approaching. An immense feeling of resolve overtook him.

Palermo has a fighting chance.

CHAPTER 69

THE FRIGHTENED Palermo citizens swarming on the *Cassaru* parted like the Red Sea, watching in fascination as two women emerged on horseback and rode through them, toward the city gate.

Gripping the leather reins, *Siciliana* swayed confidently on the saddle as her large warhorse moved through the dirty street, its enormous hooves sending out plumes of dust with every step. She gazed down the length of the road leading to the sea. Her face dripped with red-and-yellow war paint, her hair braided up away from her neck, her long stiletto strapped tightly to her abdomen.

Siciliana carried a long spear mounted in her stirrup. Tied to the tip of the spear was a large *bannera* snapping briskly in the wind.

The flag gleamed red and gold, the colors bisected diagonally, red on top, gold on the bottom. Emblazoned onto the dual-tone fabric was the heraldry of the *Gorgoneion Trinacria*. And between each bent leg of Medusa were stitched three new symbols. Symbols that hadn't previously existed there before. *Siciliana's* finishing touch. Between each bent leg was stitched the crude image of an artichoke bud, the *cosca*, their sharp petals gleaming defiantly from the *bannera*. Sicily was nothing without *cosca* . . . without family.

Siciliana called her final masterpiece *Bannera dâ Sicilia* . . . Sicily's flag.

Tziporah Solazzo trailed steadily behind her, her bow and quiver hanging from the side of her horse. She glanced down to see the men and women scatter in front of them, looking up with wide eyes.

Fathers held their daughters and mothers held their sons as they watched Sicily's great hero pass before their very eyes. A young girl watched in awe and pumped her fist into the air as the two warriors moved through the street.

As *Siciliana* approached the stone archway of the *Porta Felice*, the endless expanse of the sea came into full view. She beheld an enormous fleet of warships quickly approaching on the horizon.

Teutoni captain Roger Mastrangelo moved up to meet her.

"Can you believe it?" Mastrangelo shook his head. "Sicilians willing to fight their own kind for those Angevin bastards."

Siciliana shot him a grim look.

"Messina's families are starving, *Capitano*, like ours," she said. "There is no man more desperate than one whose hunger is not only in his own famished gut, but in the miserable bellies of his children. He has a fear beyond any other."

Mastrangelo nodded his head in agreement, gripping the hilt of his sword for comfort. "Damn them for forcing us into this position."

Siciliana raised her liquid green eyes toward the horizon. With each passing second, the fleet of Messinese galleys drew closer. She quickly lashed her horse and galloped toward the front of the *Teutoni* and rebel army amassed on the shoreline. As she passed the men on her horse, each brave Sicilian drew his own sword, spear, or whatever arms they had scrounged up over the past weeks since seizing Palermo.

Siciliana turned toward the crowd. "Spread out and gather all of the Messinese flags that every home, church, and vendor can spare. Bring them back here immediately, and pass them out among one another."

The rebels shouted in agreement as they scrambled in all directions.

Siciliana turned to Tziporah, flashing her an assured glance. Shifting in her saddle, Tziporah squinted back at her with a look of concern, forcing a smile.

Siciliana sat quietly on her horse. The muscular beast released a soft snort, becoming restless as men and women armed with swords and clubs moved anxiously into position around her. Patting the horse gently on the neck, *Siciliana* lifted her gaze to the approaching fleet.

Tziporah watched in silence as Mastrangelo and his cavalry of *Teutoni* Knights mounted up on horseback and set off to the other side of the harbor, extending their numbers as far as humanly possible. She then noticed a band of five women dressed in black move to the front of the line, their heads wrapped in black cloth and each gripping long, polished stiletto blades. Years prior, Angevin soldiers arrested and executed each of their husbands, and ever since the Vespers uprising, the five women had banded together in their own protective *cosca* to protect the only home they had left—each other.

"What now?" Tziporah whispered.

Siciliana glanced at her. She then tapped the side of her finger to her temple. "Trust me."

A long line of Sicilian rebels stood at the ready on the shoreline. The men and women of Palermo gripped their weapons tightly, shifting anxiously at the awesome sight of Messina's naval force bearing down upon them.

Siciliana held her breath and waited. A moment of truth was before her. Like a Greek temple ruin, the *rebellamentu* was faltering, collapsing on itself . . . and who better to uphold it than a *cavaleri* always *en occhinero*.

CHAPTER 70

Mediterranean Sea, Route to Palermo
April 18, 1282
1:14 p.m.

DON RICCARDO RISO stood at the bow of the lead galley, watching Palermo's harbor materialize in the far distance. An unstoppable force to reckon with, his fleet of eleven Messinese war galleys moved in a pyramid-shaped formation, carving their way through the choppy waters of the Mediterranean Sea toward the main port of Palermo. The enormous wooden war vessels were adorned in armor plates, three massive sails towering above, and each with forty long oars that extended out from the ports and carved their way through the water. Each ship carried a crew of two hundred Messinese sailors, totaling an army of over two thousand soldiers strong—a fearsome sight to any unsuspecting spectator from the distant shoreline.

Despite his notorious reputation as a naval hero, Riso had always feared the day his naval strength would be pitted against the people of his own island. No stranger to dangerous odds, he had earned his fame two decades prior when he had dared launch a strike with merely a few vessels against an enormous Pisan fleet.

On this morning, Riso charged forward into battle once again, prepared to lose his honor and his immortal soul in civil war against his own people, albeit wanted criminals against the crown.

Today we fight our own brothers and sisters, he thought. *When this is over, I will leave my inheritance to my sons and retire to Amalfi, spending my final days collecting rare artifacts and tending to my lemon groves.*

He looked as if his personal attendant had polished him to a fine luster. Exquisitely dressed in a crimson Messinese naval officer uniform, Riso tightened the rapier scabbard hanging at his side. *Battle-ready.*

Riso pressed his palm onto the wooden banister and closed his eyelids. He had been awake for almost twenty-four hours, restless, mentally preparing himself for the massive task that lay ahead. He ordered a full attack on Palermo harbor. He would then force a blockade, restricting all further harbor activity, travel, and commerce. If he struck quickly and mercilessly, he knew this impending insurrection could be swiftly crushed.

Riso took a deep breath, attempting to loosen his muscles. He carried a heavy hesitation in his heart. Like most everyone in Messina, he had heard of the horrifying acts of violence that took place in Palermo a fortnight earlier.

Riso shook his head, clearing his mind of troubling thoughts. He lifted his gaze slowly to the horizon. As Palermo's harbor drifted closer into view, in an instant he beheld a sight that sent a chill up his spine.

He had heard the stories before departing Messina but often questioned their authenticity. Stories of a savage woman who had led an army of Sicilians across the island's interior, carving her way through French soldiers like a knife through tender lamb meat, and perceived as such a threat to the French Crown that a generous bounty had been set for her capture or death.

Gazing out toward the harbor, what he observed was as real as the sturdy, wooden hull of his ship. A woman, sitting high atop an imposing warhorse, her stone face drenched in yellow-and-red war paint, a long, curved sword strapped to her back.

Riso felt a thick lump lodge somewhere beneath his Adam's apple. In that moment, he knew deep in his bones that he was entering the hardest fight of his life, not only because of Palermo's brute ferocity, but because of something much more terrifying.

He was going to war with the savage, *Siciliana*.

CHAPTER 71

Palermo, Sicily
April 18, 1282
1:26 p.m.

Siciliana REINED in her restless horse, bringing it to a stop on the edge of the sandy beach. She turned back toward the men and women forming ranks behind her. She could see the fear in their eyes. Returned from the city, a drove of citizens carried folded Messinese flags that they started passing out among the crowd and throwing up to those perched on the walls.

Siciliana raised her fist. The rebels fell silent.

"Daughters and sons of Sicily!" she shouted.

A deafening roar rumbled through the Sicilian ranks. *Siciliana* smiled, feeling as if her *patri* were whispering in her ears. She felt him moving through her as she spoke words that came as easily from her mouth as her own breath. "Two weeks ago, we showed the world our true strength," she shouted. "In a moment's time, the forces of Messina will slam upon these very shores. To give up hope now will only bring destruction. Our forces are sufficient to raze this whole island." She thrust her finger out toward the impending fleet. "The hearts of Messina, our own brothers and sisters, must not belong to the enemy."

And the army of Sicilians united in an uproar that made the ground shake, thrusting their fists high into the sky.

"Rebellamentu!" they screamed in union. Every man, woman, and child felt the thunderous roar reverberate deep in their chests, their hearts pounding as they realized they were part of something bigger than themselves, bigger than their history.

Tziporah looked on in awe as the entire harbor surged with energy. A proud smile crossed her face. She turned back to face *Siciliana* and moved up beside her. Together with two hundred men, they marched forward onto the expansive beach, where the Messinese contingent was approaching. Gripping her reins, she took in a deep breath as she watched the warships slowly approach the harbor, her muscles tightening with apprehension.

I hope she knows what she's doing, Tziporah thought.

CHAPTER 72

TWO THOUSAND Messinese troops were massed above deck on the imposing battle fleets now sitting in Palermo's harbor. They stood in ordered ranks—archers, infantry, lancers. It was the largest army that Messina had mustered with the single purpose of total assault—an army unlike the people of Palermo had ever seen. The Messinese weapons and armor were polished and expertly worked, gleaming in the blinding sun.

The rebels' armor was not nearly as advanced, with makeshift breastplates and helmets made of rawhide, leather, and heavy cloth. Some wielded fragile, heirloom swords passed down from generation to generation; some carried sharp tools once used for farming, now turned into weapons of war. The people of Palermo always made do with what they had. Their confidence held in the integrity of the weapon's wielder more than the weapons themselves.

Down on the beach, Don Riccardo Riso approached on horseback, leading a squadron of Messinese troops. The soldiers marched forward, flying the *banneras* of both Messina and the golden *fleur-de-lis*, the heraldry of their Angevin overlords.

The *Teutoni* Knights and Sicilian *cavaleri* fell silent.

Don Riso approached carefully. He knew his soldiers had superior weapons and training, but he had also heard of *Siciliana*'s unpredictable barbarity and the macabre fate of Justiciar Jean de Saint-Remy.

Siciliana rode forward to meet Don Riso in the middle of the beach, her red-and-gold-painted face made of stone. Both armies were lined up directly behind their leaders, primed for battle. Don Riso's weaselly face scowled with indignation at the defiant woman before him.

"In the name of the royal vicar Herbert Orleans, you stand to face punishment for your crimes against *Re Carlu* and the glorious Angevin Crown," Don Riso shouted.

The line of rebels shifted and grumbled. They shot anxious glances toward one another, gripping their blades tightly and digging their heels into the dirt.

Siciliana didn't flinch. *You first.*

Don Riso continued to spit his menacing threats like venom. "Those who survive here today will be dragged back under the shameful yoke of bondage from which they came. And those who perish shall have their heads removed from their pathetic corpses and piled upon these very shores."

Siciliana glared at the vile don. She then lifted her gaze to the lines of Messinese infantry massed behind Don Riso.

"Brothers of Messina!" she shouted into the enormous group of soldiers. "Have you forgotten that we share the same history, the same language, the same past shame and present strength?" She pointed back toward the walls of Palermo. "Right now, all of Sicily is stained with the blood of our Angevin tormentors. She is strong in the courage of her daughters and sons, in the ruggedness of her mountains and ruins, in the protection of her seas that are her embankments. We will never go back to the oppression and atrocities that *Re Carlu* has inflicted upon us."

The Messinese soldiers shifted. *Siciliana* noticed the men exchanging concerned glances.

"Remember, we are Sicilians!" she continued. "And that he or she who draws a single blade on this beach is a traitor to their own nation. A Sicilian nation! Let us instead combine our arms and go forth together against our tyrant oppressors, as one. Together, we can take back our past. Together, we can seize our future. Together, we *will* dare to live in *rebellamentu!*"

At that moment, the rebels hoisted the heraldry of the Cross of Messina among their ranks on the beach and dropped the flags down from the city walls. The Messinese soldiers watched in fascination as the *banneras* of their home city were strung up and hoisted high above the harbor like a well-timed marionette show. The flags were tossed up to the windows of homes overlooking the beach and draped majestically over their balconies. In a matter of minutes, the entire harbor was draped in the *bannera* of Messina.

Two cities united as one.

The Messinese soldiers were taken aback by this sudden and valiant display of unity.

Don Riso bared his teeth and craned his neck back toward his men. "Hold your position! We cannot allow ourselves to be deceived by—"

Suddenly, a Messinese soldier shoved past him, knocking the wind from Don Riso's lungs. The Messinese soldier walked slowly to face *Siciliana* sitting on horseback. He gripped the hilt of his rapier and pulled the sword slowly from its scabbard. There was the long, sharp scraping of polished metal. Then, just as soon as he removed the rapier, he thrust it blade-first into the cold sand. He then gazed up at *Siciliana* and pressed his closed fist into his chest.

Another Messinese soldier emerged behind him, and then another, and another.

The soldiers pushed past Don Riso. One thousand swords sang as they were ripped from their scabbards and slammed into the sand.

At first, the *Teutoni* Knights and rebels looked on warily, fearing it was a trick. But seeing the Messinese soldiers unarm themselves one by one, they holstered their own weapons and approached the soldiers on the beach.

Siciliana looked on in satisfaction as the rebels moved past her to join the Messinese soldiers. Both lines of warriors approached one another in the center of the beach, extending their hands outward and opening their arms. Hands clasped hands. Soldiers and peasants met one another with a hearty embrace. They exchanged personal effects, gauntlets, badges, buttons. Cries of joy and Sicilian songs erupted among the ranks. The Messinese infantry docked their enormous warships, the men piling down the gangplanks to join the celebration.

Tziporah watched the men come together with a bewildered look plastered to her face. She then slowly turned her head toward *Siciliana*, gazing upon her in admiration.

From across the harbor, *Teutoni* captain Roger Mastrangelo and his cavalry of knights looked on with a slack jaw, watching the events unfold as if in slow motion.

The men and women standing along Palermo's wall embankments marveled at the miraculous display of peace unveiling before them.

Ignaziu Luciu slowly lowered his sword, his face softening.

Siciliana pulled back the leather reins and spun her horse around. Gripping the Sicilian flag in her stirrup, she hoisted it high in the air and thrust it into the sand. The flag sliced into the ground and flapped defiantly for all the world to see.

Siciliana flashed Tziporah a knowing smirk before kicking her heels into her horse's ribs. The horse snorted and took off toward the city wall.

Tziporah stared at her for a long moment, trying to process what had just happened. Snapping out of her trance, Tziporah lashed her horse and quickly moved to keep up with her friend.

High above Palermo in the cathedral's bell tower, young Concetta peered out over the scene, her bright eyes wide in bewilderment. She watched *Siciliana* ride away from the beach as if in slow motion, making her way through the city gates and down the length of the *Cassaru*, where a chorus of roaring applause greeted her.

Siciliana had helped save thousands of lives.

Concetta's face beamed as she watched *Siciliana* disappear into the crowd. She moved away from the bell tower's edge, spotting a long rapier leaning against the side of the wall. The sword was nearly twice her size. She slowly unsheathed the blade, holding it in front of her face with two small hands. A shaft of sunlight struck the blade's surface, casting a thin beam of golden light across her small face. *Siciliana* had suddenly conjured a feeling within her.

For the first time in her short life, Concetta felt the strange sensation swelling in her heart.

Hope.

CHAPTER 73

Matagrifone
Messina, Sicily
April 19, 1282
8:41 a.m. // Twentieth day of Vespers

AN ALARM rang out. Lady Manon Orleans darted from her bedroom chamber to meet a crowd of soldiers, handmaidens, and servants gathering near the main gates of the fortress. The large swath of people milled around the gates, pushing one another to get a better look at the source of the commotion.

Manon approached the gates and pushed her way into the crowd. Moments later, her eyes widened in horror. The grisly sight before her would haunt her dreams for the rest of her days.

Archbishop Salvatore Malu's mutilated, nude corpse lay sprawled across the stone.

Manon clasped her hands in front of her mouth. Gazing upon the maimed corpse, she immediately knew the truth deep in her bones. No one was safe from the savage woman they called *Siciliana*. Not even the privileged Sicilian archbishop, sanctioned by the pope himself, who all had thought was truly untouchable. And now the question remained for all at *Matagrifone*: Who would be next?

"My claim over this realm suffers because of Malu's incompetence," Vicar Herbert Orleans said, pounding his fist on the table. "These people insult me!"

Vicar Orleans sat at the head of a long table in the war council chamber, surrounded by Angevin officers. The mood in the room was tense and explosive. General Guy de Rochefort loomed behind Vicar Orleans, exuding his hulking dominance.

Manon Orleans stood in the corner of the room alone, her back pressed against the wall, her hands clasped. "Quite impressive for a woman they call a savage," Manon said under her breath.

Orleans craned his neck to face Manon, his eyes bulging from his head. "My insolent daughter," Orleans growled to himself, his jowls shaking like a dog's. Orleans snapped his head to one of the Angevin officers sitting around the table. "What of Riso's operation in Palermo?"

The officer cleared his throat. "Foiled, my lord."

"Foiled?"

"The Messinese soldiers refused to fight their own kind. Palermo is lost."

Orleans's eyes flashed with anger. He glared down his nose at the officer.

The officer shifted in his seat.

Orleans slammed his hand down, knocking over the military figurines sprawled across a map on the table. "Riso, that worthless fool. I should have never sent a Sicilian to do a Frenchman's job."

Orleans fumed for a long moment, staring down at the map spread out on the table. Suddenly something in his eyes seemed to change. He slowly turned toward General Rochefort and beckoned him forward. The hulking general approached the vicar, his heavy boots scraping the stone floor with each step.

"End this," Orleans said.

General Rochefort loomed over the war council. "This savage has the people's loyalty. They protect her. They protect each other. I can capture her for you. But to do so will require the use of certain practices."

"What practices?" an officer challenged.

Rochefort glanced over to Manon with a scorching glare, his black eyes void of all humanity, filled with bloodlust. "Total extermination," he said, letting his eyes linger on Manon.

Manon kept her chin high but felt herself shrink under his gaze.

Rochefort turned back to face the war council. "Sicilians are a dirty people with dirty blood. Blood of gypsies. Savages. I will cleanse this dismal island of every last one of them," he said, raising his gauntlet and closing his fist. "When I'm finished, it will be as if they never existed at all."

CHAPTER 74

Taormina, Sicily
April 19, 1282
4:04 p.m.

THE MESSINESE knight *Fra'Diavulu* sauntered out onto the perimeter wall, pressing his palms against the ledge. He glanced up toward the sky to see an enormous golden eagle circling above among the roiling clouds, creating a sweeping shadow that moved across the perimeter wall. The eagle shrieked down from overhead.

Fra'Diavulu lowered his gaze to the east and spotted something moving up the road. It was a large *bannera* fluttering briskly in the wind, carried on horseback. The rider, dressed in black from head to toe, a cloth wrapped around his face like an Arab warrior, came into view.

Heading directly toward the *Porta Messina*, Taormina's main gate to the city, the rider carried a long spear he had mounted in the stirrup. Tied to the spear's tip was the red-and-gold *bannera*, embroidered with the shrieking face of Medusa, three bent human legs, and three *cosca* buds.

Angevin soldiers fanned out along the perimeter embankment with their swords drawn. Archers fell into formation and swiftly nocked razor-sharp arrows and drew their bowstrings.

The rider in black cantered slowly toward the main gate, the large and unusual flag waving defiantly, then reined his horse to a full stop. The golden eagle circled above before swooping down to perch on the rider's gauntlet. From the perimeter wall, a hundred arrows pointed downward, all aimed directly at the rider's heart.

Fra'Diavulu noted hints of the rider's features beneath a Saracen war mask in the shape of a falcon's beak. He had curly black hair, a beard, and olive skin. Two stiletto blades crossed over one another on his abdomen.

"Who are you, and why are you here?" *Fra'Diavulu* said.

"I come to you carrying *Bannera dâ Sicilia*—Sicily's flag—with a message from one *Siciliana*."

Fra'Diavulu's eyes widened. *Siciliana?*

The men along the perimeter exchanged anxious glances.

An Angevin soldier leaned over to *Fra'Diavulu*. "You know what she did to my brothers at Vicari?"

Fra'Diavulu raised a hand to silence him. "Open the gate."

"Sir?" the soldier asked.

"I'm going down to meet him," *Fra'Diavulu* said. With that, he lowered his mask.

· ❦ ·

Don Rapaci sat upright, his head held high, as the gates of Taormina groaned open. *Fra'Diavulu* emerged from the city gates, two Angevin guards at his side. The soldiers cautiously approached his position and came to a stop.

"I understand you have claimed the name *Fra'Diavulu*," *Don Rapaci* said.

Fra'Diavulu straightened his stance and stared forward through his scowling mask. "I claim nothing."

"Except for the right to oppress our people," *Don Rapaci* said.

An Angevin guard leaned over and growled to *Fra'Diavulu* in French. "A dirty Sicilian dog. Let our archers strike him down where he stands."

The other guard bellowed with laughter.

Not missing a beat, *Don Rapaci* summoned his best French and responded in kind. "I would gladly die a thousand deaths rather than serve your king."

The two guards looked on in astonishment.

"What message do you bring?" *Fra'Diavulu* said.

"*Siciliana* demands your immediate surrender of the city," *Don Rapaci* said.

Fra'Diavulu shook his head. "I'm afraid you rode all of this way in vain. This is the king's favored city."

"If that is your position, I'm afraid you and your men will perish in a day's time," *Don Rapaci* said.

Fra'Diavulu scoffed, lifting his chin. "Tough words for a man with one hundred arrows pointed at his heart."

Don Rapaci lifted his gaze to the walls above. Archers lined the length of the perimeter, their sharp arrows gleaming in the sunlight. He was unfazed. "*Siciliana* is camped at the *Valle del Bove* on the volcano, Mount Etna," he said. "She will wait for you there."

With that, *Don Rapaci* gnashed his teeth and lashed the reins of his horse. With a loud cry, he spun the beast around, kicked it hard in the rib cage, and galloped away.

Fra'Diavulu watched as the rider in black galloped away at breakneck speed, his flag flying overhead. As the rider disappeared down the winding road, a single thought gnawed at the back of *Fra'Diavulu*'s mind. He knew what he had to do. *I must meet her.*

Fra'Diavulu turned to face his men. The entire garrison looked on in silence, eyes blinking, anticipating his orders. *Fra'Diavulu* scanned the perimeter wall, his eyes moving from man to man. "Ready the garrison. We ride at dawn."

CHAPTER 75

Valle del Bove
Mount Etna, Sicily
April 20, 1282
7:38 a.m. // Twenty-first day of Vespers

THE *VALLE DEL BOVE*, or Valley of the Ox, was a gargantuan horseshoe-shaped crater on the eastern slope of Mount Etna. Numerous glowing fissures and explosive steam vents along the crater's flanks produced slow-moving lava flows, ejecting ash and lava debris with great force. For centuries, these dangerous flows threatened roads, farming, and the safety of villages surrounding the volatile region.

Siciliana and Tziporah rode their horses toward the front of the Sicilian rebel army of three hundred men assembling on the stark expanse of black volcanic soil. To *Siciliana*'s left, a glowing river of red lava serpentined down the side of the crater, and on her right, steam vents exploded and hurled rock and ash at random intervals, raining down debris over the gathering rebels. As the rebels took up their positions, *Don Rapaci* rode up to meet *Siciliana*. He was clothed in black, his face wrapped behind a dark cloth revealing only his harrowed eyes.

"You brought us to the gates of hell," *Don Rapaci* said, glancing around the horseshoe-shaped crater closing in on all sides.

Siciliana smirked and gazed forward, concentrating on the task at hand.

On the opposite side of the volcanic field, *Siciliana* observed a knight sitting high on horseback, surrounded by a unit of over five hundred Angevin infantry stacked ten rows deep. An impressive, imposing sight. The knight wore a steel war mask, obscuring his entire face. A flexible curtain of chain mail was attached to the skull of his helmet and extended downward to cover his throat and neck. His polished armor gleamed silver in the hazy sunlight. He had already begun to ride out to the center of the field.

Don Rapaci moved up beside *Siciliana*. "*Fra'Diavulu*."

"He intends to strike terms," *Siciliana* said. "I will ride out to meet him."

Don Rapaci nodded. "You are not alone. We stand with you."

Siciliana flashed him a keen look.

With that, *Don Rapaci* extended a long spear to her. Tied to its tip was *Bannera dâ Sicilia* that she had given him only days earlier. "Sicily stands with you."

Siciliana stared at the flag for a long moment. She reached out and gripped the spear, accepting the *bannera* the same way she had accepted her fate in defining a nation she now found herself leading. She carefully couched the spear firmly into her saddle's stirrup. A short breath snorted out from her horse's nostrils into the sulfuric, volcanic air.

Siciliana gritted her teeth and lashed her horse, cantering up the long line of men. She thrust the spear into the air, displaying the *bannera* in full glory, urging her men to make some noise. The entire army of scrappy rebels howled, their hearts swelling with pride. They cheered for the *bannera*. They cheered for their new nation. A Sicilian nation of their own.

"*Rebellamentu!*" the rebels thundered, shaking the soil beneath their feet.

Siciliana reared her horse back, flashing an assured look to *Don Rapaci* and Tziporah. She then turned to face the imposing Angevin forces looming across the valley.

Siciliana's heart pounded as she stared down the steely spectacle of the most brutal army in the Mediterranean. The fate of her people was now solely in her hands. She took a deep breath and lashed her horse, tearing off toward the center of the battlefield, gripping *Bannera dâ Sicilia*.

The bold Sicilian flag snapped in the hot wind as *Siciliana* rode out to meet the notorious masked knight known as *Fra'Diavulu*.

CHAPTER 76

Fra'Diavulu **PEERED** out over the black charred land. Glowing red lava serpentined down the side of the crater, slithering slowly around them like a viper of destruction. Steam vents expelled hot ash and volcanic rocks, launching debris high into the air. Hot projectiles flew through the air and crashed into the soil, exploding loudly throughout the valley, reminding him of the Saracen stones hurled against the walls of Jerusalem when it was seized during the Holy Crusades.

Siciliana has brought us to hell, he thought.

Fra'Diavulu tightened his grip on his horse's reins and lifted his gaze to the opposite end of the battlefield. He witnessed *Siciliana* riding down the lines of her men as they roared with anger. She then holstered the flag in her stirrup and turned her horse toward the center of the valley.

"Now is our chance," an Angevin officer whispered. "Send an arrow directly into her heart."

"Hold your fire, Sergeant," *Fra'Diavulu* ordered.

"With all due respect," the officer said, "she murdered Justiciar Saint-Remy, the king's own cousin."

"*Silencieux!*" *Fra'Diavulu* barked. "I will ride out to meet her."

Fra'Diavulu gazed forward through his devil war mask as *Siciliana* approached the center of the battlefield. Even through the yellow-and-red war paint dripping from her face, he could see the fire in her eyes, scorching the earth in front of her. She had a look in her eyes he had seen only once before, while hunting *Teutoni* Knights. *The look of blind belief.*

Fra'Diavulu kicked his heels into his horse and galloped forward to the center of the battlefield.

The two diametrically opposed warhorses snorted breaths of hot air from their large nostrils as their riders approached one another from opposite ends of the volcanic valley.

Fra'Diavulu stared through the rolling black dust and observed the shape of a woman materialize into view.

Out of the dust rode *Siciliana.*

The savage woman was clothed in leather armor, her face dripping with red-and-yellow face paint, a long stiletto holstered to her abdomen. In her right hand she grasped a mounted spear that displayed the same grotesque *bannera* he had seen a day earlier at the gates in Taormina: the shrieking face of Medusa with three bent legs emerging from behind her head, and emblazoned with three *cosca* buds.

Fra'Diavulu slowly rode closer, rearing his beast to a stop in front of *Siciliana*'s horse so they were nearly nose to nose.

Fra'Diavulu inched forward, looking closely at the fierce insurgent as they glared silently upon one another. The Messinese knight decided to speak first. *What does one say to a savage?*

He took a deep breath and chose his next words carefully.

CHAPTER 77

Siciliana **inched** forward on her horse and glared at the knight, his face hidden behind the polished war mask, the image of Satan grinning back at her. This was a truly professional soldier, a pure agent of carnage.

But then again, so am I.

"These are my terms," *Fra'Diavulu* said. "Lay down your arms on this battlefield, surrender yourselves as my prisoners, and none of your men will die today."

Siciliana spat at the ground where the knight's horse stood. "I have terms for *you*. Surrender Taormina and declare Sicily a free nation."

"That's impossible," *Fra'Diavulu* said.

"*Silenziu!* I'm not finished," she shot back. "You will declare Sicily a free nation, and then march straight back to the sea from where you came, stopping at every Sicilian farm along the way to beg forgiveness for years of oppression, rape, and murder."

Fra'Diavulu held his ground. "I don't have the power to give such an order."

"*Vaffanculu.* Then you and your Angevin dogs will burn in hell."

Fra'Diavulu, unshaken, spoke with an assured tone. "If you lay down your arms, I can help you negotiate a surrender."

"You mean submission," *Siciliana* barked. "Slavery."

Fra'Diavulu shook his head. "Listen to me. You have slaughtered over three thousand of *Re Carlu*'s soldiers, including French civilians, and his own cousin. You have yet to taste the full power of his retaliation."

Siciliana felt a surge of anger course through her veins. *How dare he threaten me?*

Fra'Diavulu continued. "It is only a matter of time before you are crushed under the weight of the largest military the Mediterranean has seen since the Roman Empire. If you surrender to me now, I will help you bring terms to the royal seat of Messina."

Siciliana's heart pounded. These words only enraged her even more. She gazed at the Angevin army over the knight's shoulder; they were armored and at full attention. She then glanced back at her own band of scrappy Sicilian rebels, not nearly as armed or protected. However, she knew their true weapon was their resolve.

Siciliana turned back toward *Fra'Diavulu*. "If you ride against my army, you will be shown no mercy."

The two warriors glared at each other for a long moment.

"Who are you?" *Fra'Diavulu* asked.

"I am Sicily." With that, *Siciliana* reined her horse in, steering it back toward her army. A deadly calm fell over the battlefield. *Fra'Diavulu* nodded his head as he gripped the reins on his own horse.

"So be it," he said with a hint of regret. "*Simmo surfaru.*"

Siciliana suddenly pulled tightly on the leather reins, bringing her horse to a stop in its tracks. *Those words.* They gnawed at the back of her mind, sounding awfully familiar.

They were words she half remembered from a lost childhood. Words she heard the vineyard workers speak to one another. Bad words that her father told her never to speak again.

We are nothing but sulfur, she told herself.

Sitting on her horse in the middle of the volcanic valley, *Siciliana* craned her neck and turned back around, staring into *Fra'Diavulu's* scowling war mask.

Summoning all of her emotional strength, she opened her mouth to speak, daring to utter only a single word.

"Cicero?"

CHAPTER 78

FRA'DIAVULU'S JAW dropped. He watched as the savage warrior pressed her palm against her left cheek, smearing away the red-and-yellow paint from the surface of her bronze olive skin. As the paint wiped away, he saw it.

A crescent-shaped scar.

Fra'Diavulu felt his heart explode inside his chest as if smashed with a battering ram. He slowly pulled off his mask, revealing his black curly hair and large hazel eyes.

"Aetna?" he gasped.

CHAPTER 79

SICILIANA'S EYES rapidly flooded. A single tear fell from her eyelid and trickled down her cheek. The stunned Messinese knight gazed back at her.

"Say his name," *Siciliana* said.

"What?" *Fra'Diavulu* said.

"Say *Patri's* name."

Fra'Diavulu's chest heaved in and out, seeming barely able to contain himself. "Don Vittorio Vespiri."

"And his favorite marionette show?" she said.

"What is the meaning of this?"

"Say it!"

Fra'Diavulu stared at her for a long moment. *"The Song of Orlando."*

Siciliana couldn't believe what was happening. As a child, she dreamed of living in a time as valiant and honorable as Orlando's. And now here she was, on the slopes of Mount Etna, in the greatest kingdom in the world, staring down her own brother in a battle of the ages. A battle worthy of the greatest marionette epics of Sicilian generations to come.

And here she was, like the perfect knight Orlando, faced with protecting that which she loved most from her own kin.

"Aetna, we don't have a lot of time," *Fra'Diavulu* said, his tone sounding more urgent. "Our men think we are negotiating terms, and will expect a result."

Siciliana snapped her focus back to the present moment. "My terms stand firm. Surrender Taormina and declare Sicily a free nation."

Fra'Diavulu shook his head. "That will lead only to more violence, more death."

Siciliana growled. "I will vanquish every last Angevin soldier with air in his lungs, so help me God."

Fra'Diavulu looked up into the dark sky, desperately seeking an answer, when suddenly he was struck with an idea. He glanced back down, his gaze sharpening. "What if we work together?"

Siciliana stared at him.

"You will surrender to me," *Fra'Diavulu* continued. "I'll take you and your men into my custody. We'll move out immediately to Messina. Vicar Orleans is a weak man. He is on the brink of insanity due to this insurrection you started. The mere sight of you bound and chained would immediately lower his defenses. Upon entering *Matagrifone*, you and your men will slaughter every last soldier inside, just as you did in Palermo, in Vicari, ending the Angevin occupation of Sicily once and for all. You and me. For Aunt Paola. For *Patri*. For our home."

Siciliana was silent for a long moment. An introspective frown formed on her lips as she seemed to consider the offer. In a sudden motion, she gripped *Fra'Diavulu* by his cheeks, squeezing his face tightly in her hands. "Remember when we used to play on the crater as children?"

Fra'Diavulu's instinct kicked in, and he immediately gripped her forearms, struggling to pull her off.

Siciliana's breathing quickened. "We used to watch the lava crawl down the side of the mountain. It devoured everything in its path, as if those things had no business ever being there in the first place." She leaned in slowly, whispering one last phrase into her brother's ear. "I am lava."

Fra'Diavulu felt a chill shoot up his spine at the sound of her words.

Siciliana pulled him in even closer. "Every Angevin on this island will be devoured in my path, as they had no business ever being here in the first place." Suddenly, *Siciliana* pressed her lips into her brother's. "*Addiu*, Cicero."

Siciliana released him from her grip and pushed him away. She raised her fist into the air, glaring at her brother in cold blood. She then pulled back her reins and galloped across the battlefield toward her men.

CHAPTER 80

SITTING ATOP his warhorse, *Fra'Diavulu* sat stunned as he watched his sister, back from the dead, gallop away toward her army across the expansive battlefield. He reached under his armor and pulled out a prickly pear. He sank his teeth into the juicy fruit, its red liquid dribbling down his chin like blood. He lowered his war mask over his face, gazing upon the swath of angry insurgents. He shook his head and sat up straight, finding his center of gravity. His heavy armor and breastplate gleamed silver for all the world to see. A perfect machine of war. He unsheathed his blade and held it out as a page ran up to douse it with oil. Another soldier approached with a torch and ignited the sword in a blazing inferno.

Fra'Diavulu hoisted the flaming sword high into the sky for all the world to see. Suddenly, he started cackling. The laughing became maniacal and demonic as it reverberated from behind the scowling devil mask. Louder and louder.

The red glow of lava illuminated the black-soiled battlefield. Frequent vent explosions threw rocks and hot debris into the air, raining down like hellfire.

Fra'Diavulu reached under his breastplate and pulled out a small crucifix necklace. He slowly pressed his lips against the cross, then tucked it back under his breastplate. He refocused his mind on the present moment. He slowly unsheathed his sword, the sound of scraping metal reverberating among the ranks. He hoisted his sword high into the air.

"All who betray *Re Carlu* shall die a traitor's death!" he bellowed for all of his men to hear.

With that, he kicked his heels into his horse's rib cage. The horse let out a loud snort as the captain pushed forward. At his order, the entire company of soldiers ground into motion, marching in perfect unison toward their destiny.

Fra'Diavulu raised his flaming blade high into the air, and then pointed it forward. *"Assalto!"*

Siciliana galloped at full speed back to her army, plowing to a stop in front of the men. Tziporah rode up next to her, noticing a glint of sadness in her eyes.

"What is it?" Tziporah said.

Siciliana shot her a disconcerted glance, gazing at her friend for a long moment before peeling her eyes away. In that instant, *Siciliana* opened her mouth to let out a scream as she thrust the flag spear into the soil, her nation's new flag fluttering in the wind.

Bannera dâ Sicilia.

Siciliana reined her horse around to face her army. The men stared back at her with conviction in their eyes. They were ready for war.

Don Rapaci and Tziporah nodded in solidarity.

Siciliana cracked a smirk and spun her horse around to face the line of rebels.

"Brothers of Sicily!" she bellowed. "We are about to embark on the most important fight in the history of our great people. The Angevins are a ferocious enemy, but so are we. They will show us no mercy and take no prisoners, so neither will we."

Siciliana pulled back the reins of her horse as it snorted with excitement. Spinning it around to face her men, she thrust a finger toward *Bannera dâ Sicilia.* "Our formidable *bannera.* A symbol of our new nation. Observe where I have laid stake into the soil. We do not retreat past that spot until we have won or died fighting."

There was the sound of singing metal as *Siciliana* unsheathed her stiletto, hoisting it high into the sky. A shaft of sunlight broke through the clouded sky and gleamed off the long sword, creating a shimmering glare for all to see.

The rebels raised their swords, shouting over one another. *"Rebellamentu!"*

CHAPTER 81

SICILIANA **DUG** her heels into her horse, leading a charge with *Don Rapaci* and Tziporah riding at her side. The screaming Sicilian rebels barreled forward across the black soil at lumbering speeds. The Angevin soldiers advanced toward them from the far end of the battlefield.

The opposing armies closed in. Two hundred yards . . . one hundred yards . . . fifty yards . . .

The Sicilian stampede thundered across the massive volcanic field. Frenzied and wild-eyed, the rebels burst through the black dust being churned up as they ran, screaming insanely. Directly ahead, a great tidal wave of armored Angevin foot soldiers barreled closer, rapiers and spears hoisted steadily to meet the onslaught.

Siciliana raised her sword high, her eyes filled with exhilaration as the army rushed toward their inevitable collision. *"Rebellamentu!"* she cried at the top of her lungs.

Undeterred, the Angevins didn't let up as they met the Sicilians' first line like storm waves crashing upon the shore. The opposing armies smashed into one another at full gallop,

Sicilians and Angevins clashing with ferocity in hand-to-hand combat.

Siciliana hacked through the Angevin ranks with long roundhouse swings of her sword, leaving a trail of maimed corpses in her wake.

Don Rapaci deflected a flurry of blows with his shield and plowed down a flank of foot soldiers before they could react.

Tziporah clenched her horse's rib cage tightly between her thighs, balancing on her saddle as she nocked an arrow into her longbow. She drew back the bowstring and fired the arrow directly at an Angevin soldier. The arrow whistled through the air and struck the man through the left eye, sending him spinning face-first into the dirt.

Fueled by an ancient rage, the Sicilian rebels flung themselves through the air, twisting and turning over their heavier opponents, plunging their blades and spears into their oppressors. Angevin fists collided with Sicilian cheekbones, crushing them with brute force. A multitude of bloodcurdling screams rose above the tumultuous fury of battle. Swords and maces flashed, impaling armor and flesh, drawing blood and innards.

Siciliana spun back her horse and circled around for another charge. As she galloped into the mayhem of clashing bodies, she leapt from her horse and crashed hard into an Angevin soldier, smashing her blade square into his chest. She deflected heavy blows from the soldiers descending upon her. Every swing of her blade created an Angevin corpse.

Maneuvering to her feet and regaining her footing, *Siciliana* spotted a soldier bull-rushing her with a rapier. She deflected his blow with her blade, sidestepping him as he barreled past her. She thrust her stiletto in a backhanded stroke. The soldier howled as he crashed to the ground, screaming in his native tongue.

Angevin soldiers lunged at *Siciliana* three and four at a time, though their efforts were sloppy and uncoordinated, and the coarse volcanic stone hampered their footing, slowing their speed. In the heat of the fight, *Siciliana* maintained mental clarity and awareness of her surroundings. *A cavaleri always en occhinero.* She moved in a blur of motion, finding her rhythm in the chaos, closing the gap from man to man before they could even raise their sword to strike.

The Sicilian rebels swarmed together, pressing forward, driving their oppressors back against the glowing lava flows. Angevin archers in the wings looked on in panic, unable to find a clear shot without striking their own men. The foot soldiers realized they were too heavily armored to move quickly and efficiently in the loose soil that was slippery beneath their boots.

Siciliana waded through the horde of clashing bodies, scanning the terrain like a desperate predator. She slashed her sword with every step as hundreds of bloodied men grappled around her.

Suddenly, a panicked Angevin soldier stumbled into her path. *Siciliana* quickly thrust her blade down upon his helmetless head, cleaving his skull in two. Blood streamed from the gaping wound. As the man dropped to his knees, she spotted a swirling armored figure moving toward her. His flaming blade raged like an inferno from his fist.

Fra'Diavulu, she told herself. *My own brother. My enemy.*

The deadly knight carved a swath through her countrymen, rebels falling as his flaming blade never stopped moving, deflecting blows and striking with ruthless strength and velocity. Sparks flew with every strike. *Fra'Diavulu* moved gracefully between attackers. Eyeballs to eyeballs. There one moment, gone the next. A grim realization washed over *Siciliana* as she recognized the deadly fighting style of a stiletto master *en occhinero.*

Fra'Diavulu plunged his blade through the back of a Sicilian rebel, wrapping his free arm around the rebel's head and snapping his neck in one fell blow. At the same time, he bludgeoned another rebel in the gut with the back of his gauntlet, then kicked another's teeth in with his boot heel.

In that instant, a pocket cleared between *Siciliana* and *Fra'Diavulu* as they came face to face once again on the battlefield. The two *cavaleri* slowly approached one another across the bloodstained volcanic soil as heavy smoke and sulfur drifted between them.

Fra'Diavulu gazed upon his sister.

Siciliana stood before him, her face paint dripping as a heavy sweat soaked her brow.

"*Simmo surfaru,*" *Fra'Diavulu* said, extending his flaming sword forward.

Siciliana's heart hung heavily as the cruel strings of destiny brought her into a fatal showdown with her own brother. Here on her own volcano. *He should've surrendered Taormina.* Instead, he betrayed her, his own blood. *His own family.* And so, he would perish with the rest of the Angevin dogs here on the volcano they had once called home.

"No . . . ," *Siciliana* growled. "No matter where we are thrown, we always land standing."

In that instant, an explosion rocked the earth.

A nearby steam vent burst to life, hurling hot volcanic rocks through the air, showering down over the two *cavaleri.* *Fra'Diavulu* flinched, turning his head away from the explosion. Not fearing the pain, *Siciliana* stood firm as the hot rocks seared her cheeks. She then sprung forward with all of her strength, leaping into the air and slashing her stiletto down on her brother.

Fra'Diavulu parried the incoming blow with a reverberating clang, ducking and weaving away from the attack. At once he summoned his own *occhinero,* slashing with surgical blows against his sister. *Siciliana* moved effortlessly with his strikes as if performing a grotesque dance, deflecting the momentum of the sharp steel away from her torso.

Siciliana struck again. She slashed with power and speed as *Fra'Diavulu* backed away, now using the tip of his blade to keep her at a distance. Despite his best defense, the edge of *Siciliana*'s blade sliced him across the arms and thighs, cutting dangerously deep into the back of his calf.

The two long-lost siblings clashed like Roman gladiators in the middle of the valley, surrounded by the brawling conflict. *Siciliana* was astonished by *Fra'Diavulu*'s skill. He didn't fight like any Angevin soldier she had met in close quarters. He fought like she did. He fought like a true *cavaleri*.

Fra'Diavulu summoned a second reserve of strength and parried *Siciliana*'s incoming strike. He spun in a full circle and drove her backward into the bodies of her men with a rapid series of blows.

Siciliana staggered backward, on the defensive, deflecting her brother's attacks. The fire from his blade singed her arms. But she was no stranger to pain. It would take more than a fiery sword to keep her from her destiny.

Fra'Diavulu then thrust his fist forward, smashing directly into her sternum, knocking the wind from her lungs. Her eyes widened in shock as she felt suffocated by her own body.

· ❦ ·

Immediately, *Fra'Diavulu* barraged *Siciliana* with a series of quick blows. She raised her blade with each strike, deflecting each blow as she gasped desperately for breath.

Suddenly, *Fra'Diavulu* adjusted his footing and maneuvered effortlessly around *Siciliana*'s back. He grappled to get his hands around her throat in an attempt to crush her windpipe. As he tightened his grip around her neck, he felt his heart breaking.

This is how my sister dies, he thought. *By my own hands.*

CHAPTER 82

FEELING HER brother's strong grip tightening around her neck, *Siciliana* reeled backward, the burning sweat rolling down her forehead and stinging her eyes. With all of her remaining strength, *Siciliana* clasped her hands together and thrust her fists backward, connecting directly with *Fra'Diavulu*'s devil war mask. The blow sent a painful reverberation through his skull, stunning him and sending him staggering back into the mass of bodies.

Snarling, *Siciliana* weaved around the soldiers and hurled herself at *Fra'Diavulu*, lifting him off his feet and causing them to crash together in the black dirt. In a flash, she pinned the heel of her foot down on his shoulder as she reached for a large rock. Without letting up, she smashed the rock repeatedly into *Fra'Diavulu*'s mask like a hammer. The rock cracked in her hand with each strike. *Fra'Diavulu* grunted in agony under the crushing blows.

Siciliana then clamped her arm around his neck, holding him in a tight grip between her forearm and closed bicep. She pressed her palm into his head, pushing it forward into her elbow.

The intended effect was instantaneous.

Fra'Diavulu felt the blood flow to his skull cut off immediately. A sudden disorienting feeling of dizziness washed over him.

The Saracen mercy lock!

Writhing in agony, *Fra'Diavulu* stared up in desperation into the fierce green eyes of his sister. He knew it was only a matter of seconds before he lost consciousness. "You're not going to kill me."

Tears trickled down from *Siciliana*'s cheeks as she gazed upon him.

Moments later, *Fra'Diavulu*'s eyelids began to flutter as he lost all sense of himself, falling limp in her arms.

Siciliana rolled *Fra'Diavulu* onto his stomach, positioning his limbs in an awkward fashion to make him appear dead so that he might remain unharmed in the tumult of battle.

Dizzy and barely able to stand, *Siciliana* rose to her feet and surveyed the valley. The cries and clangs of war had begun to fade.

The Angevin infantry scrambled to regroup. They banded together to prepare for a counterattack when *Don Rapaci* burst through the sulfuric fog and came crashing into their flank, his dueling swords puncturing their jugulars. The remaining helpless soldiers were inevitably crushed under the hooves of the massive beast.

The end was imminent.

Siciliana watched the last of the Angevin soldiers scramble in every direction in utter panic, begging for their lives, being cut down where they knelt. Over the past three weeks, the Sicilians had continued to taste something their people had not felt for centuries. *Vinciri*, she thought. *Victory.*

Siciliana scanned the aftermath of the battle. She beheld mangled corpses in the black volcanic earth. Dying Angevins impaled with swords and spears. The soil slick with blood and entrails.

Feeling a rush of vindication and sadness course through her veins, *Siciliana* tightened her grip around the hilt of her stiletto. She raised her arm above her head and thrust the sword into the air.

"Rebellamentu!" she shouted at the top of her lungs.

The scrappy rebel army, outarmed and outmatched, their faces bloodied and dirty, struggled to catch their breath as they took up the victorious chant. The rebels cried as one voice, one people, one nation.

"Rebellamentu! Rebellamentu! Rebellamentu!"

CHAPTER 83

Valle del Bove
Mount Etna, Sicily
April 20, 1282
12:08 p.m.

Fra'Diavulu SLOWLY opened his eyes and felt a crushing pain, as if every bone in his body had been smashed to pieces. His vision blurry, he tried to make sense of his surroundings. To his horror, he found himself lying in the gore-soaked soil in a heap of mangled Angevin corpses. The groans and cries of battle had all but receded, leaving nothing but the rancid stench of rotting flesh and sulfuric gas in the air.

Fra'Diavulu watched helplessly as the Sicilian rebels scrambled to and fro. Some were already dressing the wounded. Others sauntered among the corpses strewn about the valley, probing with their spears for any signs of life. Any Angevin soldier found squirming was quickly executed with a merciful stab through the heart.

Fra'Diavulu attempted to flail his limbs to get their attention. He knew that if they saw him, they would come and put him out of his misery.

A deserving death, he thought.

But he found that his energy was hopelessly depleted. He was unable to move as he watched the aftermath unfold before him.

Suddenly, *Fra'Diavulu* heard shouting in the distance. The voices became louder and more panicked. He slowly turned his head and watched as a group of rebels dashed past his blurry field of vision. Grimacing, *Fra'Diavulu* craned his neck in the rebels' direction, tracing their path to the source of the commotion at the opposite end of the field.

Fra'Diavulu was no stranger to death in his long and tumultuous career, yet what he was about to observe would haunt him for the rest of his days.

CHAPTER 84

SICILIANA **WALKED** freely among the dead and dying. Splattered with blood and dirt, she inhaled deep breaths, feeling the juices of rage slowly drain from her body. She relaxed her sword-wielding arm, letting it hang loosely at her side as she stepped over Angevin and Sicilian corpses.

Siciliana turned and gazed out over the volcanic valley of death, now a grisly scene rivaling the bowels of hell. She made her way toward the central gathering point, frequently stopping and grabbing the arms of her wounded brethren, offering soft words of solace and gratitude.

"For Sicily," she whispered to her men. "For *cosca*."

In that instant, her ears perked as she heard a commotion coming from across the field. There were cries from her men echoing in the distance.

Siciliana furrowed her brow, picked up her feet, and ran. As she moved across the field toward the sounds of panicked shouting, she came upon the cluster of men gathering together in a semicircle.

"What's wrong?" *Siciliana* asked. She pushed her way through the men. As she emerged from the cluster of bodies, her heart dropped into her stomach as she beheld the sight before her.

Tziporah sat alone in the dirt with her back pressed against a large boulder, exhaling slowly, a stunned look on her face. *"Rebellamentu,"* Tziporah whispered, almost incoherently.

"Tziporah?" *Siciliana* said, alarmed.

Don Rapaci was already in motion, dodging corpses strewn about the ground as he moved up alongside *Siciliana*, seeing the worry in her eyes. A few other men scrambled over, clutching their own wounded limbs. Time slammed to a standstill as they looked upon the same grisly sight.

Sitting there in the dirt, Tziporah glanced down in astonishment at the pool of blood forming rapidly at her waist. An Angevin rapier emerged halfway from her sternum.

"Tziporah!" *Siciliana* cried, rushing over to her friend and collapsing to her knees, looking over the blood-leaching rapier.

Tziporah struggled to breathe as she wrapped her small hands around the rapier's hilt.

"No!" *Siciliana* screamed.

In one abrupt motion, Tziporah yanked the sword from her abdomen. A stream of blood gushed from the gaping hole.

Siciliana's eyes widened in horror. *"Medicu!"* she screamed into the air. Stricken with agony, she scooped Tziporah into her arms.

The young girl's eyes were frozen in an expression of shock.

Suddenly, rebels leapt into action. In a flurry, they tore linen from their own clothing to create a tourniquet. One rebel ripped down *Bannera dâ Sicilia* from its spear and threw it over to *Siciliana*. She quickly unraveled the Sicilian flag and pressed it into Tziporah's sternum, desperately trying to stop the bleeding.

"I failed you," Tziporah said.

"Don't speak," *Siciliana* said.

Don Rapaci tore open Tziporah's tunic at her abdomen, revealing the nature of the horrific wound.

"*Cristu*," Don Rapaci said, hunkering over the bleeding girl. He pressed his own hand over *Siciliana*'s, helping to plug the wound.

Everyone was shouting and talking at once. Other hands moved in an attempt to create a tourniquet around Tziporah's waist.

Siciliana could see her friend fading as the men worked around her. "Tziporah, listen to my voice," she whispered. "Focus on the sound of my voice."

Tziporah shivered. She gulped a breath of air, but it was more of a sob. "I can't feel my legs."

Don Rapaci gently placed his hands on either side of her abdomen and slowly moved her onto her side. He slid his free hand up the small of her back, feeling the gaping exit wound. The blood drained from *Don Rapaci*'s face as he gently rolled her back over, realizing the full extent of the damage. Her lower spinal cord had been severed.

"How does it look?" Tziporah sputtered.

Don Rapaci glanced at *Siciliana* and shook his head.

Tziporah looked up at *Siciliana* with distant eyes, smiling weakly. She extended her hand outward, opening her palm. *Siciliana* reached out and grabbed it, clasping it in her own.

Siciliana gazed down at her young friend, stroking the girl's face with her hands. She brushed her dark hair back, trying to keep her comfortable.

Tziporah lifted her eyes to *Siciliana*, her gaze narrowing. With a single look, the young girl sent her sister in arms an unmistakable message: *Let me be.*

"No," *Siciliana* said, shaking her head.

"I've lived long enough . . . ," Tziporah muttered.

"Don't you give up on me," *Siciliana* said.

Tziporah glanced down at the blood-soaked Sicilian flag pressed against her abdomen. "I've lived long enough to know what it means to be a free *Siciliana*, thanks to you."

Siciliana's face soured. She was unable to stop her bottom lip from quivering as she wrapped her hands around Tziporah's fragile head, pressing her forehead against her own.

The young girl withdrew her hand slowly, letting it fall limp at her side. "*T'amu.* I love you, Aetna." Tziporah smiled weakly at her best friend, her eyes glazing over. She then rested her head softly against *Siciliana*'s shoulder. It was time to rest. The muscles in her face slowly relaxed as her eyelids fluttered shut for the last time.

In that instant, *Siciliana* felt Tziporah's life force leaving her body, slipping away beneath her bloodied hands.

Tziporah was gone.

A sulfuric wind blew across the ugly soil.

Siciliana held Tziporah's body firmly against her own. Her face twisted in anguish.

The rebels gathered around her. For a long moment, they looked on in silence. No one offered any prayers of comfort or words of anger as they stared in shock at their dead sister in arms. Stealing looks toward *Siciliana*, each man knew her grief-stricken expression carried the blame for this young girl's death.

The Sicilians had been sitting together in silence only a few minutes when suddenly they heard a low growl echoing in the distance.

All heads whipped toward the pile of corpses strewn in the middle of the field.

Fra'Diavulu crawled out from the heap of bodies, staggering to his feet momentarily before collapsing back to the dirt. Blood trickled down his forehead from beneath his helmet.

The men snarled.

The rebel Adrianu Amici grabbed the nearest sword and barreled toward the Messinese knight, who sat fearlessly in a daze. He approached *Fra'Diavulu* and butted the hilt of his blade directly into the knight's head. He then kicked *Fra'Diavulu* in the torso repeatedly.

"Bastard!" Adrianu cried.

The men sneered and sharpened their blades with a sick pleasure as Adrianu moved in and pulled *Fra'Diavulu* to his feet.

It would be a swift execution.

CHAPTER 85

"**ANY FINAL** words from the Messinese dog?" Adrianu sneered.

Fra'Diavulu could barely stand as he stared down his executioner. *"Vaffanculu,"* he spat. He wanted them to strike fast, and to strike true. A welcome release from a life of pain and regret.

The men burst into laughter as a rebel moved up behind the Messinese knight. A piece of torn cloth emerged from the rebel's hands as he tied a blindfold around *Fra'Diavulu's* eyes, yanking it tight. With a quick snap of his heel, the angry rebel kicked *Fra'Diavulu* to his knees.

The rebel raised his blade over *Fra'Diavulu's* head, staring down at the spot on the back of his head, where he would cleave his skull in two. "Burn in hell," the rebel growled.

"Stay your weapon!" *Siciliana* shouted.

All heads turned slowly as *Siciliana* approached, sheathing her stiletto, eyes hooded with a hunter's detachment. "We need him alive."

Adrianu blinked in disbelief. "This man has fought with our oppressors."

"He's the protector of Taormina," *Siciliana* rebuked, shooting *Fra'Diavulu* a grim look. "He is still useful to our fight. Our Trojan horse."

Adrianu scoffed. "*Cristu*, this is war. Not some foolish Greek drama."

Without warning, *Siciliana* raised her arm and smashed the back of her hand into Adrianu's face, cracking into his cheekbone. Seconds later, her stiletto flashed forward and came to rest against his jugular. She bared her teeth. "We need him alive."

All eyes were now on *Siciliana*.

Don Rapaci moved in, patting Adrianu aside as he yanked the blindfold from *Fra'Diavulu*'s eyes. He gripped him by the collar and pulled him to his feet. The two men's eyes met as they stood nose to nose. Suddenly, *Fra'Diavulu* glanced up with a surprised look of recognition. His face contorted with outrage. "You . . ."

Don Rapaci raised his eyebrows, taken aback by the sudden aggression.

Fra'Diavulu's nostrils flared like a bull's, his breathing becoming heavier. Hot Sicilian blood coursed through his veins like the steaming lava flows creeping down the mountain around them.

"The *Teutoni* fugitive!" *Fra'Diavulu* snarled, lunging at *Don Rapaci*'s throat and tackling him to the ground. "It's all your fault!"

The two men grappled with one another on the coarse black soil.

"*Patri* would still be alive if it weren't for you!" *Fra'Diavulu* yelled, tightening his grip around *Don Rapaci*'s throat.

Don Rapaci stared up at *Fra'Diavulu* in disbelief. "Impossible."

Fra'Diavulu growled. "You led them straight to our home."

The rebels moved in and pulled *Fra'Diavulu* off *Don Rapaci* before throwing him face-first back into the black dirt.

A rebel snapped out his blade. "I've heard enough from the Angevin dog."

Siciliana stepped forward, throwing up her palm. "No." She turned to *Fra'Diavulu*. "What are you talking about?"

Fra'Diavulu craned his neck up from the ground, spitting dirt from his mouth "That man knew *Patri*."

"*Sì*, he was *Patri*'s teacher," *Siciliana* said.

Don Rapaci rubbed his throat, catching his breath.

Adrianu flashed his brother, Gaetano, an inquisitive look and mouthed, *Patri?* Gaetano shrugged.

Fra'Diavulu grimaced as he pushed himself to his feet. "He was the *Teutoni* Knight who led the Angevins to our home. I've spent my entire life looking for him."

Adrianu snorted an uncomfortable laugh. "What the hell is going on here? Why is he talking like this?"

Siciliana gazed into *Fra'Diavulu*'s eyes for a long moment. A pained look fell across her face. "He's my brother."

Adrianu's and Gaetano's jaws dropped. All heads turned toward *Siciliana*.

She continued. "We were separated as children when the Angevins destroyed our home and murdered our father. I thought he was dead."

Gaetano leaned over to his brother. "*Fra'Diavulu* is *Siciliana*'s blood kin?"

Adrianu nodded in shock.

"I'm afraid he's telling the truth," a deep voice bellowed. *Don Rapaci* stepped forward, sheathing his blades in his belt.

Siciliana swiveled to him. She closed the gap between herself and *Don Rapaci*. Her voice cracked with a muted anger. "You led them to our home? My *patri* would still be alive?"

Nobody moved. All eyes were now on *Siciliana* and *Don Rapaci*.

· ❦ ·

Don Rapaci was just standing there, motionless. He exhaled a deep breath. The memories still haunted him, but it was time she knew the truth. "I'm afraid I have not been forthright with you, Aetna."

Siciliana furrowed her brow.

Don Rapaci cleared his throat and lifted his chin. "It was I who showed up at your family's vineyard that fateful day many years ago. It was I who activated Captain Roger Mastrangelo and the *Teutoni* Knights of Palermo."

Siciliana took another step forward. "What are you saying?"

Don Rapaci stared at her grimly. "I am the secret grand master of the *Ordu Teutoni*."

CHAPTER 86

DON RAPACI gazed at *Siciliana*. He noticed a look of consternation fall across her face.

"You're a *Teutoni* Knight?" *Siciliana* pressed.

Don Rapaci lifted his eyes to Mount Etna's smoking cone. His voice turned somber, as if about to tell a mother her son had been slain in battle.

"My name was once *Capu* Andrea Bonelli, high commander of the *Ordu Teutoni*," he began. "It was fourteen years ago when *Re Carlu* moved his army from France to the northernmost territory of the kingdom of Sicily—the Palentine Plains. Angevins were raiding villages all along the valley. Innocent women were being molested while their husbands were forced to watch. *Teutoni* Knights rode out with Prince Conradin's army to stop them and attempt to thwart *Re Carlu's* impending invasion of Sicily."

Don Rapaci made quick eye movements as he remembered the scene in graphic detail.

"The young prince deployed his army in three divisions. At first, we dominated the battle. We overwhelmed *Re Carlu's* first two waves and forced them into a retreat. Amidst the tumult of clashing bodies, I killed a large man wearing *Re Carlu*'s armor and captured his *bannera*. I waved the flag of our enemy in the air for the world to see. Victory was within our grasp. Believing the battle was won, Conradin's army split up. Some pursued the fleeing men; others pillaged the Angevin camp for weapons and nourishment. We didn't realize that the man I had slain was not actually *Re Carlu*, but a decoy. It was then that the shrewd French warlord sprung his trap. A cavalry reserve of over two hundred Angevin horsemen stormed over the ridgeline and decimated our divided army. I retreated from the battlefield with a handful of knights, escaping with my life. The young prince was not so lucky. He was captured and handed over to *Re Carlu*."

Don Rapaci paused, fighting that familiar feeling of shame that often dragged his mind back in time, locking him once again on the Palentine Plains as a younger man. The memories came as they always did, like waves crashing against the shore . . . the reek of human blood and entrails . . . the stench of death . . .

Galloping from the battlefield under a barrage of arrows, *Capu* Andrea Bonelli rode across the countryside in a frenzy, killing the horse underneath him. His stomach growled with hunger. With every passing second, the dream of a free Sicily slipped further and further into oblivion. The reign of Conradin was vanquished that day. And Sicilians would be subject to the rule of a lustful and murderous tyrant. The *Teutoni* commander's heart and mind were utterly defeated, but he knew he had to stay focused. Calm.

It's the panic that betrays you.

A week later, Bonelli arrived in Napoli incognito in time to witness Conradin's public execution. Magistrates were bribed to officially arraign Conradin as a war criminal. A scaffold was built on the site of the *Campo Moricino*. Colorful tapestries hung from the castle walls; flower petals carpeted the stone floor. *Re Carlu* wanted the memory of the young prince's death seared into the minds of every Napolitano citizen in attendance. It was the only glimpse they had of the spirited sixteen-year-old boy who might have been their king.

Bonelli gazed up at the guillotine platform as the shamed teenage monarch was pushed onto his knees. He watched as Conradin defiantly hoisted his gauntlet in the air for all to see. It was emblazoned with the black Imperial Eagle on a golden shield, its wings spread outward, its red tongue extending from its beak. The coat of arms of Sicilian kings. The young prince then threw it out into the watching crowd in a final act of resistance.

Seconds later, the hooded executioner pressed Conradin's head into the wooden block. The hulking man raised his sharpened sword into the air above the prince's neck and held it there for a fleeting moment, then . . . *whoosh!*

Conradin opened his mouth and screamed. The blade sliced through the air and severed his head from his body. A dead silence fell over the piazza.

The executioner picked up the prince's bloodied head, gripping it tightly by its thick golden hair, and lifted it out over the crowd. Its lifeless expression was frozen in a perpetual state of shock.

"Long live Charles the First, king of Sicily!" an Angevin page cried from the platform. "All hail King Charles!"

Bonelli bowed his head in hopeless grief. He made the sign of the cross and quickly moved to the spot where Conradin's gauntlet had fallen. He gently stepped over it and discreetly picked it up under his hooded cape, slipping it onto his forearm. He disappeared into the crowd with a single thought lingering in his mind: for the people of Sicily to survive, there was one last mission for him to undertake.

I must find the winemaker.

With Prince Conradin dead, and the *Ordu Teutoni* driven underground, the commander knew it would be a long and treacherous journey to Mount Etna. Now that he was a hunted man, his main concern was not to get caught. He'd have to travel off the main roads, settling into a town for days or months at a time before moving on to the next. It would take a year. Maybe more. But it was a journey that he decided was worth his life.

Standing in the *Valle del Bove* among the Sicilian rebels, *Don Rapaci* carefully unwound the black wrap of his sleeve and exposed a glimmering object beneath. He raised his forearm and revealed a gauntlet emblazoned with the black Imperial Eagle against a golden shield.

Siciliana remained silent while the men standing around her gazed forward, transfixed.

Gaetano Amici turned to Adrianu with wide eyes. *"La Guanto di Sfida!"* he whispered. "The Gauntlet of Defiance."

Don Rapaci lowered his eyes and continued. "There was only one man left who could protect the people of Sicily now. He was once my greatest student. A man of *occhinero* who loved his people and defended those less fortunate than him."

Siciliana's eyes narrowed. *"Patri."*

Don Rapaci nodded. *"O Santo Cavaleri.* A perfect Sicilian knight who could rise up, protect this land, and end the tyranny that has crippled it. So that the people may finally know a country of their own."

Siciliana nodded. "Conradin's promise."

Don Rapaci frowned. "A conquered prince granting his power back to the people of Sicily . . ." He shook his head and blew air from his lips. "I'm afraid to confess that Conradin never made such a promise. It was nothing more than a myth that I created to muster the red-blooded Sicilian spirit into *rebellamentu* and instill your father with the moral authority that this land was now truly *ours*—sanctioned by the prince himself, under the dutiful guard of the *Ordu Teutoni*."

The men murmured among themselves, exchanging anxious glances.

Siciliana couldn't help but be impressed by the audacity of such a tale. But when she finally spoke, her words were cold with insulted dignity, her face trembling and flushed bloodred. "You lied to me? You lied to my *patri*?"

Don Rapaci stepped closer. "No."

Siciliana fumed. "You tried to trick him into helping you as if playing a demented game of chess with his life?"

Don Rapaci shook his head, his eyes pleading with her. "I tried to help him realize his destiny as protector of Sicily: to rise up under the protection of the *Ordu Teutoni* and lead a people's resistance against *Re Carlu*. But he refused to fight. He turned his back on Sicily when we needed him most."

Adrianu leaned over to *Siciliana* and growled under his teeth. "We don't have to listen to this."

Siciliana thrust a hand upward to silence him. She looked gravely at *Don Rapaci*. "Continue . . ."

Don Rapaci frowned in thought, then said, "When the Angevins arrived that terrible day, I was captured and taken away, along with the young Vespiri boy." He paused and shot an ashamed glance over to *Fra'Diavulu*. "During a routine rest stop en route to Messina, I quietly slipped from my bindings as the men slept and escaped General Rochefort's grasp."

Fra'Diavulu's brow narrowed. "You left me to die."

Don Rapaci had a pained look on his face. "They would've executed me as soon as we entered Messina. I had to make a choice."

"What choice?" *Fra'Diavulu* said.

"My life . . . or yours," *Don Rapaci* said. "I knew that for better or worse the Angevins would take you in. I knew you had the heart to survive."

Fra'Diavulu smoldered. "Why didn't you take me with you?"

"I was a hunted man," *Don Rapaci* said, his expression solemn. "There was no way I could care for a child. A father's strength is a blessing I can only imagine."

Siciliana stepped forward, her face cold without a hint of sympathy. "So you fled to Palermo."

Don Rapaci turned toward *Siciliana* and nodded. "I did what I was trained to do. I went underground, assumed the rank of grand master, and built up a clandestine network of *Teutoni* Knights. I knew your father would teach you the Cistercian Trail—the secret pathway off the main roads that led directly to the *Santo Spirito*. I vowed to myself that I would keep watch over you, and protect you, until the day you were ready."

"Ready?"

"To make true the legend I created all those years ago," *Don Rapaci* said. "Don Vespiri lost his *occhinero* when it mattered most. But you, Aetna, are greater than your father. *You* are a perfect Sicilian knight. *Rebellamentu* is your destiny."

Don Rapaci then lifted his eyes to the sky. He had nothing left to say.

Siciliana became quiet, seeming to retreat into herself, as if watching a loved one die. "My *patri* chose to protect his family, even in the face of certain death. Sicily is *cosca*, or it is nothing."

Don Rapaci straightened his back, attempting to stand taller. "*Sì*. Family *is* everything. I was merely a boy when Frederick the Second ruled Sicily and decreed that all Arab Sicilians were a malicious threat to the kingdom's security . . . and expelled them from the island." He pointed a finger at himself. "What then becomes of the orphaned sons and daughters whose families were torn apart? What if a Sicily free of tyranny and intolerance was the only family *we* had left?"

For several seconds, *Don Rapaci* stared into *Siciliana*'s eyes, feeling the air hanging heavy between them.

Siciliana was curt, shaking her head with willfulness. "I'm truly sorry for your loss. I'm sorry for everything life has taken from you. But it's time we parted ways."

Don Rapaci was taken aback by the vehemence of her response. His face contorted in grief. "Aetna . . ."

With that, *Siciliana* slid her stiletto into her scabbard, spun on her heel, and turned her head back one last time. "Return to Palermo . . . *Capu* Andrea Bonelli."

Don Rapaci said nothing. He only nodded, ashamed. He knew *Siciliana* was her father's daughter, full of stubborn resolve, and didn't expect sympathy, or even absolution.

Don Rapaci mounted his horse as the men around him looked on, stunned into silence. Rosalia's piercing screech echoed sorrowfully across the valley as her gigantic wings spread open, lifting her upward into the sky, circling above.

Don Rapaci kicked his heels into the sides of the large horse. He galloped away toward the surrounding black hills until he disappeared, obliterated by the thick volcanic dust.

CHAPTER 87

SICILIANA **HEAVED** a breath. Her face twitched with perplexity as she watched not only her mentor and friend recede over the mountain, but worse, the promise that Sicily ever belonged to them in the first place. How could she have been so foolish to believe such a story? *Siciliana* clenched her fists. Royal promise or not, she decided that Sicily *was* theirs. No king or tyrant would take it from them. *We are the judges of kings.*

Siciliana turned back toward the men. "Gather all weapons and ammunition you can carry. We make for the highest peak and set up camp for the night." She then directed Adrianu to clean and dress Cicero's wounds as the other men collected their gear.

Adrianu looked solemn as he scanned the corpses of their fallen brothers on the battlefield. "And what of the dead?"

Siciliana knew the rampant disease that the festering of death would spread. They would be taking no chances on this day. They had to do the unthinkable. "Burn them."

· ❧ ·

Somewhere among the piles of stinking corpses, a pair of eyelids fluttered open. A dizzy French foot soldier gazed out through bloody slits at the aftermath of the carnage. As he lay there wounded, he watched a hazy specter carrying a torch move through the sulfuric smoke in his direction.

The ghostlike figure took the shape of a skinny, war-torn Sicilian rebel, silhouetted in black against the hazy sky. As he sauntered across the valley, the young rebel pressed the flaming tip of his torch into the piles of dead men strewn across the battlefield. The flames roared as the bodies caught fire and erupted into an inferno.

The Angevin soldier slowly regained his focus, realizing he would soon be burned alive. If he was going to act, he would have to act fast. The soldier quickly probed around his immediate surroundings, finally feeling what he was searching for. He closed his hand around the cold steel handle of a rapier, yanking it free from beneath a dead soldier. Moments later, the rebel, his torch blazing, approached the pile of corpses where the soldier lay.

Suddenly, like a venomous snake, the Angevin soldier snapped into action, thrusting the razor-sharp blade upward, skewering the young man right through the sternum.

The unsuspecting rebel gasped, his eyes widening in horror as the wind was knocked from his lungs. As the torch slipped from his hands and fell gently to the volcanic soil, the Angevin sprung to his feet and wrapped his arms around the man's face, twisting it sideways. There was a sickening pop.

Without hesitation, he heaved the rebel onto the pile, picked up the burning torch, and tossed it onto the heap of bodies. The corpses went up in flames.

The wounded Angevin then picked up his feet, turned, and limped away as quickly as he could, disappearing into the encroaching sulfuric fog.

CHAPTER 88

Cattedrale di Palermo
Palermo, Sicily
Seralcadio District
April 20, 1282
10:54 p.m.

BLACK STORM clouds roiled above Palermo Cathedral. A flash of lightning lit up the sky followed by a loud clap of thunder. Sitting at his workstation in front of the *Stupor Mundi*'s tomb and sarcophagus, *Teutoni* captain Roger Mastrangelo crushed a letter from *Siciliana* in his fist. The troubling contents of the letter landed like shards of glass in his gut. The envoy they had deployed to Rome had failed. The Holy See refused to acknowledge Sicily as a sovereign state and further endorsed *Re Carlu*'s dominion over the island.

Mastrangelo bit his lip, staring a hole in the ground. In that moment, he knew the worst was now upon them. The brutal, shrewd royal commander of the most powerful army in the Mediterranean would soon be turning his sights right on them. The same brutal commander who decimated Prince Conradin and the royal lineage of the old kingdom of Sicily.

Mastrangelo's mind reeled back to that fateful Vespers night. The plan had seemed so perfect. It was around the cold hour of three a.m. that the last screams of dying Angevins were heard echoing through the streets. Then dead silence, save the bonfires and festivities happening among the squares.

Mastrangelo remembered the sounds of the heavy raindrops pelting the Norman stone roof of the ominous *Magione Basilica*, the last church built by the Norman kings and the secret command of the *Ordu Teutoni*.

Two *Teutoni* Knights in full regalia stood guard outside the church's entrance with their swords drawn. They wore sparkling white tunics emblazoned with the black cross of the *Ordu Teutoni*. Their helmets and armor were perfectly polished. Their faces were like stone as their eyes pierced the night like cold blades, scanning for intruders. They knew this night of all nights was worth everything.

Inside the inner sanctum of the command, on the far side of the church's cloister, two dozen *Teutoni* Knights in full regalia gathered around a massive oak table in the church's great hall. The legs of the table were fashioned by large stones removed from a nearby mosque built centuries earlier. Hanging on the wall behind them was a gleaming silver shield bearing the black cross of the *Ordu Teutoni*.

Fueled by nerves, most of the *Teutoni* Knights were standing. That way they didn't have to unstrap their broadswords girdled to their belts. The knights in the chamber bore names like Mastrangelo, Baverio, Ortoleva, Coppola, and Lonfredo. In the men's faces were all of the colors of Sicily. Complexions fair and dark. Blond and black and red beards of Normans, Arabs, and Greeks. Eyes of brown, blue, and green. The younger knights among them were weaned on stories of Frederick II, the *Stupor Mundi*, the Wonder of the World, the greatest Sicilian king to ever walk the earth, who died thirty years prior.

Maps of Sicily were unrolled across the large oak table and scrutinized, some hung on the walls. Squires took turns replacing the torches that illuminated the room. Others brought out hot platters of fried *arancini* rice balls, grilled artichokes, and roasted boar sent from the Arabs of the surrounding *Kalsa* district.

Teutoni captain Roger Mastrangelo stood at the head of the table. He looked proudly upon the contingent of knights who had spent years in hiding, now returned in full glory.

Lu parlamentu secretu contra Re Carlu, the secret parliament against King Charles, was expected to last until dawn.

Mastrangelo stabbed a thick finger into the tattered map of Sicily lying on the table. "We must organize all able knights around the island to raise their blades in their towns and villages. We must act immediately. The element of surprise is an advantage. A necessity."

The knights nodded.

Mastrangelo glanced around the room. "We can then engage the Angevin forces city by city and buy ourselves enough time," Mastrangelo said. He then stooped his head back to the map, bringing his fingers to his chin and surveying the various routes between the cities.

The knights furrowed their brows and exchanged confused glances.

One knight cleared his throat. "I'm sorry, sir, but enough time for what?"

Mastrangelo regarded his men, a knowing look in his eye. "To appeal to a new monarch, of course."

The knights exchanged more glances.

Mastrangelo paused, distracted by a sudden movement in the shadows. Heavy footsteps entered the inner sanctum.

"Who's there?" Mastrangelo called out. "Announce yourself at once!"

Metal sang as all of the knights in the room unsheathed their swords, snapping into a combat-ready position. Glaring into the shadows, Mastrangelo beheld a tall, lean man dressed in full *Teutoni* regalia. He wore a Saracen war mask that concealed his face entirely to protect his identity. The man lifted his gauntlet, revealing the heraldry of a gold shield bearing the black Imperial Eagle, its wings spread open and a red tongue hanging from its mouth.

"*La Guanto di Sfida!*" one knight gasped.

Mastrangelo's eyes widened. He bowed his head in reverence. "Grand Master."

The knights and pages around the room gazed on, transfixed. They immediately lowered their swords and bowed their heads.

The *Teutoni* grand master stepped forward into the torchlight. "The monarchy is no more," the grand master said. "The *Ordu Teutoni* will fulfill Prince Conradin's last promise. We will give power back to the people of Sicily and end the oppression that has crippled them."

Mastrangelo shook his head. "Our oath is to restore the glory of the old kingdom to its rightful heir, Prince Conradin's own cousin . . . Constanza II of Aragon."

One knight shot him a surprised look. "The queen of Spain?"

"*Sì.*" Mastrangelo nodded. "We must appeal to Constanza II, and offer her our crown."

The other knights burst out into impassioned murmurs, exchanging concerned glances.

"Enough!" the grand master growled, slamming a fist on the table. "The time of kings and queens is no more. Sicily now belongs to the people."

A thick silence hung in the air.

"The Sicilian people, you say?" Mastrangelo growled. "Fishermen. Shepherds. Farmers. Who will lead them?"

"*O Santo Cavaleri*," the grand master said.

More murmuring among the knights. The young pages' faces lit up around the room. If there was a Sicilian more revered than the *Stupor Mundi*, it was the great *cavaleri* Don Vittorio Vespiri, Sicily's perfect knight.

"*O Santo Cavaleri* is dead," Mastrangelo said.

The grand master stepped forward, shaking his head, his tone becoming urgent. "The winemaker's daughter lives. She is ready to take up her father's mantle and fulfill Conradin's promise."

Mastrangelo raised a brow. "How do you know this?"

"I was there when the bells of the *Santo Spirito* tolled for Vespers," the grand master said. "The daughter of *O Santo Cavaleri* was the *Siciliana* who raised her blade and cried '*Moranu li Francisi*' into the night. I saw her fierce conviction with my own eyes. She will lead the people in *rebellamentu*."

A scowl hung on Mastrangelo's face. "*Rebellamentu* is a dream. Kings are the judges of Sicily. That is our lot in life."

The grand master glared at the captain through his black mask for a long moment. He then peered around the room, looking each man in the eye. "Kings may be the judges of Sicily, but *we* are the judges of kings."

The knights around the room nodded their heads, their eyes wide with resolve.

The grand master continued. "At sunrise, I will escort this *Siciliana* to Palermo Cathedral. There you will arrive and announce your allegiance to her. Then together we will stir the hearts and minds of the people and reclaim Sicily in the name of our families, our orphans, and all Sicilians who have had everything taken from them." The grand master paused, reflecting inwardly on those final words. *Everything taken from me.*

The knights around the table lifted their chins proudly, nodding their heads. Then they all turned to face Mastrangelo.

Mastrangelo stared at the grand master for a long moment. He then lowered his eyes to the map of Sicily sprawled out before him. He noted the various towns and villages spread around the island where they might have knights still hidden, waiting to be activated. Mastrangelo bit his lip and nodded.

"So be it," Mastrangelo said. "Let us reclaim our island once and for all."

Back in Palermo Cathedral, *Teutoni* captain Roger Mastrangelo looked down helplessly at the crumpled letter now in his hands. With the Holy See refusing protection, and further endorsing *Re Carlu*'s dominion over the island, it was only a matter of time before the largest army in the Mediterranean would bear down on their small island. He knew that the army *Re Carlu* was amassing for the invasion of Constantinople, an invasion for the ages, would soon be pointed directly at them.

Mastrangelo lifted his palm to his neck. He rubbed his throat and swallowed a large lump. He knew *Re Carlu*'s ultimate punishment. The same punishment he gave their fallen prince. And Mastrangelo liked his head very much where it was.

CHAPTER 89

Matagrifone
Messina, Sicily
April 21, 1282
12:26 a.m. // Twenty-second day of Vespers

SHAFTS OF silver moonlight poured into Lady Manon Orleans's bedroom chamber as she threw on her hunter's attire and slid into her black leather riding boots. She grabbed a blade and sat down in front of a mirror, staring at her ashen-blond hair for a long moment.

"For easier it is by far to strip of bark and bough all the forests of the world than to subdue my own heart," Manon said. "For if it were done, I would have shorn my hair off like a nun."

In that instant, she made a decision.

Manon lifted her blade to her face and grabbed a clump of hair in her palm. Taking a deep breath, with quick flicks of her wrist, she sheared off large swaths. With each yank of her blade, her ashen-blond locks fell to the floor in large handfuls. She looked at herself in the mirror for a long moment. Her hair was now cropped close to her chin, more so resembling a page boy than a lady of the court. She pursed her lips and nodded to herself.

Turning away from the mirror, Manon moved quickly across her bedroom, snatching up her Moorish throwing knives. She cracked the bedroom door open and carefully peered into the hallway.

Four soldiers on patrol.

Just as she had feared. Vicar Orleans had assigned a curfew for all the women of the king's court and stationed his garrison all around *Matagrifone* to ensure it was enforced. The Sicilians proved to be a volatile people, and it was for their own protection, he reassured them.

Biting her lip, Manon slid back into her room, pacing back and forth. She squinted as the moon's bright light fell in from the window and into her eyes. She stared into the moonlight for a short moment, pressing her palm softly against her abdomen, sensing the precious new life she carried inside her. She would soon have a family. A family of her own. And that was worth her life.

Manon felt all fear shed from her body like a wildcat's winter coat. In that instant, her escape plan revealed itself. She would make a break for the stables and ride off for Taormina.

Leaping into action, she strapped her knives tightly around her waist and dashed for the window. She swung her legs over the ledge and jumped to the ground below. She moved silently along the perimeter of the castle wall, disappearing into the thick shadows.

Nothing on earth would stop her.

CHAPTER 90

Valle del Bove
Mount Etna, Sicily
April 21, 1282
1:01 a.m.

SICILIANA SAT alone by her campfire, gazing endlessly into the dancing flames. The bloodied Sicilian flag that had stood the test of battle was draped over her shoulders. She longed to wash the smell of death off her skin. The pungent aroma of smoke stained her hair and clothing. With every breath, she exhaled the trauma of the night. The cries of the dying reverberated in her ears, in her blood.

A black shroud blanketed the night sky, pinholes of starlight filling in the void. Sicilian moonlight had washed over the volcanic terrain, bathing *Siciliana* and her men in glowing ivory, the crackling of the campfires the only sounds breaking the dead silence of the night. A strained quiet had fallen over the encampment as men tended their wounds, many already asleep. *Siciliana*'s scrappy army of Sicilian warriors, which had begun the day two hundred fifty strong, had been tragically reduced to fewer than eighty, shattered by a single deadly battle that dramatically shifted the course of the war. The flickering campfires threw long shadows of the soldiers across the black volcanic earth, which danced in the glowing light.

Fra'Diavulu limped over to *Siciliana* and sat beside the fire, watching his sister sharpen her stiletto with a small stone. The two estranged siblings sat in silence for a long moment.

"You hunted *Teutoni* Knights. Why?" *Siciliana* asked.

Her words seemed to break into *Fra'Diavulu*'s memory. He blew out a deep breath. "*Capu* Andrea Bonelli led the Angevins directly to our home. If it weren't for him, *Patri* might still be alive. We'd still be a *cosca*." *Fra'Diavulu* turned inward, as if sorting through his thoughts. "The night he escaped from Rochefort's contingent, we had been tied together at the wrists. When I fell asleep, he was there beside me. The next morning, he was gone . . . like a raptor on the wind."

Siciliana shook her head. "*Don Rapaci.*"

Fra'Diavulu muttered in a seething tone. "He took everything from us and then left me to die. I thought my anger alone would kill me. Choking my grief until it coursed like a poison through my veins. In that moment, I made a vow to *Patri* that I'd find him and exact justice in the name of the Vespiri family—even if it meant destroying the entire *Ordu Teutoni.*"

As she gazed into the fire, *Siciliana*'s eyes widened at the pure boldness of the idea. To take on a blood feud with an entire order of legendary knights in the name of family. *Rispettu.* She nodded to herself. *Respect.*

"Is it true?" she asked. "Did *Patri* refuse to fight?"

Fra'Diavulu glanced over to catch her gaze. "It doesn't matter."

"Did he?"

"He chose to protect us," *Fra'Diavulu* said. "To protect *cosca.*"

Siciliana scoffed. For some reason, the words landed like shards of glass in her gut. Her mind moved toward thoughts of Tziporah. The only *cosca* she had known. Now gone.

"Our *cosca* will never be safe if we don't have a home to call our own," *Siciliana* said, beckoning out across the landscape. "*Patri* was a great man. But I'm disappointed in his inability to think larger than himself."

Fra'Diavulu paused for a moment, carefully choosing his next words. "Maybe he was afraid. Even great men feel fear."

Siciliana shook her head. "A *cavaleri* always looks their enemies in the black of the eyes even in the face of pain and death. Where was his *occhinero*?"

"You believe *Patri* was a coward?" *Fra'Diavulu* asked.

She turned to *Fra'Diavulu*, a grave look on her face. "I believe that when you fight to protect *cosca*, you don't have the luxury of fear."

Fra'Diavulu frowned, seeming to understand her point.

A sharp wind whipped between them.

Fra'Diavulu glanced up and gazed out into the night, as if searching the heavens for something. "I wonder what she would think about all of this."

Siciliana stared intently at her blade. It suddenly felt strange to think that the man who had just tried to kill her, who was responsible for the deaths of nearly half of her men, was asking about her *patri*. That they had shared a *patri* to begin with. "Who?"

"*Matri*," *Fra'Diavulu* said. "Remember the stories *Patri* used to tell us about her? Her gentle face. Her nurturing embrace. The golden wheat of Sicily herself."

Siciliana felt her eyes suddenly well up with tears. "*Sì*," she said softly.

"What would she think about the atrocities we've committed on her volcano?" *Fra'Diavulu* said.

Siciliana looked up. "This was nothing compared to what we did to your friends on Vespers night."

Fra'Diavulu furrowed his brow. "My friends? Aetna, the Angevins aren't my friends."

"You fought with them as if they were."

Fra'Diavulu shook his head. "War was the last thing I wanted. More innocent lives lost. Families ripped apart." He stabbed a finger out into the darkness. "I wanted to save Sicily, like you."

"You wanted to save Sicily? You stood in Sicily's way on that battlefield."

"There are more paths to freedom than death," *Fra'Diavulu* said. "Better paths."

"What kind of paths?"

"*Diplomazia.* Diplomacy with the Angevins in the name of a Sicilian nation."

Siciliana spat at his feet. "Rapists and murderers. There will be no peace."

Fra'Diavulu pursed his lips and nodded silently. A frustrated smile crossed his lips as he swallowed his words, relenting. He said, "I left Taormina with five hundred men. I will return alone. This will not go unnoticed—"

Siciliana raised an impatient hand to silence him, never looking up from her sword. She explained coolly. "Your mission is simple. In a few hours, when the sun rises, you'll return to Taormina with your page—one of mine in disguise. This will no doubt create a swirl of mystery as you enter the city walls and proceed to the Taormina fortress. Once you arrive at the castle, you'll call a meeting with the entire Angevin garrison and deliver the following news . . ."

Fra'Diavulu furrowed his brow, leaning in closer.

She continued. "The insurrection is over. The savage known as the *Siciliana* is defeated. Your men stayed behind to transport her and the rebel army to Messina for their execution.

You'll order for the city's finest wines to be brought to the fortress so you may imbibe in celebration and victory into the night. Then my men enter the city unopposed and kill every last drunken Angevin inside."

Fra'Diavulu nodded. "There's a hidden entrance carved into the cliffs that takes you up through its cistern. You and your men can infiltrate from there."

Siciliana nodded grimly. "Once the vicar discovers he lost *Re Carlu*'s prized city, he'll react in fear and send a counterattack. We'll draw out his remaining forces from Messina. Wave by wave. Until the people of Messina gather the courage to rise up as we did in Palermo. Then, together, we will take back Sicily for the ages."

With that, *Siciliana* sent sparks flying down the edge of her blade with her sharpening stone.

Fra'Diavulu nodded. "This might work."

"It *will* work."

"But there's only one thing."

Siciliana glanced up.

Fra'Diavulu said reluctantly, "When I return to Taormina, how will they know that I succeeded here? That you have surrendered?"

With that, *Siciliana* pulled the tattered Sicilian flag off her shoulders and pressed it into his large hands. The flag's emblazoned emblem was still stained with Tziporah's blood. "You'll carry this."

Fra'Diavulu grabbed the *bannera*, holding it carefully in his hands. The blood-soaked flag of a new nation. *A Sicilian nation.* He bowed his head and said in a strangled voice, "I will protect this with my life."

Siciliana looked upon her brother. A brother who seemed like a stranger. A moment of silence passed between the two siblings. Then, a skeptical smirk crossed her lips. "So, you're the *Fra'Diavulu . . ."*

Fra'Diavulu snorted. "And you're the *Siciliana*."

Siciliana nodded, realizing in that moment that they had both clawed their way out of their own personal hells and had become larger and more legendary than they could have ever imagined. *Cent'anni,* she thought. *May we live forever, indeed.*

Siciliana stood up and brushed her hands on her thighs. "You move out in three hours. Try to catch some sleep." She picked up her blade and walked away.

Feeling a sudden chill, *Fra'Diavulu* gulped in a deep breath and pulled a blanket over his legs. He tilted his head toward the sky. The night was dark and black. But little did he suspect the darkest of nights were yet to come.

CHAPTER 91

Castello Saraceno
Taormina, Sicily
April 21, 1282
9:31 a.m.

STEERING HIS horse up the cliffside street toward *Castello Saraceno, Fra'Diavulu* felt pleased with his choice of page. Gaetano Amici was disguised in an Angevin page's uniform, the clothes taken off a corpse pulled from the battlefield of Mount Etna. Riding confidently ahead of the Messinese knight, the page clearly knew what he was doing.

As *Fra'Diavulu* approached the end of the narrow street, he craned his neck and peered up to the high walls of the Saracen Fortress rising above. It seemed as solemn as it was when he had arrived a week earlier. With one hand, *Fra'Diavulu* steered his horse by the reins; with the other, he gripped a long spear planted firmly in his stirrup. Fluttering from the spear's tip was the bloodied *Bannera dâ Sicilia*.

As the two soldiers continued to climb, resentful locals clogged the winding roads leading in and out of the fortress's perimeter. *Fra'Diavulu* could feel the icy glances searing into the back of his head as they pushed through the crowd.

"They look at us as if we murdered their greatest hero," Gaetano muttered.

"Keep quiet and follow my lead," *Fra'Diavulu* said.

The two men approached the fortress's cliffside entrance. *Fra'Diavulu* observed there was little discernible activity save the usual Angevin soldiers patrolling the perimeter, their regular blue-and-white uniforms dirtied and unkempt. To his left, the cliff dropped off to the city streets below, and just beyond, the vast expanse of the Ionian Sea stretching endlessly toward the horizon. Today the sea was as gray as the dark clouds that hung overhead.

Fra'Diavulu led the horses to the foot of the fortress's main staircase. Gaetano threw his leg over his horse and dismounted, hitching the steed. *Fra'Diavulu* dismounted his own horse as a large haggard soldier lumbered over to meet the men eye to eye.

"Where is the army?" the soldier sneered.

Ignoring him, *Fra'Diavulu* dislodged the Sicilian flag and sauntered up the staircase. "Summon the finest of wines from the village below. We have much to celebrate tonight."

The soldier turned and followed him on his heels.

Fra'Diavulu approached the oaken doors of the castle and with a hefty push heaved them open.

Entering the fortress's main hall, *Fra'Diavulu* screeched to a halt. Instantly, he felt a surge of uneasiness as he beheld the sight before him. A grim figure sat in a high-backed chair at the end of the hall. Angevin royal guards of Messina surrounded the perimeter of the room.

"The Brother Devil returns," the grim figure said.

Fra'Diavulu hesitated as the figure's fiery gaze scorched him from across the room, cutting through the darkness. He watched as the hulking figure rose from his seat and sauntered forward. Heavy boots cracked against the stone floor with each step.

Fra'Diavulu watched as the orange glow of torchlight fell upon the man's face, revealing small slits of eyes and a grotesque scar on his cheek.

General Guy de Rochefort had arrived in Taormina.

CHAPTER 92

"ARREST HIM," Rochefort said.

Rochefort's elite guards moved in with the force of a thousand men.

"Gaetano, run!" *Fra'Diavulu* shouted as he was tackled to the ground.

Gaetano's eyes widened with fear. The skinny Sicilian snatched *Bannera dâ Sicilia* from *Fra'Diavulu*'s belt, spun on his heel, and darted from the castle.

Rochefort extended his arm and threw a book at *Fra'Diavulu*'s feet. The book hit the ground with a thud, sending up a plume of dust. *Fra'Diavulu* slowly glanced down. He swallowed a hard lump as he read the cover: *Contrasto*. The book of Sicilian poetry he had taken from the *Teutoni* catacomb. His gift to Manon.

"Thou shall not covet another man's wife," Rochefort said.

Fra'Diavulu stared down at the book, speechless.

Instantly, Rochefort raised a heavy hand and smashed it into *Fra'Diavulu*'s cheekbone.

Fra'Diavulu's vision burst with flashes of light, his skull throbbing. He gnashed his teeth and with all his strength lunged for Rochefort. The guards kept him heavily subdued.

Rochefort glared down his nose at *Fra'Diavulu*. "A garrison of my most vile and brutal men have Taormina under full occupation. They await my orders, rather impatiently, to cleanse this city of its population. But not before enjoying the carnal spoils for every wet and luscious encounter they are worth."

Fra'Diavulu slowly raised his eyes to Rochefort's until he could see the black of his eyes. He knew the entire game had changed. Even if Gaetano escaped and warned *Siciliana* of his capture, her remaining men wouldn't have the strength in numbers to match Rochefort's brutal garrison of deviants and murderers. Every Sicilian soul within the city's walls would be executed in cold blood.

"Now, tell me the location of this savage woman they call *Siciliana*," Rochefort said.

Fra'Diavulu searched his thoughts. He knew he had only one option left to protect the future of Sicily as he knew it. To protect his sister. His *cosca*.

"I don't know," he snapped. *Omertà.*

Moments later, a soldier grumbled from the back of the room, pushing his way forward. "He lies."

Recognition crossed *Fra'Diavulu's* face as the soldier stepped into the light. The man was from the contingent he had taken out to Mount Etna the day prior.

"He led us into battle against the insurgents. Our army was obliterated," the soldier said.

Rochefort studied *Fra'Diavulu* for a long moment, like a predator eyeing up its meal. "The savage woman would never let an enemy soldier leave the field of battle with his head intact." Suddenly, he gripped a tuft of *Fra'Diavulu's* hair and yanked his neck backward, in the same instant pressing a blade to his throat. A murderous grin crossed his lips. "They are working together."

Fra'Diavulu remained silent, refusing to give them anything.

"An adulterer *and* a traitor," Rochefort said.

The soldiers exchanged surprised glances. The Brother Devil himself, whose flaming blade had skewered many *Teutoni* Knights, was working with the Sicilian insurgents?

Rochefort released *Fra'Diavulu* from his grip and thrust him backward into the arms of his guards. "He dies tonight . . . in the *Teatro Greco*. Mandate the entire city come witness the mercenary *Fra'Diavulu* lose his head, and his head placed on a pike for all the world to see."

The men in the room broke out into devious laughter.

"And what of the *Siciliana*?" one soldier asked.

Rochefort's expression turned grim. "You don't chase a wolf. For they are far too cunning."

"What do we do?" the soldier pressed.

"You make your presence known in its territory . . . Let it approach you . . . then—" Rochefort abruptly grabbed the soldier by the collar, pushing his blade into the soldier's sternum.

The soldier's eyes bugged out from his skull, a vein bursting from his forehead, as the general turned the razor-sharp blade upward into the soldier's chest cavity, mincing his heart to mush from the inside. The soldier's eyes rolled back as he lurched forward, falling flat-faced to the ground.

Rochefort turned toward his men. His wide eyes were filled with the insatiable bloodlust of a great destroyer. The Destroyer of Sicily. "Lock the city gates and secure the perimeter walls. I'm placing Taormina under siege."

CHAPTER 93

In a dank prison cell beneath *Castello Saraceno,* an Angevin sergeant looked upon *Fra'Diavulu* in bewilderment as he was shackled to the wall. "I still can't believe it," the sergeant said. "*Fra'Diavulu,* the bane of the *Ordu Teutoni,* in league with the insurgents."

Fra'Diavulu kept his gaze trained forward as the guards tightened his chains. "What is Rochefort doing in Taormina?"

A grizzled soldier slugged *Fra'Diavulu* across the mouth. "This is the sergeant's prison. Only the sergeant asks the questions."

Fra'Diavulu lurched forward and groaned as blood oozed from his mouth and nose.

The sergeant approached him slowly. "The general was ordered by Vicar Orleans himself to crush the insurgency by any means necessary."

Fra'Diavulu spat defiantly to the sergeant's feet. "*Vaffanculu.*"

"You stand accused of the worst of crimes," the sergeant said. "High treason."

"Against whom?"

"Your king, of course," the sergeant said. "Have you anything to say?"

Fra'Diavulu's face hardened. "Kings may be the judges of Sicily, but we are the judges of kings."

The sergeant moved in closer. "Are you afraid?"

Fra'Diavulu remained silent.

The sergeant grew impatient, his face turning red. "Are . . . you . . . afraid?"

Fra'Diavulu's gaze suddenly sharpened as his eyebrows pulled together. He began to mumble under his breath in Sicilian. "I am Cicero Vespiri . . . son of Don Vittorio Vespiri . . . *O Santo Cavaleri.*"

The Angevin soldiers exchanged confused glances.

"What is he saying?" a soldier said.

Fra'Diavulu's breathing became heavier, angrier. "I am Cicero Vespiri . . . son of Don Vittorio Vespiri . . . *O Santo Cavaleri,*" Cicero Vespiri growled. "And you will all soon feel the fury of *Siciliana.*"

CHAPTER 94

Porta Messina
Taormina, Sicily
April 21, 1282
1:41 p.m.

DONNING A green hooded hunter's cape, Lady Manon Orleans beheld the massive iron gates of Taormina's landmark entrance, the *Porta Messina*. The figure looking down on her from the perimeter walls was an Angevin lieutenant, surrounded by fifty elite archers spread out on either side, arrows drawn tight. But it was the man behind him in the shadows who sent a shiver down her spine.

General Guy de Rochefort stepped forward, his expression hardened. He lifted his palm into the air, instructing the archers to hold their fire. "The city is closed," the general growled. "Give me one good reason why my archers shouldn't strike you down where you stand."

Manon removed her hood, revealing her freshly chopped ashen-blond hair. "I demand you open these gates at once."

A murmuring of surprise spread among the archers.

"My dearly betrothed," Rochefort growled, his fist tightening, "you deliberately violated my orders to remain within the confines of *Matagrifone.*"

Manon pursed her lips. "I'm here to see the Messinese knight *Fra'Diavulu.*"

"I'm afraid there are no knights here," Rochefort sneered. "We do possess a traitor who will die tonight."

Manon felt a surge of trepidation rush through her. *A traitor?* She didn't want to believe him but sensed in that moment that something wasn't right. Fra'Diavulu *is in danger,* she thought. Manon shifted in her saddle, sitting straighter. "You lie."

Rochefort grinned, his gaze lingering on the fair maiden before him. He then glanced at his archers on either side of him, their arrows drawn and aim steady. He knew a simple motion of his hand could unleash a flurry of arrows down on the defenseless countess. He could throw her maimed corpse over the cliffside into the Ionian Sea, erasing her from history forever, and no one would be the wiser. A simple motion of his hand and the vicar's noble lineage in Sicily would be all but vanquished. It was an intriguing premise. But then again, why waste such desirable flesh, which would soon be his for the taking?

"Listen to me carefully," Rochefort said. "I am hereby detaining you in Taormina Fortress for violation of your curfew. You will be held there until a transport returns you to Messina under the custody of your father. If you resist, my archers will strike you down on the very horse you sit on. And they are excellent marksmen. Do you understand what I am telling you?"

Manon glared a hole through the general. The totality of his order took her off guard. She glanced over her shoulder, gauging the distance to safe cover. But an attempt to rear her horse and flee would be suicide. She knew Rochefort's bloodlust knew no bounds, and wasn't prepared to test its limits. It was clear to her that she had no choice in the matter.

Manon's face hardened as the city gates groaned open. A contingent of armed guards fanned out in two semicircles around the young countess, moving in slowly, swords drawn.

Manon scowled as the men dragged her away.

CHAPTER 95

Valle del Bove
Mount Etna, Sicily
April 21, 1282
4:47 p.m.

SICILIANA **STOLE** an anxious glance at the afternoon sun sinking beneath the slopes of Mount Etna's crater. The falling light did little to ease her mind as she received the troubling news from Taormina. She glanced down at the bloodied *Bannera dà Sicilia* in her hands.

Gaetano Amici fell to his knees for a long moment, trying to catch his breath.

"Tonight?" she asked. "Are you certain of this?"

"*Sì*," Gaetano sputtered, nodding his head between large gulps of air. "General Rochefort has taken the city under siege. *Fra'Diavulu* was arrested. He dies tonight at the *Teatro Greco*."

One of the Sicilian rebels stepped forward, a stalky man with dark circles under his eyes. "I say let him die," he said. "The bastard chose the Angevin yoke over his own kind."

All heads whipped toward *Siciliana*. She glanced up at him through her wild hair.

Another rebel nodded, raising his voice. "We don't need Taormina. And if what Amici says about General Rochefort is true, that means Messina is vulnerable."

"This is the distraction we hoped for," another said. "Now is the time to end this once and for all."

Adrianu Amici became angered. "Listen, you *Mamluks*. He is still one of us. He is of Sicilian blood. We cannot leave him to die."

The men grumbled.

"At the expense of our cause?" the stalky rebel scoffed, approaching *Siciliana* like an angry ox. "And what of the lives of the men *we've* lost? Do they not matter?"

Adrianu stepped in front of *Siciliana*, shielding her from the man's advance. "How dare you speak to the *Siciliana* in that tone. After all she's done for us, for Sicily."

The stalky rebel ignored the considerable reprimand. "*Vaffanculu*. At the rate we're losing our men, there won't be much of a Sicily left."

Snarling his lips, Adrianu clenched a tight fist and slugged the man hard across the face. The rebel tumbled to the ground and snorted a contemptuous laugh, lifting his fingers to his bleeding nose.

Adrianu was now on top of the insolent rebel. "Shut up and fall in line."

Siciliana was just standing there, motionless, expressionless.

The stalky rebel pushed himself up, brushing the dusty black soot from his clothing. "I won't be part of this any longer. I'm going back to Palermo."

Adrianu's eyes turned black with rage. "Don't you turn your back on your people."

The rebel spat at Adrianu's feet, turning and walking away.

Siciliana watched with a cool detachment as the rebel grabbed his gear and sauntered off.

Gaetano turned to *Siciliana* and flashed her a look of desperation. "You must do something!"

But *Siciliana* said nothing.

All eyes turned toward the deserting rebel. The same thought seemed to wash over the men at once. In that moment, the ragtag unit of surviving rebels nodded in agreement. One by one, they turned away from one another and quietly gathered their personal effects, holstering their weapons, slinging heavy sacks of supplies over their shoulders.

The brothers Adrianu and Gaetano blinked in disbelief as the remaining men fell in line behind the defector, limping off together toward the horizon. Bones creaking, gear clanking. What was left of *Siciliana's* rebel army disappeared over the crater's ridgeline.

Siciliana remained silent, turning away from the two brothers. She saw a nearby pile of supplies and went to it. She walked over and knelt over the pile, gathering her weaponry and armor, wondering how the hell it had come to this. *Rebellamentu.* The hope for a free country of their own, falling apart before her eyes.

Gaetano turned and shuffled back to *Siciliana*. "Are you going to let this happen?"

Siciliana kept her gaze trained on her sword. She turned inward, awash in her own thoughts. "Now I understand," she told herself. "I *am* the daughter of *O Santo Cavaleri.*"

Adrianu and Gaetano exchanged confused glances.

Siciliana stood up and faced the two men. "What kind of Sicilian abandons their own family?" she said. "I don't want to live in a Sicily where we leave our own kind to perish at the hands of our oppressor. Sicily is *cosca*, or it is nothing." With that, *Siciliana* sheathed her blade. "I'm leaving for Taormina."

Adrianu gazed at her for a long moment. He took a deep breath.

"You are outnumbered. Rochefort's forces are far too strong," Adrianu said. "You go to certain death."

Siciliana looked up to him with a steely resolve. As a little girl, she would dream, wondering if only she had been lucky enough to live in another place, another time, would she have fought as valiantly as the perfect knight, Orlando? Today she had her answer. In that moment, she heard Orlando's words come flowing into her mind: *Then I will live forever.*

Adrianu shook his head in disbelief. He anxiously ran his fingers through his oily black hair, trying to process her reasoning.

Siciliana approached the two brothers. She placed her palms gently on their shoulders, a tender smile crossing her lips. "When you find a friend, you find a treasure. I need my friends now more than ever. Go back to Palermo and tell Captain Mastrangelo what happened here."

Adrianu and Gaetano gazed at her for a long moment. They knew what they had to do. The two men nodded and turned to collect their personal effects.

"How will you fight a thousand men without an army?" Gaetano said.

"I have an army," she said.

Gaetano looked up at her with a curious stare, slinging a supply sack over his shoulder.

Siciliana lifted her finger toward the eastern horizon. "The people of Taormina," she said. "It's time to wake them up."

CHAPTER 96

Castello Saraceno
Taormina, Sicily
April 21, 1282
5:27 p.m.

IN THE prison beneath *Castello Saraceno*, the notorious Messinese knight named Cicero Vespiri was alone in his cell, shackled in rusted chains. He couldn't stand at his full height due to the connecting chain from his wrists to his ankles, forcing him into a hunched stoop. This was meant to create the posture of submission. But he was unafraid. *I deserve death.* A rightful punishment for doing nothing when the woman whom he loved begged for his help as his brothers and sisters suffered around him.

What have I become?

Cicero couldn't begin to imagine what Lady Manon Orleans ever saw in him. He remembered the day they met like it was yesterday.

The afternoon was cold and dreary. Standing alone at a smithing station in *Matagrifone*'s military barracks, fifteen-year-old Cicero Vespiri held a long, glowing blade against an anvil and banged it hard with a hammer, sending out a plume of red-hot embers into the air. *Clank!* The blade glowed white as he pounded it flatter, sharper. *Clank! Clank!* He then tossed it into a nearby trough. The scorching blade hissed and steamed like a fire-breathing dragon as it struck the water.

Suddenly, there was a commotion near the main yard. Cicero raised his eyes from the anvil to see the vicar's own daughter riding atop a white stallion straight into the camp. She was a stunning young girl of about sixteen; her ashen-blond hair, glistening silver in the sun, was braided intricately behind her slender neck.

Lady Manon Orleans confidently approached a cluster of Angevin recruits milling about the grounds. She pulled back the leather reins, bringing her horse to a stop in front of the young men. "My father is seeking a page to serve the great Messinese lord Don Riccardo Riso."

The eager recruits flocked toward her, pushing one another out of the way, laughing and raising their hands.

Cicero remained at his workstation, lowering his eyes and pretending not to notice her. A near-futile exercise, like pretending not to notice the radiant Sicilian sun.

Manon eyed the recruits moving toward her. She didn't seem interested in any of them. Sighing to herself, she gazed out over the group of boys, spotting Cicero working alone at a forge. She kicked her horse and trotted toward him.

"You there," she called out. "The Messinese lord Don Riccardo Riso is seeking a page."

Cicero kept his eyes trained downward. "I'm no page." He brushed his curly black hair away from his eyes. "I'm a *cavaleri.*"

Manon raised an eyebrow as she reined her horse to a stop. "A Sicilian knight?"

Instantly, Cicero snapped out a stiletto blade and twirled it effortlessly between his fingers. *"Sì."*

Manon's eyes narrowed, seemingly transfixed by the dangerous motions of the blade spinning in his hand. "What are you doing here?"

Cicero shook his head and snorted. A prying question. "I have nowhere else to go. My family is dead."

Manon frowned, a look of consternation crossing her face. "What's your name?"

Cicero glanced up, continuing to twirl his stiletto. "The others call me Brother Devil."

An inquisitive look fell across Manon's face, as if she didn't quite know what to make of the strange boy standing before her. "A devil with the blade, indeed."

Cicero rolled his eyes and sheathed his stiletto. He grabbed a prickly pear fruit from his pocket and tore into its fleshy skin with his front teeth. Red juice dribbled down his chin. He wiped his mouth with his sleeve, leaving bright red stains on his white tunic that made it appear as if he were bleeding from multiple stab wounds.

He glanced down and recognized the royal *fleur-de-lis* seal emblazoned on the front of the horse's breast strap. He took another bite of the prickly pear and said, "This is the vicar's prized breeding stallion."

Manon pursed her lips and nodded with a hint of defiance. "*Oui*. I'm riding him to the *Megaliti* this morning."

Cicero raised a suspicious eyebrow. He pointed to a set of Moorish throwing knives strapped to the horse's saddle. "Planning to run into much armed resistance among those rocks?"

An impish grin crossed Manon's lips as if she had been caught red-handed. "Look . . . I'd rather my father didn't know about me borrowing—"

Cicero held up his hand and smirked. In that instant, he couldn't help but feel a surge of admiration for her blatant audacity—sneaking off into the province's interior with the vicar's priceless horse. "The way I see it"—he swept his arm in a broad arc—"all of this will belong to you one day anyway."

Manon grinned, her gaze softening. She tightened her grip on the reins. "Good knights are in short supply. I'll be sure Don Riso hears of you."

Cicero nodded affirmatively. "Milady."

Manon eyed him curiously, then turned her horse and trotted away.

Cicero's brow furrowed over the bridge of his nose, his gaze sharpening. *The entire world will hear of me.* With that, he slammed the hammer hard into the anvil.

Clank!

As Cicero stood in the dark prison cell beneath Taormina Fortress, his eyes jolted open. He was alarmed by the sounds of an altercation coming from outside the chamber. Muffled voices.

Confused, he stood a moment in silence and listened. Suddenly, there was a fumbling of large iron keys. Then the bolts of the door began to turn slowly.

· ❧❦ ·

Outside the cell, a prison guard leapt to his feet as a figure appeared at the base of the stone stairwell. Lady Manon Orleans stepped forward from the shadows, wearing a hooded cloak. She pushed a skinny soldier in front of her, a Moorish throwing knife held against his throat.

"Lady Orleans?" the guard stammered. "You're not allowed down here."

"I will see the prisoner immediately," she commanded.

"We are under strict orders from the general," he said. "No one sees the prisoner until the execution."

In that instant, Manon unsheathed another Moorish throwing knife from beneath her cloak and flicked it up tightly against the man's groin. "When my father hears of my treatment here, I will see to it that you're shipped to the diseased trenches of Albania if you do not open this cell at once."

The guard nodded and fumbled for the keys, opening the gate.

Manon released the knife from the soldier's throat and stepped into the reeking cell. She could barely contain her emotions at the sight of her beloved knight.

The guard moved into the cell and grabbed Cicero, yanking him upright against the force of the chain. "Look alive, Sicilian filth."

Cicero grimaced.

"Enough!" Manon said. "Now leave us."

Reluctantly, the guard sneered at her and sauntered out of the cell.

Manon turned to Cicero, her face softening. "I didn't want to believe it when they told me."

Cicero gazed back at her. He fought every urge to break from his chains and embrace her.

"Is it true?" she asked.

"Is what true?"

"Are you in league with the rebels?" she said.

Cicero pursed his lips. *"Sì."*

Manon searched Cicero's eyes. She knew he was telling the truth. A long, uncomfortable moment passed between the two lovers. Finally, she nodded her head. "Good."

Cicero's brow furrowed. He cocked his head in confusion.

"My father is a selfish man," Manon said. "His cruelty knows no bounds. The world would be a better place without men like him."

Cicero frowned, bowing his head in regret. "No one should have to say that about their own *patri.*"

Manon blew out a deep breath. "There's something you need to know." She grasped Cicero's palm and rested it on her abdomen. "I'm pregnant with your child."

Cicero's jaw dropped. *"Spinarosa?"*

Manon lifted her chin and nodded.

Cicero looked speechless. He held her hand tightly in his own. He spoke softly, carefully. "This is incredible news. You must go, then. Raise our Sicilian child as an act of *rebellamentu*."

Manon pursed her lips and shook her head. "Rochefort has the city under siege. He's going to massacre the entire population tonight. No one will be spared."

Cicero's face contorted with a mix of sadness and anger. He gritted his teeth and yanked viciously on his shackles. His strength sapping quickly, he finally relented to his restraints. His chest heaved up and down.

Manon's eyes fell to her abdomen. She placed her palm firmly over her stomach. "I carry Sicilian blood. I will stand and die with them."

Cicero's eyes turned wide. "No. Run. Escape tonight."

Manon shook her head defiantly. There was conviction in her eyes. Willfulness.

Cicero's brow narrowed. *"Spinarosa*, no . . ."

Manon heard the jailer shift outside the cell. She backed up, still looking at Cicero. Her eyes brimmed with love and loss. Then she turned and rushed away into the lightless stairwell, her cloak flowing behind her.

"Manon!" Cicero yelled, left alone to watch helplessly as all traces of her disappeared, swallowed forever by the darkness.

CHAPTER 97

Valle del Bove
Mount Etna, Sicily
April 21, 1282
7:45 p.m.

MY BROTHER is alive.

Siciliana stood alone on the crater's edge, remembering the exact moment she had that realization. Now that she knew the truth, everything in her life suddenly fell into place. She no longer needed sleep. Her fatigue was gone, her weaknesses forgotten. She felt her spirit awash in the full glory of *rebella-mentu*, and *occhinero*.

We will be cosca *again,* she told herself. *Sicily is family . . . or it is nothing.*

A blood-scarlet sunset fell over the landscape, twinging the clouds with a hellish glow. A cauldron of *Vespertilio* bats flew out from the surrounding volcanic caves, a large swath of flapping bodies screeching together as one mass across the darkened sky.

Siciliana watched the winged beasts disappear into the night as she methodically snapped on her gauntlets, her leather chest plate, and her belt, then strapped her stiletto to her abdomen, giving the snug leather straps a tug. She braided her raven-black hair back and away from her eyes, then wiped vibrant red-and-gold paint across her face in a diagonal pattern. She unfolded *Bannera dâ Sicilia* and wrapped it tightly around her shoulders, securing it like a cape.

No matter where I am thrown, I will always land standing.

General Guy de Rochefort had challenged her.

Tonight, *Siciliana* would rise to that challenge.

CHAPTER 98

Teatro Greco
Taormina, Sicily
April 21, 1282
9:16 p.m.

THE *TEATRO Greco* was one of the largest ancient Greek amphitheaters in Sicily. Clinging to the side of Taormina's most southern cliff, and with a diameter over three hundred feet, the amphitheater's horseshoe-shaped seating enclosure culminated in an expansive stage. Far off in the distance, framed perfectly between the stage's main pillars, Mount Etna's crater could be seen spewing forth spectacular lava fountains and fiery balls of molten rock, illuminating the night sky in a hellish red glow. Plumes of smoke and ash ascended into the sky like a great cypress tree. Lightning flashed from the roiling clouds.

Tonight, five thousand Sicilians, the largest crowd the *Teatro Greco* could hold, were gathered in the theater and waiting to bear witness to another spectacle for the ages—the execution of the notorious Messinese knight *Fra'Diavulu*.

In the outer passages below the theater, Cicero Vespiri, shackled at the wrists and ankles, was marched along a rear corridor by a squad of Angevin soldiers. The sound of chains jangled on the floor, accompanied by the heavy scraping of boots in the sandy dirt.

Cicero was bruised and bloodied, but unshaken. He kept his back straight and his chin high. A *cavaleri* was always *en occhinero*. Even in the face of death. Passing a group of fifteen prisoners, they stood in silent tribute as *Fra'Diavulu* marched toward his doom.

Angevin soldiers dragged Cicero up the passageway to the entrance, into the amphitheater. Torchlight fell onto his face, cutting through the darkness, the air carrying the sounds of the massive crowd beyond.

General Guy de Rochefort waited in front of the entranceway amidst the pillar ruins of the amphitheater's atrium. He was garbed in a silver breastplate, a wolfskin draped across his armor's shoulder plates. Beside him was his escort of elite guards. The approaching soldiers handed over Cicero to Rochefort. The brute general gestured to the guards to begin preparing Cicero to enter the amphitheater. Cicero braced himself, almost expecting to be killed in that instant.

Rochefort walked up to Cicero and scowled, looking down his nose without remorse. "Was she worth it? The whore soon to be my wife?"

Cicero glared into his eyes, never breaking eye contact.

Rochefort studied him for a long moment, when a look of recognition crossed his face. "It's been eating away at me since the first day you arrived at *Matagrifone*," he sneered, studying his features. "That stupid boy from the vineyard . . ."

Cicero's brow furrowed over the bridge of his nose, his eyes narrowing into an icy glare.

"Whose father cried like a coward," Rochefort said.

Cicero's breathing became heavier. He felt in that moment as if he could break free of the chains and wrap his hands around the general's throat.

Rochefort stood over Cicero. "Tonight, a great cleansing of Sicilian blood will begin, starting with you." He turned to the guard. "Take him away."

CHAPTER 99

Castello Saraceno
Taormina, Sicily
April 21, 1282
9:19 p.m.

HIGH ABOVE the city in the *Castello Saraceno*, Lady Manon
Orleans stood alone in her quarters. The father of her child
would soon be executed, and along with him the city's entire
population. Fathers, sons, mothers, daughters. *Innocent
Sicilian families.* Manon placed a palm over her abdomen
and closed her eyes. A feeling of strength and resolve surged
through her. She was ready to die as one of them.

Shaking the troubling thoughts from her mind, Manon let
out a deep breath and moved to the window overlooking the
city below. She beheld the dramatic eruption of Mount Etna on
the horizon. A forked river of lava serpentined down the face
of the mountain, consuming everything in its path. Suddenly,
a flash of lightning brightened the night sky. In that instant,
Manon thought she saw the figure of a woman racing swiftly
across the city's rooftops.

The woman had long dark hair braided back and up, a blade strapped to her waist, a cape billowing in the wind.

Manon's eyes widened, transfixed. The figure moved gracefully from roof to roof, never losing footing, maintaining perfect balance. Poise. It was *her*. The free woman who decimated Angevin strongholds and fortresses with the stroke of her sword.

Manon backed away from the window, clenching her fists. Deep down, she sensed it might not be a dire night after all.

The *Siciliana* had arrived in Taormina.

And with her . . . *hope*.

CHAPTER 100

SICILIANA **SOARED** effortlessly over the rooftops of Taormina, sprinting and leaping from roof to roof as she traversed the length of the cliffside city.

In one of the homes—its walls painted pale yellow and festooned with pink wildflowers—a young girl toddled out onto the balcony. Suddenly just below her, the girl glimpsed a fiery-looking woman whoosh past her like a Greek goddess blazing down from the sky. Flapping behind her like a cape was a red-and-gold *bannera* emblazoned with the fearsome face of Medusa, crowned by three human legs bent at the knee, and three *cosca* buds.

The young girl's eyes widened with wonder and then excitement. *"Mamma!"* the girl cried, thrusting a finger into the air. *"Siciliana!"*

Panicked, the mother ran and scooped the girl off the balcony, holding her in her arms and turning back into the house.

The little girl never looked away, grinning from ear to ear as she watched *Siciliana* dash away over the rooftops.

CHAPTER 101

Teatro Greco
Taormina, Sicily
April 21, 1282
9:21 p.m.

GRIM MAGISTRATES prodded Cicero Vespiri, pushing him onto the execution platform. On the platform sat a single chopping block and an enormous polished ax.

Cicero didn't look away from these implements of death as he felt a strong hand press into his shoulder and push him to the ground, his kneecaps cracking into the stone floor.

The executioner then laid his palm on Cicero's head and pressed it tightly on the wooden anvil as an aide wrapped a gnarly rope around Cicero's neck, securing him tightly to the wooden block.

Cicero lifted his eyes up to the crowd and saw thousands of glassy gazes trained on him. The audience sat in shock and horror. *Fra'Diavulu*, the Brother Devil, was about to lose his head here at the *Teatro Greco* in Taormina.

Oh Sicily, Cicero thought, *you take your best and turn them to ashes.*

Cicero turned to see a royal magistrate step forward onto the platform and unravel a large scroll. The chief magistrate had a facial tic that made his nose twitch like a rat's. He looked at the crowd with bored, apathetic eyes.

"You stand on charges of high treason and conspiracy," the magistrate boomed. "You will be beheaded, drawn, and quartered. Your head will be placed on a pike to be displayed in the city of Messina, and each of your limbs sent to the three corners of this island. Have you any last words?"

Cicero accepted his death but would not accept the charges before him. He unstrapped his gauntlet and, in a final act of defiance, tossed it out toward the audience. The gauntlet seemed to fly through the air in slow motion before landing on the ground at their feet. A gauntlet of defiance. *"Vaffanculu,"* Cicero sneered one last time.

The entire crowd gasped.

Unmoved, the magistrate nodded to the executioner.

The crowd fell silent as the executioner hoisted his ax, feeling its weight, before raising it above his head into a striking position.

Cicero's eyes rolled toward the crowd. A thousand horrified faces blinked back at him. There was utter silence. Then his eyes fluttered shut as he resigned himself to his fate.

CHAPTER 102

SICILIANA GRIPPED the brick and pulled herself up, peering over the ledge of the back wall of the ancient *Teatro Greco*'s highest seating section. Lit by the orange glow of flickering torches, the rear wall of the theater's seating bowl backed right into the edge of a steep mountain face rising from the rocky shoreline below. The climb up along the back face of the theater would've proved difficult to the average rock climber, but the *Siciliana* wasn't average.

Peering over the ledge, *Siciliana* narrowed her gaze, surveying the entire scene before her. From her position, she could hear the magistrate declaring Cicero's sentence into the amphitheater, the rumblings of the tense crowd. Angevin guards were stationed at the tops of each of the theater's six aisles, jeering and laughing at the spectacle on the stage below. With the guards' backs to her, *Siciliana* knew this was her only way forward.

She saw the plan materializing in her mind as clearly as the firelight from Etna's eruption filled the night sky. First, she knew she would have less than ten seconds to swiftly and silently dispatch each of the six guards, wasting no movement, no single breath. One could not be given even a second to alert the next. Once the guards were taken down, she had to go right for Cicero. She would sprint down the middle aisle, where she'd have the clearest shot, and whip her blade at the executioner. The trained soldier instinct in Cicero would kick him into action. He would free himself, and they'd turn the crowd on the Angevin contingent.

General Rochefort's garrison would soon know the fury of the Sicilians on Vespers night.

Siciliana closed her eyes, gulping a deep breath into her lungs. *This is it.* She would have to be swift. Gritting her teeth, *Siciliana* hoisted herself up, throwing her legs gracefully over the ledge. Without one wasted motion, she turned on the balls of her feet and rushed the first guard.

Seconds later, the guard dropped to his knees, rolling onto his stomach. Behind him, a soldier hidden from view leapt forward, snarling.

Before she knew it, the weighted balls of a net whipped forward and wrapped themselves around *Siciliana*, ensnaring her in a tight, inescapable web. She growled loudly as the six men plowed forward and tackled her to the ground, sending a shock wave through her system.

A trap, she thought.

Squirming violently, she growled as the men overpowered her and hoisted her up, carrying her down into the amphitheater.

CHAPTER 103

A SCREAM rang out.

The crowd gasped in shock as Angevin soldiers emerged down the center aisle, carrying a woman thrashing in a net. Her cries echoed through the entire amphitheater.

Cicero Vespiri's eyes snapped open. He watched helplessly as the soldiers moved down the aisle toward the stage. Seconds later, the prisoner they carried came fully into view through the meshed netting. Cicero beheld her long raven-black hair and face covered with red-and-gold war paint.

Aetna, he thought, his face contorting in anguish.

General Rochefort's eyes turned black with deadly satisfaction as the prisoner was carried forward.

The men moved *Siciliana* onto the stage, cutting the net away and pushing her into the impossibly large arms of the executioner.

"Citizens of Taormina . . . people of Sicily!" *Siciliana* cried. "The Angevins murdered my father, Don Vittorio Vespiri, *O Santo Cavaleri!*"

"Silence!" the executioner growled, slugging her across the face.

Siciliana spat blood from her mouth. "Your families are next! Rochefort will slaughter everyone in this city. Rise up now against our oppressor!"

A wave of distress moved over the murmuring audience, whose members exchanged concerned looks. Their anxiety quickly turned to anger.

As the air seemed to thicken among the crowd, the executioner dragged *Siciliana* up onto the platform as they rolled out another chopping block, nothing more than a splintered oaken log. The executioner grabbed *Siciliana* by the back of the head and pressed her facedown onto the wood, holding her in place under his foot as another solider bound her hands.

Siciliana and Cicero found themselves facing each other, gazing into each other's eyes across the execution stage.

Cicero shook his head and thrashed in place, attempting to summon all of his strength to break the gnarled bonds of the rope. But he hadn't eaten in over a day, and suddenly he felt the strength sap from his body. "Why, Aetna?" he said. "Why did you come here? The fight for Sicily is worth more than my life."

Siciliana didn't make a sound. It was as if the world fell silent around her. She only lay there, her neck on the chopping block, her body pressed to the ground, as she gazed fondly upon her long-lost brother. "Sicily is *cosca*, or it is nothing."

General Rochefort sensed the tense and explosive energy growing in the crowd. He stepped forward and thundered into the ancient theater with the booming gravity of a thespian villain declaring his cruel intentions, just like the great Greek actors had done here centuries earlier. "If any of you utter one sound, I will have the entire city rounded up and beheaded on this very stage . . . one by one . . . with your heads placed in straw baskets and strewn from the side of these very cliffs onto the villages below."

General Rochefort turned toward the executioner and gave him a nod.

The executioner approached Cicero and hoisted his large ax, its surface polished and gleaming in the orange torchlight that surrounded the perimeter of the stage and theater.

Siciliana and Cicero kept their gazes trained on one another as the executioner lowered the tip of the ax gently to *Siciliana*'s neck as he steadied his stance over the young captain. Even with a light touch, the ax's razor-sharp edge cut into *Siciliana*'s sweaty flesh, the salty liquid stinging the open wound.

Staring into the ax's large reflection before him, Cicero observed what appeared to be a terrible feathered beast flutter out of the darkness like a fearsome griffon. The beast came to rest on the back wall of the theater's bowl perimeter, gripping the stone with its sharp talons, retracting its immense wingspan into its chest. The creature's powerful build and hooked beak were silhouetted against the night sky. In that moment, Cicero's face softened, a wild smirk forming on his lips as he beheld the familiar form of a great Sicilian golden eagle.

Cicero's eyes widened, his lungs filling with breath. Then, he burst into laughter. It was the same bellowing, bloodcurdling howl he reserved for unleashing his worst upon his victims.

The audience gasped in horror as the devilish knight crowed maniacally in the face of his own oblivion. *Fra'Diavulu*'s notorious laughter. The men and women closed their eyes and made the sign of the cross as the executioner steadied his blade.

Suddenly, a man in black sprung up from the middle of the crowd. He pushed his way through the heap of Sicilians, dashing for the main aisle.

General Rochefort's eyes widened with rage. He thrust a powerful finger into the audience. "Kill him!"

Stupefied, the Angevins stared on in shock, paralyzed with astonishment.

As the man in black reached the aisle steps, as if in slow motion, he threw off his cloak to reveal Arabic-style leather armor and gauntlets, armed with two stiletto blades crossing his abdomen. He had olive skin, curly black hair, and a thick beard.

Don Rapaci.

In one fell motion, *Don Rapaci* unsheathed his dueling swords and leapt through the air as Rosalia opened her wings and soared down toward the stage, letting out a piercing cry. *Don Rapaci* whipped the blades hard over his head, throwing them at the executioner. The blades whooshed heavily through the air and smashed into the executioner's burly chest.

The executioner let out a loud gasp as the blow sent him hurtling backward, dropping the ax in front of Cicero's head, the ax nearly cleaving off the front of his face.

Not wasting a precious second, *Siciliana* sprung to her feet and sawed the ropes binding her wrists against the ax's sharp edge. An Angevin soldier was already charging her position when the golden eagle shrieked and dropped from the night sky, plunging its sharp talons into his eyeballs. The soldier clutched his face and screamed as he tripped off the platform, breaking his neck on the stone floor below.

Don Rapaci unsheathed another sword strapped to his back, carefully flipping it around and whipping it hilt-first up to *Siciliana*.

Siciliana snatched it easily from the air and swung it around to meet an attacking soldier. With one fell swoop, she slashed the blade across the soldier's neck, then brought its edge down against the rope binding Cicero.

Cicero immediately leapt to his feet and caught the maimed soldier, pulling the rapier from his hands. He then turned to deflect another soldier's incoming blow.

Don Rapaci vaulted onto the stage and retracted his blades from the fallen executioner's chest, joining his friends on the killing ground.

The three Sicilians worked together, striking and parrying as the Angevins fell upon them from all sides.

"Moranu li Francisi!" Siciliana cried into the night.

Suddenly, the men and women in the crowd seemed to feel their hearts fill with a deadly mix of anger and resolve. As one force in the night, those who had arms drew their blades, rose up from their seats, and fell upon the scrambling Angevin contingent.

In the tumult of chaos, General Rochefort gnashed his teeth and bolted toward the exit. He leapt onto a horse and lashed the reins, galloping off down the narrow street toward *Castello Saraceno.*

Through the throng of clashing bodies, *Siciliana* watched Rochefort storm off.

Baring her teeth, she removed Sicily's flag strapped to her back and tied it to the end of a spear. She hoisted it high into the sky for all to see, framed by the magnificent display of Mount Etna erupting violently on the horizon, lava thrashing from her crater like a boiling *sugo* sauce.

As the men and women gazed up at *Bannera dâ Sicilia* waving majestically before them, *Siciliana* saw reflected in each of their liquid eyes ten thousand flags of Sicily staring back at her. She thrust the spear in the direction of *Castello Saraceno.*

"Tonight, the Angevins will know the fury of Vespers!" *Siciliana* cried. "For your families! For Sicily! *Moranu li Francisi!"*

Yelling as one voice, the angry throng of Sicilians thrust their swords into the air. "Death to the Angevins!"

CHAPTER 104

LIKE A fleet of galleons lurching away from their moorings, five thousand Sicilians stormed from the amphitheater, barreling down the narrow street. The rebels plowed a path straight to the city's main open-air piazza, culminating in front of the *Palazzo Corvaja*, a tenth-century Arab palace that loomed over the square. Dim torchlight cast an ominous orange glow along the solemn face of the fortress, its long lancet windows towering over the piazza.

Amidst the confusion, dozens of Angevin soldiers organized their numbers and pushed forward up the street, barreling faster and faster toward the advancing rebels.

Cicero Vespiri moved out in front of the rebels, starting into a dead run. He dunked his rapier into a barrel of oil and then slammed it into a burning torch. The flame licked the oil, igniting down the length of the blade.

"Assalto!" Cicero cried.

Before the men and women of Taormina had time to consider the danger, they ran after Cicero, lining up behind the notorious knight they knew as *Fra'Diavulu*. The Taorminians stormed forward in an attack, shouting into the night sky.

The two armies, Sicilian and Angevin, barreled toward one another down the street at breakneck speed.

Cicero pointed himself like an arrow at a soldier carrying the royal *fleur-de-lis* heraldry of *Re Carlu*. He lowered his shoulder and crashed into the soldier, flipping him backward into the air. Then he swung his flaming rapier and cracked another soldier across the skull.

Don Rapaci ran beside the Messinese knight, matching him move for move, slashing his way into the Angevin ranks.

Rushing head-on into the main piazza, the rebels smashed into the melee of Angevin soldiers, crying with a feverish rage not heard since Vespers night.

Amidst the tumult of battle, Cicero glanced upward. A smirk crossed his lips as he beheld *Siciliana* flying across the rooftops just above them, keeping up with their charge. She wielded *Bannera dâ Sicilia* tied to the tip of a long spear, the flag flying in the wind as she ran.

Siciliana leapt effortlessly from roof to roof, hoisting the Sicilian flag high for all to see.

On the ground below, an Angevin lieutenant stood his ground as the rebels advanced, hacking left and right with his sword.

Don Rapaci spun around him on his heel and thrust it into his back, piercing his lungs from behind. He then rushed past the lieutenant as he dropped to his knees, his eyes wide with shock.

In that moment, *Siciliana* whipped the flag spear down into the fray. Its sharp tip smashed into the lieutenant's sternum. The dying lieutenant looked down at the spear protruding from his chest. He gripped the spear tightly as his legs gave out, falling backward to the ground. A throng of rebels swarmed around him, each taking turns thrusting their blades into his torso.

Siciliana launched herself from the rooftop, grabbing a thick clothesline hanging between two building structures. The clothesline snapped and swung her down. She flew over the melee of clashing bodies and hit the ground hard. She strode across the battlefield, unsheathing her stiletto, deflecting incoming strikes with every step. The Angevins thought they had an easy target. But they were wrong.

With each blow she absorbed, *Siciliana* felt herself becoming stronger. Her pace quickened, then, picking up her feet, she sprinted up the city's main artery away from the clashing bodies, turning on the narrow street leading to *Castello Saraceno*. General Rochefort had retreated for the fortress, and she was determined not to let him escape.

The Angevins closed their ranks and moved in on the advancing rebels.

Cicero and *Don Rapaci* rushed toward them, swords swinging in unison. As they advanced, they were assaulted from all sides by four soldiers. Cicero cracked the hilt of his sword into one soldier's face as *Don Rapaci* spun on his heel and maneuvered his blades in swift, precise motions. In the blink of an eye, the remaining three soldiers dropped to their knees with holes through their hearts.

Don Rapaci winked at Cicero, before running off to engage more approaching soldiers.

Cicero was in the center of the clashing bodies when he saw a hulking Angevin step out from the *Palazzo Corvaja*. The giant man had a horribly scarred face with only one eye, like a cyclops. It was a haggard face that had seen too much war.

To Cicero, the hulking soldier seemed to step right out of a harrowing Homer epic. The Angevin cyclops carried a two-handed steel mace with eight knife-edged hinged flanges. Two

limber swordsmen swarmed around the giant Angevin, protecting his flanks as he bludgeoned helpless rebels from above
with his mace.

Cicero's eyes widened in horror as he beheld rebel skulls
crushed beneath the cyclops's mace, sending fountains of
blood running into the streets. Cicero gripped his rapier and
gritted his teeth, steeling himself for the fight of his life.

CHAPTER 105

SICILIANA **MOVED** carefully and silently as she entered the secret cliffside entrance leading into *Castello Saraceno*'s small cistern, dimly lit by sparse sconces on the wall. The stagnant water quickly soaked her leather boots up to the midcalf as she entered the liquid chamber.

The cistern, built into the cliff directly beneath the castle, stored a small water supply for the fortress. The moldy smell wafting in the chamber told her that this water tank had been long neglected. Dank, diseased, putrid.

Spotting a single soldier emerge in the dark, *Siciliana* crept up behind him and slashed her blade across the guard's throat. He splashed face-first into the water. Suddenly, another soldier sprung from the shadows, lunging for her from behind. Her stiletto, already at her back, caught him right through the sternum, like hooking a fish through the gill.

Siciliana retracted her blade and dashed up the small staircase leading out of the cistern. She entered a long hallway lit only by flickering torches and so narrow, it could fit only one person wide.

Siciliana slammed to a stop as she saw five Angevin royal guards hovering down the length of the hallway. Each man was heavily armored with their rapiers drawn. These hulking brutes were trained for one thing and one thing only—cold-blooded murder. *Siciliana* knew she would have to move fast among them, eyeballs to eyeballs.

Summoning all of her *occhinero*, *Siciliana* inhaled a deep breath and charged the line of deadly guards. She sprinted toward the first guard, flipping directly over him and landing between him and the second guard. With her blade, she swiftly stabbed the first in the back, then the second in the chest.

Unu ... dui ...

Siciliana retracted her blade and spun to the ground, immediately maneuvering around the third guard's extended rapier. She moved in and wrapped her arm around his throat. She tightened her biceps and, with a sharp twist, snapped his neck.

Tri ...

Using her forward momentum, *Siciliana* kicked the guard's corpse directly into the fourth guard, who instinctively extended his arms to catch his fallen comrade. She then leapt into the air and projected herself against the side of the wall, jumping over them both.

In one fell swoop, she thrust her blade backward and upward into the guard's groin canal. Flicking her wrist, she gave her blade a sharp twist for good measure.

Quattru ...

She grabbed a dagger from the guard's belt and whipped it forward. The dagger zipped through the air and plunged right into the fifth soldier's windpipe. He dropped hard to his knees, then fell face-first to the wet stone with a sickening crack as his skull bones were broken, sending shards of bone matter into his brain.

Cincu.

Taking a deep breath, *Siciliana* picked up her feet and ran up the sloping pathway into the fortress's main hall full of Angevin soldiers. She dashed across the room and clotheslined a man with her forearm. She kicked a heavy wooden table that flipped into the air and crashed into a group of soldiers, knocking them to the floor. She then flipped and twirled high into the air, slashing each man across the face as she spun forward. A whirlwind of death.

Seconds later, a hulking armored figure stomped into the fray, wielding a two-handed claymore broadsword. The giant swung it heavily down toward her, each blow sending sparks up from the stone floor.

General Guy de Rochefort lumbered toward her, swinging his claymore harder and harder with each step. A powerful war machine.

Siciliana parried the onslaught of incoming soldiers between Rochefort's attacks. In a flurry of motion, she swung her sword, punched, kicked, and swept the soldiers closing in around her. In the midst of the chaos, *Siciliana* watched Rochefort disappear down the hallway leading back to the cistern. Running at full tilt, she slammed her shoulder into the last remaining soldier, driving him into the ground and running him through with the tip of her blade.

Siciliana then picked up her feet and made chase.

CHAPTER 106

DON RAPACI barreled toward a heavily armed carriage holding a dozen Angevin troops outside of the *Palazzo Corvaja*.

With a demented cry, one soldier leapt from the carriage and rushed forward with his blade lowered. Before the soldier could attack, his head was snapped to one side by the impact of a sharp stone, thrown by a rebel from the fray.

From that point on, *Don Rapaci* never stopped moving. He charged forward, snatching up the fallen soldier's rapier. This was the *Falcon of Palermo*. A don who had mastered the lifelong practice of *occhinero*.

With focused eyes, *Don Rapaci* swirled in and around the carriage like a cyclone of death. He thrust his blade into one man's clavicle, pulled it out, and whipped it into the throat of another. An archer tried to aim his bow, but in a panic, he misjudged *Don Rapaci*'s speed and dexterity. *Don Rapaci* swung his blade, slashing open the archer's face, severing his nose, then shattered his jaw with his fist. The man splashed into a pool of blood.

Howling in terror, the last surviving soldier in the squad veered away from the carriage and stumbled in the piazza's grassy center, falling face-first into the dirt.

Don Rapaci made chase and leapt on top of him. The soldier rolled onto his back. He raised his hands and begged for his life.

As the tumultuous sounds of battle raged around him, *Don Rapaci* either didn't hear him, or refused to hear him. But in that moment, from behind the black of his eyes were all of the fallen families and orphans of Sicily glaring from the afterlife.

Don Rapaci swung down hard, plunging the blade deep into the soldier's chest. He then worked it free and lunged down again. The soldier's eyes snapped back into his head. He was clearly dead. But *Don Rapaci* swung down again, and again, hacking the soldier into a pulp, covering himself completely in blood.

A stab for each Sicilian soul that lived inside him.

Cicero Vespiri inhaled a deep breath and moved toward the hulking Angevin cyclops and his two flanking swordsmen.

A soldier charged forward from Cicero's blind spot, thrusting his blade out. Cicero instinctively deflected the blow and slugged the man across the face, breaking his jaw. He turned and saw the cyclops glaring right at him. The giant's mace was already coming down at Cicero's head. Cicero dove sideways as the mace crashed to the ground. Landing hard on his stomach, Cicero felt the air knocked from his lungs. He gasped desperately for breath as the two swordsmen stabbed their blades down at him.

As the first blade came down, Cicero rolled to his left, then to his right as the second blade hit. Unable to breathe, Cicero gripped his flaming sword and sprung to his feet. He slashed with power and speed as the two swordsmen backed away while at the same time dodging incoming blows from the giant's mace. One man maneuvered around Cicero and sliced him across the back of the shoulder.

Cicero felt a searing pain as he arched his back and screamed into the night sky.

The giant's mace swung toward his head. Dropping his sword, Cicero clenched his teeth and ducked back. The bulbous mace whooshed past his head and smashed into the chest of one of the two swordsmen. The blow smashed through the man's rib cage.

Cicero rolled away as the mace came down again, just missing his torso. Left with only his stiletto, Cicero found himself in an increasingly hopeless situation. The more they fought, the more control the giant Angevin gained.

Cicero deflected several blows from the remaining swordsman. His only option was to disarm his opponent, but he needed the man to be closer. Cicero stepped into the attacking swordsman, who took the opening and speared him through the shoulder.

In that instant, with the blade through his upper body, Cicero reached out and grabbed the soldier by the back of the neck, gripping the scruff of skin like a dog. He pulled the swordsman forward, slamming his exposed neck right along the edge of the razor-sharp rapier. The swordsman's neck arteries burst open, spouting blood.

Cicero yanked the sword from his shoulder and doubled over. As he looked up, he noticed the cyclops smiling through his rotten teeth.

Staggering backward, Cicero tried to run, but his legs gave out. He sank to his knees, kneeling on the ground. He gazed out across the embattled streets of Taormina, watching as his fellow Sicilians lost their momentum against the waves of Angevins pouring down from the streets all around them.

Bannera dâ Sicilia dropped to the ground near him, the cloth crumpling as it was trampled by retreating rebels.

Cicero made no further attempt to defend himself. He saw an Angevin dagger lying nearby and crawled forward to pick it up, his head pounding as he moved. He pushed himself up to where the cyclops was standing and swung at him again. The cyclops immediately parried downward, smashing the dagger from Cicero's hand.

Pain shot through Cicero's body like a bolt of lightning. His arms shot out to the sides as he barreled over and collapsed to his knees. He felt his limbs go limp but still possessed the strength to reach for the Sicilian flag, gripping the long spear in his hand. He heard the heavy boots of the cyclops saunter up behind him to deliver the final blow.

"Tonight, I will send the Brother Devil back to hell!" the giant Angevin bellowed.

Cicero, kneeling like a condemned man for the executioner, tightened his grip around the flag spear. He could sense the cyclops moving behind him, measuring his killing stroke. He knew he would feel the mace smashing into the back of his skull at any moment. But as he heard the mace whooshing through the air, Cicero ducked sideways with surprising speed, and in one fell swoop brought the spear around, planting its end firmly into the ground and thrusting its tip upward. As the cyclops lumbered forward with all of his weight, Cicero thrust the flag spear up into his stomach and through his back, giving it a sharp twist and severing his spine.

The cyclops's ugly face contorted in pain.

"You first," Cicero growled, slowly retracting the flag spear from the hulking Angevin's stomach. He stood there, watching the last light of life snuff out from the soldier's only eye.

Barely able to stand, Cicero dropped the flag spear at his side and fell face-first to the ground. His shoulder wound bled into the street beneath him. He was unable to move, unable to think.

The rebels around him were now in full retreat, dispersing in all directions away from the approaching Angevin reinforcements, tossing their weapons as they ran. Some rebels leapt onto abandoned horses, tearing off toward the city gates in haste.

The fight for Taormina, Cicero knew, would soon be lost, and worse, so would the future of *rebellamentu*.

CHAPTER 107

SICILIANA **MOVED** swiftly down the steps leading into the dark of *Castello Saraceno*'s cistern. She noticed the sconces lining the walls had been extinguished, long trails of smoke filling the air. Staying quiet and pressed against the wall, she moved into the great black oblivion, as though entering the gates of Hades. She slowed her breathing, willing her senses to adjust quickly to the dark and quiet. She maneuvered down the staircase and stepped into the water, her boots once again becoming soaked with stagnant water.

Suddenly, *Siciliana* felt the painful squeeze of a metal vise clamp shut around her neck. Instinct kicking in, she couldn't stop her hand from immediately grabbing the vise and attempting to tug it away. The vise squeezed her neck, choking her with each tug.

Siciliana knew deep in her bones what it was.

This was the device that had killed her *patri.*

"You!" she said. "You took everything from me . . . You murdered my family!"

Siciliana tugged the vise furiously, sweat pouring down her forehead.

"It's the panic that kills you," Rochefort said.

With that, Rochefort swung his heavy claymore upward and thrust it downward. *Siciliana* deflected the force of the blow with her stiletto and spun away in the direction of his momentum. Before she could land her footing, the large claymore arced through the air, directly at her forehead. Struggling to make a choice, *Siciliana* pushed back on her heels and fell into the pool of water, splashing down hard. She tugged on the vise, only making its stranglehold worse.

Rochefort's claymore swung down hard again toward *Siciliana*'s groin. With all of the strength in her heels, she pushed herself backward, the heavy sword smashing, spraying dirty water into *Siciliana*'s eyes. The giant battle sword swung down again and again as *Siciliana* scraped her way across the cistern's floor. Her arms and legs burned. She tugged at the device furiously. She felt the blood swelling dangerously in her head. Bursts of light started flashing before her eyes. She could barely breathe.

Rochefort stopped swinging, halting his onslaught, giving *Siciliana* a chance to panic and feel the effects of the vise. He couldn't put himself through the patient art of stalking to let the moment be ruined by the tip of his claymore. Silently, he stepped forward.

On her knees, *Siciliana* looked up as Rochefort sauntered closer, standing over her. "It's the panic that kills you," he said.

Siciliana tried to move, but her legs were fatigued and unresponsive. She gasped for breath. She knew it was only a matter of minutes before she'd black out. Then, an instant later, she noticed the movement of an apparition lingering in the darkness behind Rochefort.

The attack came with stunning, deadly swiftness.

Thwack!

Rochefort let out a pained gasp as a curved Moorish blade slammed directly into his spine. His eyes shot open in shock.

Siciliana snapped to attention, narrowing her gaze to the razor-sharp blade staring her directly in the face.

Thwack!

Another blade punched into his back.

Thwack! Thwack!

Two more blades burst from Rochefort's sternum in tight groups, each nearly on top of the next. This was a true marksman.

Struggling for breath, Rochefort felt his lungs fill up with his own blood. He let out a pained cough as blood vomited from his mouth, oozing down his chin.

Rochefort dropped to his knees, splashing into the stagnant water, coming face to face with *Siciliana*. He glared at her for a long moment through his bloodshot eyes.

Siciliana watched as his eyes rolled back into his head and he choked on his own blood. Rochefort's legs gave out, and he fell forward, splashing face-first into his watery grave.

As the general's corpse floated lifelessly in front of her, *Siciliana* slowly lifted her gaze toward the apparition, standing in the darkness of the cistern.

Siciliana's eyes widened as she watched her savior step forward into the light.

CHAPTER 108

"Diavulu!" **Don Rapaci** yelled across the killing ground of the *Palazzo Corvaja.* "Our numbers are faltering!"

His ears ringing, Cicero Vespiri lifted his gaze up toward the streets in front of him. It was pandemonium. Sicilian rebels scattered in all directions as a new Angevin regiment charged down the hill from *Castello Saraceno.* Cicero watched helplessly as rebels around him dropped their arms and ran for their lives. *No,* he thought. *No retreat.*

The Messinese knight noticed the tattered Sicilian flag strewn across the stone before him as rebels stampeded over it, imprinting their dirtied footprints into the bloodstained cloth. In that moment, Cicero's gaze sharpened with resolve. He made a decision that sprung deep from his true Sicilian heart. Arms trembling, he slowly pushed himself off the ground with one hand, gripping the flag spear in the other.

Standing upright, Cicero gritted his teeth and thrust the flag high into the black sky as red glowing embers swirled overhead. He screamed at the top of his lungs. *"Rebellamentu!"*

Lifting one boot in front of the other, he stormed forward against the onslaught of Angevin soldiers. Shocked bystanders watched as a single Sicilian, tired and outnumbered, smashed shoulder-first into the massive body of armored Angevins.

Don Rapaci blinked in astonishment. With a howl, he picked up his feet and chased after Cicero.

"No retreat!" Cicero cried to the men and women around him. "Push forward!"

Cicero barreled on through the nightmare landscape, plowing his way through waves of oncoming soldiers. Moving up the narrow street, he could see the city's prized square, *Piazza IX Aprile*, in the distance. The historic piazza stood high and impregnable atop the steep cliffs. On the horizon, Mount Etna glowed like a furious red-orange lighthouse, spewing pillars of smoke and fire into the sky.

Arrows zipped through the air, cutting down rebels on both sides. Cicero and *Don Rapaci* ran near one another, screaming.

An Angevin archer came close and drew his bowstring. *Don Rapaci* knocked him backward with a broad slash of his sword. The Angevin fell to the ground, gasping, holding his mortal wound tightly.

Gripping the Sicilian flag, Cicero continued uphill, pushing against the tide.

From every corner, every staircase, every window overlooking the main street, Sicilians gazed up and saw Sicily's flag unfurled and pushing forward to the *Piazza IX Aprile*.

The sight emboldened the Sicilian rebels.

The fleeing men and women stopped in a moment of utter bewilderment as Cicero plowed through the Angevins, oblivious to the death bearing down on him from all sides. In a sudden burst of courage and audacity, the rebels lifted their swords and turned to follow him. *"Rebellamentu!"* they shouted among themselves.

Cicero pushed ahead until he barreled into the expansive *Piazza IX Aprile*, and then fought his way up to the cliff's edge, where the Angevin numbers were clustering.

With the flag spear as his only weapon, Cicero crashed his way through the men, leaving them to the angry Sicilian blades charging up behind him. As he approached the sheer cliff ledge, he grabbed an Angevin by the chest plate and pushed him backward over the side. The Angevin howled as he tumbled down thousands of feet to a bone-crushing death on the rocks below.

Don Rapaci moved like a serpent in and around the Angevins as he guarded Cicero's flank. Soldiers dropped face-first into pools of blood around him.

Cicero hoisted himself up onto the cliff ledge, firmly planting his boots into the stone. He stood up tall, lifting his chin high as he hoisted *Bannera dâ Sicilia* into the air.

Tears welled in Cicero's hazel eyes as he waved the Sicilian flag back and forth in a broad, sweeping motion. Far above the city, the red-and-gold flag shimmered into the night sky.

The shrieking face of Medusa, Sicily's Great Protector, cried out to the Sicilian people through the night.

A beacon of rebellamentu.

In that moment, the rebels fighting for their lives in Taormina looked up to the flag emblematic of their new nation. An intense swelling of pride and patriotism filled their hearts. They raised their swords and their voices as they fell upon their oppressors as one brute force, overwhelming the Angevin infantry.

The panicked soldiers couldn't keep up with the endless throng of Sicilians who poured into the streets. They emerged from their homes and ran up and down from the various staircases that connected the stacked levels of the cliffside city.

Some Angevins started tossing their weapons aside and ran away from the battlefield, breaking into a headlong retreat.

But to their horror, they quickly found there was nowhere to go. Every street corner, every staircase, every alleyway had the sharp tip of a blade waiting for them.

Cicero took long, deep breaths as his muscular arms waved the Sicilian flag to and fro. He watched in astonishment as the Angevins attempted to flee, only to be overpowered by the Sicilian rebels. In that moment, deep in his heart, he felt only one thing: *Sicily is ours!*

CHAPTER 109

THE TORTUROUS vise gripped *Siciliana*'s throat, turning her face blue. Her head felt swollen with blood as she sensed herself approaching unconsciousness.

As Rochefort's body splashed face-first into the water, *Siciliana* saw the figure appear behind him.

Lady Manon Orleans stood confidently in the cistern, holding her Moorish throwing knives, her chest heaving. "I am *Spinarosa*," she said confidently. "A rose among thorns."

Siciliana gazed upon her with a mix of shock and relief. The two women stared at one other, a mutual look of solace washing over both of them.

Manon dropped the throwing knife and dashed over to *Siciliana*. "Don't touch it. It's a trap!"

In that instant, *Siciliana*'s eyes widened in realization. *It's the panic that kills you,* she thought to herself.

Manon splashed to her knees, extending her hands in assistance. But *Siciliana* raised her palm, signaling Manon to stay put. *Siciliana* closed her eyes, taking long and deliberate breaths, attempting to slow her breathing, quiet her mind. The rage and fury of battle and death had relentlessly clouded her mind over the past few weeks. As she retreated inward, she wanted to remember who she was, where she came from, and what she had accomplished.

The history that I made, she thought.

A bold new idea that was a people's Sicily would live on for all time, in the face of oppressors bent on spoiling her perfect soil, kept by a nourishing people, who were humble stewards of the gifts the bountiful island provided them. Sicily's crashing shorelines and salty sea air. Her ancient markets. Her velvet *Etna Rosso* wines. Her piquant red and yellow spices. The Greek ruins and Arab mosques and Norman fortresses that dotted her cities and countryside. Millennia of cultures carved in the faces of her people.

Siciliana struggled for a last breath. Soon to be snuffed from existence. But Sicily would not. Sicily would never. Sicily would go on forever.

Then, like a bolt of lightning, the spark came from above. An idea that struck *Siciliana* as if thrust into her mind like a spear directly from the goddess Athena.

Calmo, she thought to herself.

Relaxing the tension in her muscles, *Siciliana* gently raised both her middle fingers to either side of the neck vise. She slowly probed her fingers forward, then backward, studying the grooves of the metal, looking for something.

Then she felt her fingers fall into an indented groove.

Siciliana's gaze narrowed forward with steely purpose. Her green eyes glowed with the light of retribution. Her lips curled up into a half smile. By way of a cognition that now filled her brain, she uttered three empowering words through her teeth. "I am lava." With that, *Siciliana* gently pressed her fingers into the vise's grooves.

Clack!

A trigger unlatched, releasing the tension from the tightening spring inside. The vise slipped easily from *Siciliana*'s neck, falling into her hands.

Siciliana gazed down at the deadly device in her palms. She suddenly felt the thousands of innocent lives that left this world through the sharp and angry jaws of this horrific monster, including her own *patri*.

Siciliana lifted her eyes to Manon, who knelt directly in front of her. Manon gazed back at *Siciliana* with the look of an ally. A friend. Both women suddenly lunged forward, wrapping their arms around one another, squeezing one another tight. Neither made a sound, only the lapping water of the cistern against its stone pillars breaking the silence.

The two women embraced, kneeling together in peace and strength.

CHAPTER 110

Piazza IX Aprile
Taormina, Sicily
April 22, 1282
12:03 a.m. // Twenty-third day of Vespers

THE LAST remaining cries of dying Angevin soldiers pierced the air. Among the dwindling tumult of battle, the exuberant rebels of Taormina came together in the *Piazza IX Aprile*, offering one another hugs, handshakes, and tears of gratitude.

Bannera dâ Sicilia snapped defiantly from its position on the cliff ledge for the whole world to see.

Men and women lit torches, strung out celebratory candles, and laid out long wooden tables in the streets, where they put their best food and other rations. A local baker rolled up with a wooden cart. She offered the rebels her entire shop of goods—cannoli, almond cakes, marzipan, hazelnuts, and the most decadent of them all, Sicily's culinary treasure, the cassatini.

"Mangiatevi!" she admonished, beckoning them all forward. "Please, you must eat now."

A hundred hands stretched forward, grabbing every sweet within reach from the baker's cart, stuffing their mouths with the sugary treats, filling themselves with renewed energy.

Suddenly, a man in the crowd noticed a pair of figures approaching in the distance. His eyes lit up as he pointed down the street. "Over there!"

Like specters from the fog, *Siciliana* and Manon Orleans emerged from the mist and stepped forward onto the *Piazza IX Aprile*, grasping each other's hands. Their faces were worn, their hair mangled, their clothes wet and dirtied, but they stared forward as sharp as blades.

Cicero Vespiri, *Don Rapaci*, and a throng of tired rebels looked on as *Siciliana* and Manon held one another as they approached the piazza. *Siciliana* carried Rochefort's wolfskin over her shoulder.

Cicero's tired eyes widened in astonishment. Reaching the piazza, Manon leapt forward into his arms, planting her parched lips against his own, a single tear trickling down her cheeks.

The rebels poured in and immediately began offering medical aid.

Don Rapaci approached *Siciliana*, the red-orange torch-light illuminating her face. She looked upon him for a long moment, then handed him the wolfskin.

Don Rapaci carefully took it from her, holding it between his palms. He gazed down intently at the silver fur hide that seemed to gleam in the moonlight. It suddenly hit him. A strong punch of retribution right in his gut. The brutal general responsible for the murders of thousands of men, women, and children was dead.

Siciliana looked solemn. "There never was a promise for a free Sicily?"

"There was *one*," *Don Rapaci* responded, pressing a finger into his own heart. "A promise that an orphan son once made to his family . . ." He then pointed his finger toward *Siciliana*'s heart. "To your family. And isn't that as good a promise as any prince or king?" With that, he wrapped the wolfskin around *Siciliana*'s shoulders.

Siciliana looked down at her vanquished enemy's fur hide and nodded with conviction. "I promise that our Sicily will be a home for all Sicilians . . . *in posterum.*"

Amidst the celebration, Cicero Vespiri turned his head toward his sister. His expression implied more than pride. More than approval. *Re Carlu*'s prized city had fallen into Sicilian hands.

Who knows what the future holds for Sicily? he thought. Though there was one thing he did know. *Our people will endure.*

The rebels of Taormina relished in this historic achievement as they swarmed through the city, surveying the damage, and thrust their blades into every last Angevin soldier holding breath in their lungs.

A small oaken table was set out on the *Piazza IX Aprile* amidst the festivities and celebrations of the night. Four rebels sat together.

Their names were *Siciliana, Fra'Diavulu, Don Rapaci,* and *Spinarosa.* Each took turns placing their blade on the table, crisscrossing one another, as if forming the spiny, tightly knit leaves of an artichoke. Sharp. Impenetrable. Deadly. *Cosca.*

Glowing orange torchlight danced across their laughing faces as they smiled, swapped stories, twirled and slurped pasta, and gulped wine, remembering loved ones and the fallen.

From that humble oaken table strewn out on the piazza, four kindred spirits seemed to soar up into the stars, out over the shimmering sea, and high above the island they called their own. They had come from four walks of life, bringing together four complex histories, hopes, and dreams.

They came together as warriors.

They came together as *cosca*, as family.

A Sicilian Family.

CHAPTER 111

Matagrifone
Messina, Sicily
April 23, 1282
11:51 a.m. // Twenty-fourth day of Vespers

RAIN PELTED the roofs of Messina the day General Guy de Rochefort's naked corpse was thrown at the foot of the gates of *Matagrifone*, his bare chest carved with three curved lines emerging from a center point.

The body lay spread-eagled on its back. Rochefort's jaw hung open, his empty eyes gazing lifelessly at the sky. Pools of rainwater formed around the corpse, streams of red blood webbing through the puddles.

The battle for Taormina was over. And France's most brutal general, murderer, and perpetrator of all unthinkable Angevin atrocities throughout Sicily was dead.

Shortly after Rochefort's corpse arrived at *Matagrifone*, Vicar Herbert Orleans locked himself in his personal chambers, refusing to open his doors for his attendants. It was whispered throughout the castle that he was slowly going mad.

Cornered, weak men always broke.

Lying in his bedchamber, Vicar Orleans clutched his silk
sheets, shivering violently. His eyes were haunted with terror.
France's deadliest general had been maimed and murdered
by the Sicilian insurgents. His daughter had gone missing.
Fra'Diavulu was probably dead.

Hearing a commotion rising outside, Orleans turned his
head and looked at his chamber window. It was the sound of a
terrible gathering swelling before the fortress's gates. He heard
it as clearly as if he himself were the one strewn naked on the
streets below.

The murmurs turned to grumblings that turned to deafening jeers that reverberated through the stone castle fortress. By
now, the rain had stopped, but the clouds remained heavy and
dark, drooping low over the distant sea.

Orleans knew it was only a matter of time before the one
they called the *Siciliana* carved a path directly to his doorstep.

A gust of wind swept over the dusty grounds of *Viticultura
Vespiri*. Wild, unkempt grapevines had begun to blossom
across the abandoned property as *Siciliana* walked across the
black volcanic soil.

Siciliana moved toward the old stone manor near the center of the vineyard and found the clearing she was looking for.
She knelt on one knee and scraped her fingernails into the
dirt, carving out a small hole. She reached behind her hair and
unlatched Vittorio's *Gorgoneion Trinacria* pendant. She carefully laid it in the hollow, in the very spot where her *patri* had
died. She brushed the soil back over the hole, packing it tightly
with the black earth that had carried her loved one's blood.

"He would be proud of you," a soft voice said behind her.

The Messinese knight Cicero Vespiri moved up behind her, guiding a horse by the reins. He held his devil war mask in one hand. An army of Sicilians stood behind him.

Siciliana stood up slowly, keeping her eyes on the ground. She turned to face her brother.

"He would be proud of *us*," she said.

"I'll ride ahead to Messina," Cicero said. "Your men will be waiting there for your word."

"And what of Manon?"

Cicero paused for a long moment. He knew he had to tell her the life-changing news. That he would be bringing a child into this new world they had created. But he decided, in that moment, it would have to wait.

Siciliana looked at him, sensing a point coming.

"After Messina falls, Vicar Orleans, her father, will be executed . . . ," Cicero said.

Siciliana grinned. "By my own hands, if I can help it."

Cicero nodded solemnly. "That is why Manon must stay in Taormina," he said. "It will be safe for her there."

Siciliana nodded in return.

The two Sicilians gazed at one another for a long moment. Standing on the very ground where their own painful journeys had started, now reclaiming their home and the life that was taken from them.

Cicero stepped forward. He pulled his sister into a tight embrace, kissing her softly on the cheek. He then looked around at the wild vineyard, its tattered *Gorgoneion Trinacria bannera* still hanging at the entrance, standing the test of time.

"What will you do with this place?" Cicero said.

Siciliana gazed fondly around the vineyard grounds. "Perhaps one day, when Sicily is ours," she said, "we can call this our home once more."

Cicero nodded. "Until we see each other again, Aetna . . . my sister."

Siciliana shook her head. "Aetna Vespiri is no more," she said. "There is only *Siciliana*."

Cicero nodded his head, pressing his fist to his chest. "*Cent'anni . . . Siciliana*."

Siciliana smiled and nodded, pressing her own fist to her chest. "*Cent'anni . . . Fra'Diavulu*."

"*Fra'Diavulu* is no more," he said. "There is only Don Vespiri."

Siciliana nodded. An assured smile beamed from her face. "A true *cavaleri*, indeed."

With that, Cicero mounted his horse, gave it a hearty kick, and tore off. The army of Sicilians trailed behind him. A gust of wind swept a cloud of volcanic dust across the earth.

Siciliana's heart hung heavy as she watched her brother ride away. She saw him glance back just once at the spot of dirt where Vittorio's pendant now lay. And in her final moments standing there alone on her family's soil, she looked up and glimpsed someone materialize in the distant fields. He was beautiful, smiling, calm. He was *O Santo Cavaleri*.

He was her *patri*.

CHAPTER 112

Cattedrale di Palermo
Palermo, Sicily
Seralcadio District
April 23, 1282
1:43 p.m.

CAPTAIN ROGER MASTRANGELO sat at his makeshift work-station in Palermo Cathedral, presiding over a pile of corre-spondence. His aides, Baverio and Ortoleva, hovered beside him, feeding him letters one by one. Mastrangelo looked up curiously at the two hapless men standing before him.

"*Siciliana* attacked Taormina by herself?" Mastrangelo asked.

"*Sì.*" The Amici brothers, Adrianu and Gaetano, nodded simultaneously.

"Because her long-lost brother is *Fra'Diavulu*," Mastrangelo said.

"*Sì,*" the Amici brothers said again.

"And her army is decimated?"

"*No,*" the brothers responded, smiling. "The people of Taormina are her army. She went to wake them up." The two brothers shot assured glances toward one another.

Mastrangelo shook his head. "*Rebellamentu* is a lost cause. The most brutal war king in the Mediterranean will soon set his sights upon these very shores, and we are fighting like insurgent savages. We will not survive the spring." Mastrangelo slowly rubbed his throat with his palm. "It's time we appealed to a higher power."

The men around him looked confused.

"You want to pray, sir?" Baverio asked.

In that moment, Mastrangelo snapped his gaze upward.

From where they stood, the Amici brothers seemed to notice something flash in Mastrangelo's eyes. Something dangerous.

"Fetch a blank scroll and our official seal," Mastrangelo ordered. "I will dictate a letter on behalf of the *Ordu Teutoni* of Sicily."

A page scrambled for a scroll while the men around the room shot one another concerned glances. Just as quickly as he left, the page returned and plopped himself down in a wooden chair. He nervously prepared his materials to inscribe the captain's direction.

Mastrangelo leaned back in his chair and blew a long breath out his nostrils. He pressed his fingers to his chin, choosing his next words carefully. Strategically.

"To Her Most Beautiful, Sublime, and Exquisite of All Jewels in the Mediterranean and Rightful Heir to the Old Kingdom of Sicily," he said. "Her Royal Majesty Constanza II of Aragon . . . Illustrious Queen of Spain . . ."

· ❦ ·

Adrianu and Gaetano Amici exchanged worried glances as
Mastrangelo dictated the troubling content of the letter.

Adrianu looked furtively between the various *Teutoni*
Knights and aides in the room, scanning for any possible signs
of protest. But they never came. In that instant, the unset-
tling implications of the present moment hit him like a ton of
Moorish stones: Roger Mastrangelo, venerated captain of the
Ordu Teutoni, had turned his back on the promise of a people's
Sicily.

He had turned his back on *Siciliana*.

EPILOGUE

Mount Etna, Sicily
April 24, 1282
7:56 a.m. // Twenty-fifth day of Vespers

FULLY ARMORED, *Don Rapaci* sat on horseback at the top of the black volcanic crater, Rosalia perched majestically on his forearm. The clouds above were gray and roiling, casting him in dark silhouette as a glowing red river of lava serpentined down the cliff beside him, sending up occasional bursts of fire and sulfur.

Siciliana approached on horseback, observing *Bannera dà Sicilia*, her fearsome Sicilian flag, hoisted from *Don Rapaci's* stirrup, snapping stiffly in the wind. Its bright red-and-gold colors gleamed in pristine condition against the gray sky.

The maiden turned monster turned myth, she told herself.

Looking up solemnly at the Sicilian flag, *Siciliana* remembered the lives of all the men and women who died protecting it, for those to be born under it, for all who would fight for it long after they were gone. She remembered her *patri*, the Sicilian families torn apart by Angevin brutality, the orphans of Sicily left to fend for themselves. She remembered Tziporah.

Never in her entire life did *Siciliana* dream that she would be the harbinger of *rebellamentu*, sending thousands of their oppressors directly to hell.

"You've turned the tides of history," *Don Rapaci* said. "Angevin soldiers are fleeing from our cities all across the island . . . *Hope* lives once more in Sicilian hearts . . ."

A breath of air hung between them.

Siciliana sensed something else coming. "But?"

"Messina is *Re Carlu*'s last stronghold in Sicily," he said. "Home to the most powerful navy in the Mediterranean."

Siciliana looked unshaken. "The people will rise," she said assuredly. "Messina *will* fall."

"What about retaliation?" *Don Rapaci* pressed.

Siciliana furrowed her brow inquisitively.

Don Rapaci fished in his breast pocket and pulled out a sealed scroll, extending his hand outward. "The latest from our spies in Napoli."

Siciliana took the scroll stamped with the French royal seal. She opened it and read the edict. *Re Carlu* had directed all available Angevin warships stationed across the Mediterranean to mount a full invasion against Messina's shores.

"The good news is we have thwarted *Re Carlu*'s great war with Constantinople," *Don Rapaci* said. "The bad news is he has now turned his very gaze toward our own soil."

Siciliana bit her lip and nodded. Confronting this level of brute military strength would be their greatest trial yet.

"It seems our *rebellamentu* is now a war of worlds," *Don Rapaci* said.

Siciliana nodded coolly and gently folded the letter, handing it back to *Don Rapaci*.

"*Una guerra in la primavera,*" she smirked. "Nothing like a war in the spring."

A beguiling grin spread across *Don Rapaci*'s lips. "A War of the Vespers!"

With that, *Don Rapaci* laughed with gusto and thrust Rosalia from his forearm, the golden eagle's enormous wings expanding out and flapping into the sky. The winged beast let out a piercing cry as she circled overhead as the hazy glow of the sun burned through the sky's gray veil of clouds.

Siciliana lifted her eyes upward. There was a tenderness in her face as she watched the majestic raptor circle above. She then grabbed the long flag spear from *Don Rapaci* and planted it firmly in her leather stirrup. "I never thanked you," she said, "for saving my life."

Don Rapaci lifted his gaze to hers, flashing *Siciliana* one last look of affirmation. "Sicily is *cosca,* or it is nothing."

The two Sicilians grinned and kicked their horses, tearing off together down the volcanic cliff. An oozing river of lava illuminated the edges of the mountain path. Great black and silver rocks glowed with orange light. And *Bannera dâ Sicilia* snapped strongly in the wind as the golden eagle soared down from the sky on a shaft of sunlight.

VIOLENCE IS a detestable act and should be avoided at all costs.

But the violent ferocity of the Sicilians who rose up in Palermo on that bloody night in March forged the identity of a new nation and dramatically altered the face of the Mediterranean forever. Brave fathers and daughters and mothers and sons came together as cosca and turned their defensive blades against a French oppressor—freeing themselves from the yoke of tyranny.

The lessons of the Sicilian Vespers came to serve as a solemn warning to those cruel and self-serving lords of kingdoms and lands who craved absolute power at the detriment of the peoples' health and prosperity.

History would speak of an arrogant king who once warned a foreign emissary that he could conquer all of Italy by the seat of his saddle and stroke of his sword.

"I'll seize Roma for breakfast," the king gloated, "and Napoli for supper."

The emissary snorted defiantly. "Then I pray your Highness reaches Palermo in time for Vespers."

—From *War of the Vespers*
by *Don Rapaci*, 1282

SICILIANA

RECIPES

SALSA RUBBINU ALLA SICILIANA

"Siciliana's *Ruby Sauce*"

Serves: 6 to 8

- ½ cup olive oil (you can never use enough olive oil)
- 1 large onion, chopped
- 6 cloves garlic, sliced finely
- 1 (6-ounce) can fresh tomato paste
- 1 (28-ounce) can peeled tomatoes
- 6 sprigs Sicilian basil (and a few additional fresh sprigs to garnish before serving)
- 1 tablespoon sea salt, to taste
- 1 teaspoon pepper, to taste
- 1 cup chicken broth
- 1 tablespoon sugar

1. Heat oil in saucepot.
2. Sauté onion and garlic until golden brown.
3. Add tomato paste and sauté for three minutes.
4. Add tomatoes, basil, sea salt, pepper, chicken broth, and sugar. Bring to a boil.
5. Cover and simmer slowly for one hour.
6. Cut with chicken broth, as needed.

7. Discard basil sprigs before serving.
8. Garnish with fresh Sicilian basil leaves.

PANELLE DI AETNA

"Aetna's Panelle"

Serves: 4 to 6

- 1½ cups chickpea flour
- 3 cups water
- 1 teaspoon sea salt
- Freshly ground pepper
- ¼ cup olive oil
- 4 sprigs parsley, minced
- 1 lemon
- Vegetable oil for frying

1. Combine chickpea flour, water, sea salt, pepper, and olive oil in saucepot over medium heat and whisk until it creates a smooth and glossy batter. Stir in parsley.
2. Pour batter onto a parchment-lined baking pan and spread it quickly with a spatula, about ¼-inch thick.
3. Set aside in refrigerator and let cool for one hour, until firm.
4. Once cooled, cut the firmed mixture into squares and fry over hot vegetable oil for approximately three minutes on each side, or until golden brown.
5. Place panelle on a paper-toweled plate, douse with lemon, and serve hot.

ABOUT THE AUTHOR

CARLO TREVISO grew up in Milwaukee, Wisconsin, and graduated from Columbia College Chicago with a degree in film directing. Traversing the worlds of Hollywood and advertising, Treviso has written and produced commercial broadcast campaigns for well-known brands all over the world. The son of a Sicilian immigrant, Treviso enjoys bringing his passion and appreciation for Sicily to his readers. He is a proud advocate and supporter of conservation organizations UNESCO, LIFE ConRaSi, and World Wildlife Fund—all of which work to protect the beauty and grandeur of Sicily's engrossing past, resilient culture, and vibrant biodiversity. Treviso resides in Chicago, Illinois.

Printed in Great Britain
by Amazon

13177378R00277